George Vincent Higgins, formerly Assistant DA for the District of Massachusetts, now runs his own law office. Born in Brockton, Massachusetts in 1939, he graduated from Boston College and received an MA in English from Stanford University. His first job was as a truck driver for Coca-Cola, but he dropped that to become a reporter for the *Providence Journal* and the Associated Press. He went on to obtain a law degree from Boston College Law School in 1967. For three years he was a lawyer in the Massachusetts Attorney General's Office, in the Organised Crime Section and the Criminal Division.

George V. Higgins's first published novel, *The Friends of Eddie Coyle*, was made into a film starring Robert Mitchum. Among his other novels are *The Digger's Game*, *Cogan's Trade*, *A City on the Hill*, *The Judgement of Deke Hunter* and *Dreamland*. He has also written two non-fiction books, *The Friends of Richard Nixon* and *Style vs. Substance*, as well as short stories, numerous book reviews and articles. He has most recently been working on scripts for the American television series *Hill Street Blues*.

George V. Higgins

IMPOSTORS

First published in Great Britain by
André Deutsch Limited 1986
Published in Abacus by
Sphere Books Ltd 1987
27 Wrights Lane, London W8 5TZ

Set in Times

Printed and bound in Great Britain by
Collins, Glasgow

1

The District Attorney for Bristol County had told the receptionist in the foyer of North American Group's main office on the 20th floor of 200 Federal Street in Boston that he had an appointment with Mr. Baldwin, and she had smiled and asked him to have a seat. The District Attorney was fifty-three years old and had his best suit on, a slubbed silk glen plaid with a muted red stripe he had had custom-tailored at Jason's, the best men's store in New Bedford. His necktie was a Sulka repp stripe that had cost him forty dollars in New York, and he was wearing his Johnston and Murphy black tasseled loafers. He was nonplussed when she asked him to sit down. He glanced over his shoulder at the blue crushed velvet armchairs and three-cushion couch grouped around the glass coffee table, but did not move from in front of her desk. He looked at his watch, a gold Audemars Piguet that said 10:30, and spoke to the receptionist again.

"I do have an appointment," he said, trying to conceal his irritation and dismay under a tone of firm command. "I called Mister Baldwin personally two days ago, and my office called back yesterday afternoon to make sure it was still on. I've driven quite a distance to get here this morning on time. I wouldn't want Mister Baldwin to think I arrived late, after making so much trouble."

The receptionist nodded. She was a stylish woman in her early forties in a clinging ivory jersey dress which made it clear that she had taken care of her body. When she folded her hands on the desk blotter, she was as careful to display the large diamond and wedding rings on her left hand. "I understand that, Mister Taves," she said. "If you'll just have a seat, I'm sure someone will come out to see you very soon."

The District Attorney exhaled. He went to the coffee table in front of the couch. He put his hands in his pockets and looked at the brushed chromium logos on the beige suede-textured wall behind the couch. The large block letters at the top headlined North American

Media Group, Inc.'s inventory of newspapers, magazines, television and radio stations. Under the parent company name, in slightly smaller Gothic letters, was "The Boston Commoner." Below that on the left ran a column of much smaller letters listing eight other newspapers: Albany, Tulsa, Fort Lauderdale, Santa Barbara, Spokane, Council Bluffs, Santa Fe and Crystal City, Georgia. In the center of the wall in the same size letters was a list of broadcasting call letters, some beginning with *W* and some with *K*; nine had *TV* after the first four letters; seven had *AM* and eight had *FM* as the last two letters.

On the right a third column listed the names of eleven magazines; the District Attorney had purchased and read two issues of *Journeyer* which he still had in his office in a thick file of publications he had sampled during his first term. The District Attorney smiled. He recognized the names of two other magazines — *Innovation* and *Style* — as reference works Judith had relied upon for decorating plans that had cost him a great deal of money when they purchased their new home in Fairhaven. The names of other magazines meant nothing to him. He turned back toward the receptionist and cleared his throat. When she looked up inquiringly, he said, smiling: "Say, uh, is *Perfect Pleasure* about what I think it's about, or is it something else?"

The receptionist looked puzzled. "I don't know, Mister Taves," she said. "It's about travel and leisure. Places to go? Restaurants, hotels?"

"Oh," he said.

"What did you think it was about?" she said.

"Well," the District Attorney said, "I didn't know. I know *Journeyer*, there, the one about dykes? I've seen that one sometimes. But the other one, I didn't know."

The receptionist looked more puzzled. A door opened to her left in the corner of the sueded wall and another woman emerged. She was about twenty-five and wore a black skirted suit with an ivory silk stock and blouse. "Mister Taves?" she said. The District Attorney nodded. "If you'll come with me?" she said. He followed her through the door as the receptionist's perplexed expression softened into a smile.

In the interior corridor there was beige tweed carpeting on the floor and there were pictures of clipper ships and men of war on the pale green grasscloth walls. He followed her past smaller, window-less reception areas enclosed by glass walls framed in dark wood. The desks in those areas were larger and better polished than the one he had in his office in the courthouse in New Bedford, and the women who sat behind the desks and operated IBM Correcting Selectric typewriters were all very well-dressed. There was virtually no sound. The woman in the black suit came to a large glass case set on a wooden chest at the end of the hall — it contained a big model of the US *Constitution* under full sail with the ports open on her starboard side and the cannons run out for action. The woman turned right and led him down another corridor decorated like the first, but now the glassed-in reception areas presented views of the Boston skyline to the north. At the end of the corridor there was a larger reception area behind a glass wall. The woman opened the glass door and held it for the District Attorney to enter.

He registered two small blue couches in crushed velour and several abstract pictures which had black lettering at the bottom of the colors; it seemed to give the names of things and after them, the dates. The woman peeked into the office opening off the reception area and said: "Mister Baldwin? Mister Taves is here." The District Attorney heard Mark Baldwin reply: "Send him in, Anne." The District Attorney glanced at his watch as he started across the thick tan pile carpet. It was 10:50. She saw him do it. As he passed her and entered Baldwin's office, he was sure she was mouthing some message behind him.

2

Mark Baldwin had a deeper tan than late June in New England explained. He was standing behind a refectory table twelve feet long and four feet wide, two harness-leather In boxes piled with files within reaching distance near the corner to his left, two Out boxes of the same material partially filled to his right. The table was positioned cater-cornered in the northeast corner of the room, so that Baldwin's tall brown leather chair put his back to the column that divided the windows giving off to the north and the view of the Tobin Bridge, and those to the east which looked out on the harbor and Logan Airport. Baldwin was wearing a narrow black knitted tie, a white button-down Oxford cloth shirt and grey slacks. He stood up slowly and put out his hand. "Billy," Mark Baldwin said, "long time and no see."

The District Attorney had to stretch to shake Baldwin's hand. He felt his suit coat tightening across his paunch as he did it. "Twenty minutes longer'n it should've been," he said. He sat down in the chair next to the In box corner; his suit coat bloused up from the top button as he sat. He snuffled and stared at Mark Baldwin. He nodded. "What I hear's true," he said. "I should've known it was. Guy's three years older'n I am, looks fifteen or twenty younger. How you do it, Mark? Magic or monkey glands?"

Baldwin looked without expression at the District Attorney. He said: "Would you like some coffee, Billy?" He eased himself into his chair, wincing slightly as he sat.

Taves grunted. He shifted in his chair. He raised his left hand and pretended to study his fingernails while looking at the artwork on the west wall above the cream-colored leather couch. It was a collection of three posters promoting European Grand Prix competitions at Monte Carlo, Spa and Nurburgring in 1962. He shook his head. "Uh uh," he said. "I had coffee 'fore I left Fairhaven. Yesterday, I think it was. What I'd like is an explanation, why I had to wait. Near as I remember, I never kept you waiting like this, twenty years ago. You come down to the courthouse in hysterics or something, you had to have the story now? I never kept you hanging fire, sucking your thumb in the lobby. And then, then when there was that little problem with that Italian family there, I forget their name, then did I keep you waiting when you just hadda talk? I don't think I did, Mark. I don't think I did. I think I always saw you, the minute you showed up. But now, now when I come here to see you, and you're a mucky-muck, now I have to wait. I drive alla way up here, I'm trying, do you a favor, and you treat me like this?"

Baldwin pursed his lips. He shook his head. The District Attorney heard the door to Baldwin's office shut behind him. He leaned back in his chair. "Twenty years," he said musingly. "Is it really twenty years?"

"It's more'n twenty years," Taves said. "It's closer to twenty-five years. It's a long time, anyway."

"And you're trying to do me a favor," Baldwin said.

The District Attorney raised his eyebrows. He exhaled noisily. He leaned forward in his chair, the suit coat blousing still more. He reached down with his right hand and undid the top button. "Well," he said, "I don't know. I thought I was. And hoping to do myself a little good at the same time, of course — you know how us pols are. No, your *newspaper* knows how us pols are. Maybe you personally actually don't. But yeah, since you mention it, I'm being nice to you. Unless you think somebody bringing bad news isn't being nice. That I can't help you with."

Baldwin reached forward and moved the file folder on the top of the outside Out box to the center of the table. "I'm not sure I follow," he said. "Is the District Attorney of Bristol County telling me that his decision to seek a fourth term is bad news for me?"

"Uh huh," Taves said, "so that was it. I cool my heels in the lobby for twenty minutes so you can call up the files on me and see if this is an election year. That's pretty crude, I think. All you had to do was ask me, I called for this appointment. If whether I'm up this year is something you need to know before you see me, the fuck didn't you ask me, huh? Or ask my secretary? Or have your secretary ask my secretary, the idea a man running for re-election makes your stomach queasy? I'm not ashamed of it, Mark. I tell everybody. 'Yup, another term. A fourth one. Just like FDR. Tell your loved ones and your neighbors: that's what I am after.' You guys owned something besides the *Commoner* and pervert magazines, you had regular papers like the ones in my district, you would know I am like that."

" 'Pervert magazines?' " Baldwin said. He looked amused. "What 'pervert magazines,' exactly, Billy, do you think we own?"

"*Journeyer*," the District Attorney said. "You put out *Journeyer*, and I know that thing. I have read it, all right? I've seen that it's garbage. My first term, all right? Father Gomes, down at Saints James 'n' Joe, Father Gomes is all upset, and he gets the Holy Name, and the Knights as well, so they are all upset. And all of sudden I have got this regular thing every night where the papers come out and there's all this stuff about pornography and all, and people're marching, and they're having candlelight vigils, and all that kind of shit, and so I go out and buy it. 'This is pornography,' they say? I will look at it myself." He paused. He nodded. "So, Mister Baldwin, I have seen your magazine. I know what it is. And it's pornography. It's about women screwing women, and how great it is. And if that isn't pornography, I don't know what is."

"Well," Baldwin said, "if it's pornography in your mind, and you are the DA, why not prosecute? I mean: why didn't you? It was your decision."

"Because," the District Attorney said, moving around in his chair, "because inna first place, those cases . . . . I don't have to go scouting around for cases to bring, not in my district, all right? We got plenty of poverty, plenty of immigrants, plenty of people that can't find a job, and a pretty good number don't want to. That don't want a job, and they'd just as soon have more cash on them than the welfare gives to them. So they do things, and we got plenty to do in my office as a result, just keeping up with them. And in the second place, Father Gomes died. Had a cerebral hemorrhage, and he was a young man. And that sort of took everybody's mind off of it, and they sort of forgot about it. And nobody came along to remind them. So I just let it die.

"I got prosecutorial discretion. I can do what I want, and nobody can stop me." He paused again. He smirked.

"Which I am trying to use now," he said, "in a prudent and judicious manner, and what thanks do I get for it? I get to drive about sixty miles and then cool my heels out in the hall while the great Baldwin reads my file. To find out if I am running for re-election. Honest to God. I should have my head examined."

Baldwin took a deep breath. He hunched his shoulders and rested his elbows on the refectory table. "Now look, Billy," he said, "you have got to understand. I'm in an awkward position here."

"If I didn't understand it, Mark," Taves said, "I would not be here."

Baldwin showed irritation. "Let me finish, willya, for God's sake?" he said. "You are running for re-election. The *Commoner*'s everybody's whipping-boy down in Bristol as it is. I am seeing you, alone. You've got two opponents who've announced so far, and one more at least who's waiting in the wings. I know two of those guys. They are cockamamie jerks. You think I like the idea, interviewing them? I haven't got time to do that, sit here entertaining a bunch of stupid Bravas, one after the other, having them yell at me in Portuguese, so I can waste my time telling every one of them that I run North American, not the *Commoner*, and I don't tell the *Commoner* which guy to endorse. But if I talk to you like this, I may have to talk to them. Give them the same access you've had, or get in a mess if I don't. I may have to do that, and damnit all, Bill, I don't want to. That's the way I feel."

"You've got a short memory," Taves said. "That's what you have got."

"What did I forget, Bill?" Baldwin said. "Say what I forgot."

"Where did you first know me?" Taves said.

"DA's office, Plymouth County," Baldwin said promptly. "You were a wet-behind-the-ears-assistant on the *Lavalle* case. I was a wet-behind-the-ears reporter on the *Commoner*. I went to you to get news, which you gave to me. Then I had a little problem, which after a while went away, and I appreciated the fact it went away, I seem to recall. I appreciated it and my family appreciated it and my friends as far away as New York, some of them, appreciated it. If you'd kept what we sent you to show my appreciation, you wouldn't've needed to win the election. You could've retired right then."

"You recall what that election was?" Taves said. "You got anything in your memory about the reason why I went back, Bristol County, when I made that run? You knew then why I did that, Mark, why I moved back to Bristol County when I ran for DA. You know why, today?"

"I assumed," Baldwin said, "if I assumed anything, that you thought you could win in Bristol, and you couldn't in Plymouth. And besides, you didn't want to challenge your friend Mister Keane."

"You were right," the District Attorney said. "And it wasn't an assumption. It was what I said to you. Do you recall why I told you I couldn't win in Plymouth, but I could in Bristol County?"

"Actually, no," Baldwin said. "This was over twenty years ago, Bill. I should get one break."

"You'll need more'n one," Taves said. "I told you I was moving to Bristol because I wanted to be the DA and I didn't have a chance in Plymouth even if Ward stepped down, because I was Cape Verdean and there weren't enough of us in Plymouth. Whereas in Bristol, there were plenty."

"Oh yeah," Baldwin said. He hunched his shoulders and leaned back in his chair.

"Uh huh," Taves said. "One of those stupid Bravas, I believe you just called us? Talks in Portuguese?"

"I believe I did say that," Baldwin said.

"I believe you did," Taves said. "But being a regular kind of guy, I am going to speak to you in English now, because I don't speak French like you do. You and me, Mark, got a problem, and I don't know whose problem's worse."

"Tell me what those problems are," Baldwin said. "Let me be the judge of that."

"Okay," Taves said. "I got the video-taped statement of the guy who killed Thomas Brutus with a twelve-gauge shotgun. He wasn't interested in talking about that, shooting Thomas Brutus. What he wanted to chat about was how Mel Shaw killed Timmy Lavalle with a winch handle and got away with it."

"Mel Shaw?" Baldwin said. "Mel Shaw killed Timmy Lavelle?"

"That's what my defendant says," Taves said. "He's very firm about it, and I think he's probably right. But he can't prove it, and so neither can Ward Keane. And he can't give us anybody else who can prove it either. So we're stuck. But we believe him."

"Tell me something if you know offhand," Baldwin said. "How long's Shaw been gone as bureau chief down in Waterford? Is it ten years or so?"

Taves shrugged. "I dunno," he said. "Five or six, at least. Ward says he thinks Shaw quit when that development business down there with the mall and everything, when that really started to take off. Which I think was about six, seven years ago. Or Ward does, anyway. It was long after you and I left — I know that."

Baldwin leaned forward and pushed a button on his telephone console. "Annie," he said, "have Personnel rustle up Mel Shaw's file for me, will you, please?" She answered over the speakerphone: "The whole jacket, Mister Baldwin? Or just the summary?" He snorted. "Oh hell," he said, "Just the summary. I haven't got time to read all his old columns again. Just the career summary." He leaned back again. He clasped his hands behind his head. "Get that much straight, at least. Not that I can see right now what the hell I'm going to do with the information after I get it. I assume you and Keane, you're not planning to bring this out, what you suspect and all. You're not, are you?"

The District Attorney sighed. "I'm not," he said. "He is. The guy that had the gun.

"Look," he said, "all right? This guy is not traveling with a full basket. I don't mean he's not competent to stand trial, because he is. He just got out of a treatment program, a medical program, about six weeks before he did it, and he was under constant observation and evaluation all during that, and he talked to some people the day before he did it and they all agree: he's sane. He knew what he was doing, I mean. And he premeditated it. And he knew right from wrong and all that good old stuff. But he's obsessed, you know? He wants to tell his story. He's *determined* to tell his story. And he's going to tell his story, it looks like, because he's going to trial. At which trial, he tells us, and I've got every reason to believe him, he is going to take the stand in his own defense and explain to everyone who'll listen that the reason he had to kill Thomas Brutus himself was because the system, which of course is guys like me and Ward Keane, the system doesn't punish killers even when it knows who they are. 'And don't tell me it isn't relevant,' he said. 'If I get up at my own trial and want to say something, no judge on earth's going tell a man in that kind of situation he can't say what's on his mind.'

"So you see?" Taves said. "The guy isn't crazy. He may even have a point, you come right down to it. I don't think he's gonna get very far with the jury, making it, and I have told him that. And I think he even agrees with me a little bit. But, like he says, he's gonna try. He's gonna do his best." Taves paused. "And I've got to say, Mark, knowing this guy, he might surprise some people. He's good on his feet."

"What's his lawyer have to say about this?" Baldwin said. "Having a murder defendant take the stand? That's a risky business. He figure the guy's got nothing to lose, might as well take his shot?"

"He doesn't have a lawyer," Taves said.

"Well, he can get one appointed for him, can't he?" Baldwin said. "I mean, the Reagan people've cut a lot of the poverty programs and stuff, but they're still allowing lawyers for indigents, aren't they?"

"He isn't indigent," Taves said. "He's got plenty of money. Well, I say 'plenty of money,' I don't mean he's got as much money as you, of course. But he's comfortable enough. He could afford a lawyer. He just doesn't want one. Says he doesn't need one. 'Case's got nothing to do with the law,' he says. 'That's what this case is about: that the law's irrelevant. The hell do I need a lawyer for, if the whole reason I did what I did and the reason I'm doing what I'm doing is because lawyers're irrelevant?' Judge Mills at the arraignment tried to assign somebody to represent him just for purposes of those proceedings, have one of the Mass. Defenders represent him until he had time to hire his own lawyer. He wanted no part of it. 'I'm appearing *pro se*, Your Honor,' he said. 'That's how I intend to try this case. Myself. No lawyer.' So Judge Mills gets all antsy, as any district court judge's going to when it's a murder case and here's the defendant creating a situation right off the bat where something could get screwed up that taints his conviction three years down the line, and the appeals court hands down a reversal that talks about how stupid the district court judge was for not appointing a lawyer, and Mills starts to read the guy his rights. And the guy laughs at him. 'I know all my rights,' he says, and he recites them. So that's the end of that."

Taves paused and reflected. "Guy does have a point, I suppose. Like he said to Judge Mills, all the years he's been hanging around police stations, talking to cops, watching court trials, it is pretty ridiculous to think he doesn't know his rights."

Baldwin cleared his throat. "Billy," he said, "I've got the strangest feeling I don't want to ask the next question because I don't want to know the answer to it."

The District Attorney smiled and nodded. "You don't," he said. "It's for the same exact reason I had the same feeling when the

Fairhaven cops call me up when they take this guy in and tell me how they've got him in custody and he's not making any trouble and won't even call a lawyer because he says he doesn't need one and he knows all that shit. And I say: 'How does he know it? What is he, some kind of cop himself?' And I'm thinking of course, that my God, he's a lawyer and he's shot this guy and that's how he knows all his rights, because I don't even know yet who's been shot, you know? If I had've, I would've. Known who did it right off, I mean. And they say, the cops say: 'No, he's a reporter. We got Joe Logan here.' "

"Oh my God," Baldwin said. His shoulders sagged. The door opened behind Taves and the secretary came in with an orange folder tabbed *Shaw, Melvin R.*, put it on the desk and started back toward the door. "Annie," Baldwin said, "thanks for this one. Now I need another one. And this one I want the whole barrowload. Clips, correspondence, used Kleenex — everything we've got on Joseph Logan."

The secretary frowned. "That name's familiar," she said. "Why do I recognize it?"

3

"You see what I mean?" Taves said, when the secretary had shut the door. "You see what I mean when I say I think we have got a problem? That lady probably never saw Joe Logan in her life. Didn't know the guy was on the earth. But a few weeks ago, right? He blows a guy to mincemeat with a damned shotgun, and all of a sudden this smiling son of a bitch that every old lady in my county depends on to give her the evening news while she gums her fish sticks to death turns out to be this vigilante, revenging the death of his family."

"Well," Baldwin said, shifting uncomfortably in his chair, "I see some of what you mean. Certainly I do. If the judge lets him tell his whole story on the grounds it shows his state of mind . . . ."

"Which he will," Taves said grimly. "Joe's dead right when he says that. If he decides he wants to get up on the stand and recite the Yellow Pages, the judge is gonna let him. The judge is gonna have to, just to keep the record clean."

". . . then he'll certainly be in a position to embarrass the hell out of Mel Shaw. Certainly his trial will be news statewide at least. So if he gets up on his hind legs and calls Mel Shaw a murderous queer at his own murder trial, it will get coverage.

"But other than that," Baldwin said, "trying to look at the matter objectively, it's not a big problem for me. Like I said, all I have to tell the *Commoner* people to do is grasp their nettles firmly and make no bones about the fact that Shaw was working for us when he committed the heinous act. *If* he committed the heinous act, and all that sort of thing."

"Yeah, yeah, yeah," Taves said. "And: blah, blah, blah. Look, whaddaya say you and me stop playing the games here right now — you think we could do that?"

"Come again?" Baldwin said.

"Let's quit fucking around here and play a little golf," Taves said.

"You know exactly what I'm talking about. You're just not sure how much I know, and therefore you're playing it cozy. But that's my problem, you see: I know what Logan says he knows, which is that this cocksucker Shaw apparently had some kind of a fight with his boyfriend and banged him on the head. I didn't know it when I could've looked for the corroboration I would've needed to go to Ward and the two of us go in the grand jury and get an indictment, but I know it now, and so does Logan.

"My problem is," Taves said, "that's basically *all* I know. For sure. But suppose by the time this case of his rolls around for trial, all right? Suppose by then Joe's decided there's some other interesting little tidbits he'd like to tell the jury about. Like when Gina Rivera met this wealthy, handsome guy at the Texaco station one night at the Sagamore rotary, and along with giving her some money for his coffee he also gave her some sweet talk and she ended up going with him and spending the night with him at his nice house in Cataumet, all right? Nothing like young love, I always say, except that when the guy's about thirty and the girl's fourteen, the law says that's too young. What was that line Bobo Rivera kept using that day in Ward's office? 'Statutory rape,' I think." He stared at Baldwin and grinned. Baldwin did not say anything.

"Uh huh," Taves said, nodding, "keep control. Right to remain silent, all that kind of thing. But let me ask you something, Mark, all right? Does Logan know the story about that little matter?"

"I doubt it," Baldwin said. "That happened the year before he came to Waterford. The only ones who knew about it, so far as I know, except for you and me and Keane and the Riveras were Shaw and Oscar Deese. Oscar's dead. Anything he knew died along with him."

"How about Dan Munroe?" Taves said. "Dan was the detective then. Wouldn't he have known? And how about Helen Deese — wouldn't Oscar've told his wife?"

Baldwin frowned. "He could've," he said. "Oscar might've done that, yes."

"Of course he did," Taves said. "We got to assume that Logan knows something about how me and Ward and Shaw and Oscar worked on Bobo and his fat wife there to make them drop those fucking charges."

Baldwin shrugged. "Okay," he said, "assumed. Is Logan likely to make that part of his recitation? Far as I know, Joe and I got along all right. No hard feelings I recall. So he's a loose cannon on a rolling deck now. So he maybe does have some dim idea of how the Riveras got convinced they didn't want their darling daughter put through testifying in open court. So what? He isn't mad at me."

"No," Taves said, "he's mad at me. I didn't put Tom Brutus away for killing Joe's wife and his kid. Not for long enough, at least. Mark, you should see this guy when I try to talk to him. Talk about obvious contempt — if I looked at a judge the way he looks at me, I'd be in Walpole by nightfall. So far he hasn't come right out and told me he thinks I'm an asshole to my face, but he's not far from doing that. What if he's sitting in his house down there in Mattapoisett right this very minute and thinking about fixing my ass at the same trial where he leaves Mel Shaw for dead? Can he do that to me without bringing you into it?"

"Sure," Baldwin said.

"But will he?" Taves said. "Why should he leave you out, when he's getting even with everybody else he ever met? Tell me how that makes sense."

"I never did anything to him," Baldwin said. "I told you: I always got along fine with Joe. Whatever his obsessions may be now, the causes for them arose long after he and I passed like ships in the night. He's got no beef with me."

"That's what you think, at least," Taves said.

"Yes, it is," Baldwin said.

"But you don't *know* that, do you?" Taves said. "You hope it, so you think it, but you don't really know.

"You really think you can predict what the guy's going to do? You think it's possible he might've changed some since the last time you saw him? You think he hasn't changed, since the first time *I* met him? Mark, I've been in daily contact practically with this guy ever since he came in with the new ownership of SET. For over ten years, I know Joe Logan. Like him. Get along with him. Have a couple drinks with him, shoot the shit and have some laughs. Not one of my bosom buddies, not my closest pal, but an honest-to-God nice guy — trust him with anything.

"Now," Taves said, "I'm not saying I can't understand, a guy's wife and son get wiped out by a guy that everybody ever met him knew was sooner or later gonna kill some people driving. Of course I

can understand. Thing like th
him, Mark, cripes — it was like
all right? He don't, he's decided a
rules, all right? Living the way he's
keeps his word, never does nobody a
was being a jerk. Now, now he thinks th
when I prosecute somebody, it's some kind
That when the judges sentence somebody, it'
what I mean? And he's going to get even. Wh
once."

Taves stood up. He wriggled in his suit and sat b
He used his hands in a spreading gesture. "Everything
now," he said. "As far as Joe's concerned, everything'

"Now," he said, "if I was you, which I am not, I woul
wonder how much Joe knows about what me and Shaw and
did for you, all right? I would wonder that. And I would also wo
whether Joe knows how much campaign money I got from you a
people you knew after all of that."

"Well," Baldwin said, "but there was no real campaign disclosure
law in those days. I mean, it'd be pretty hard for him to find out,
after all these years. Don't you think?"

"I dunno," Taves said. "I wasn't a reporter. You're the one, did
that. Keep in mind, Mark, you're starting to think like I am here,
like you had my job. And the thing of it is with this damned thing,
it's the other way around. What I got to do is think like you do,
which is as a newspaperman, you know? Like Joe Logan thinks,
which is still as a reporter or an editor, or something. You bastards,
you don't have to prove it. If you're satisfied it's true, well, you just
go ahead and print it, and as far's the public's concerned, well, that's
the end of the guy that you print it about. Don't matter what he says.
Whether it's true or not. Which is what Logan's gonna do when he
gets up in court. He's gonna tell that judge his state of mind when he
killed Brutus was that all these things he's seen all his life — all these
guys getting off when they were guilty, not even getting prosecuted,
all these guys making deals and so forth — that was what made him
decide to get the shotgun out and finish Brutus off. And you could be
part of that, Mister Baldwin. Your name could be on that list, and
that should worry you."

Baldwin sat back in his chair as the secretary knocked and

losed the door
vant to find out
t he is liable to

the District

can make a
before the

at'd wreck me, too. But what it did to
it made him into a different person.
those years he was playing by the
supposed to, good to his family,
harm? He decided now he
whole thing's a joke. That
of an act I'm putting on.
all just a big show. See
everybody. All at
ck down again.
's opened up
fair game.
kind of
Oscar
nder
nd

sking him
back to
putting
until I
you're not
...noag, I assume,' he is
...there's an interesting idea. How
...Baldwin for something? Like maybe he must've
...Shaw in the Lavalle thing, and didn't turn him in because Shaw had the hammer down on him for the Rivera case.' Or how about: 'When Oscar Deese and all those folks in Waterford're sneaking around all those years buying up land onna sly, how come Mel Shaw that runs the paper there didn't ever print anything about how all the people getting screwed? Baldwin knows all those people. They're all like him now, lots of money. How come Mark Baldwin up in Boston that by then is Mel Shaw's boss, how come Baldwin didn't tell him: "Put that stuff inna paper, Mel, or kiss your job goodbye"? I think I'll tell the jury that, something more to think about.' And that idea, I might give him ideas, that does not appeal to me much, if you know what I mean."

"I think I do," Baldwin said.

"What we got to do, I think" Taves said, "well, what you have got to do, since I can't do it myself, is, we have got to find some way to persuade this guy to tell us, or somebody else who will then tell us, what he is going to do."

"I see," Baldwin said.

"So at least," Taves said anxiously, "so at least we get some idea what to expect when he goes into that courtroom in the fall. All right?"

"Yes," Baldwin said, "that does make sense. I do see what you mean."

"And, well," Taves said, "that's what I had in mind, I guess. What I came up here to tell you. To see if maybe you think of some way that somebody can go to see this guy, probably somebody he never met in his life before, that doesn't know us or him, that could get him to tell his story. Because keep in mind, publicity is why he's doing this. He's got an ax to grind."

"In other words," Baldwin said, "one of our reporters?"

Taves frowned. "That I don't know," he said. "I leave that up to you."

4

Roger Kidd in a dark-grey pinstriped flannel suit put his hands in his pockets and rocked back on his heels while he surveyed the Charter Club bar on the 36th floor of 200 Federal Street. He had had his sandy hair cut short and neat around the ears, and Edward in the Ritz Barber Shop had left it a little wet; the wire frames of his glasses pressed it down against his scalp. He recognized no one seated at the four tables along the westerly windows, and the trio occupying the table at the southwest corner was not familiar to him. But beyond them at the table partially concealed by the bar and the people seated at it was John M. Flaherty of Doran & Flaherty Advertising. Flaherty interested Kidd a lot. Flaherty was having a martini on the rocks with a twist and eating peanuts. Seated with him was an Oriental woman in her early thirties. She was wearing a lime-colored linen suit and she was very animated. Flaherty said something that made her put her head back to laugh and arch her back slightly in the black leather chair, so that her breasts became prominent against her white blouse. Flaherty grinned hugely and took another handful of peanuts. Kidd, his lips pursed, was still studying Flaherty when Mark Baldwin in a blue blazer came up behind him and put his left hand on Kidd's left shoulder. "John Dean, I presume?" Baldwin said.

Kidd glanced to his left to verify Baldwin's identity. "Hullo, Mark," he said. "Actually you, running newspapers and all, ought to know this: Dean wore tortoise-shell frames. As did I. And why I do not, anymore."

"The things a man learns from talking to lawyers," Baldwin said.

"The things a lawyer learns, out in the world," Kidd said. He nodded toward the southerly windows. "See that fella down there, beefy chap in a grey suit, got his legs crossed at the table?"

Baldwin squinted and stared. "One with the red Nantucket tie with the blue whales on it?" he said.

"That's the one," Kidd said. "John Michael Flaherty, as I live and breathe. Doran and Flaherty. Know the lady with him?"

"No," Baldwin said, "I do not. And I regret that fact."

"You surprise me, Mark," Kidd said. "I thought you knew all the ladies."

"Roger," Baldwin said, "I thought I did. All the ones that look as good as she does, at least. Heavenly days."

"Unless I am very much mistaken," Kidd said, "the lady being entertained by Mister Flaherty is Emma Sung, who is his doxie. But I would like to be sure."

" 'His doxie?' " Baldwin said. "Roger, bless my soul. I haven't heard that word in years. Victoria Regina was still on the throne, I believe. The last time I heard it, I think, was when my mother thought I was asleep and she used it to my father to describe the secretary in his New York office. I couldn't've been more'n six years old. I was nine before I found out what it meant. And that my mother was right."

"Well," Kidd said, rocking again, "at Kincaid, Bailey and Kincaid, as you know, we like to maintain a certain sense of decorum. The proprieties, as Bayliss says."

"And your client Flaherty is not observing them?" Baldwin said. "I'm surprised you're not over at his table this very minute, rebuking him for this conduct."

"Mister Flaherty," Kidd said, "is not our client. Mister Flaherty's *wife* is our client. Jane Flaherty is under the impression that John Michael Flaherty is consorting with a woman other than herself for sexual purposes, and engaged us originally to see that no financial harm befall her in the event he decides to end his marital relationship with her in order to formalize his relationship with this other person. That was several months ago. Now Jane's wish is that we conduct proceedings to dissolve the marriage, making sure that maximum financial harm befalls him."

"I see," Baldwin said.

"The information that Jane gave us," Kidd said, nodding toward the table, "was to the effect that his paramour is of Oriental ancestry. Which leads to my suspicion that his companion of the day is in fact the paramour. But I may be mistaken."

"They all look alike," Baldwin said, mocking sympathy, "all those paramours."

Kidd gave him a sharp look.

"I'm sorry, Roger," Baldwin said. "Can we go in and eat now, if I promise to behave?"

Kidd pretended to consider. "I believe so," he said. He nodded toward the far table again. "I sure would like to know for sure, though, if she is the chippie. Fine-looking woman, I must say. Can't say's I blame old John."

Baldwin steered him toward the hostess who escorted them through the dining room to the table at the extreme northeast corner, pausing when they were accosted by other men in pinstriped suits who looked up from their luncheons to exchange greetings. At the table she ascertained that Kidd would have a Sprite straight up and Baldwin would have his usual Campari-soda, and then left them alone. Baldwin lowered himself into his chair gingerly. "Jane's a bit plain, is she now?" Baldwin said.

"Jane is dowdy," Kidd said.

"She's probably a rocket in bed," Baldwin said.

"No," Kidd said, now studying the menu, "she is not."

"Oh ho," Baldwin said. "And how do you know that, may I ask?"

Kidd chuckled once. "Not the way you're thinking, Mark, not that way at all. I don't know how to go about all that extramarital stuff I hear so much about. Which means if I tried it, I'd get caught, and then Polly would hire somebody like me to give me a gelding. Financially, I mean. No roll in the sack I've ever heard about is worth that kind of grief. Especially one with Jane. Jane told me she isn't. Can you imagine that? Telling her lawyer in her divorce that she's always hated sex? And then telling him to nail her husband for screwing this Asian girl?"

"What the hell did she expect him to do?" Baldwin said.

"I don't know," Kidd said, shaking his head as the waitress brought the drinks. "I confess I don't know. The thought has crossed my mind that this is in fact what she wanted. For him to get another woman so she could go after his money and make him pay her for the liberty to do with somebody else what she doesn't want to do with him. The thought has crossed my mind."

"But you're representing her," Baldwin said.

"Of course we are," Kidd said irritably. "She's a client. She has money. She's entitled to representation if she wants it, isn't she? Of course she is. We're not sex therapists. Or marriage counsellors. Why marriages fall apart is no concern of ours. We're lawyers. We represent survivors."

Baldwin sighed. He picked up his menu and opened it. "I'm glad I never practiced," he said.

"So are the clients," Kidd said, "and so are the rest of us lawyers." Baldwin snickered.

"Why did you ask me here, Mark?" Kidd said. "Was it for the scrod?"

"Actually, no," Baldwin said. "I recommend the veal."

"Veal it is," Kidd said. He took a drink of Sprite. He sat back in his chair. He clasped his hands across his stomach. He appraised Baldwin. He nodded and smiled. "You look very good, Mark," he said. "Have you been in France?"

"Uh huh," Baldwin said.

"I thought so," Kidd said with satisfaction. "You always look good when you come back from France." He took another drink of Sprite. "You should remarry Lucille."

Baldwin laughed. "Go back with Lucille? Are you out of your mind? The gallery she opened in Beaulieu with what she got out of me almost thirty years ago, for God's sake — have you got any idea what another one of those settlements would cost me today? Lucille's great in bed, Roger, but another long-term booking could easily run me a couple million bucks. She's not that good."

"Probably not that much, actually," Kidd said thoughtfully, as the waitress approached. "The franc was trading at nine-point-eight to the dollar this morning. You could probably do it for less."

"You're incredible," Baldwin said. They ordered medallions of veal in lemon sauce, Baldwin writing the choices on the form provided. Baldwin invited Kidd to share a bottle of Côtes du Rhône '78 he described as "adequate." Kidd declined and requested another Sprite, which he described as "non-alcoholic" and Baldwin ordered half a carafe of the house California red wine. The waitress accepted the completed order and went away.

"I don't see what's so incredible," Kidd said. "I think I'm practical. Twice a year you go away. You always go to France. When you leave, you always look as though you really need a vacation. When you come back, you always look as though you've had one. Which very few people can claim these days, that they come back from a trip looking like they've actually rested and relaxed."

"Oh sure," Baldwin said. "Except of course I made my usual mistake and went up to Pelouse de Bagatelle and got myself involved in a match with a bunch of six-goal players and several strange ponies. So as a result my back is out. And I had another one of my patented runs of luck in Saint Jean-Cap Ferrat which always do so much to make Claude glad he runs the casino and make me wonder if I was dropped on my head as an infant. But I spent a lot of time by the pool in the sun, and Lucille closed the gallery by mid-afternoon most days and made sure I wasn't lonesome by myself at the hotel." He reflected. "She really is an extremely accomplished woman." He sighed.

"Too accomplished, perhaps?" Kidd said.

"That's a gentle way of putting it," Baldwin said. "It's a paradox, I think, that I still feel as I do about her. The principal reason that she still attracts me is that even after all these years and all the other experiences I've had, I still have never found her equal in bed. I come home and from time to time I think about her, and I know that all I have to do to have her every day is move back there to stay. And I wonder sometimes why I don't do that. I'd have to leave my work, of course, but that's really not that big a deal. I still thrive on the job, but after almost twenty years, I can't say the thrill's the same. We're a mature company now. I consolidate and I conserve; I do not innovate."

"The excitement's gone, is it?" Kidd said.

"Pretty much, uh huh," Baldwin said, as the waitress brought their salads and the half carafe of wine. "When the Group bought out the Goulds, you know, and I shifted over from doing the reporting and the writing to administration, I wasn't kidding myself. The only reason they wanted me to stay was their own insecurity. The *Commoner* was the biggest outlet they had ever owned. They only kept me on because they were afraid there'd be stupid mistakes made if they shifted one of their yokel publishers out of Oklahoma or someplace like that and planked him down to oversee *The Boston Commoner*. That there'd be dissension in the ranks and pretty soon this enormously complicated, sophisticated, powerful engine would start to misfire and finally seize up. I was continuity. They didn't want me for my executive abilities, which then even I didn't really know I had. They wanted me because I was close to the Goulds, identified with them, and I'd worked in the trenches, and I was symbolic reassurance to all the other *Commoner* people that they didn't want to lose, that the only changes made would be administrative, on the business end.

"I never expected to stay this long," Baldwin said. "I figured they'd keep me around for a couple of years and then either my usefulness to them would be over, or I'd be bored sitting in an office and I'd start looking for a job with one of the networks. Something that would get me back out in the world. Maybe covering the war or something else I hadn't done." He paused and grinned. "What's that line about your life being what happens to you while you're planning something else? When I signed up with Group, Richard Nixon was in the first year of his first term and we were fighting Ho Chi Minh. They settled the war without me some time ago and I'm still where I was back when that was going on." He began to cut his salad. "Funny," he said. "Funny."

"So," Kidd said, "why don't you do it then?"

"Quit my job and move to France?" Baldwin said. "Spend the rest of my days making leisurely love to Lucille, and dining at La Reserve?"

"Sure," Kidd said, chewing on lettuce, "no reason why you can't. You've certainly got the money, so that's not a barrier."

"The trusts're still in good shape, are they?" Baldwin said, smiling.

"Yes indeed, tip-top," Kidd said. "Checked the books this morning and everything's just fine."

"Roger, I'm impressed," Baldwin said.

"Well," Kidd said, "after all, this was rather sudden, when you called me up. It's not something you've made a habit of doing, in all the years I've known you. So naturally I had to wonder what was up. Are you planning some big change in your life, for which the condition of your estate is a relevant concern? Or are you planning some big change in *my* life, such as telling me that Kincaid, Bailey isn't going to be the trustee for the Baldwin family holdings anymore and you're putting it all into Sears no-load no-frills mutual funds?" Kidd smiled. "I must say I'm relieved to hear it seems to be the former sort of change you have in mind. You're an important client. I'd have trouble explaining to Bayliss and the other partners how losing you was not my fault. They would be annoyed."

Baldwin laughed. "Well," he said, "it's a tempting thought. But actually, I don't think I want to do it. As central as sex is to my life, I don't think it's overwhelming enough to make it possible for me to live out my years just for twenty minutes a day of ecstasy. As routine as my job's become, it is something to do. I need that, to fill up the idle hours."

"Oh for heaven's sake, Mark," Kidd said, pushing his salad plate away as the waitress brought their entrées, "aren't you a little old for this by now? This sex thing of yours?" The waitress's eyebrows rose as she set the plates down.

"I don't think so," Baldwin said, looking at her with amusement. She blushed and quickly left the table. "Does it matter if I am? It's the way I'm built. It's the way Lucille's built too, even more so." Kidd snorted and began cutting his veal.

"Well," Baldwin said, "I can't explain it to you, Roger, you know. Either you're so constructed that sex is an important and necessary, regular part of your life, and you don't feel comfortable doing anything else unless you have your releases, or else you're not so constructed and it doesn't matter much." Kidd looked up sharply. "Now don't get upset, Roger," Baldwin said, "I'm not casting aspersions. I'm just stating facts. Which if I had been fully aware of them when I was twenty-eight years old might have caused me to be fully contented with a relationship something short of marriage to Lucille, and saved me a lot of heartache. Not to mention money. Or, if it didn't do that, might have made me wise enough to see that leaving Lucille unattended on the Côte d'Azur while I gallivanted around Europe for that summer with Team Lotus was not a smart move at all. Which, if I'd stayed put, might've meant she wouldn't't've gotten involved the way she did with Chris LeGrasse and God knows how many others, and I would not have dumped her. Information is always valuable, Roger, especially information about yourself. Even when it's on a subject that you find unsavory. Maybe: *especially* when it is."

Kidd sat back in his chair and dabbed at his lips with the napkin. There was not a morsel of veal left on his plate. "That was delicious," he said.

"Glad you enjoyed it," Baldwin said, taking his fourth bite.

"So," Kidd said, as Baldwin ate, "since you didn't ask me here to discharge me as trustee, and you didn't ask me here to inform me that you've decided to quit your job and move to France, why did you ask me here in such a rush?"

"Good," Baldwin said, nodding, "on to business." He sat back from his half-finished lunch and wiped his mouth. "Little too much flour, I think. Little too much flour." He drank some wine. "What I've got on my mind, Roger," he said, "is a problem that I don't know what to do about."

"Involving the Group, I take it?" Kidd said.

"Involving the Group very much," Baldwin said. "More specifically the *Commoner* than the Group as a whole, but still a problem for the Group, so it doesn't really matter."

"Let me ask you this," Kidd said. "Why . . ."

" . . . didn't I just get on the elevator and go up to the twenty-ninth floor and talk to Don Joyce at Rand, Hayes," Baldwin said.

"Well," Kidd said, "after all, they do represent the Group, and they're set up to handle questions that newspapers encounter. I'm flattered that you call me, Mark, and you know Kincaid, Bailey will always be grateful for any new business you want to send our way. But there are only eight of us in the office full-time, now that Bayliss only works a sixty-hour week . . . . "

" . . . while still billing, of course, for the usual ninety," Baldwin said.

"Now don't make fun of Bayliss," Kidd said. "He's been greedy now since Teddy Roosevelt was President. You can't expect him to change his habits overnight. His problem is greed, just as yours is sex. You believe you can't get too much sex, and he believes he can't make too much money. You should be tolerant."

"I suppose," Baldwin said.

"Of course," Kidd said. "But my point is that we're all trusts and estates, you know, and taxes. And the occasional wretched divorce that affects one of our regular clients. But that's all we do, that sort of thing. Not newspaper matters or corporate problems. We don't have the expertise. We're not set up to handle them."

"This isn't exactly a corporate problem," Baldwin said, as the waitress returned for their plates. Baldwin ordered coffee for himself, and tea with lemon for Kidd. "Let me tell you," he said after she had gone, "about a conversation I had this morning with the District Attorney of Bristol County."

5

"Tell me more about this man Taves," Kidd said, pouring the last of his tea.

"He's one of those dangerous louts," Baldwin said. "You know the type I mean. Redneck-shrewd. Mucker-canny. Made his way to prosperity and expensive suits that don't fit him right not by being smarter than the competition, but by staying up later, cutting more corners, sticking more knives into backs. Always on the lookout for a slight. Sees them where none have occurred. Hypersensitive about his modest origins, his ethnic background — which I inadvertently and stupidly slurred this morning, thoroughly pissing him off — and his reputation. His image, I suppose he would call it. But he has power, real power. That's why he's dangerous. Those district attorneys are like medieval lords with their fiefs, when they choose to be."

"Which made him feel comfortable about coming into your office and threatening you," Kidd said.

"Well," Baldwin said, "I wouldn't put it that strongly, that he threatened me. And I'm sure he wouldn't use that term, if you asked him to describe our conversation. More in the nature of an effort on his part to make me understand the urgency of a shared situation of some legitimate concern to both of us. More his concern than mine, I think he'd admit, but still mutual."

"So he threatened you," Kidd said.

"Well," Baldwin said, "you couldn't call that a threat, exactly. Whatever Gina's parents and Gina thought of me over twenty years ago, the statute of limitations is long gone."

"In the courts it has," Kidd said. "In less formal surroundings, it probably hasn't. You might be able to weather it in Boston, pass it off as a youthful impetuosity. Although I must say, you were what then, about thirty?"

"Exactly thirty, when it happened," Baldwin said. "Gina was my surprise birthday present to myself. And a very nice little package she was, too, even if she was a little misleading on the subject of her age."

"Mark," Kidd said, "fourteen? I mean, I know she told you she was eighteen, but after all, you were a man of the world. Which is exactly what the reaction of most people would be if you told them you were still a reckless youth after three decades on earth. You perhaps couldn't know she was fourteen, but you certainly couldn't have believed she was as old as she claimed to be. You took advantage of a child. A sexually-precocious child, perhaps, but the law's intended to protect such children from people like you."

"I figured her for about sixteen," Baldwin said. "A very old sixteen. She was old enough for what I wanted, Roger. And what she wanted, too."

"Good," Kidd said. "Keep that little speech in mind, Mark, in case Taves or someone else gets it into his head to tell that story to your board. You'll need every rationalization you can muster if that happy day arrives."

"Yes," Baldwin said, "I know that and you know that, what a nice little scandal, even twenty-five years stale, would do to my standing with the board. I can just see the look on Paul Rundle's face, getting a phone call out there in Saint Cloud that his CEO's a rapist. He'd be beside himself.

"Thing of it is," Baldwin said, "what you and I know is not data in possession of Billy Taves. So if a threat exists it's a threat he doesn't know about, and didn't mean to make."

"But we still have to deal with it, Mark," Kidd said. "It's something we have to take into account. It's one thing for you to tell me that ennui's setting in for you in your job, and you'd just as soon quit it and relax. It's quite another to be chucked out on the street, fired on grounds of moral turpitude."

"Yes," Baldwin said, "it is."

"And, it seems to me," Kidd said, "we have to think about other implications. Just how much did you funnel into his campaign after that bothersome case went away?"

"Only ten or twelve thousand," Baldwin said. "Even allowing for inflation since then, Billy was fairly cheap. And I think Keane got five or six, when he ran again."

Kidd sucked his breath in through clenched teeth.

"Roger, Roger," Baldwin said. "It was all perfectly legal under the campaign laws then. And it was perfectly permissible under the *Commoner*'s ethics code — we couldn't run for office, but there wasn't any prohibition against contributing to somebody else's campaign."

"Mark," Kidd said, "please, don't be disingenuous. You know how delighted the *Herald* would be to pounce on you. First the juicy story of how the CEO of its biggest competitor seduced a mere child. Then the even juicier story of how the case was bagged."

" 'Bagged'?" Baldwin said, raising an eyebrow.

"Bagged," Kidd said firmly. "That's the name you put on it when you proposed doing it back then, to my dismay, and that's the name you put on it after you did it, against my advice."

"Keep your voice down, Roger," Baldwin said, looking amused. "Everyone may not be as sophisticated as we are."

Kidd looked around. "There's nobody but Flaherty and his lady friend here," he said in a lower voice, "and they're not here to eavesdrop on us.

"What you did," Kidd said, leaning over the table, "and what the *Herald* or any other self-respecting tabloid will be only too happy to headline, was how you mobilized your contacts as a *Commoner* reporter and your financial resources as a son of the wealthy Baldwin family, first to frighten off the people who'd press charges, and then to reward the prosecutors who swept the affair under the rug. That will destroy you, Mark, destroy you utterly. A corrupt publisher who bought off prosecutors to squelch a sex charge. It would finish you."

"It wouldn't help," Baldwin said.

"And whatever 'data,' as you put it, that Taves lacks," Kidd said, "he's got to have at least a vague notion of the danger to you. Therefore what he said has to be construed as a threat, and taken as one, regardless of what he meant."

"As always, Roger," Baldwin said, "you have a talent for boring straight to the heart of things. That's why I rely on you."

Kidd waved off the remark. "Never mind that, Mark," he said, "let's get on to the matter at hand. We know that Taves was corrupt in those days, because you corrupted him."

"Use a different word, Roger," Baldwin said. "Three people I know made contributions of funds in cashier's checks to the man's campaign. A fourth person contributed the same kind of checks to

Ward Keane's campaign. No lists were made. No documents were preserved. None of them had any personal interest in any matter then or previously pending in either DA's office. People can suspect what they like, and dream up all the innuendos that they want, but if the *Commoner* proposed to print something like that about some-body else, and call it 'corruption,' Dan Joyce and the Rand libel boys would go into cardiac arrest. It'd be *prima facie* defamation, libel *per se*, plain and simple, a lawsuit we never could win. And any other paper that you care to name, any TV station or radio outfit, their lawyers looking over the same story will tell them the same thing."

"All right," Kidd said, "you arranged through friends to pay him off, and pay off Keane as well. That suit you any better?"

"Marginally," Baldwin said. "Only marginally."

"Now," Kidd said, "that leaves us with the question I was getting to before this semantic dispute. We know what Taves was in the early Sixties: he would take a bribe, if it was discreetly paid. The question now is: whether he's corrupt today? In other words: what are we dealing with here? Is this fellow playing as straight as he's capable of playing when he says that what he wants is for you to get involved in a *sub rosa* partnership with him to find out what Logan's going to do? Or is this a crafty subterfuge on his part, some sort of ploy to get you thinking exactly along the lines we're thinking now, and get you nervous enough to offer him another, probably far more generous gratuity, in order to buy off this Logan prosecution that he claims disturbs him so?"

Baldwin frowned. "That's a good question," he said. "But I don't see a gambit here. I would say he can't be bought. Or even rented for a while. He probably would *like* to be corrupt, but he's afraid he'd get caught. He wouldn't expose himself like that, do something that might give some other scrambler the weapons to do him in. No, I don't think he's on the take. He lives pretty well, by his standards at least, but back when he first ran for office he could be DA and have a private practice, too. Which he did, with Ward Keane, who is still the DA in Plymouth County. And I'd imagine that the two of them worked the usual dodges that don't smell like perfume but were perfectly legal back then.

"You know," Baldwin said, "the guy up on drunken driving gets nailed to the cross in the criminal case, so the lawyer that's handling the civil case for the victim's family has a pretty easy time of it collecting from the insurance company. And the civil lawyer knows where to refer the next zoning board case that comes in — right to the DA's law firm. Keep in mind, he and Keane didn't *nol pross* the Rivera case. They didn't take any active part at all in explaining to Bobo and bride how nasty it was going to be when my defense lawyers got their chance to cross-examine Gina. Oscar Deese and Mel Shaw did that, Oscar giving them all these solemn warnings about what was going to happen, Mel just by way of no harm calling them up and saying he's a reporter from one of the Cape papers and scaring the devil out of them that he was going to publish that their daughter was a tramp. The Riveras, on what they thought was their own, made the decision to drop the case. Billy and Ward respected their wishes. Billy and Ward were rascals, maybe, but they were cagey rascals, and even though the laws've gotten a lot stricter now, and the media much more vigilant, both of them're still in office, still doing quite well. I don't think Billy wants a bribe. He would be too wary."

"So he's not after money from you then," Kidd said. "Or, if not from you directly, from this former employee, Mel Shaw."

"I don't think so," Baldwin said. "I think Billy was on the level this morning. He genuinely doesn't want to try this *Logan* case. Look at the position he's in. Joe killed this insignificant old bastard in broad daylight, in front of several witnesses, with a TV minicam crew up the road. And he didn't do it quietly. He fired three loads of double-O buckshot into this Brutus from a range of fifteen feet. That's three ounces of ball bearings moving at around eight hundred feet a second. Ever kill a deer?"

"No," Kidd said. John Flaherty's companion's laughter pealed across the room.

"I have," Baldwin said. "You never get a shot at a deer under thirty yards or so. The pattern of the pellets, 'the spread,' disperses geometrically with the distance from the muzzle. Double-O buck loads are made to assure that if even one of the ball bearings hits a vital spot, your animal is down. Can you imagine what three dozen of those things do to the average human torso at a range of fifteen feet? It looks like hamburger."

Roger Kidd winced.

"Taves has video-tape of that body taken by the WSET film crew immediately after Logan ejected the last spent shell. No exaggeration, Roger. If what Billy tells me is true the blood comes out like the Fountains of Rome. It is gory stuff.

"Now," Baldwin said, "put yourself in Taves's position. It's an election year. He has got competition, and one of his opponents is trying to do to Billy this year what Billy did to old Fred Barlow back in Nineteen-sixty-six. Persuade the voters to throw out the incumbent because he's obviously middle-aged and the contender's prettier. Billy's got this grisly murder case which on the face of it he cannot lose. But when you look at it a little closer, you see he cannot win.

"The defendant is well-known in the community, and he is well-liked, too. He was the evening and late news anchorman on WSET-TV for ten or twelve years. The people in the New Bedford area think he's their trusted friend. They're not going to want to convict him of murder. Joe is a nice guy.

"Now look at his motive. It's one any peasant can understand. Thomas Brutus killed Joe Logan's wife and son, and for doing it he got two lousy years in jail. Two years, Roger. One year for killing Rosemary Logan. One year for killing Ricky Logan. That punishment was the joint handiwork of Billy Taves's office, which prosecuted the case, and the retarded judge who sentenced Brutus on his ninth offense for driving under the influence when he caused the fatal crash.

"So here is poor Billy in an election year, with a case he *has* to prosecute, against a TV personality. He's reasonably apprehensive that the jury will acquit.

"How does Billy win?" Baldwin said. "He's a scrapper, Billy is. They are realistic. If he convicts Logan on Murder One, and Logan gets the chair, or life without parole, Billy is the villain. Billy therefore deserves to lose the election. If he doesn't convict Logan on at least second degree, which on the facts would be pretty hard to justify anyway, then his opposition yells that Billy went into the tank for a popular defendant with a sob story defense. And Billy loses the election. If Logan had all his marbles, Billy could look for a plea. But Logan's got a cause he wants to present. He's not going to plead.

"So," Baldwin said, "when Billy Taves chokes down his pride and comes up to see me, whose paper endorsed his opponent in the last election, and he tells me that this case is a real problem, I think he is right. I think he's hoping I will find some way he hasn't thought of, and couldn't implement if he did, to stop this case from coming to trial."

"And, I take it," Kidd said, "there's no way that the two of us, looking at what he said, can disagree with him that you would like to do that for him, if you possibly can."

"Yes, I would," Baldwin said. "And not just for selfish reasons, either."

"What others, may I ask?" Kidd said.

"Oh, in the last analysis, I suppose," Baldwin said, as Flaherty and his companion, laughing joyously, got up from their table to leave, "in the last analysis, they'd turn out to be selfish, I guess. Almost all motives do, if you look hard enough. But not entirely that, pure selfishness, I mean. I'm the only *Commoner* holdover left in the Group's top echelon. All the other lingerers and malingerers from the Gould ownership days've either died or retired. All the other people who remember the Goulds and the way they ran the paper as a real forum for the public interest, and damn those who opposed it: all those people are gone. Except for me. The rest of the board of directors consists of former yokels and outside eminences and people who used to be ambassadors or almost were governors, or once served an interim appointment as U.S. Senator. Their grasp of balance sheets is firm, but they have absolutely no feel whatsoever for the operation of a great newspaper.

"Don't laugh at me here now, Roger," Baldwin said, "because I'm serious. Yesterday I spent fooling around with bids and proposals to convert our offices here and all our other operations around the country from the mishmash of data-processing systems and IBM Selectrics and God knows what else to one uniform, interlinked system that will interface, I believe the term is, all our operations. All our newspapers. All our broadcast outlets, and all our magazines. It's boring, tedious work, and it's harder because it should've been done long ago, and it makes me yearn for France. But somebody has to do it correctly. If I or anybody tackling this conversion makes a mistake, it will harpoon the *Commoner*'s potential ability to access, as they say, instant reports of virtually anything that happens in the United States. That ability will make the *Commoner* a better newspaper, and also make our other papers and our broadcasting outlets better because they'll have access to the *Commoner*'s reports. I'm the only one in the Group hierarchy who has any real appreciation for the journalistic implications of decisions like that for the *Commoner*.

"I can enforce my decisions," Baldwin said, "because I have credibility. If I lose that credibility, pretty soon purely economic judgments by some buffalo from Wichita will begin to diminish *The Boston Commoner*. At this stage of my life, Roger, it seems unlikely that I will leave any children behind me. None I know about, at least. I have my faults, as you know, but I take the *Commoner* very seriously.

"Now this two-bit DA from the boondocks" Baldwin said, "comes into my office and tells me that he's got a case that's out of control, and likely to damage the *Commoner*. Billy Taves doesn't know what I've just told you. Nobody's told him, and he isn't bright enough to figure it out by himself. But somewhere in the dim recesses of his scheming brain, he has managed to perceive that Joe Logan poses a threat to me as well. And he is correct. If Logan takes the stand and says that Mel Shaw of the *Commoner*'s Waterford bureau evaded prosecution for murdering his fag boyfriend by covering up crooked real estate deals, the *Commoner*'s going to look like a hill of shit, you should pardon the expression. Here is this great defender of the public interest, this great thundering voice against official corruption, unmasked as a pitiful, helpless giant used as a tool of public corruption by its own bureau chief. Doesn't matter to the paper what Shaw's motive was for doing it, that it was exposure to a murder charge and not just simple greed. Doesn't matter to the paper what my motive might have been for not preventing Shaw from doing it, my own exposure to scandal. All that matters to the *Commoner* is that its corporate integrity, its .reputation for truthfulness and independence, has been compromised in public. Maybe even fatally compromised." He sighed. "I'd hate to think I was responsible for that, for that happening."

Then he laughed, one bark. "Suppose," he said, "just suppose that Logan doesn't have any hard feelings for me, that he really doesn't know anything about the Rivera case. Suppose I get off scot-free, when he starts his arias. As far as anyone knows, I'm as pure as the driven snow. Except, of course, that as CEO of the paper, I didn't watch my people carefully enough to make sure no one compromised it.

"If you were the buffalo from Wichita," Baldwin said, "would you bring that up at the next executive committee meeting when I announce that no expense, such as the one for this new data-processing system, is too great to assure you the continued journalistic integrity and excellence of *The Boston Commoner*? Or would you just laugh in my face?"

"I would laugh in your face," Kidd said.

"Do you, perhaps," Baldwin said, "begin to see why it is that I did not bring this matter to the attention of Dan Joyce at Rand, Hayes, which represents the said board as a whole, along with the *Commoner*?"

"I believe I do," Kidd said, "What I do not see is what exactly you want me to do."

6

"All right," Baldwin said in his office. "Let me try out a few notions on you and see whether you think any of them leads us to the penitentiary."

"You're making me nervous," Kidd said. "I'm not a criminal lawyer. I don't want to be one, and I don't want to need one. I live a placid life, Mark. I like it that way. I do not crave excitement. I didn't like it the first time that you came to me with a questionable errand, seeing the Rivera family for you, and I told you so then. Then, after they refused the hush money, and you told me your next idea, I told you I'd be no part of it. That those so-called 'contributions' you planned to make could backfire dangerously some day. Well you did it anyway, and what did it take? Over twenty years? Longer than I expected, at any rate. I figured you'd be up before the grand jury before the year was out.

"But the point is, it has happened," Kidd said. "Not when, perhaps, but just as I said it would. Now I'm older, and even more nervous. I can't stop you today any more than I could then from taking action that seems risky to me, but I won't help you plan or execute it. So, watch your loose talk around me. I'm easily distressed."

"You do know criminal lawyers, though," Baldwin said.

"I do," Kidd said. "When you and I were at Andover back when Grant was taking Richmond, I knew a townie twenty-one who would buy beer for us. And I used his services. Sparingly, as you recall, with utmost discretion, and consequently no repercussions from the authorities. I do the same sort of thing with the criminal lawyers that I know today. When the firm feels that a client of ours requires the advice of counsel on potentially criminal matters, I call one of the criminal lawyers that I know, and I dispose of it. That need does not arise very often, I am glad to say. When it does, we use our wits, and get rid of it.

"Fortunately," Kidd said, "nothing you've told me so far seems to me to indicate any criminal exposure on your part. Unless there's something you haven't told me that you think carries that danger. So, why the need of someone who does that kind of work?"

"After Billy Taves ruined my morning," Baldwin said, "the first thing that occurred to me was that what I need is information. I need a sharp son of a bitch of my own to dig into this can of worms and tell me what is going on."

"Well, for heaven's sake, Mark," Kidd said, "you've got a posse of reporters over at the paper who specialize in that sort of thing. Pick your hungriest and turn him loose. One phone call should do that, and it won't cost you a penny more than you'll spend anyway."

"Taves had the same bright idea," Baldwin said. "Can't do that, Roger. You are not thinking."

"I don't see why you can't," Kidd said. "They all work for you. Maybe not directly, but they will do what you say."

"They all work for me, Roger," Baldwin said, "to get things to put in the paper. I don't *want* what I want in this instance to come out in the paper."

"Oh, yes," Kidd said, touching his upper lip with the first two fingers of his right hand. "Yes. I can see where that could be a problem."

"You know what happens when you get a good reporter all haired up to get a story, and he gets it, and then you say to him: 'Oh, by the way, can't print it'?" Baldwin snickered. "It's like putting a cherry bomb under a pail. You get not only the bang you would've gotten anyway, but also a pail flying through the air to conk you on the head."

"That was stupid of me," Kidd said. "Let me think some more."

"Obviously," Baldwin said, "I've got to keep the paper a good hundred yards from this. Obviously Billy Taves and I should not be seen playing kissy-face while this damned thing is going on. So I need a cover for somebody who's good to find out whether there's a way Billy Taves hasn't thought of to stick this case down the porcelain convenience before we get crap on ourselves.

"You must know somebody, some lawyer or investigator, who can find out things like that. What about Mrs. Flaherty's case? Haven't you got some sneaky private eye tailing him around?"

Kidd shifted on the couch and looked uneasy. "No," he said.

" '*No*' "? Baldwin said. "What do you mean, 'No'? How's she going to prove adultery without a private snoop?"

Kidd shifted again. "Well actually, Mark," he said, "that's a bit of a sore point in the firm just now. Whether Jane should allege adultery. Our preference now is that irretrievable breakdown should always be the grounds alleged in the libel or complaint, regardless of the actual, proximate cause of the collapse of the marriage." He looked earnest. "Almost nobody gets divorced in a vacuum," he said. "Our clients usually have children, and even those few that don't, have relatives, mutual good friends, business associates and so forth. Dragging dirty laundry into court and waving it around like flags hurts others as well as the intended victim, and those wounds don't heal."

He exhaled heavily. "Or so we try to tell our clients, at least," he said. "In Mrs. Flaherty's instance, I must say we're meeting quite a lot of resistance." He shook his head. "It's hard for me to understand how people get into these situations where their overriding aim becomes to hurt somebody they once loved. I suppose it's because I've never been in such a position, where I've been badly hurt and just wanted to strike back. That's what Bayliss says, at least, and he claims he's always right.

"But anyway," Kidd said, looking pained and wistful, "the answer to your question is that so far, at least, we don't have a detective on John Flaherty. By this time next week, I suspect we probably will, and he'll get what Jane has in mind despite all our advice to the contrary. And then we'll try again to convince her that the best use to be made of the material, for the sake of everyone involved, is to present it to her husband's attorney and see if it prompts his lawyer to advise him to offer a generous settlement in exchange for a quiet divorce. And hope for the best."

"Well," Baldwin said, "what about that guy, then, to work for me in this?"

"Oh," Kidd said, crossing his legs and shaking his head, "no, Mark, I don't think so. The man we use in these situations is a retired cop whose first name I can never remember. They call him 'Bad Eye Mulvey.' He's got a lazy eye. We got him through Jerry Kennedy, who used to do whatever occasional criminal work our clients needed done. I don't think he's very good, actually, this Mulvey character. I guess his work's all right, the kind that we need done.

He doesn't strike me as having a first-rate mind."

"He strikes you as stupid, you mean," Baldwin said.

Kidd grinned. "He's very thorough," he said. "He's very patient, and scrupulous about following directions. And he's cheap, to boot. Which is why I think Bayliss finds his work satisfactory. But what you seem to have in mind strikes me as requiring a little more intelligence, good judgment and discretion, than I think it likely Bad Eye has at his command. If you follow me." He chuckled.

"Okay," Baldwin said, "what about the guy who sent him, this Kennedy character? Should I talk to him?"

Kidd looked worried. "Ah," he said, "tough question. Five years ago, three years ago, my answer would have been 'Yes.' A little hesitant, perhaps, but I would have answered 'Yes.' Today? I don't think so. Jerry's been going through some bad times of his own. Had himself a public battle with some idiot judge that got on television and caused a general disgrace. I heard he's been drinking more than he should, and Ed Maguire in the federal court told me confidentially he's in some sort of difficulty with the IRS." Kidd frowned.

"I don't know, Mark," he said. "I've known Jerry a long time, and I like him. He's a bit of a roughneck, I suppose, thinks of himself as an outlaw and a rebel, but all of those criminal types do that. All the ones I know. I suppose he's still reliable enough, but I can't be sure. I don't think I'd call on him right now. Not for something this sensitive.

"See, your problem here, Mark," Kidd said, "is really one of concealment. If you send in an investigator or a lawyer, he's going to have to tell people who he represents. People're more sophisticated than they used to be. Sooner or later somebody's going to press your man on why he's asking questions. And if he doesn't answer plausibly, there will be trouble. But you don't want your involvement disclosed. So your operative is going to have to lie.

"Well," Kidd said, "let's be practical for a moment: what lie's he going to tell? And what will be the consequences of any lie he tells? If it's believed, of course, no problem. You will get away with it. But if it's not believed, and either the police or this fellow Logan get wind of it and start to figure things out, you could find yourself in a worse mess than you're in already.

"My guess is that if you send in either an investigator or a lawyer, your chances of being detected, the *Commoner*'s chances of being damaged still further, are virtually certain. A lawyer has to have a client, paying him to talk to people. An investigator has to have either a lawyer who's paying him on behalf of a client, or a client who's paying him directly. Unless what you want to know is contained entirely in public records, like deeds and that sort of thing, you have to have some sort of credentials to tap into it. You can't provide any. That's the sticking point. The only way I can see for you to do this is to dress somebody up as a reporter for one of your publications, and send that person in."

"An impostor, in other words," Baldwin said.

"You can put it that way," Kidd said.

"Well, I have to, don't I?" Baldwin said. "If what you're saying is correct, I can't use a regular lawyer or a private eye. And I know very well I can't use a real reporter. So what I have to do is hire somebody to impersonate a reporter, and do it convincingly enough so that by the time anybody gets wise, he's gotten what I wanted and made a clean getaway."

"Is that a problem?" Kidd said.

"In theory, no," Baldwin said. "We own enough regrettably-obscure publications so it wouldn't be too tough to find a slot. Create one, I mean. And the editors of those publications are obedient. They will do what I say, and accredit someone if I tell them to.

"The problem," Baldwin said, "the problem is finding someone who can't be connected to me, and therefore by definition must be someone I don't know, that I can trust enough to put in a position to do me a lot of harm if he decides to defect. What I'm asking for is somebody who's so good at deception he can bring off this charade, but not so good at it that he'll also doublecross me. The thought makes me uneasy."

Kidd frowned and cleared his throat. "Terry Gleason may have the person you need," he said.

"Terry Gleason," Baldwin said. "Do I know this guy?"

"Probably not," Kidd said. "He was in the Suffolk DA's office for a number of years before he went out on his own. When Kennedy began to have his troubles, and we began to have our reservations about their effect on his work, we found ourselves with a valuable client whose son has a drug problem and needed a criminal lawyer. So we asked around, and one of the judges that Bayliss knew mentioned Terry's name. I bounced it off Ed Maguire. He said Gleason'd had a case before him, and he'd found him capable. So we recommended him and our client went to see him, and I gather the matter turned out reasonably well. The boy didn't go to jail, at least, so I assume it turned out well."

"But if he's a lawyer . . .," Baldwin said.

"I'm coming to that," Kidd said. "Apparently Gleason prefers to work pretty much alone, but he's doing well enough these days so that he's had to hire an independent paralegal to handle preparation for him. She came in to see us because she needed some background on the boy's family, and his father wouldn't talk to her without our okay. I was impressed by what I saw. She was smart, thorough, makes a good appearance. And appeared to be the soul of discretion. Her name is Constance Gates."

Baldwin shook his head. "I dunno, Roger," he said. "I haven't met this woman, but I have got my doubts that some glorified twenty-one-year-old secretary can waltz into this and do what I want without making things worse."

"That's not what she is," Kidd said. "You'd want to meet her, of course, and form your own opinions. But Connie's a bit more qualified than you assume. In the first place, she's about thirty-five, give or take a year. She has a bachelor's degree from Wheaton, early Seventies. This freelance paralegal business is recent, something she got into when her marriage ended."

"A hobbyist?" Baldwin said. "Living on her alimony and getting cheap thrills in the law?"

"Hardly that," Kidd said. "She made it clear to me that she went into it because she wanted to use her brain. She said her profession before she married and had children was not the kind of work where that activity was likely, and she thought she'd try something new. And she said it's working out. Only takes assignments that look interesting to her. Works on a fee basis, and takes as much time to complete her jobs as she thinks that they require."

"What was her previous profession, made her think the law takes smarts?" Baldwin said. "Airline stewardess?"

Kidd laughed. "She was a reporter, Mark. A newspaper reporter."

"Score two points for Mister Kidd," Baldwin said. "How do I talk to her? Call this Gleason fellow?"

"Better not," Kidd said. "I'm not that well-acquainted with Terry. Although I assume he's trustworthy, the fewer people that know about this, the better. I have her number at the office. Let me sound her out, without being specific of course, and I'll get back to you."

"I'd be obliged," Baldwin said.

Pleading his bad back, Baldwin did not get up to escort Kidd from the office. He sat in his leather chair and swiveled around so that he looked out the easterly windows to the airport across the harbor, where the silver planes rose and descended in the mid-afternoon sun. When he was sure Kidd was gone, he swiveled back and punched the intercom button. "Anne," he said, "get me Bob Doran, please."

"Doran and Flaherty?" she said.

"Uh huh," he said. "And check my book, if you would. What've I got on tonight?"

"The Catholic Charities committee dinner," she said. "Eight at the Saint Botolph."

"Wonderful," Baldwin said dryly. "Okay, get Doran."

When the call to Doran came through, Baldwin was succinct. "Reason I called you, Bobby," he said, "I think it might be a good idea, you had a chat with Jack." He paused. "Yes," he said, "precisely about that. The Chinese piano lady." He paused again. "I know it's none of your personal business, Bob," he said. "I know how you feel about Jack. But I think the time has come where if you don't get involved in it, you may personally regret it later." He listened and nodded. "Because it may have bad repercussions for your company: that's why." He paused again. "She's off the reservation, Bob. Jane is after his balls. She's out of control. I can't give you details and I'm not going to. But listen to me, please: If you talk to Jack, and he doesn't listen, try to buy him out." He paused again. "Yes, Bob," he said, "that serious." He listened again. "You're entirely welcome, Bob," he said. "I like to help my friends."

He put the phone down and looked out the window again. He shifted in the chair and groped once in his crotch. He picked up the phone again and punched an outside line. He dialed the main number for North American Group. The receptionist at the front desk answered. "Sylvia," he said, "I don't know how much longer my back's going to take to heal, but I know it's going to be longer than I can wait."

"Five-forty-five?" she said softly.

"Is that okay?" he said.

"If I leave much earlier," she said warmly, "it may cause cheap talk."

Baldwin laughed. "Five-forty-five," he said.

7

Sylvia Francis found the newsstand in the lobby of 200 Federal Street crowded with other people leaving the building between 5:15 and 5:30. She made her way among them in the narrow aisles like an infiltrator. She went to the notions counter; no salesperson was there. She inspected the contents of the small sewing kits displayed, selecting one priced at four dollars; she served herself as well to two packages of the L'Eggs panty hose arranged on the black metal rack between her and the cashier. She took seventh place in the line of people at the cash register. By the time she had moved up to fourth, she had palmed the sewing kit into her handbag. She presented the panty-hose to the cashier, paid for them and left the store.

There were three cabs outside the easterly doors of the building in the turnaround; she took the first in line and said: "One-sixty Beacon, please." She settled back against the cushion as the driver pulled away from the curb and pressed her thighs together, enjoying the warm moisture in her crotch.

At 160 Beacon, she paid off the driver and went quickly through the black wrought-iron gate and down the three steps to the front walk, fishing in her handbag for the appropriate set of keys. She unlocked the front door and then the inside door, shutting each of them carefully behind her making sure they locked again. She crossed the pale beige Oriental rug in the foyer to the elevator; its door opened when she pushed the button. She got in and punched "5" on the scale of six and leaned back against the handrail at the rear of the car. She clamped her legs together again and for the first time since leaving her desk in the reception area of North American Group, allowed herself to smile.

She deactivated the digital alarm system inside the door to the one-bedroom apartment on the fifth floor within the thirty seconds it allowed. She closed and locked the door behind her, looked at her Movado museum watch for what little guidance it gave to the passage of thirty seconds, exhaled in exasperation, tapped her foot, and when the watch indicated that it was approximately 5:40, reset the alarm. She got away with that, too; the alarm did not go off.

To her right as she faced the hall door was the door into the kitchen. Behind her the living room was bisected horizontally by a three-cushion grey tweed couch facing the picture window. There were two putty-colored leather Eames chairs in the corners by the window; a wide circular glass coffee table formed the center of the grouping. Below the window was a Sony television monitor on a pedestal, flanked by two large speakers in walnut cabinets. Between the couch and the door where she stood was a Swedish modern oak dining table with four off-white leather chairs. The carpeting was light blue wall-to-wall. Beyond the window the Charles River against the backdrop of MIT was blue in the late spring afternoon, and small boats with striped sails from the Sailing Club plied back and forth in the light winds of June.

Sylvia Francis paid no attention to the view. She went into the bedroom to the right off the living room, flipping the light switch for the bathroom as she passed the door. She heard the fluorescent tubes over the double sinks clinking on as she reached the king-sized bed. It was covered with a blue and white striped comforter. She pulled down the corner nearest to the double closet doors and saw that the linen was fresh. She nodded approval. She put her handbag down on the bed and used her left hand to steady herself against the wall behind the headboard while she removed her right shoe. Teetering a little on the other high heel, she reversed her position and took that shoe off as well. Flat-footed now, she pressed her lips tightly together and pulled her dress off over her head. She turned back to the closet, opened it, and put the dress on a padded hanger. There were four other dresses in the closet, two of them in plastic bags fresh from the cleaner's; two pairs of embroidered jeans; and five pairs of high-heeled shoes on the floor. There were also a pair of brown boots and a pair of white Nike sneakers. On a hook next to the rod hung a white negligée.

Expanding the elastic waist of her white half slip she let it drop to the floor and then sat down on the bed to remove her panty-hose, first pinching the cotton crotch liner to revive the excitement she felt in the newsstand and the cab. She dropped the hose on the bed and unhooked her white bra, letting it slide down her arms, catching it and dropping it on top of the hose. When she pulled down her white bikini panties, the crotch was darkly wet. She stood up and went quickly around the bed, pausing briefly to admire her body in the mirror. Her dark pubic hair glistened, and she rubbed it hard with her hand, reaching deep between her legs to spread the moisture. Then she went over to the windows, opened the beige drapes and stood at the middle of the window and looked out over the river shining in the late sunlight, trying to decide if she could see the figures in the boats clearly enough to make it likely they could see her. She decided they could not, but that the people in the cars passing along Storrow Drive could. She liked that idea, and plucked at her crotch hair again. She looked down at her breasts and pinched her left nipple. It was very hard, and so was the right one.

She walked quickly into the bathroom, opened the medicine cabinet and took out a bottle of Guerlain "L'heure bleue" cologne. She set it on the counter. She opened the other side of the medicine cabinet and removed a small canister of spermicidal foam and a clear plastic applicator plunger. She filled the applicator and backed up to the toilet, reaching with her left hand to make sure the seat was down. She urinated, holding the plunger aloft with her right hand, then transferring it to her left in order to use tissue. She spread her legs wider and inserted the plunger into her vagina, emptying the foam into herself. In front of the mirror she put cologne behind her ears, under her breasts and generously into her crotch hair. She also put some behind her knees. Looking at herself in the mirror, she smiled again. She inserted the middle finger of her right hand into her vagina and stroked her clitoris. She felt herself lubricating again and continued for a few seconds, stopping soon enough to deny herself orgasm. She looked at her face in the mirror and saw that the color in her cheeks was very high. She hugged herself and shivered. She heard the door open and close. She went out of the bathroom, stood in the doorway to the living room, and looked at her watch. "Where have you been, Mark?" she said in a low voice. "I thought you'd never get here."

Baldwin was looking at his Rolex GMT. He glanced at her and smiled. He looked back at his watch. "Ten minutes," he said. He grinned at her. "It's really that bad?"

"Ten minutes plus three days and seven weeks," she said, moving toward him and reaching out to take his blazer off. She laid it on the back of the couch. When she turned back to him, he was removing the black knit tie and heading for the bathroom. "Hurry up," she said.

"I am," he said, "I am. Just got to take a leak here, you know, while I'm still relaxed enough to get an angle on the flush." She hugged herself again in the living room and shivered. Then she went into the bedroom, hearing him in the bathroom. She took her handbag and her underwear off the bed and put them on the dresser. She went to the window again. She was standing there when he came out of the bathroom.

"Putting on a show?" he said. He unbuttoned his shirt at the cuffs as well as the front plaquet.

"I don't know," she said. She turned to face him, resting her buttocks on the cold window sill. "I don't know what's happening to me. Ever since I was a little girl, I've had this idea that I'd like to go naked in public. Let people see me, you know? But I never did it, of course. And then when Jason and I were first married, we got married in the fall and we took our honeymoon on the Cape, and there was one day when we were down at Coast Guard Beach and there was nobody else around, and I did it. I just took off my suit and he was horrified. Absolutely horrified. Well, of course I told him there wasn't anyone around, but he wouldn't take off his and do what I really wanted to do, and then when we were leaving, one of the forest rangers or whatever they are drove up to our car and said: 'No harm done, folks, this time. But nude bathing's not allowed here.' And then he drove off, and Jason was mortified. But I wasn't. I wasn't at all."

Baldwin was moving carefully as he began to get out of his shirt. He winced as he moved. "Oh," she said, "your back. I should have thought." She went to him and took the shirt off his torso.

"Thanks," he said. He used the toe of each foot to hold down the counters of his Bally loafers so he could get out of them. He unbuckled his belt and undid his trouser clasp, letting the pants fall but standing almost upright while he did it. She steadied him with her arm around his waist and he stepped out of the pants without bending. She stopped and picked up the trousers, folding them at the crease and opening the other half of the double closet to hang them up while he moved carefully toward the bed in his socks and boxer shorts. He sat down slowly and bent as little as possible while he took off his socks. Then he eased himself out of his shorts and pivoted on his buttocks before lying down on his back. His penis was tumescent but not fully erect.

She stood at the foot of the bed and showed concern on her face. "Are you sure this is all right for you, Mark?" she said. "I don't want to hurt you."

He managed to combine a grimace and a smile. He raised his right hand and beckoned to her. "Cut it out, Sylvia," he said. "Come here and work your magic. Just treat me like a piece of fine china instead of a piece of ass, and everything'll be fine. I'm going to explode if I don't get some pretty soon."

She grinned and walked quickly around to the other side of the bed, whipping the covers back and sliding in so that she lay on her left side next to him, her left breast resting on his right bicep. She rubbed his stomach with her right hand, moving it down to the root of his penis and then under his scrotum to caress his testicles. He became fully erect. "Take it easy," he said softly. "It feels wonderful, but you do it much longer and I'm going to be the only one here having any fun."

She rose up and straddled him gingerly, allowing him to guide her with his hands at her waist. She inserted his penis and leaned back in the kneeling position with her hands on his knees. She closed her eyes and said: "Ahh." Then she leaned forward again and put her hands on the bed so that she crouched over him. "Let me do the work," she said.

"I wouldn't change a thing," he said. She pumped four times, feeling his expansion in her. He ejaculated in five bursts bracketing her orgasm. They both shuddered. She allowed herself to lie down on his chest. "Is this all right now?" she said. "I'm not hurting you, am I?"

"You'd know if you were," he said. "Secrets like that I can't keep." He could feel the warm fluid coming out of her and dripping down his scrotum. "We're not doing the sheets any good, though," he said. "Maid'll get a few laughs when she changes them this week."

She giggled. "Don't complain," she said. "I do the best I can for you, but when it's been this long, you know, there's more from both of us than I can hold."

They lay back like that for a while and his penis started to become flaccid inside her. She allowed it to retract about halfway and then carefully rolled off him to his left, so that she could sit on the edge of the bed. "Want some wine?" she said.

"Yeah," he said. "That'd be nice. Little Montrachet? That's the trouble with quitting smoking. Drives you to drink for something to do, after you've gotten laid. What I wouldn't give for a Lucky right now."

"Ten years of your life is what you would give," she said, "the way you smoked those things." She started toward the kitchen.

"Yeah," he said, "I know. But now, even after almost two years off them, it still doesn't feel complete. Without a cigarette after. 'The three best things in the world,' " he said, " 'a martini before and a cigarette after. And only one of them's good for you.' "

"None of them, actually," she said on her way through the living room. "If you grew up in the sisters' schools like I did, all of them were bad."

She came back with two glasses of wine and sat on the edge of the bed. He pulled himself up into a sitting position and accepted the glass. "To insatiable sexual appetites," he said.

"Makes the world go 'round," she said. They clinked and drank. She put her glass down on to the floor, crossed her right leg over her left and clasped the right with both hands. "I missed you," she said. "That's the trouble with my insatiable appetite: When you take yours out of the country for six weeks, and get yourself so bent out of shape you can't do anything for another week and a half after you get back, it's perfect hell for me. I got so horny I was thinking about going down to the Navy Yard and asking if they had any sailors around who'd like to have some fun."

He chuckled. "You should read *Journeyer*," he said. "We'll get you a complimentary subscription. Don't they have advice in there, techniques for ladies in your deprived state and all that kind of thing?"

She gave him a mock punch to the chest. "Thanks a lot," she said. "The day I fall in love with a vibrator's the day I'll know I'm ready for the Home."

"Is that what they push in that book?" Baldwin said. "I must admit I haven't seen it more'n twice since Macalester got obsessed with the feminist market — what, three years ago? And said we had to buy it. I thought it was mostly for lesbians, what I saw of it. Not very bright lesbians, either. Fairly stupid lesbians who had to have directions. But what the hell, right? Maybe I'm wrong. Or maybe Macalester's one of those guys, gets his jollies looking at pictures of women with women. Harmless enough, I suppose."

"Yeah," Sylvia said, "but that's not what your caller this morning thought, sir. He thinks it's a dirty book."

Baldwin laughed again and reached out to fondle her left breast with his left hand. "Oh," he said, "did the Honorable Billy Taves speak to you about it too?"

"Uh huh," she said. "Guys like that really make me laugh. Here's this fat guy getting old, comes into the office and practically strips me with his eyes, and then he gets all moral about a magazine."

"Well," Baldwin said, sipping some wine, "that's what makes moral people so righteous, you know? Their minds are filled with swinish thoughts that they'd like very much to act out. But they're afraid to do it. They're chicken. So when they see somebody else doing what they'd do themselves, if they had the balls, they get envious. That's what makes them so mean."

She unclasped her hands and turned slightly so that she could grasp his penis with her left hand. "Speaking of what people would like to do," she said. She squeezed it gently. "You know what I'd like to do?"

"Unless I'm very much mistaken," he said, looking down, "I think I have an inkling. Did I leave you up in the air there, my dear?"

She continued to handle him. "Absolutely not," she said. "I was perfectly all right. But that was almost ten minutes ago, and it's been a long time between drinks. So, if you can manage it, I would not object to a second course."

" 'If I can manage it,' " he said. "Going to get my masculine pride involved here? Is that what you're doing, scheming wench?"

She slid off the bed without letting go of his penis and knelt on the floor so that she could place both hands at his crotch. She began to knead his genitals and he became erect again. She stood up fast. "Okay," she said, "don't move."

"Move?" he said. "How the hell can I move? I haven't got any skin left."

She went to the dresser and opened her handbag. She took out the stolen sewing kit. She opened it up. She started back toward the bed.

"Hey," he said, "what're you doing? You're not going to sew my cock up."

"It's occurred to me," she said, taking the tape measure out of the kit. She removed the clip that held it folded and let it unroll to the floor. "Put a neat little hem in the end of it there, and see what that French bitch does then." She sat down on the bed again and grabbed his penis at the root.

"Hey," he said again.

"Shut up," she said, "and drink your wine." She wrapped the tape measure around his penis. She marked it. She took it off and looked at it. "I was right," she said.

"You were right about what?" he said.

"I was right about your fat cock," she said. "Ever since the first time I had that thing in me, I knew there was something different, from what I had before. Then while you were away, Jason got one of the three annual erections he gets since the docs put him on his medicine. And Jason's cock is fairly long. He's never let me measure it, even back before he had his attack, but it's a pretty good-sized tool. And when he gets one of those few hard-ons that he gets now, well, I was sort of looking forward to it. Yours being away and all. And his didn't do the job. So I started thinking, well, it must be the thickness then. You know you're almost as thick as you are long? Your thing's almost six inches around."

"Yes," he said.

"Oh," she said. "You son of a bitch."

"Well, I'm sorry," he said. "You asked me a question. I answered the question you asked."

She gripped him hard. He used his left hand to return the favor. "What am I going to do with you?" she said.

"You mean: Now?" he said. He fingered her clitoris. "Or are we talking about the long-term, here?"

She laughed and got back onto the bed. "I know what we're going to do now," she said, "and I'm damned glad of it, too."

8

Constance Gates in a tan khaki suit over a white silk blouse entered the reception area of North American Group just before 11:30 A.M. The blouse was open to the third button. She was slender. She had very good legs to which she called modest attention by wearing pale maroon shaded stockings and oxblood high heels. She carried a thin attaché case in tan suede. She wore a thin gold chain at her throat, a gold Rolex watch, and no other jewelry. She had dark hair with henna highlights, done in a chignon. She had Porsche sunglasses perched on her hair.

Sylvia Francis was talking on the intercom to Anne Leeds in Baldwin's office. "Just now," Sylvia said, appraising Gates, "uh huh. Definitely. I think Nieman Marcus is too dear. Maybe, Lord and Taylor? No, not the Talbots', not at all. Hate that pink and green." She laughed. "Talk to you later, Anne," she said, and put the handset down. "May I help you?" she said to Gates.

"That's a lovely ring," Gates said. "Did it come from Long's?"

Sylvia extended her left ring finger to inspect her own diamond. "Actually, no," she said. "Shreve's, as I recall."

"It's very beautiful," Gates said. "I am Mister Baldwin's eleven-thirty appointment." She put subtle emphasis on the verb.

Sylvia pursed her lips and picked up the handset. She looked at Gates demurely. "May I give him your name?" she said.

"Constance Gates," Gates said, turning away from the reception desk and starting toward the chairs. She was sitting with her attaché case beside her when Anne Leeds opened the door. "Miz. Gates?" she said invitingly, opening the door wider. "Won't you come with me?" Gates went into the interior corridor ahead of Leeds, so that Leeds had an instant to exchange knowing looks with Sylvia. Sylvia, finishing her second inspection of Gates's trim rear end, scowled at Leeds, nodded twice in agreement, and with her lips set, turned to answer the phone.

In Baldwin's office Gates took the leather director's chair nearest the two Out boxes on the refectory table and put her attaché case on the floor. "It's perfectly all right," she said. "My ex-husband had that problem and it drove him nearly crazy. I used to tell him it was a good thing for him that lawyers don't do heavy lifting."

"Did he ever find anyone who could do anything for it, by chance?" Baldwin said, carefully adjusting his torso in his chair.

"Uh huh," Gates said, "yes, he did. I think he did, at least."

"Are you on speaking terms with him?" Baldwin said, showing interest.

She shrugged and smiled. "There's a certain amount of speaking necessary," she said, "with the kids and all. Why?"

"Because I want you to ask him for me who it is that fixed his back," Baldwin said. "That's not what I asked you to come here for today, but if you can get me that name, I'll pay you double what you're asking for the job I have in mind."

She put her head back and laughed. "I don't have to ask," she said. "I know who it is. But it's his second wife. I don't think she's accepting new clients. I don't think Jeff allows it."

"Damn," Baldwin said.

"I know it," Gates said sympathetically. "But he's always been a dog in a manger. You know how they are." She let him study her for a few moments. She sat almost perfectly still and kept her gaze focused on his eyes, waiting for him to look down at her breasts. He didn't do it.

Baldwin broke the inspection. He leaned back very slowly in his chair and steepled his fingers. "Tell me about myself," he said.

"Beg pardon," she said. She opened her eyes wide and permitted herself a small smile. "Tell you about you?"

"That's what I said," he said.

"Okay," she said. She took a breath. " 'Father: Angus; mother: Amy, maiden name was Cross, I think. Born August eighteen, 'thirty-two. Andover, 'forty-nine. Harvard, 'fifty-three. Harvard Law School, 'fifty-six. Fletcher School, Law and Diplomacy, 'fifty-eight. Department of State, 'fifty-eight-'sixty. Team Lotus, 'sixty-one-two. *Boston Commoner*, 'sixty-two-seven. North American Group, 'sixty-seven-date. Married Lucille Bede Barrow, 'sixty-one. Divorced, nineteen sixty-two. Clubs . . . . ' "

He was grinning. "That's enough," he said. "I seldom go to them anyway, except the Charter upstairs. You're very good."

She nodded acknowledgment. "Thank you," she said. "It seemed like a reasonable thing to do. Mister Kidd was very secretive about why you wanted to see me. All Terry Gleason knew was that you had something to do with the newspaper. I was curious. Marquis publishes *Who's Who* for people like me." She paused. "So, now do I get to ask what it is, that you want me to do?"

"Not quite yet," Baldwin said. "First you have to tell me about you."

"You're not making this easy," she said.

"It's not an easy job I have in mind for you to do," he said. The humor had left his face. "I need to know something about you before I decide whether you're the person I want to do it."

She showed impatience on her face. She crossed her legs and frowned. "Mister Baldwin," she said, "I don't know what Mister Kidd told you, and I don't know what interpretation you put on what he may have said. But in case there's some misunderstanding here that's not anybody's fault, I think you ought to know precisely what I do. I prepare cases for trial. I work hard at it and I'm good at it, and it's all I want to do. I do it for money. I'm a professional. Mister Kidd gave you my name because, I assume, he thinks I'm good at what I do. My background and private life are none of your business."

Baldwin sighed. "Oh dear," he said. He unsteepled his fingers and leaned forward carefully. He reached into the nearest In box. He took out the third file from the top. It was a thin manila folder, tabbed *Gates, Constance (Holly)*. He opened it as he leaned back in the chair again. He began to read. "Born, Gloucester, October ninth, Nineteen-forty-nine. Gloucester High School, class of Nineteen-sixty-six. Wheaton College, *cum laude*, Nineteen-seventy. Reporter, Newburyport *Transcript*, Nineteen-seventy-seventy-six. Married Jeffrey L. Gates, June, Nineteen-seventy-five. Two children, Estelle and Jeffrey. Divorced, May, Nineteen-eighty-two. Residence: Five China Wharf, Boston. Credit rating: poor, based on reports from three department stores, two gasoline companies, and Wharf Furniture Company, which apparently believes you still owe them two hundred and eighty dollars for a rug you bought two years ago. Motor vehicle, Nineteen-eighty-one BMW three-twenty-eye,

Mass. registration two-two-four, MNS, color metallic green. Two Boston parking violations outstanding, both evening, both on Newbury Street between Exeter and Fairfield. One, Cambridge, Brattle Street. Vehicle registration was suspended last December for non-payment of insurance premiums, and again in April for non-payment of excise taxes. Reinstated in each instance upon proof of payment presented within three days of notice." He snapped the folder shut and put it in the nearest Out box. "You'd better pay those tickets, Miz. Gates," he said. "They'll hang a Denver boot on that lovely little sled, and you'll end up walking home. And if you somehow dodge that, your license comes up for renewal this October and they won't give you a new one until you get square with the law."

Her face was red. "Part of me," she said, "wants to tell you that you're pretty good yourself."

He waved it away. "I hire good people," he said. "That's what I'm trying to do now. I look good because my people are good. You did me by yourself."

"The other part of me," she said, "wants to tell you what you can do with whatever this job is that you've got in mind, pick up my traps and stomp out of here."

"Your choice," he said.

"My choice," she said.

"That's right," he said. "I'd prefer you didn't do that, but if you do it, let's face it, I can find somebody else. And I will."

"I'm sure you will," she said.

"Depend on it," he said. "I'm offering an assignment that pays twenty thousand dollars. It will take no more than four months of hard work. Frankly, I think it'll be closer to two, but I'm guessing. All expenses reimbursed. How much trouble do you think I'm going to have, getting somebody I like?"

"Not a lot," she said.

"That's what I think, too," he said.

"Just out of curiosity," she said, "what are the precise terms of this assignment?"

"The person I hire," he said, "will be accredited by *Journeyer* to do a detailed study, no limit on length, of the details of a murder case."

"A murder case for *Journeyer*?" she said.

He sighed. "I know, I know," he said.

"Well," she said, "have you read it?"

"Not lately," he said. "I've had other things on my mind." He cleared his throat. "The person selected will be a writer for hire. Upon execution of the contract, that person will be paid ten thousand dollars, plus two hundred dollars advance against expenses. That person will be given several files of background material which will require at least a month of study, not necessarily all at once. A good deal of field interviewing will be required. The finished manuscript need not be delivered to me until October fifteenth, but I will expect regular and complete updates of the progress of the project starting a month from hire."

"What about rewrites?" she said.

"No rewrites will be required," he said.

"Look," she said, "bear with me here. I can't claim that the work I did for the *Transcript* was Pulitzer Prize stuff, but everything I did, from the garden club to my big bank fraud story, all went through an editor."

"I'm sure they did," he said.

"And the editor changed them," she said, "and quite often, had me rewrite them."

"They often do that," he said. "But this time will be different. I'm the editor."

"You're not an editor," she said.

"I am if I say I am," he said.

"But if I'm working for *Journeyer*," she said, "why am I delivering my story to you?"

"Look," Baldwin said, "I really don't have time to Dick-and-Jane this thing for you." He hunched his shoulders and immediately winced. "I'm looking for somebody to accept credentials as a freelance reporter on assignment for *Journeyer*. The assignment is to do a long report, a story, about a murder case. The pay is ten grand in front, plus two grand against expenses, and ten grand on delivery, plus all additional expenses.

"That's all you need to worry about. Whether you want the job. My company owns *Journeyer*," he said. "The editor of *Journeyer* is a lady named Lisa something-or-other, and the publisher's a woman named Joan. I don't have to ask them whether I can commission a story for my magazine on a murder case. I can do anything I want. They're the ones who have to ask. They have to ask me whether they can tell the printers to publish next month's issue, because they aren't making any money and I can sink that thing with one phone call, any time I want. They do what I say. Right off."

"And that's what you want me to do," she said, "whatever you say and right off. You're a very unpleasant man."

He slouched in the chair and laughed. "That's what I *wanted* you to do," he said. "When you came in here, that is what I had in mind. Now I can see you're not going to, and we've both been wasting our time." He began to get out of the chair, using both hands on its arms to lever himself to a standing position. It took him a little while.

"Cripes," she said, "you weren't kidding, not standing when I came in."

"My dear," he said, rubbing the small of his back, "nothing in this amusing discussion has been kidding, I assure you. Nothing whatsoever at all." He stopped rubbing and extended his right hand. "Miz. Gates," he said, "thanks for coming. Sorry we couldn't do business."

She didn't get up. "I didn't say that," she said.

"I know," he said, "I did. Interview's over. Nice of you to come in. Tell Anne on your way out I said to pay you whatever your time charge is. She'll give you a chit. You fill it out and you send it in, and Accounting will send you a check."

She remained seated. "You're really something," she said. "You know I don't work by the clock. Mister Kidd told me, he told you that. Who do you think you are?"

He arched his back. He relaxed. He began to sit down once again. "I know who I am, Constance Gates," he said. "I didn't ask you here to find out. I asked you here to offer you a job. You're not interested. Fine. Beat it. Nice to've talked to you."

She looked down to her lap. "I am interested," she said.

"Of course you are. You have to be interested," he said. "You're not stupid. You're chronically strapped for cash. The department stores say you take a long time to pay. Big expenses like automobile insurance that you didn't have to think about when you were married catch you by surprise now, with no money to pay them. So you have to go to someone who trusts you and negotiate a small loan, or an advance against future earnings, in order to get your plates back. A person like you doesn't like being in that position, cadging cash to meet ordinary expenses. It's embarrassing and humiliating, and it makes you feel small and incompetent when you find yourself forced to do it." He cleared his throat. "I'm offering you what amounts to twenty percent of the lump sum you settled for when you and Jeffrey broke up. For about two months' work. That proposal has to interest you. It's a first-class ticket out of this grinding little cycle you're in, of never quite catching up. It has to look good to you."

He shrugged. "Unfortunately," he said, "while you're considering it, you're at the same time developing this personal aversion to me. Which you apparently are ready to allow to overcome your better judgment."

"How do you know that?" she said. "About the settlement?"

"Oh, for heaven's sakes," he said, "it's public record. All I had to do was have one of our people go up to the courthouse in Essex County and look it up. Your husband went for custody of the kids. You didn't object. Which means either that you didn't dare to or you didn't care to, for what reasons I don't know and I'm not asking you about. But anyway, you didn't. And he bought you out for a hundred grand. Zeroed out the deal. Which, given your age and his circumstances, was the best bargain he's ever likely to see. You had a lawyer who breathes through her mouth, apparently, because you don't live extravagantly, and you work pretty hard, but less than two years after you got that settlement, you started having trouble paying your bills. Which makes me think you had to pay straight income taxes on most of that money, which is your lawyer's fault, and you're just about cleaned out.

"The biggest payday you've had since you blew most of what you had left on the condo and the car's been four grand from Kidd on a lousy drug case," Baldwin said. "That I know about, at least, and not too much gets by me." He paused again. "I can see you're really tough," he said. "I admire that in a person, and I'm certainly not going to advise anybody to compromise her principles or lose her self-respect. But I really wonder whether you can afford that luxury right now."

"You've got one point, at least," she said. "Not much gets by you."

"You really did have a lousy divorce lawyer, I must say," he said. "I wish to God Lucille'd hired her, back when we split up."

"Well," she said, "Linda was my classmate at college, and she was just setting up her practice, and you know how it is when you don't know what you're doing—you hire a friend to do it. You help each other out."

"No, I don't," he said. "I hire someone who's good."

She laughed. "Okay," she said, "you don't do that. But that is what I did. I just wanted it over with anyway. It was my fault as much as hers. I took his first offer."

"But you're not taking mine," he said. "Learned your lesson, is it?"

"I don't know," she said. "That's possible, I guess." She paused, and frowned. "Let me ask you something," she said. "Knowing all you know about me, why did you see me at all?"

"Why wouldn't I?" he said.

"Well," she said, "I don't know. You seem to think I'm a fool. I come in here and you try to browbeat me. When that doesn't work, you try to humiliate me. So, all right. Now you've succeeded. But as you say, you're a busy man. Why go through all this?"

He frowned and shook his head. He rubbed his forehead with his left hand, shutting his eyes behind it. "Miz. Gates," he said, "you misunderstand." He took his hand down and opened his eyes. He folded his hands in his lap. "Roger Kidd said you were tough. He was right, as usual." He smiled. "You're too tough for me, I guess, and maybe too tough for yourself." He hesitated. "But I don't regret the visit."

She stood up fast. "Mister Baldwin," she said, "can I have a copy of that writer-for-hire contract, and twenty-four hours to think about it?"

Anne Leeds watched Constance Gates put the blank contract into her attaché case, and close the case. She accepted Gates's assurance that she could find her own way out. Leeds waited until Gates was about ten yards down the corridor before she buzzed Sylvia Francis. "You can relax," Leeds said. "This is not one of his love-at-first-sight specials." She listened. "I don't think they got along too hot, Sylvia," she said. She picked up a pack of Vantage cigarettes from her desk, took one out, and lit it with a gold-toned Colibri lighter. She laughed. "No," she said, "one of them struck the other one out in there. I'm just not sure which one did what." She paused. " 'Base on balls?' " she said. "That's good, Sylvia," she said. "That is very good."

9

Constance Gates said she appreciated her ex-husband's willingness to see her on short notice. "Think nothing of it," Jeffrey Gates said, unwrapping a tuna salad sandwich on a bulkie roll on his desk; he used the can of Diet Pepsi to hold one corner of the waxed paper wrapper down as an improvised placemat on the blotter. He put the small bag of Ruffles potato chips on the opposite corner. He put the wad of paper napkins in the wastebasket behind him.

"Just wish you'd phoned ahead." He picked up the sandwich and took a bite out of it. He still talked with his mouth full, one of several of his habits of which she'd been unable to break him. "Would've had Carla get you a sandwich."

He also still chewed with his mouth open. And she was not surprised to see that he was still getting at least two days out of each clean shirt. The lenses of his horn-rimmed glasses were cloudy and when he tilted his head at a slight angle she could see fingerprints on the lenses, which meant that he had not yet mastered the skill of removing them or adjusting them on his face, and remained unbothered by that fact. He needed a haircut, too; the greying strands, slightly greasy, curled up at the back over his collar.

"I'm not hungry," she said, starting to feel faintly nauseated. "It's all right. I'm just grateful you could see me."

" 'S all right," he said, munching. "Thing of it is, I just hope I can help you. June, you know. Things get a little tight, around this time of year."

"Tight?" she said.

"Yeah," he said, nodding and chewing. "Tough here, naturally, 'cause we made the dumb mistake of doing what Fred said and taking a fiscal year that ends March thirty-first. Which naturally means all our clients that use calendar year pay us out, end of December, and all our corporates that use July one, pay us out end of this month. Which means when we get our big chunks of cash, you know, well, one's over five months ago, and the other one's still a couple weeks away.

"And then," he said, "personally, well, I don't need to tell you that. You used to go through it with me." He paused and took another bite of sandwich. "Although I'm not sure how much of it actually registered on you." He chewed. "But the kids finish the school in June, and the camps want their money right off, bang, or else they won't hold the places. Say they won't, at least. Which is probably a lie, but I take the safe bet and believe it, that they got hundreds of frantic parents standing in line all over the place to fork over two, three grand apiece so Junior and Miss Junior can learn to sail Ensigns. How the hell do I know? They say it, I believe them. Who knows? It might be true."

"I don't follow you," she said. He had gotten some mayonnaise on his lower lip, but appeared not to notice it. It held her gaze.

"Well," he said, swallowing, "I mean, you called me and I assume you need some help. What is it this time? They change the date they bill you, the damned car insurance? I thought that was October. What'd you do, switch carriers? Not that I'd blame you, if you did. Fisherman's Casualty, they've turned into a real buncha bastards since Allied took them over. 'Pay a claim? We don't pay claims. We collect premiums — that is what we do.' We had several clients, got in pissing contests with them when they claimed under their policies."

"What the hell're you talking about, Jeffrey?" she said.

"Your car insurance," he said. "Or something. I assumed that's why you called. I was just telling you, you know I'm always glad to help you out and all. If I can. But this's a bad time for me. You can wait a week or three, I can do it fairly easy. But right now happens to be tough. If it's more'n a grand or two, I'm gonna have to whack a loan myself down at the bank. Which I will do for you, if it's an emergency, can't get your car on the road or something. But it's going to be tough."

She gritted her teeth. "Jeffrey," she said, "I am not here to ask you for money."

He interrupted his chewing. "Oh," he said. He faltered. "I just sort of assumed, you know? Because the other times like this, that you hadda see me right off, that was what it was."

"I thought you always told me," she said, " 'a good lawyer never assumes.' "

He grinned. "I did," he said. "But we try to learn from experience, right? I just thought that's what it was. What it probably was, at least. And I just wanted you to know, you know, that any time you really need help, you shouldn't hesitate to come to me. But there're times, like now, when I might not be able to just write a check and give it to you, and I didn't want you to think I was reneging on something. That's all."

"Well, it isn't," she said. "I am not here for money. I am here for some legal advice." She paused and smirked. "Which may be even worse, from your point of view," she said, "since I want it for free." She lifted her attaché case from the floor and opened it on her lap. She took out the contract and put it on his desk. "I want you to look at this," she said, "and tell me what it means."

He glanced at it but did not read it. He took another bite of sandwich and another swig of Pepsi and chewed energetically. "Tell me what it is," he said. "Contracts're my line, but not all contracts are the same."

She summarized her conversation with Mark Baldwin. "I don't know this man," she said. "I never saw him before in my life. He looks like a barracuda to me, a real sharp predator. But the job he offers tempts me, tempts me very much. So much that I really want to take it, even though my women's intuition, as you used to describe it, tells me I may regret it if I get involved with him."

Jeffrey snorted. "Huh," he said, "is that so? Well, you're getting a little smarter, at least. After that last gem you picked for companionship."

"Jeff," she said warningly, "leave him out of this. You had a couple of beauties yourself, before you married again. Everybody's entitled to a few mistakes. And each of us began this whole phase of our lives with a big one on our records, which was marrying the other one. Try to keep that in mind. This is a business deal I'm seeking advice on. Not a personal relationship. Or anything like that."

"It will be, though, before you're through," he said. "We both know that, don't we?"

She sighed. "Jeff," she said, "I came here for a favor. Do it for me, will you, and look at the contract for me? I need some advice. On that. Just that. Nothing else."

He studied her. "Okay," he said, "if that's the way you want it." He put the sandwich down. He inspected his left hand. He scowled, turned in his chair, picked the paper napkins out of the wastebasket behind him, and turned back to the desk. He scrubbed his left hand vigorously. He picked up the contract with his left hand and read it carefully, frowning and moving his lips, shaking his head, resting his forehead on his right hand, setting the document down and picking up a pencil to tap at passages that he read to himself again. He sat back in his swivel chair when he had finished, and resumed chewing. His forehead shone dully from grease that had been on his hand.

"Okay," he said, "I've read it. I'm not sure that helps you a lot, but I have read the thing." He picked up the sandwich again and took another bite. "What help I can give you, I mean," he said. "This copyright-entertainment-law crap's a little out of my line."

"Well," she said, unable to stop watching him chew and suck bits of chips out of the crevices in his teeth, "it is a contract, Jeff, that he's offering to me. And you do do contracts, don't you?"

"Sure," he said, using the nail of his right forefinger to dig a particle of chip out of his left lower jaw. He inspected it, put it back into his mouth, and picked up the sandwich again. "But the contracts I work on are for three years of employment of members of Retail Clerks Local Six-fifty-one by New England Computer Stores. Not for six performances of *Rigoletto* by Placido Domingo. These things are full of terms of art, that I don't understand."

"Mister Baldwin," she said, "is not asking me to sing opera."

"Good thing," he said, chewing again. "One of things about you that I never will forget is that awful racket you made in the shower."

"Is Andrea's voice better?" she said sweetly.

"I dunno," he said equably. "Probably not, but it doesn't matter. She can't even remember jokes, let alone the words to the whole score of *Hair*." He bit again and chewed. Through the food he said: "You have no idea the difference it makes in a man's outlook when the day starts without anybody mentioning the age of Aquarius. It's really wonderful."

She shook her head, partly to clear it and partly to force her to stop looking at his mouth. "Well, I'm glad for both of you," she said. "But even though I did sing to you, and even though you say you don't know these things, would you tell me what you think? What does it mean, 'writer for hire'? That mean *anything* to you?"

He leaned back again and slowly shook his head. "The only thing it means to me," he said, "is that it doesn't mean anything to me. Which in turn probably means that it *does* mean something, something serious, and that *Journeyer* magazine is going to like that meaning a whole lot more than the person who signs this agreement with it." He sighed. He took another bite. He picked up the contract and studied it again. He put it down. "But what it is, I don't know."

"Is there anybody in the firm who might know?" she said.

He shrugged. "Archie Coleman," he said. "Archie used to represent Glynnis Fearing, handled her divorce, and her husband used to write. So Archie had some experience with reading his contracts and all. But Archie's unfortunately dead."

"He probably won't be much help to me then," she said.

"Although it is possible, now that I think of it," he said, "that Richard might have some idea of what this about. Richard represents a couple of those fancy art galleries on Newbury Street and he's always hanging around with that artsy-cutesy crowd. Richard might know."

"Could you ask Richard to look at it?" she said.

"Could if he was in," Jeffrey said. He looked at his watch. "Twelve-fifty? Doubt that he is. Richard goes *out* to lunch days. Richard says it's 'simply *unhealthy* to eat lunch at your desk every day.' " Jeffrey pursed his lips and tossed his head. He leaned forward and poised his hand over the intercom button.

"Richard is 'that way' now?" she said.

Jeffrey used his tongue to get food particles from his teeth. "Uh huh," he said. "Very much so. Oh, he doesn't make a big production out of it, or anything, but times've changed a lot since Richard really tried to cover up. He says he lives alone with his kitty, but Richard's not telling the truth. Richard lives with Dexter. Dexter's his boyfriend." He punched the intercom. There was an immediate "Yes?" He nodded. "Harriet," he said, "is Mister Pond in, or has he gone to lunch?" "Gone to lunch," the voice said. "Said he'll be late today. He's meeting Mister Francis from Appalachian Investors at the Harvard Club." Jeffrey nodded wryly. "Thank you, Harriet," he said.

He sat back in his chair. "That's Richard for you, all the way," he said. "Richard is meticulous. He always leaves word where he is, and with whom."

"So the rest of you won't get suspicious that he's in some

bathhouse somewhere," she said, "doing naughty things? Do you all care that much?"

"Care?" Jeffrey said. He snorted. He folded his hands over his paunch. "Hellfire, woman, we don't care. Richard can do it with a tomcat if he wants. No, he leaves word where he's gone and with whom so that when that person comes in as a client and starts paying the firm *mucho* money, Richard will be sure we remember why that new business came in. And hold us up for a bigger share of it." He shook his head again. "Dunno how he does it," Jeffrey said. "They can't all of them be queer, but once Richard gets them listening, they line up at the front door. And these are substantial clients, too. Very profitable accounts. Richard's valuable to us."

"Well," she said, "I'm glad to hear it, what with Estelle talking Brown these days, and Jeffrey set on Yale." She paused. "If he can get his grades up, of course," she said.

Her ex-husband smiled at her. "Connie, Connie," he said, "can those digs, all right? You know and I know that Jeffrey Gates the fourth is not going to go to Yale. Jeffrey the fourth is going to Dartmouth, just as did Jeffrey the first through the third. Jeffrey the fourth just doesn't know it yet. But he will. Believe me, he will."

"You should let the kid pick his own school," she said. "I'm not all over Estelle's back because she kissed Wheaton off, when she was six years old."

"I will let the kid pick his own nose," Jeffrey said. "I will not let him pick his school. And my reasons for that are much stronger than yours are for not trying to influence Estelle. My family's gone to Dartmouth for three generations. My son isn't going to break that tradition, and I'm going to see that he doesn't."

She exhaled. "I know you'll try," she said. "I just hope it doesn't do anything to him in the process."

"It won't," he said.

"I still worry," she said.

He came forward in the chair fast, slightly startling her as he always had when he chose to demonstrate that an apparently-placid, out-of-shape man could react very quickly when he wished to do so. "Cut it out, Connie," he said in a hard voice. "The reason I'm raising those kids is that you didn't want to do it. I told you a long time ago that if you weren't going to do it, I was, and I would do it my way. You didn't want to do it when they were two and three years old, you're not going to reverse yourself now. Estelle's only nine. She'll change her mind a hundred times before she graduates from Concord and decides where she'll go. And the same thing with Jeff. Barely eight years old? Of course I'm going to influence him. I'm going to do my damnedest. That's what parents are for."

She held up her right hand. "Okay, okay," she said. "Sorry I brought it up." She closed her attaché case and stood up. She nodded toward the contract on his desk. "Look," she said, "if I haven't pissed you off too much, could you ask Richard to look at that thing for me? I would appreciate it."

"He may charge you," Jeffrey said, not getting up. "Richard's very big on collecting fees. 'No freebies,' Richard says."

Her shoulders slumped. "I don't care," she said. "Let him charge me, all right? I can pay for ten minutes of his time. I can afford that much."

"If you're sure," he said. "You didn't put Richard through law school, you know, as you like to claim you did me."

She waved her left hand at him. "No, Jeffrey," she said, "I won't go another round just now. I've had enough for one day. Just ask him to call."

10

Richard Pond and Jason Francis emerged from the Harvard Club on Commonwealth Avenue into the afternoon sunshine with nothing resolved. They were both burly men and they both wore lightweight worsted suits — Pond's was a dark grey pinstripe; Francis wore plain grey — with red silk ties on collar-pinned white shirts, and polished black wingtip shoes. Pond's black hair was greying at the temples and his three-week-old Jamaican tan was fading somewhat. Francis's red hair was receding from the forehead, and his moustache had grey accents. They descended the steps and stood on the sidewalk just west of Massachusetts Avenue in the sunshine, and regarded each other ruefully.

"You're not being reasonable, Jason," Pond said. "You know very well that my offer beats Bolt, Samuelson all hollow. Be sensible, man. Don Samuelson's ninety years old."

"Eighty-two, I think, actually," Francis said.

"Oh, for heaven's sake," Pond said. "Retirement age is sixty-five. Seventy, the latest. Don might as well be a hundred, for all the difference that makes. He's a dying man, Jason."

"He looked pretty healthy to me, Richard," Francis said, "last time I saw him, at least. He and Bayliss Kincaid'd just finished forty-five minutes of that brand of hog-the-tee squash they both play, banging into each other and never calling lets, and Don wasn't even puffing. Do we walk or take a cab?"

"Walk," Pond said, and they started east toward Massachusetts Avenue. "We'll walk down to the Ritz and get a cab there, or if we decide to go on, we can walk across the Public Garden and look at the nice mallards. And on the way we can see if Samuel Morison's finished taking his shit."

"What're you talking about?" Francis said. "Samuel Morison's dead."

"His statue, of course," Pond said. "The one on the greensward down by Fairfield, I guess it is. He's made of bronze and wearing a slicker and sitting on a rock in the Rodin *Thinker* pose. Dexter's brother, Rodney? Owns the Mint Gallery? Rodney says Morison looks like he's taking a shit.''

Francis put his head back and laughed.

"I wish you'd be serious, Jason," Pond said.

"How can I be serious, Richard," Francis said, "when you're telling me stories like that?"

"You know what I mean, Jason," Pond said. "Ever since Runciman Wire and Cable was acquired by Cleveland Bridge, Don's been scrambling to keep the billing up. And you know how he's been doing it as well as I do. You know *better* than I do. You've been paying it. He's churning the files."

"They've given us very good service, Richard," Francis said. "I've had no complaints from my board about their charges. We're harrowing old ground here, gnawing on old bones."

"But Jason," Pond said, "how would your board react if you came to them and said you'd *saved* the stockholders twenty, twenty-five percent by changing legal counsel? Just in the first year? They'd be ecstatic, Jason. They'd give you a raise."

Francis smiled at Pond. "Richard," he said, "be sensible. The first thing my board would do if I suggested we change would be to ask me why on earth we'd want to. Don's firm's done good work. Truly, Richard, they have."

"It's routine work, Jason," Pond said. "Anyone could do it. My bunch could do it, and would do it, much cheaper for you."

"I disagree with you," Francis said. "In the first place, you and I both know the discount would be for the first year. The second year we'd find ourselves paying you what we're paying Bolt, plus a little more."

"What do you care, Jason?" Pond said. "It wouldn't come out of you."

"Richard," Francis said, "I'm surprised at you. I got where I am because I treat what my board spends as though it came out of me. They know that and they trust me. I'm not going to jeopardize that trust."

"Oh, pooh," Pond said. They crossed Massachusetts Avenue and continued east toward Hereford. The June sunlight highlighted the new leaves on the trees and people walked their dogs on the esplanade between the roadways.

" 'Oh, pooh' nothing," Francis said. "You've known me long enough and well enough to know better than that. Those people trust me to administer their money carefully, to the best of my ability. That is what I do."

"That's what I'm telling you, Jason," Pond said. "That you could do a better job for them if you took your legal business out of Bolt, Samuelson, and shifted it to us."

"I can't do that," Francis said. "I'm not going to tell you tales out of school, but much of what was involved in our expansion has been extremely sensitive. Don's firm's done yeoman service. The banking commission? You can talk all day about deregulation and all that sort of thing, but the fact of the matter is that I can't fault them, Richard. When we went into Plymouth County, that was potential dynamite. They did a masterful job. I have no grounds to propose they be replaced."

"None?" Pond said.

"Richard," Francis said, "Richard, do be serious. That's not a reason to propose replacing them with you — that's a reason to shy away from you. My board has no idea, and I assure you, that's the way I want it. I don't know what they'd do, if word got out. Yes, I do — they'd fire me."

"Jason," Pond said, "this is the twentieth century. Times have changed. People get elected now, when that fact is known."

"The voters are nowhere near as conservative in that respect as my board is," Francis said. "Adultery's as far as their tolerance goes, and it's grudging for that. Believe me, I know. David Mandel's little embarrassment last year when the madam's files were seized very nearly knocked him off the board. No, I won't risk that. If they ever found out about me, the first thing they'd do is panic that I might give them all AIDS, using the same water carafe in the conference room. The second thing they'd do is give me my notice. Bank on it, Richard — that's what they would do. And I'm not going to risk that, Richard. Not for you or anyone."

"You're not being fair," Pond said.

Francis stopped in his tracks. "*That* isn't fair," he said. "I've got a fiduciary responsibility to the people who employ me. If you want me to strike a blow for liberty, ask me to do something that only affects me. Don't ask me to show you a professional preference for a private reason. You know I can't do that."

Pond reached into his right hand pants pocket. He took out two twenty-dollar bills and a ten, folded together. "All right, Jason," he said, "take this back. And let Dexter take her to court. Then you can divorce her, and it won't cost you any money."

Francis said: "No."

"Well, Jason," Pond said, "didn't you just tell me, if I wanted you to strike a blow for liberty, I should ask you to do something that affects you personally? Did you just say that?"

"Yes, I did," Francis said. "But not that. I won't do that for you. Put that back in your pocket before some junkie jumps you, and we get in a fight."

"Well, then," Pond said, "what will you do? For me or anybody else?"

"I don't know," Francis said, as they approached Hereford Street. "Nothing that offends my principles, I guess."

"Your *principles*," Pond said, as they waited for the light. "You've got no more principles than any other fag, Jason, and it's high time you started admitting it. You're just like everybody else. But you've only got about one arm out of the closet. You're a sissy fag."

"Oh, shut up, Richard," Francis said. "You're so rich you could sell out Dexter's newsstand and retire with him to Morocco. Don't you be telling me what I can and cannot do."

"I certainly will," Pond said, as they crossed Hereford Street. "Just look at yourself. It's craven what you're doing. Letting that bitch use you like this. You know she's fucking Baldwin. You know she's a common thief. And what do you do since you know it? You protect her — that's what you do. Once a month you call Dexter, under the table, and ask how much she's stolen. Then you call me for lunch, and give me some money, and then you go back to your job. That's servile, Jason. It's debased. You're degrading yourself. You ought to divorce that twat, you know, and begin living your life. You're getting old, Jason. Time doesn't wait."

Francis stopped again. He took a deep breath. "Richard," he said very slowly, "the only reason I'm taking this abuse from you is because I've known you a long time and I know you think you have my best interests at heart. But you're wrong. I do know what I'm doing. I have a reason for everything I do. Sylvia and I have an understanding. It's very important to me and my career that the details of my private life don't come out. She's very loyal, Richard. If

I'm protecting her, she's protecting me more. I was twenty-three years old when we got married, and I didn't want to believe what I now know to be the truth. I was thirty-seven years old before I finally realized that it didn't matter what I wanted to be the truth — the truth was what it was, no matter what I did.

"I realized that in a hospital bed," he said. "When I came out of the sedation that they gave for the seizures, I realized that I had to stop denying the dominant side of my nature. I was killing myself.

"She's never asked me what happened," he said. "I think she guessed, but I don't know. She's never pressed me, never questioned my explanation that the reason I don't do it with her anymore isn't because I don't want to, but because I'm impotent. She's kind to me. I owe her. I owe her for living with me and I owe her for being loyal, and I'm not going to repay that debt with disloyalty of mine.

"I'm not like you, Richard," he said. "I don't dislike women at all."

"I don't dislike women," Pond said. "A lot of them are my friends."

"But none of those women happens to be married to one of your boyfriends," Francis said, "and that's the difference with us. Sylvia is a good woman. I'm trying to be a good man. I know what she's doing. She's staying married to me and hoping it lasts until Baldwin decides he wants her. If that day ever comes, she will ask me for a divorce, and I will give it to her. Then my board will sympathize with me, cuckolded by that well-known rake, Mark Baldwin, and understand that I'm so hurt I never want to get involved with another woman again. At which point, I will owe Sylvia even more. But the timetable's hers to adjust."

"And besides," Pond said, "she tells you what Baldwin tells her, in his pillow talk. And that probably turns you on." He stopped and grasped Francis by the sleeve. "Is that it, Jason? Is that what it is? Does it turn you on to hear what Mark Baldwin does in bed with your wife?"

Francis jerked his sleeve away. "Don't be a damned fool, Richard," he said. "She tells me nothing that goes on."

"I don't believe it," Pond said. "I don't believe it at all."

"Richard," Francis said, "I do believe you're sick. I honestly think there's a fair chance that you are mentally ill. The way you talk about Mark Baldwin is not the conversation of a person in control."

Pond smirked at him. "Jason," he said, "you don't know Mark as I do. If you did, you'd hate him too. I'd like to see him dead. I expect to someday, too. Dead, or close enough to dead so being dead would be better."

"That's enough," Francis said. He stepped to the curb.

"Where are you going, Jason?" Pond said.

"Back to my office," Francis said. "Go and fuck a duck."

11

Constance Gates crossed Commercial Street in the hot sun, and turned onto China Wharf. There were two young men leaning on the mailbox at the corner. The brick sidewalk was uneven, hard to walk on in high heels, and the other people who had leased angle-parking spaces there had done the same thing with their Jaguars, Mercedes and Porsches that she had done with her BMW — tucked the left front wheels right up against the curb so that transients coming into the lot in Cadillacs and Lincolns would not crease the rear fenders of the residents' cars. The front bumpers left about eighteen inches of passageway on the sidewalk between the rough granite wall of the building and the overhang of the parked cars; she had to swivel as she walked. One of the two young men whistled. "*Very* nice," he said. When she reached the doorway to 5 China Wharf, set back from the sidewalk and up two steps, she went into the entryway, checked her mailbox and found nothing, stuck her key in the outside door, deactivated the digital alarm in the entry, opened the door, went inside, slammed it shut behind her and rearmed the alarm.

The designers who had converted the old granite warehouse into three floors of residential and professional condominium space had done it by installing gypsum partitions across it every thirty feet. That created unimproved interior units which could be split into adjoining rooms to make three-room residences with kitchens and baths and cramped closet spaces, the entirety amounting to about 600 square feet of usable space. The business operations on the first floor generally were double units. The partitioning met the granite interior wall that had bisected the building into two long rows of cargo bins, so that the northerly walls of all spaces on her side of the building were visually pleasing but cold grey stone that became damp in humid weather, almost slimy to the touch.

The architects had made their priority conservation of the interior spaces; the gypsum board was thin, so that office equipment noises and Muzak bought by managers to mask the racket filtered into the stairwells. That made the experience of residents returning home in the daytime vaguely disorienting. The cramped stairwells were fitted with soft pine risers and treads initially and repeatedly painted white to conceal the grime they collected and the rapidity of wear they showed in the centers. Tenants and visitors, maintenance people and deliverymen: everyone who used the uneven stairs in a hurry tended to carom off the gypsum. The residents who kept yachts docked at the marina on the other side of the parking lot and the Porsche owners who took pride in doing their own routine service right outside left grease and oil deposits on the wallboard coming home from their exertions. She ascended carefully, trying not to brush her clothing against the gritty wallboard, doing her best as well to ignore the clatter from the law firm of Keitel & McGee on the first floor of her sector.

On the second floor she heard "General Hospital" murmuring out of Tina Lester's unit and desultorily considered knocking to invite herself in for a drink. She discarded that notion without any trouble; the youngish ophthalmologist who kept Tina in that setting had distracted her from fears that her twenty-second birthday ushered in her middle age by financing vanity publication of a book of her poetry. Tina, crowding twenty-three, was working on another collection of poems which Gates was sure would be just as good, and did not wish to hear recited. But if she went in and then discouraged Tina from reciting her work, Tina would fall back on one of her only two other topics of conversation, using that nasal voice either to complain some more about Leonard's continuing refusal to divorce his wife and marry her, or to recall at length with many sympathetic clucks and pats the horrors she had heard Connie suffering day and night upstairs above her in the four months she had lived with Ted. She went past Tina's door on tiptoe.

At the top of the stairs, Gates unlocked the first and the knob cylinder to enter her unit. The door opened into her kitchen, banging on the edge of her refrigerator. She had left the Mr. Coffee on "warm" all day and the cup or so remaining in the glass pot in the morning had been reduced to a brown paste with a sharp, hot smell. "Damn," she said, locking the deadbolt, putting her attaché case on the counter, and shutting the brewer off. She went around the counter into the combination living room-dining room, stopping at the couch to rest her hand on the arm to take her shoes off.

The couch was slipcovered in bright yellow. A pale orange loveseat stood against the bedroom wall to her left, with a rectangular walnut coffee table in front of it. Opposite the loveseat were two armless upholstered chairs done in nubby light blue tweed. Between the two chairs a nineteen-inch Sony television stood on a pedestal, with a cable service receiver on the top. Beneath it was a Panasonic VHS recorder. The rug was beige shag. On the wall over the loveseat hung a Utrillo print. On the wall between the two chairs there was a charcoal caricature of Mick Jagger; it was signed *Ted* in a flourishing scrawl at the lower right corner.

In her stockinged feet Gates walked to the sliding glass door that opened onto a small balcony overlooking the parking lot and the marina. She brushed aside the white translucent curtains which allowed her to dress in daylight without exhibiting herself to passersby on the far side of the dock, and opened the door. There was a little breeze off the water, and when she released the curtains, they billowed into the room, brushing against the Breuer chairs at the round butcher block table in front of the door. The breeze carried a faint aroma of oil, but it was better than the smell of scorched coffee.

She went back to the couch and turned right into the bedroom. She looked toward her desk against the interior wall. The red light on her Phone-mate was blinking. She considered for an instant whether taking her clothes off or collecting her messages seemed likeliest to make her feel better, and decided getting changed had the edge. She put her jacket on the green-and-blue flowered comforter and took off everything but her yellow bikini pants. She inspected the suit for wrinkles and decided it would have to go to the cleaners with the silk blouse; those articles she put on the shelf of her double closet. The yellow bra and the panti-hose went into the laundry hamper in the bathroom. She used the Waterpik to flush the remnants of a quick lunch out of her mouth, and brushed her teeth to remove the lingering taste.

She returned to the bedroom. She dressed in a light-blue cotton fatigue sweater and white tennis shorts, sat down at her desk and replayed her messages. There was one from Terry Gleason's secretary, Madge, who confirmed Gates's realistic fears that Warren Milano had decided to plead guilty in the federal court to a single count of falsifying records and thus would not require Gates's assistance in the preparation of his defense on eighteen counts of bank fraud. "You don't have to call back," Madge said gratuitously. "Thanks, you bitch," Gates said to the machine.

The second message was a computerized service spiel soliciting subscriptions for *The Boston Globe*. It had begun before the beep from her machine indicated readiness to record. The computer was apparently programmed according to beeps, and reacted to the Phone-mate's beep by restarting its spiel. The computer's opening beep did something to her Phone-mate's program, so that it beeped again, restarting the computer. The two machines confused each other four times before reaching the five-minute time limit enforced by the recorder. Annoyed at first, she became fascinated by the time the exchange ended, and felt almost cheerful.

The third and last call was from a woman who identified herself as "Mister Pond's office," and said that "Mister Pond wants you to know he has looked at the contract and will be more than happy to assist you in any way he can."

Gates wrote down the number, erased and rewound the tape, then got up from her desk and went over to the bed. She flopped down on her back and put her right forearm over her eyes.

After two or three minutes, she sat up again. She went barefoot out into the kitchen and took a bottle of Perrier water out of the refrigerator. She poured a glass of it and went back to her desk and stared at the telephone. She put the glass on the desk and picked up the phone. She punched seven numbers and waited.

"Hi, Brenda," she said, "this is me. Is Ted free by any chance? I don't want to disturb him if he's out in the back, creating. But if he's handy, you know?" She laughed. "Did he take the whole paper, Brenda, or just the sports section?" She laughed again. "No, I'll hang on," she said. She waited and considered whether she should file her nails.

"Hi, Ted," she said. "Can I ask you, ah, something? Sort of a favor, I guess. Yeah, something like that. Definitely something like that. Is there any chance you could stop by tonight? I dunno, maybe have dinner, drink some wine, something like that?" She paused. "Well," she said, "yeah, I know I said that, and if you're, you know, if you're all back with Donna and everything's working out, well, I don't want to screw that up." She paused again.

"No, no," she said, "that's not what I meant. Well, I meant what I said, and that, at the time, but it's just that, well, now, now I'm not sure anymore that I meant it. If that makes sense." She paused. She laughed. "No," she said, "I guess it doesn't. Well, let me try again. I guess what I'm saying is: I've had a bad day. And it's not the first bad day I've had lately. I've had a whole string of them, you know? One right after another. And I guess I'm lonesome. I miss you. We did have some real good days before all the other stuff started happening, and . . . . I want to talk to somebody and have someone talk to me. That I can do that with without worrying, you know, what impression I'm making and whether if I say something, it's going to cost me. Yeah."

She listened. She lowered her head while she was listening and shut her eyes. She used her left fore- and middle fingers to massage her left eye. "Yes," she said, "I do know that. No, I understand. Yes I do, Ted, yes I do. I really do understand. No, I don't blame you. I don't blame you a bit. It's okay. It really is." She paused. "No, I don't feel that way, Ted," she said. "And look, thanks. All right? Thanks for being so nice."

She hung up the phone. She slid back in the chair so that she sat on her coccyx. She considered whether to cry. She decided against it. She sat up straight and picked up the phone again. She punched Pond's number.

"Mister Pond," she said, when he came on, "I can't tell you how much I appreciate your courtesy."

12

Constance Gates in her grey raw silk suit and a fresh white silk blouse arrived in the Landing Bar at the Parker House precisely on time for her 6:30 P.M. appointment with Richard Pond. The bar was crowded with people who had spent the day prospering and were now enjoying that fact in loud, confident voices. She told the maître d' she would like a table for two, that she expected Mr. Pond, and that she would appreciate it if the waiter would bring her the check. The maître d' heard her out and said that Mr. Pond was waiting for her at his regular table. He escorted her to the table in the northeast corner, furthest from the door. Richard Pond rose from his tufted beige leather chair as they arrived, smiling and extending his hand. "Constance," he said, as she accepted it, "it's really been so long."

She returned his smile and sat down. She cocked her head at him. "I wasn't sure you'd remember," she said. "My plan was to pretend I thought I was imposing on a total stranger. You must have met so many of us, under those circumstances."

He made an economical gesture with his left hand as he sat. "Ah yes," he said. "Those dreadful little picnics at Blaine's place up in Marblehead for the new associates. Hot dogs and hamburgs and beer and hypocrisy, out on Blaine Ketchell's front lawn. Interchangeable young men with their interchangeable young wives and their fungible versions of safe conversations likely to ingratiate them with their new superiors. 'Very important to make the new people feel at home,' Blair used to say. 'Part of our professional family.' What a crashing bore." He paused. "Thank *God* Blaine retired. Out there every day on the Charles, rowing his silly ass off. Squash in the winter, sailing in summer, tennis each weekend, of course. But stupid? My God Blaine is stupid. He'll live forever, Blaine will. He's only seventy or so today, and in perfect shape, of course. He's going to live forever just to annoy us. But he'll never be smart, not our Blaine. What a relief when he left."

She was laughing when the waiter arrived. Pond did not give her a chance to think about a drink. "Wine spritzer, I'd say, wouldn't you?" he said brightly.

She laughed. "Mister Pond," she said, "I came here for your advice. I'm not going to start by rejecting it."

"Two spritzers," he said to the waiter. He leaned forward over the glass table and patted her left hand. "Just as I remembered you, Constance," he said. "Perfectly delightful. In among that crowd of little wrens in Country-Store-of-Concord pastels that our recruits married then. No more style than an Odd Fellows' picnic. What was it you said to Ray Fellows that day? Something about the Coast Guard?"

She giggled. "I don't remember," she said.

He smirked as the waiter brought the drinks. "Oh, nonsense, Constance," he said, "of course you do, if I do. And you can be sure that Ray does, too, even if he is the under-secretary of something or other for something or other at the State Department today. He was going on about his boat, as I recall. His bloody little boat. Man was an absolute bore on the subject, him and his bloody boat."

"The *Flying Cloud*," she said.

"That's it," Pond said delightedly, "The *Flying Cloud*, of course. That dinky little sailboat, and he named it after a clipper ship. That was Raymond all the way. And what did you say to him?"

She was unable to stop laughing. She sipped at her drink. "Oh, I don't know, exactly," she said. "He was going on and on about how he and the boat were 'one,' I think it was, and if it wasn't for the time that his 'career' took, he'd singlehand it to England." She paused and took another sip. She chuckled. "And my father was a fisherman, a lobster fisherman, where I grew up in Gloucester. And in the summertime I'd go out with him, when I was a little girl, and to keep me out of trouble, he put me in charge of the radio. When Mister What's-his-name there mentioned that his boat was the *Flying Cloud*, it just broke me up. If he wasn't aground, he was lost in the fog, and if that wasn't it, he was leaking and he had to have a pump. So, when he started in about sailing to England alone, I just thought it was so ridiculous I said that if it wasn't for the Coast Guard he couldn't sail from Corinthian to Boston on a fair day without drowning." She paused. She put the wine glass down. "And he didn't like that," she said, "me telling him he couldn't make it across

Marblehead harbor between the yacht clubs like that." She paused again. "Jeffrey didn't like it either," she said. "He said cracks like that to senior partners could hamper his career."

"Jeffrey was right, I'm sorry to say," Pond said.

"I know it," she said, looking down at her hands. "I think one of the good things that may have come out of my and Jeff's divorce is maybe that things like that don't get held against him any more. I hope so, at least. I don't mean we did it for that — *I* did it for that. Not for Jeffrey's career. But if it had to happen for other reasons, at least I hope it did that for him. Made it a little simpler for him at the firm."

"Jeffrey doesn't need to worry," Pond said. "Jeffrey's a remarkably capable lawyer."

"He really is, isn't he?" she said. "I don't think I ever really thought about it, not when he was in law school and not afterwards, either. I just took it for granted. He's a born lawyer. He's so damned competent. At everything."

"Yes," Pond said, "he is. When I bring clients in that need the kind of work Jeffrey does, I feel perfect confidence in turning them and their problems over to him, and I know none of them will ever call me in the middle of the night to bitch about Jeffrey. Never." He sighed. "If only we could spruce him up a bit."

She giggled again. "Well, my dear," Pond said, sipping his wine, "now I don't mean to be unkind, but no display of loyalty's going to convince me you don't agree. He looks like a garage sale waiting for a place to happen."

"I know," she said, between giggles, "I know, I know, I know."

"One morning on a lark," Pond said, "I went to Filene's Basement with a friend of mine who was looking for a dress. I think Nieman Marcus stuff was on sale. And here were all these women, taking their clothes off, trying things on, right in the middle of the aisles, and sweaty people stepping on other people's clothes and yelling at each other, and it was simply hotter than Hades in there, and I said to him: 'Now we know. This is where Jeffrey is dressed every day. This *must be* where Jeffrey is dressed. I'll bet if you go over to men's suits and shirts, we'll find Jeffrey in his shorts, being outfitted for work.' "

She was laughing and shaking her head at the same time. "Stop it," she said, gasping, "stop it."

"Well, it's true," Pond said. He sipped and looked over the rim of the glass at her, his eyes twinkling. "We can both sit here and say how much we admire Jeffrey, but when we get through, you know that what I said will still be true."

She shook her head again. "I tried, Mister Pond," she said. "I honestly and truly did. I was married to him for eight years. At least once a week I told him I was going to run him through the car wash without the car if he didn't get cleaned up. You can see what good it did. It's the way he is. He's never going to change."

Pond was studying her. "I was genuinely sorry when you two broke up," he said. "Our shop is filled with the most conventional of people. You had a refreshing insouciance about you. I admired it."

She hesitated. "I don't know what to say," she said, after she concluded that she didn't and would not. She made another try. "I know everybody says this," she said, "most everyone, at least. Not about me and Jeffrey but about all divorces. That they're for the best? Like people do when somebody with cancer dies. 'It's for the best.' " She began to laugh again.

"Yes," Pond said, grinning, "I like that one too. The poor devil finally gets release from his agony, and these twits say: 'It's for the best.' People who become distraught over hangnails — they're the ones who say it. Idiots."

"But in our case, it was," she said. "We didn't get along. We just didn't get along."

"Oh," he said, "forgive me. I don't mean to pry. I'm sure you had good reasons, and anyway, my motive was selfish. Even though Blaine's deadly little get-togethers are things of the past and all, there's still a certain amount of unavoidable contact, occasions of forced jollity, among members of the firm and their families. We share one of those luxury boxes at Fenway Park with one of our clients, Brayton Homes? They entertain their big customers there when the good teams are playing, and we have it when the lesser teams come to town. And we all have to go there on a rotating basis and be *social* with each other and 'get to know each other outside the office,' you know? Stupefyingly dull. And now Jeffrey has to drag along What's-her-name. Andrea?"

"Andrea," Gates said.

"And my God, she is a clot," Pond said. "I don't even like baseball that much. I mean, the only games I like to see are when the

Yankees or somebody like that's in town, and it's festival, you know. But to spend a summer afternoon watching the Cleveland Indians fall down and drop the ball, and listen to Andrea nattering on all the while about how *much* Jeffrey thinks of me and how he *loves* his work, well, I'm telling you, it's a wonder I don't just throw up my hot dog and beer over the rail down onto the real fans below."

She was laughing again.

"She's a phony, too, you know," he said. "That thought just occurred to me. Not only is she sedating me with all her dreary tales about how well the children are doing, but all that *stuff* of hers about how Jeffrey admires me is just a lot of *crap*."

"I don't know her at all," Gates said cautiously. "All I know about her is what I hear from Estelle and Jeffrey when I have visitation, and they say she's very nice. Which I'm glad to hear. It tears my heart out, of course, but I'm glad to hear it, still. She takes good care of them."

"Well, of course she takes good care of them," Pond said. "What else is she good for, anyway, besides wiping snotty noses and heating porridge up? Or whatever it is that young matrons do these days. The woman is a twit. A bimbo, would you say?"

Gates giggled again. "Now Mister Pond," she said, "you really shouldn't tempt me to disparage my successor. I'm trying to be well-behaved and nice, and it really isn't fair."

"But you agree with me," he said. "Why did Jeffrey marry her?"

"Well," she said, "I think, and I'm not being nasty here, I think he married her because she was what he wanted. And I wasn't. I don't think she makes any demands on him. I don't think she minds when he just runs everything. I think she defers to him and says: 'Yes, dear.' And: 'Certainly, dear.' And: 'Whatever you think, dear.' And I never did that. I always had to get my two cents' worth in, and I demanded a certain amount of attention. Which, Jeffrey being Jeffrey, I did not receive. And which I was never going to receive, as long as we were married. So, when I said I wanted Out, he was only too relieved. And he found somebody else, who would bow and curtsey to him and not make too much noise." She reflected. "And, she's very pretty. And she's good with the kids. She's everything he wants. I don't blame him a bit."

"Why *didn't* you seek custody?" Pond said. He sat back in the armchair and rubbed his chin with the fingers of both hands.

"Well," she said "I'm sure Jeffrey must have told you. Must've told the people in the firm something, at least, when we decided to split up."

"He was indefinite," Pond said. "I don't blame him, of course. But I've always been rather curious. I got the impression, from what he said, that you didn't want them. Was that right?"

She sighed. "Mister Pond," she said.

" 'Richard,' please," he said. "We're having such a good time, sitting here and chatting. Call me 'Richard,' please."

"Richard," she said obediently, "I really don't want to talk about why my marriage broke up. It's not that there was anything sinister or anything like that. In fact that's probably the reason that I don't want to talk about it — because the reasons are so dull. If I had something exciting to tell, maybe I would. Talk about it, I mean."

He leaned across the table again and patted her arm. "I'm sorry," he said. "I shouldn't have pried."

She shook her head again. "You're not . . . , yes, you are," she said, "I got that wrong. But even so, I would tell you, if there was just something to tell. And there isn't. I'm not even sure that the dull reasons that we — I — had were any good. And that's kind of embarrassing, you know? To think you made a decision like that and you didn't even have a good reason." She sighed. "I don't know," she said. "I felt trapped. I felt really caught, and unhappy, and . . . . I don't know what I felt, but it wasn't happy. It sure wasn't happiness. And I complained. I suppose I complained too much. And Jeffrey was very patient with me, and he started taking on more and more of what was involved in running our lives, and pretty soon it got to the point where I didn't even have to do the things that it bothered me to do anymore. Jeffrey's competent at home, too. Jeffrey's always competent. But I was just, well, superfluous. The nanny took care of the children. The housekeeper took care of the house. Hills Food Service took care of the shopping, and I took care of myself. And Jeffrey. Who doesn't require much care. And won't accept any, either."

"That's why he looks like he does," Pond said.

"That's probably it," she said. "So one morning I woke up with another empty day ahead of me, and he was making his coffee and toast in the kitchen, and I said: 'I want a divorce.' And he took the toast out of the toaster and started buttering it and said: 'So do I.'

And that was it. Not much of a story, huh? The only real item in it was that Jeffrey wasn't surprised when his wife asked for a divorce. But even that's not exciting — Jeffrey, nothing surprises Jeffrey. He is always well-prepared." She paused. "What did he say at the firm?"

"Nothing much," Pond said. "He seemed to think he had a right to treat it as a private matter, and I must say that those of us who'd gone through Ray's divorce, when he absolutely refused to consider it a private matter and got everyone involved, I must say we were relieved. We didn't ask many questions, and haven't to this day."

"Then why did you ask me tonight?" she said. She fixed her gaze on his face.

He raised his eyebrows and cocked his head. "Fair question," he said. "I'll give you the answer. Because you through Jeffrey asked me for some legal advice today, and I like to be sure that the advice which I give is properly cognizant of the client's actual needs."

"I asked Jeffrey to translate one phrase in a contract," she said. "Does that require a full history to do?"

"It might," Pond said. He finished his spritzer and signalled for another round. "Beyond the definition of the phrase that puzzled you, you see, is the ultimate issue of whether you should sign the contract which includes it. To advise you on that question, I have to take into account what I know of the other party to the contract, and what I know about you. I knew quite a bit about Mark Baldwin before you arrived tonight. I knew almost nothing about you. But what sort of person you are has a real bearing on whether I can say that you should or should not sign a contract with Mark Baldwin."

"It's not with Mark Baldwin," she said. "It's with *Journeyer* magazine."

"Nonsense," Pond said, as the waiter brought the second round. "I know Lisa Croyden very well, and I know Joan Fitch as well. Lisa is the publisher and Joan is the editor in chief, and both of them think the United States consists of Greenwich Village on the east and San Francisco on the west with some flat sort of tawny open land in between. Vague as angels, the pair of them. Lovely people, very nice, friendly, warm and silly. They just happen to have this notion that kinkier lesbian women constitute a large enough market to interest enough advertisers to support a magazine of the style they would like to put out. And four months out of seven, enough of those women, plus an undetermined number of stray men, buy the magazine off the newsstands to keep the circulation figures high enough to let them argue that another six months of subsidized publication will prove that they are right.

"There's a dilettante on Baldwin's board," Pond said, "name of Macalester. Ralphie Macalester's never worked a day in his life. He's married to a woman named Serena who's never worked a day in *her* life. Serena's into this holistic living business, and that's how she spends her macrobiotic waking hours, fooling around with biorhythms and eating sprouts or something. Ralphie gets up in the morning and confers with their astrologer, accountant and trustee, while he has his tiger's milk and pedicure. Serena has Ralphie convinced that the cosmic harmonies require that the descendants of Sappho have access to a picture magazine reflecting, shall we say, their interests, and it doesn't matter whether that magazine makes money. Ralphie has his accountant convinced that he will lose his cushy job if he argues with Ralphie. So when Ralphie comes in from his upstate New York manor house for meetings of the board of North American Group, he has his accountant's figures to buttress his case that six months more of subsidies will have *Journeyer* on a profit-making basis.

"As long as Ralphie has those figures," Pond said, "Baldwin's board doesn't argue with Ralphie either. Because Ralphie, in addition to Serena, the astrologer, the accountant and the pedicurist, has the trustee of his trust under this thumb as well. Ralph can revoke that trust, name a new trustee for it and sell off what it holds. You follow me?"

"I'm not sure," she said.

"Ralphie controls the trustee," he said. "The trustee can sell Ralphie's share of North American. And will, if Ralph tells him to. On the open market, where God knows who might buy it. The Macalester share of North American comes to approximately seven-point-three percent. Not enough to make policy, but certainly enough to screw up any policies that might be in real dispute.

"So," Pond said, "Baldwin controls his board. He likes it that way. If keeping Ralphie happy means printing *Journeyer*, well, Baldwin will print it. Unless and until he can find some white knight somewhere to buy out Ralphie if the day comes when the fight seems worth the cost. Which will never happen unless Ralphie becomes a pain in the neck, which he won't as long as *Journeyer* comes out.

"Therefore," he said, "when you say that the contract I've seen is with *Journeyer*, not Baldwin, I say: 'Nonsense.' As long as Baldwin is humoring Ralphie, any agreement with *Journeyer* is a contract with Baldwin. Himself."

"That's what he said," she said.

"Ah," Pond said. "That's interesting. I'm surprised he was so frank."

"He said the people at *Journeyer* do what he says, when he says it," she said, "and that's what he wants me to do."

"Refreshing candor," Pond said. "That's what that little clause means."

"It does?" she said.

"Uh huh," he said. "I have a friend in New York name of Simon. Simon's a talented man. Does all kinds of things that everybody knows pay absolutely nothing, and he makes a living at it. Sacred music? Simon knows everything there is to know about sacred music, and he knows it because he had a dual major in theology and music in college. And then in graduate school. Another of the things he does is freelance writing. Now, when Jeffrey showed me the document today, it meant nothing to me. But I knew it would to Simon, so I called him up and I said: 'Peter,' naturally we call him 'Peter,' all that churchy stuff, 'what does this mean, Peter?' And he told me. 'Writer for hire' means that you work for the magazine on just the same terms as a carpenter works for a homeowner. To erect, say, a fence. The carpenter is hired to put up a fence. When the fence is up, he gets paid and he's through. The homeowner now owns the fence. He can leave the fence where it is. He can chop it down. He can dig up the posts and sell it to somebody else for ten times what he paid the carpenter. The carpenter can't come back and claim that he should have more money because the homeowner resold the fence. He can't do anything to make the homeowner leave the fence up, because it's good work and the carpenter wants other customers to see it. And if somebody makes a movie out of that very fine fence, the carpenter will receive nothing."

"That's the same as it was on the paper," she said. "That's nothing new for me."

"Yes, it is new," Pond said. "It's completely different. If you wrote a story for the paper, and it was a real lulu, you could write a book about it, and you could sell that book. And the movie and all that other stuff, if the chance came along."

"On my own time," she said.

"On your own time," he said. "The contract I looked at prevents that. Any story you get out of this assignment for *Journeyer* belongs to *Journeyer*. *In toto*. Forever. It's theirs."

She frowned. "Does that matter?" she said.

"I don't know," he said. "That's what bothers me, advising you on this. Notwithstanding the shameless snooping you've allowed me to do tonight, I still don't really know a lot about you. What you want out of this contract, or what you want out of your life."

"I can tell you what I want from the contract," she said. "The other I'm not so sure about. Mister Baldwin told me that the contract, when it's filled in, will pay me twenty thousand dollars, plus all expenses. I need that money, Richard. Is he trying to cheat me?"

"Oh, goodness, no," Pond said. "I know a lot about Mark Baldwin, and I must say I don't like him. But if you had come in here tonight and said to me: 'Richard, my word is good. Mark Baldwin has promised to pay me two million dollars tomorrow, and I need a hundred bucks tonight,' I would take your draft on his account. And if you got hit by a cab on the way out the hotel tonight, and died before two A.M., I would feel no hesitation in presenting that draft to Mister Baldwin tomorrow. And it would be paid. Mark Baldwin keeps his word.

"I know a number of people," Pond said, "who deeply regret that fact. Because, you see, Mister Baldwin's word is good not only when he says he will do something *for* you, but also when he says he will do something *to* you. You can always trust him. He is not a good man to cross. If he says he will ruin you, he will."

"But why should that bother me?" she said. "I'm just a poor working girl."

Pond put his head back and laughed. "And that, dear lady," he said, "is precisely why it should bother you."

"Richard," she said, leaning back in her chair, "since we've become such good friends and all: What will it take to get you to tell me all that you know about Mark Baldwin?"

He exaggerated a simper. "Constance," he said, "didn't Jeffrey tell you *anything* about me?"

"Uh huh," she said.

He laughed again. "Shrewd bettor," he said. "You know you're not risking too much."

"I haven't got much to lose," she said.

"All right," he said, "a sporting proposition if ever I've heard one. Whatever you've heard about me, I'm no different from other men — I mean I also put food in my mouth." He laughed. "It's the story of life, isn't it? We spend most of our waking hours looking for something appealing to put in our bodies, or those of someone else. So, we'll pop over to the Marliave and you take me to dinner."

"I'd be delighted to," she said. "I mean that, too. But, ah, you don't have other plans?"

He grinned. "Constance," he said, "the General Court's in session tonight. Odds on eight or ten of them will be in there on the dinner recess, beating some lobbyist out of *pollo* and red wine. Can you imagine the consternation we'll create for those rednecks when I come in with you?"

"They don't know me," she said.

His grin vanished. His voice softened. "Constance," he said, "you poor thing. You're a beautiful woman. Don't you know that?"

She stared at him.

"Don't you?" he said.

"Well," she said after a while, "I used to. I used to think I was."

He picked up the wine glass and gestured to her to do the same. She picked up her glass. "You still are," he said, clinking glasses. "Confusion to our enemies," he said, raising his.

"I'll drink to that," she said, and did.

13

"Mark Baldwin's mother, Amy, and my mother, Suzanne," Richard Pond told Constance Gates, "were half-sisters. Amy's mother, Julia, was the first of Archie Cross's four children, two by her mother and two more by my grandmother. Amy's sister, Amelia, died of influenza in the Nineteen-twenty-eight epidemic; she was in the booby hatch at the time, a detail which is usually left out of family accounts. Julia killed herself with sleeping pills during the breakup of her second marriage to some refugee Hungarian count or something shortly before World War Two. My mother's brother, Jonathan, was killed on a combat mission over Okinawa; even though it was clearly established that Uncle Jonathan came to grief as a result of his extreme recklessness above and beyond the call of duty, he was posthumously decorated for bravery. My mother is considered a recluse by good society, which is better than having her known as the hopeless alcoholic that she is."

"Wow," Gates said. They were sitting in a high-backed booth on the southerly wall of the low-ceilinged downstairs dining room at the Marliave Restaurant. Pond had ordered a bottle of Barolo and two dishes of veal marsala without consulting her; she had been permitted to say that she preferred a salad to pasta. The small dining room was crowded and the ceiling was made of patterned tin painted white; the resulting resonance of many conversations made it almost impossible to distinguish specifics of any.

"I'll say," Pond said. He drank some wine. He put his glass down and folded his hands. "Archie Cross was a full-fledged bastard," he said. "I don't think there's any question but that the many singularities of his descendants can be traced back directly to him. Of course I imagine that if Archie were alive today to hear such charges, he'd immediately defend himself by accusing some earlier ancestor as the ultimate culprit, but the fact remains that in his own right, he was a perfect monster.

"As best I can tell," Pond said, "the most damaging of Archie's many deplorable character defects was his tendency to resort to violence when he was frustrated. I say that because the tendency to violence was the worst that I saw — he may have had worse that I don't know about. His vocation was the arrangement of investments in what today would be called 'Third World' or 'developing' countries — Cuba, Venezuela, Brazil, that sort of thing. He spent a lot of time on what were then real frontiers, which probably heightened if it didn't create his penchant for violence — he may have needed it to survive. I've seen photographs of Grampa wearing a white linen suit and a big straw hat and two enormous pistols holstered at his waist. It was obvious he was strutting when the shutter snapped. He liked wearing those guns, and he claimed he'd used them, too.

"The trouble is, he brought his swagger and his appetite for violence home. Along with all the frustrations that he must have built up dealing with natives and other infuriating people who refused to speak English to him. And he took it out on his families. He beat both his wives, unmercifully. He used his hands on all his children, all three girls and Jonathan as well — no sexist discrimination there. He convinced his daughters that their lives were worthless because they hadn't been born male, and he convinced Jonathan that he was a wretched excuse for a male. He infected Mark's grandmother with a venereal disease he'd acquired on one of his voyages, and then accused her of having contracted it herself during his absence. He used that as his grounds for divorcing her, in order to marry my grandmother. Oh, he was a prick.

"Naturally," Pond said, "sharing Grandpa Archie as we did, we semi-first cousins had quite a lot in common, and were probably much closer as a result than most real first cousins in more placid families ever get to be. We're not in regular contact now, but twenty years ago the various calamities befalling us as the results of Archie's long-past misdeeds gave us no choice but to associate. His crimes united us. Who else on earth could we tell — who else would understand? — the history behind my mother's problem with the bottle, or Amy's excruciating willingness to tolerate Mark's father's liaisons? My mother and Mark's mother gave me and my two sisters, and Mark and his younger brother, almost endless problems, all of them directly attributable to the way that Archie had treated them in their formative years. And those experiences of course left their marks on the five of us. There's simply no question about it.

"When I say that," he said, "I want you to understand that I am not trying to excuse my personal conduct or anyone else's with a lot of cheap psychobabble. Am I clear on that, Constance?"

"Very clear," she said.

"What my mother used to call my 'irregular' social life, and what I call Mark's 'satyriasis:' maybe neither of them is in the slightest way related to the history of the family," he said. "But then again, maybe it is. There's certainly no blinking the fact that we're a strange breed of cats. There must be some reason.

"That's why, when you ask me whether you should sign a 'writer for hire' contract with Mark Baldwin, I have to ask myself what kind of person you are. Because I know what kind of person he is. He is ruthless. He's a user. Not of drugs — people.

"He wasn't always that way," Pond said. "Not by any means. Until he was about thirty or so, he was a genial dabbler. His father, Angus, was a replica of Archie but without the fisticuffs and pistols. You didn't have to be Sigmund Freud to know why Amy married him. He was a money-maker, just like her daddy was. Very forceful personality, almost overbearing, tough, resilient and very, very smart. But cold. Cold as a stone in winter. His capacity for human affection was stunted. If it existed at all. Mark and his younger brother, Cal, and Mark's mother: for Angus, the three of them existed to the same extent, and had the same importance, as his Rolls-Royce Silver Ghost. They were things that he had and enjoyed, when he had the time. And when he didn't have the time, when he was otherwise engaged, he didn't think about them.

"Mark has never *had* to work," Pond said. "That's a very important aspect of him. He's never had to work, never had to think about what his talents are, or which of them would be likeliest to make him a good living. Unlike my father, who could never catch a break and was always tapping into my mother's money, just to tide him over, Angus made buckets of the stuff. Enough of it, notwithstanding the Royce and the high living that he did, enough of it stuck to his fingers so that he left Amy and his boys — and his mistress too, for that matter — very well fixed. I don't think he did it out of any love for them, mind you — I think he did it for the same reason that he tipped generously in restaurants. It was part of his image of himself to treat generously the people who gave him good service. It *amused* him, you know? Each of the boys was to come into a trust worth two or three million, either when he reached twenty-one, or their father died. Back in Nineteen-fifty-three, when Mark got out of Harvard, that was a *very* considerable sum of money."

She laughed. "I'd call it a considerable sum today." she said.

"Well," he said, "It's certainly dancing money. And now, of course, with his mother and Cal both dead, he's got a good deal more. Mark is a wealthy man. But back then, two or three million was by itself a *lot*. Mark's Jaguar cost about four thousand dollars then — do you know what those things cost today? About nine times that much. And when he got that money, well, he got freedom with it. Freedom to do anything he wanted, which was also, of course, the freedom to do nothing at all.

"I do not mean he was spoiled," Pond said. "Quite the contrary. He did all the proper things. I was, for example, barely scraping along at Harvard — I was three years behind him — and my mother's money from Archie was dwindling fast. Mark paid my university expenses for my last two years of college, and my three years at law school. All of them. Tuition, board, room — everything but spending money."

"I'd call that generous," she said.

"So did I," Pond said, "when I found out who was picking up those tabs. I called it *very* generous. See, until I was in the middle of my second year of law school, stupid me didn't know where the cash was coming from. The bills arrived and I gave them to my mother — my father was long gone by then — and that would be the last I heard about them. So I assumed she was paying them. And then one night at dinner — she was absolutely pissed, of course, all tanked up on cheap champagne and smelling like a Yale Junior Prom — I made some casually-insulting reference to Mark, about how he'd be a student all his life, and she let me know in no uncertain terms that if it weren't for Mark, I wouldn't have finished college, let alone gone to law school. Which flushed my toilet for me, I can assure you.

"So I called him up," Pond said. "He was at Fletcher then. And I tried, of course, to thank him. I was very ill at ease. And he seemed uncomfortable. He said he didn't think that, really, I had to feel as I did. That after all, he had the means, and it seemed like the ordinary thing to do, and I shouldn't feel that way.

"And I was stunned," Pond said, as the waitress brought the veal. "I was absolutely *stunned*. And I started to stammer at him how much it meant to me, and how grateful I was, and he just wouldn't hear it." He bent over his plate and inhaled the aroma. He looked up. "Smell it," he said, "it can be the best part. Even the toughest veal smells good, when it's properly cooked."

She did as he directed. "It does smell good," she said.

He was cutting the veal and nodding. "Uh huh," he said, frowning. "But now comes the hard part — chewing the stuff. If it's not pounded thin enough, it can be tougher than a biker's jacket." He put a piece in his mouth. His expression brightened. "Not bad," he said, 'Not bad at all. They must've gotten a *sous* chef with stronger forearms than the old one had. Someone who *likes* beating his meat."

She mustered a small laugh to reward him.

He nodded his appreciation, an actor taking a bow in mid-scene without disrupting the performance. "Ever since that phone call," he said, "things between us have been strained. Progressively more strained, as the years have gone by and each of us has heard things about the other of which he disapproved." He chewed and shook his head. "I'm to blame in this, of course. When Cal was killed, I made an unfortunate remark at the memorial service for which Mark has never forgiven me. And in justice to Mark, I don't suppose I would've forgiven me, either."

"What was that?" she said. She was finding the veal a little harder to chew than his remark had suggested, and she didn't want him to know it.

"I didn't mean it to be unfortunate," he said. "Cal was three years younger than I, six years younger than Mark, and after Angus died, well, he got his money early and he became a little wild. That would have been in Nineteen-fifty-five; Mark was in the first semester of his third year of law school when Angus checked out, and Cal celebrated the occasion of his father's death by getting himself thrown out of Andover the following spring, in his senior year. Well, not thrown out, but he was suspended for being drunk or something, and since Mark's mother was off somewhere on the Riviera, Mark had to go up to the school and take charge. Which he did, and Cal was readmitted and he graduated. And then Cal went to Harvard, and there were similar episodes, and finally when he was in his second year there, he was expelled for good. Which would have been when Mark was in, let's see, his first year at Fletcher. And Cal was about nineteen.

"Well," Pond said, "I was in my first year of law school then, and of course I knew everything, so when Mark invited me to lunch in Harvard Square and Cal was there in his disgrace, I thought I was supposed to offer my wisdom, even if it wasn't particularly wanted. So we were in Cronin's, that dingy beer hall that isn't there any more, and Cal announced that he was dumping college once and for all and going to become a race driver. And I thought that was just about the silliest thing I'd ever heard of, and I said so. And Cal said: 'Why shouldn't I?' And I said: 'Because you'll kill yourself, that's why. And probably kill somebody else along with yourself, someone who knows what he's doing on those tracks and doesn't expect some rich kid from Beacon Hill who thinks speeding in an MG on Route Nine is race car driving, to do something stupid on the track in front of him.'

"Now," Pond said, "I can't say I expected Cal to welcome what I said. But what I didn't expect was Mark's reaction. Which was anger. 'Why the hell shouldn't he do what he wants to do?' Mark said. 'It's his life and his money. Just because he's not like you and me, and doesn't want to spend his whole life cooped up in some damned library, why should that make a difference?' And of course I had to make a bad thing worse, and I said the only reason Mark was taking that attitude was because he was sick and tired of bailing Cal out of one scrape after another and he wanted to wash his hands of him.

"That was the last time I saw Cal alive," Pond said. "He did go to Europe, and he got himself some sort of learner's permit or something that allowed him to begin a career, and Mark finished up at Fletcher and went to State. Where, I presume, some old chum of his late father's managed to get him posted to Rome as his first assignment overseas. That was in Fifty-nine. And from Rome he went to Geneva, and from Geneva he went nuts."

She was about to give up on the veal. He noticed it. "You're not eating, my dear?" he said.

"Let me put it this way," she said, "the conversation's more interesting than the dinner. I had a late lunch. I'm just not very hungry."

"You're sure?" he said anxiously. "I can send it back, you know. A friend of mine's a very influential food critic, and they know what I can do if I'm not satisfied."

She reached out and patted his arm. "Please don't," she said. "I'm perfectly happy. You have no idea how much pleasanter this is than the evening I thought I had in front of me."

He searched her face for evidence of deceit, found none and nodded. He went back to his veal. "I must say," he said, "mine's delicious." He put another piece in his mouth, where it seemed to dissolve, and resumed. "While Mark was in Geneva," he said, "Cal was badly hurt in time trials at Nurburgring. And Mark of course at once took leave and went to him. And from what I get from my mother, who got it from Amy, Mark decided that the only way Cal was going to be able to realize his ambition without getting killed on the Grand Prix circuit was if Mark took him in hand and just shepherded him through it.

"So he did that," Pond said, "or tried to, at least. He quit State and inveigled himself into a job with Team Lotus, which I think was probably not too difficult in those days for somebody with lots of money, willing to invest in the team. And the gist of it was that he was in effect operating a racing team under Lotus auspices with an experienced professional driver, fellow by the name of Rinaldi, I think, to teach the junior driver, Cal, how to win big races. And also, I'm afraid, proving to Richard Pond that he did care what happened to his younger brother and was taking care of him.

"That lasted almost two seasons," Pond said, "during which Mark got married to Lucille Bede Barrow. Her mother was Esmé Bede. Her father was the novelist, the Nobel laureate? Louis Dane?"

"Oh," she said, "yes. *Lions in Captivity*."

"That's the one," Pond said. "Her brother was killed at Dienbienphu with the Foreign Legion — all the appropriate stuff. And Mark married her, her second husband. Well, she was as promiscuous as a cat, of course, so while Mark was off at Silverstone and so forth, she was screwing someone else who moved in their circle, and while all *that* was going on, something went wrong in the pit at Spa during a workout or something, and there was an explosion. And Cal was killed.

"So," Pond said, finishing his veal, "naturally there was a memorial service at Trinity Church, and naturally I went, and naturally I felt called upon after the memorial to tell Amy that this never would've happened if Mark had listened to me, and we haven't spoken since."

"I can understand why," she said.

"Oh," he said, picking up his glass, "it was extremely stupid and thoughtless of me. You have no idea how many times I've wished I had those words back. But I said them, and they're gone, and I can't do anything about it. And you will forgive me, I hope," he said, touching her hand, "if I say that I think Mark should know that? That I meant no malice and I'm sorry I hurt him? And if he doesn't understand that, that he should at least return my calls, so I could tell him how I feel?"

"You've called him?" she said.

"Not recently," he said. "But in the two or three years after that, I bet I called him a dozen times. And I never reached him." He shrugged. He picked up his fork and poached off her plate. "No help for it, I guess," he said, selecting a morsel of veal. "These things happen in life. But that does leave us with a question. He's a complicated man. Are you up to handling him?"

"Handling him?" she said. "How does that come up? He wants to hire me to do a job. How is that involved?"

Pond sat back and dabbed at his lips with his napkin. The waitress arrived and he nodded when she asked if she could remove the plates. He drank some wine. "There are two ways of doing business with Mark Baldwin," he said. "The first way, which is the safest, is to sell him something that he wants to buy. Deliver the goods on time, submit your bill, and get the hell out of there. The other way is to submit to his considerable charm, bow to his will, and permit him to take over your life while telling you at the same time you're freer than you ever were.

"Forgive me," he said, "but the chances of you being able to follow the first strategy seem pretty slim to me. That means you're likely to wind up this job under his control. You seem vulnerable."

"I am," she said, drinking some wine. "I hate to admit it, but I am. I'm broke. I'm alone. It bothers me to be alone.

"I try to be honest with myself," she said. "I try to look at things objectively. I got divorced at probably the worst possible time. I had two kinds of friends when that happened. Women friends, I mean. The ones I'd made for myself in college, and the ones I knew through

Jeffrey, the women who'd married his friends. My friends who are still married and with their husbands and with their children don't have time for me. Their families are what they do and what they talk about. When I try to make plans to see them, they make perfectly honest, casual remarks that really hurt, without meaning any such thing. They tell me they can't have lunch Wednesday because that's the housekeeper's day off and they have to carpool the kids around. And they can't meet for drinks or dinner because Herb or Norris comes home tired from work and wants them there to feed him. They're not trying to rub it in, that they don't envy me my freedom one bit, but just by telling me the details of their daily lives, that is what they do. When they do make time to see me, they make it abundantly clear it wasn't easy and they can't make a habit of it, and then neither one of us has a good time because we don't have anything in common anymore to talk about. I seldom see my kids now, so I can't swap those anecdotes."

"Then there's the other thing," she said, taking a deep breath. "Topic A, my sex life, now that I am on the loose. I know what my married friends are thinking. All of them, no matter how contented they are, think it must be exciting, to be available. The ones that're faithful to their husbands are sneakily convinced in the back corners of their minds that while I don't enjoy the advantages of home and hearth they have, I did get something in exchange for giving up those things. Which is a license to fuck any man I take a fancy to. On days when they're happy with their husbands and haven't been mentally undressing the supermarket bundle boys bending into the backs of their Country Squires, they think of me as a scarlet woman. On days when it seems like their hubbies will never get it up again, and they have been lusting after those firm, tight, teenaged buns, they envy the hell out of me.

"Either way," she said, "I don't like it. I don't like being expected to satisfy their desire for vicarious titilation when they're horny, and I don't like feeling their prudery when they're in their smug moods. I don't like the vibrations I get from the complacent ones, and I don't like the air of superiority I can feel when I'm sitting with some hypocrite who's having a discreet affair with the pro at the country club and therefore thinks she's better than I am because she's managed her fun better. And I *especially* don't like being nudged in a restaurant when some good-looking man goes by, and hearing: 'If I were in your shoes, Connie, I'd get introduced to him.' "

She snorted. "See why I'm so hard to live with? Contradictory: that's what I am. I don't want to be envied, and I don't want to be condemned, and one or the other reaction's what I always get from them. Because, well, what is there, really besides what you do and what you want, when it comes time to talk? Nothing, that's what there is. My married friends are useless.

"Which leaves the single ones," she said. "The ones who never got married, or whose marriages were so brief they might as well not have." She took a deep breath. "Two of them are lesbians. The others are anything but lesbians. Right after Jeff and I got divorced, one of the lesbians, a woman I knew in college and never had any trouble dealing with before made a determined effort to seduce me. It upset me a lot." She paused. "I hope you don't mind me saying that," she said.

"Goodness, no," he said. "I'm against sexual recruitment by anyone, no matter what their preference is."

"It really bothered me," Gates said. "I'd always been fond of Gail's company even though I knew she was gay and she knew I was not, or at least so I assumed. When she did that, it poisoned our friendship. I haven't seen her since.

"I can't really say my straight single friends've been that much help to me either," she said. "I don't mean they haven't tried to be, because they have. They've listened to me until all hours of the night, in person and on the phone. They've invited me to go on trips with them, spend weekends at their houses on the Cape, go out on blind dates with their former boyfriends and their new ones, and generally tried to give all the support I seem to need. And it hasn't worked. I'm still at loose ends. At first I thought it was just a matter of the divorce being recent, you know, and that in time things would get better and I'd come out of my funk. But I haven't.

"I don't know how to deal with men anymore," she said. "If I ever did — Jeff and I started going together during my freshman year of college, and I never got much practice browsing males. I know what my needs are as a woman — God, I hate that phrase — and the men that I've seen since I got divorced have made their needs *very* clear, in no uncertain terms. And I must say that for someone who was Miss Priss for a very long time, I haven't had too much trouble adjusting to the fact that sex can be a casual matter, any time you want it, with anyone's who's handy. Being available, at your sole option, can be kind of fun, at first. But still, you know, I was slightly shocked when one of my friends told me she'd had forty lovers, even though I'd had seven myself by then, if you count Jeff. I don't know whether there's a moral difference between seven and forty, or a hundred, or if it's worth making if there is one. But somewhere there has to be a line between normal sexual activity and just outright promiscuity, and I don't want to cross it. On purpose or otherwise.

"Last year," she said, "I began to get worried that that's what I was doing. So I had a heart-to-heart with myself and said: 'Self, in the past month you've been in bed with three different men, which is an annual rate of three dozen a year. When you are forty, Self, you will have had over two hundred sexual partners, at least one of whom will have to have been lying when he said he didn't have anything contagious, so you will probably be sick. And you will have a reputation as an easy lay from here to Vancouver, which will probably not improve your chances for a long-term thing. So, shape up, Self, and cross your legs, and stop sleeping around.'

"And I did," she said. "I became selective. I picked out an escort who looked promising, and pretty soon I was involved in what I thought was a major affair. He was — is — seven years younger than I am, tending bar part-time to support his art. I let him move in with me, which I let him think I was doing so that he could save up all his money for a studio. He wanted to buy a condo loft in one of those old woolens buildings, down by the Channel, you know? But what I was really up to was getting him into a position where I could work on him. And I kept telling him *he* had to shape up and realize he was never going to make it, trying to be the next Marc Chagall. Or Picasso, whoever he had in mind to be. He just wasn't good enough. Now I can see what I was doing, of course. Jeff's character was set in concrete when I met him, and he wouldn't change for me. So now I was going to find a man I could mold into what I wanted him to be. Make him dependent on me, and customize a lover.

"Ted did not like hearing what I had to say," she said. "Not at first, at least. I was right about his artistic genius, but not about his character. We had some pretty big fights that my downstairs neighbors heard through the floor, and some things went on during them I didn't like at all. I always got frightened that he'd leave me after we had a big blow-out that ended up with him hitting me, so to keep him around, I'd let him make love. And he got this idea in his head that I was starting fights so he'd hit me, because that turned me on. And nothing I could do convinced him otherwise. So, when he came around to my point of view about his talent, and realized that I was right, I was stuck with a hardworking, handsome, young graphic artist who was totally convinced I liked getting punched in the mouth. He dropped all his silly dreams, and went into commercial art. Advertising. And now he's got his own operation, six people working for him, making lots of dough. I raised him from a pup, as my father used to say, and then I had to throw him out before he murdered me. So now he's living with a lady named Donna who's much smarter than I'll ever be, and she's reaping the benefits of all I worked to do."

"How to do you mean, she's smarter," Pond said. "You seem very smart to these eyes."

"She's got him," Gates said, "and I don't. She's twenty-five years old and she's smarter than I am. I finished him off, and she took him. I must be stupid."

"Perhaps you didn't want him," Pond said.

"That's what I keep telling myself," she said. "I don't know if it's true. I'd find it easier to believe if I just had someone else."

"What is it that you want?" Pond said.

She leaned back in the booth. "I don't know," she said. "All I know is: I don't have it. That's all I can tell you."

Outside on Bosworth Street, after she had put twenty-eight dollars on her Mastercard over his objections, he bent and kissed her hand. "You're extremely nice," she said.

He held onto the hand. "I try to be," he said. He looked worried. "Can I ask you something now? Because the question will come up, and unless you're prepared to meet it when it does, you should not sign that paper."

She nodded. "Of course you can," she said. "I think I know what it is, but go ahead — what is it?"

"Are you prepared to fuck Mark Baldwin?" he said. He looked very concerned.

She hesitated. She nodded. "I think so, if it comes to that," she said. She squeezed his hand. "He's an attractive man, you know," she said. "And it's not like, you know, it was a major decision or anything." She snickered. "After all, what's the difference, really, between nine and ten? If the question comes up? Yes, I'll go to bed with him."

"It will," he said sadly. He let go of her hand. "Don't get hurt, Constance," he said. "You're too nice for that."

14

On the morning of her second visit to the headquarters of North American Group, Constance Gates was allowed to enter the inner corridor off the reception area unescorted, and to find her own way down the hall to Mark Baldwin's office. "You'll recognize her right off," Sylvia Francis said to Anne Leeds on the intercom. "She's got on white linen pants that look like they might shut off her circulation, and I hope they do. And one of those blouson sweaters you can almost see through but not quite? Which is sort of ivory. I think I hate her."

"Sylvia," Anne Leeds said, "we both know it won't last even if that is what she's after. You know how he is." She saw Gates approaching the door to Baldwin's office. "Got to go now," she said, and put the handset down. "Mister Baldwin's waiting for you," she said, smiling, as Gates entered the office. "You can go right in."

Baldwin made a perfunctory move in his chair intended to remind her that his back hurt. "Don't get up," she said. She took the chair nearest his Out boxes and sat down. She framed a big smile. "Well," she said, "I made up my mind. Thanks for seeing me on short notice. Is the job still open?"

He pushed his chair back from his refectory table about two inches and stared at her. She stood the inspection for about thirty seconds, maintaining the smile. Then she let the smile fade, and frowned. "Am I intruding or something?" she said. "You didn't have to see me."

He shook his head as though trying to clear it. "On the contrary," he said, smiling, "I did have to see you. If I didn't, my curiosity'd drive me nuts. You seemed pretty negative after our first talk. Mind if I ask what changed your mind for you?"

"Oh," she said, "I changed it for myself. I do all of my own work. It was a combination of things. I talked to a couple of people. I did some serious thinking. And, I looked at the stack of bills on my desk

— the thin envelope from the phone company with the blue notice inside that says they're going to shut you off pretty soon if you don't pay the overdue balance; the sharp little comment on the Mastercard that says they're disappointed with you because you didn't pay quite as much last month as they had in mind; the one from the department store that says the next party you'll be hearing from is their collection agency. I sort of leafed through those this morning and I thought: 'Well, what the hell, huh? What harm can it do to get solvent for a change? Might even enjoy it.' And besides, it wasn't as though, you know, I had a couple dozen other people bidding for my services, and had to juggle lots of commitments in my diary. So, I decided if I didn't tack you off so much you'd never see me again, it might be sensible to come over here and chat."

"Sounds reasonable enough," he said. He pulled the chair forward and reached into the nearest In box. He removed the top document, looked at it, nodded, and handed it to her. It was a completed contract hiring her on the terms he had described. "This meet your understanding?" he said.

She read it. She put it back on the table. "Uh huh," she said. "But I'd still like to know a little more about the job. What it actually involves, you know? Some details?"

"Sign the contract," he said.

"Before I get the details?" she said, leaning forward and reaching for his pen in the holder.

"That's correct," he said, as she signed. "No signature, no details." He picked up the document when she finished and leaned back. He nodded once. He put it in the furthest Out box. He punched the intercom. "Anne," he said, "would you make a copy of Miss Gates's contract for her, please? And bring me those files I wanted."

Anne Leeds carried three thick expandable file pouches into Baldwin's office and put them on the blotter in the center of his table. She picked up the contract and went out. Baldwin tapped the pile of folders. "A little light bedtime reading," he said. "I had these copied for you. Because I was curious, I had Anne set the counter on the copying machine. If you're interested, you have exactly eleven hundred and forty-seven pages of reading ahead of you." He grinned. "A good deal of it," he said, "consists of tear sheets from the *Commoner* from twenty-three years ago. Not very interesting then — less interesting now."

He began to lever himself out of the chair, his hands on its arms pressing down and a tense expression on his face.

"You need a chiropracter, I think," Gates said.

He shook his head. "I need a witch doctor," he said. "I need somebody who can dip a cornhusk doll in the blood of my enemy's best dog in the moonlight and mutter incantations that transfer this curse to him."

"Who's your enemy?" she said.

He had made it to his feet. He put his head back and laughed. "Oh, God," he said, "take your pick. The President, the Pope, the head of B'nai B'rith, the suffragan bishop of the Episcopal diocese of Massachusetts, the head of the UMass regents, mayor of Boston, governor of Rhode Island, the owners of the Red Sox — I've got hundreds of them. One must have a dog. Find that dog and slit its throat. Rid me of the pain."

"Is that what I just signed up to do?" she said.

He laughed again, jamming the heels of his hands into the small of his back and arching it against the pressure. "No," he said, "it's not. What you agreed to do is nowhere as exciting, or as useful to society, as far as that goes. But if you want to take on this additional assignment, I'll triple your fee on successful completion."

"My ex-husband," she said sympathetically, "used to suspend himself from the top of the door frame when his back tightened up. He looked like a vampire bat that got confused about positions, but he said it helped."

Baldwin shook his head. "Won't work," he said. "Neither does lying on the floor or getting pummeled in a clinic. What happens to me is that when I don't swim for a long time, which I didn't do as much as I should have in April because I was working day and night getting ready to go away, I lose all the flexibility in my body. Then when I start working out again, not necessarily swimming but to get the flexion back, of course I overdo it and lock everything right up. I don't wish to believe that I've been so stupid, so I pretend I haven't been and continue to exercise. And pretty soon I get myself so knotted up I can barely move." He stalked a few paces away from his table, then returned to his chair and slowly sat down.

He nodded toward the pile of folders. "If I could think of some way to cut that stack down to the point where you wouldn't need a valise to carry it," he said, "I would do it. The thing that prevents me from doing that is that I don't know what's important in there and what isn't. So as best I can tell, you're stuck with the dreary business of at least skimming through it so you'll have a working awareness of what the people involved were doing at the time when Timmy Lavelle was killed.

"You may find it initially difficult to see why the unsolved murder of a drifter over twenty years ago in a sleepy little town is a story that today's worth twenty grand to me," he said. "I have to admit I find it a little puzzling myself. I was in Waterford when Timmy was killed. I was there when they found his body. I covered the story for the *Commoner*. I liked covering the story. It was sort of exciting, a nice change from fighting off the urge to take naps at meetings of the Board of Selectmen. But even then I didn't think the death of Tim Lavalle was an epoch-making event in the history of western civilization, and I still don't today.

"These files," he said, tapping the top one, "will not provide you with any reason to disagree with me. All they do is preserve the *Commoner*'s version of that and other events. Those stories were written by Melvin Shaw and me and a fellow Joe Logan, and a woman named Didi Chenevert. The ones that are important to you in that collection are the ones that Logan and Shaw wrote, regardless of subject. You need to know all you can about the murder case. And you need to wring out of those clippings and personnel records every bit of information you can get about Logan and Shaw. Because your story is about Logan. And his story is about Shaw. His story, which Logan apparently proposes to tell in court, is that Shaw killed Lavalle and got away with it. The reason Logan will be in court at all this fall is for his trial on a set of murder charges of his own."

"Wait a minute," she said, frowning. "Is Logan the vigilante guy? The one that was on TV?"

"That's the one," Baldwin said. "Living, breathing, talkative proof that a TV anchorman can be more than just a pretty face. What you have to do is get to know him, and Shaw, and everybody else whose name crops up in these files, as intimately as you can from what they wrote and said then about the things that happened. Which will not be very well, but you will need whatever you can get when you finish this reading phase.

"After you finish that delightful historical tour," he said, "you'll be glad to hear that you'll be ready for the serious investigation. Have you got a tape recorder?"

"No," she said, taken aback. "I didn't even bring my case. I thought all I'd be doing today was signing up and so forth, and I'd get cracking on the assignment tomorrow, after I found out what it is."

"Uh huh," he said, reaching for the intercom. "Reasonable enough. But I may be able to save you some time, or at least sort of get you oriented before you wade into this." He tapped the folders again. "Anne," he said to the intercom, "get ahold of Sullivan and tell him to have one of his dingbats get up here with a tape recorder pronto for Miss Gates."

"Mini or micro?" Leeds said.

"Mini," Baldwin said. "And a box of blank tapes. And one of those Trash Eighties. And have Meyer in accounting get a phone credit card number for Miss Gates." He released the button. "You have which credit cards?" he said.

"Just Mastercard," she said. "And if it wasn't for this job, I wasn't going to have that for long."

He punched the button again. "And while you've got Meyer," he said, "get her an American Express Card and a Carte Blanche and a Visa. And one of our Mastercards, too, while he's at it. Have him make up a whole package, if you would. With the Hertz number and all the rest. And also the two checks, one for ten grand and one for two. And do one of those letters for her on *Journeyer* stationery, all that 'To Whom it May Concern' stuff about how Constance Gates is on assignment for What's-her-name, the editor, and all courtesies will be appreciated. And sign Joan's name to that. Got all of that, Anne?"

"Right away, Mister Baldwin," Leeds said.

He sat back from the table. He saw that Gates was smiling. "What's the matter with you?" he said.

"Nothing," she said, blushing. "It's just that, well, last night I took a friend to dinner and it was a lovely evening, and all I've been able to think about since I got up this morning is that I've only got about eight hundred dollars left on my limit. And then I sign your contract, with expenses in advance, and I think: 'Oh, good, I can get the card paid off,' and now you're doing all these things and it's just wonderful."

"Other people's money," he said. "It's no problem at all, when it's other people's dough. All you've got to remember is that if you do get caught short and you have to use one of our cards for something that doesn't have anything to do with the assignment, you've got to put a check in the mail for the item. Because they've got auditors down there in Meyer's office that have X-ray vision, and if you charge us for a yacht or something while you're on assignment inland, they will have your ass in jail. Or threaten to, at least."

"I wasn't planning to charge personal expenses," she said, somewhat primly.

"Aw," he said, "everybody does, sooner or later. It's human nature. And it's okay if you do. That's all I'm saying. Just make it right as soon as possible. Then you'll be okay."

"Understood," she said.

"Now," he said, rapping the folders again, "if what I heard this week is correct, what you've got here is not only what Bradlee at the *Post* calls, 'the first rough draft of history,' but one that is incomplete, mistaken and deliberately misleading. What's in this stack are employee records of two *Commoner* reporters who were in the Waterford bureau in Nineteen-sixty-two and Nineteen-sixty-three. Plus what they wrote for the paper. Mel Shaw was the bureau chief. Mel stayed with us until Nineteen-seventy-nine, when he left to get rich. Fortunately for you, he didn't write that much. The other one was Joe Logan. He wasn't there very long — just under two years — and he was a rookie so most of his work you can skim.

"The third file," he said, "is every story that the *Commoner* ever printed about Timothy Lavalle, who came to a bad end." Anne Leeds came into the office with a small Styrofoam box and a smaller one of clear plastic. She snapped open the plastic box and took out a Sony tape recorder. She installed the tape in the recorder, pressed the "record" button, saw that the tape was running, and put the machine on the table. "Thank you, Anne," he said. "You're welcome," she said with a small curtsey. "Sullivan says he hopes this one comes back to him some day."

"Noted," Baldwin said. "I suggest what you do, Miss Gates," he said, as Leeds left the room, "is use this machine as a backup. In other words, take your notes, or whatever method you used when you were reporting, and just let the machine run along. Label your tapes: date, time, person interviewed, location. When you accumulate half a dozen or so, ship them to Anne. She'll have someone in the pool transcribe them, and send you the transcripts. And the same thing with the TRS Eighty, the portable computer we're checking out to you. Get used to it. Learn to use it. Then when you're ready to start doing drafts of your stuff, do them on the machine, plug it into the phone, ship the material to us and let the computers print it for you. We'll have printed copy back to you in a day. Save you some more time."

"That would be great," she said.

"Well," he said, "there is a time factor involved in this project. By breaking backs and whipping people, we can cut *Journeyer*'s lead time between submission and publication to around six weeks. Which we don't ordinarily do because it comes with a big red flag that says *Overtime* on it for all kinds of union types, and it costs like the devil. But our feeling is that when Logan's case starts to get closer, you're going to see cable news operations making plans for continuous coverage, and reporters from national magazines jockeying for seats, and people with book contracts bumping into each other to get at the principals. Because this is a naturally trendy story, Miss Gates. This is a respected member of the community whose mind snapped after his family was killed by a drunken driver. Because the response of society to this horrible thing that'd happened to him was to slap the killer's wrists with a light jail term. So Logan took law into his own hands and shot the man who had ruined his life, and that's why he's on trial. You got the drunk driving crusade that's a big thing these days. You got the death penalty question, which never goes away. And you have got the general Bernhard Goetz vigilante issue of when it's right for the outraged citizen to revenge himself on criminals when the law proves ineffective."

"Clint Eastwood in the movie?" she said.

Baldwin nodded. "Wouldn't surprise me," he said. "Him or Charles Bronson. Or maybe Sylvester Stallone. I'm too old now and I've been around too long not to know that there aren't at least a hundred reasons out there why this case may fade away. Logan may snap again, and kill himself this time. Or he may just decide he's too tired to go through a trial after all that he's gone through, and just throw in the sponge. Any number of things could happen. But I've also been around long enough to know that when it looks like a blockbuster's building, you go out and watch that block.

"You do it especially," he said, "when it's a natural magazine story, one that needs a lot of space on a one-shot deal to tell it intelligently. I don't mean the *Commoner* isn't going to cover it, and cover it aggressively, or that the other outlets won't. I hope they do, in fact, because that will heighten the interest in it. But it will still be a natural for a periodical. Now, when you've a magazine as feeble as *Journeyer* is, one that desperately needs to attract some attention and a wider audience if it's going to survive, combined with a swing-vote member of your board of directors who *insists* that the rag will survive, a story possibility like that sort of grabs your attention. If it were my decision alone, I would scuttle that operation yesterday afternoon and make the decision retroactive to the day after we bought the lousy thing some years ago, but it isn't so I can't, and I'm doing this instead. Which is gearing up to get that story covered and skedding it for *Journeyer*, and making plans for an advertising blitz that'll knock the nation on its ear if the story comes through." He paused. "The last time we talked you had some reservations about how much rewrite might be needed."

"Yes, I did," she said. "I still do. It's been a long time since I did any writing for publication, and the stuff I did then wasn't in this league at all. You're paying me a lot of money. Suppose I can't deliver?"

"Well," he said, "now you know the reason why you got no details until you were signed up. I happen to be in a unique position as far as this story's concerned. There's no other national publication in possession of my information about the Logan case. If I'm going to make any use of it, the use I have in mind, I have to keep it that way as long as possible. Until I have the benefit of that head start I've got. The minute I start interviewing established writers, and talking to their agents, I nullify that advantage. They're a gabby lot, and anything I tell one of them today will be all over New York tonight. So therefore, I talked to you, outside the trade but still capable of doing what I need most to have done. As for rewrite? I'll do that, if any's necessary. I certainly won't broadcast our secret. You will get the byline and the twenty thousand dollars, and I will get a fighting chance to rebuild that magazine." He grinned. "Stick with me, sweetie," he said, "and you'll wear real zircons."

She nodded.

"If we're going to go to all this effort and expense," he said, "we are damned right well going to be first on the newsstands with this story. Which makes time a big factor in your work. I'd rather have you spending it on completing the story than doing clerical drudgery someone else can easily do. This tape here, of course, that's running now, you may want to keep just for possible reference. It won't be playing any part in your story, at least that I can foresee."

"Does that mean you don't want to be quoted?" she said.

"What it means, I think," he said, "is that I can't imagine how anything I'd have to say about this case would be germane to your article. If what I saw when Lavalle was killed turns out to be relevant, I'll do a sidebar which I'll sign, and get you off the hook."

"Okay," she said.

"When I joined the *Commoner*," he said, "I had as you know done a number of things that hadn't turned out too well. I was sort of at a loss for something to do, and, it seemed as though, with my thirtieth birthday coming up, it might be a good idea for me to try honest work for a while. My parents had been friendly for years with the Gould family, which still owned the paper then, and it was relatively easy for me to make a call and get a job." He paused. "I say that because I want you to undersand that I'm not under any illusions that my journalist's credentials landed me the slot. Quite the opposite. I didn't have any credentials. Without that influence, I wouldn't have caught on."

"I'm not shocked," she said. "Nepotism, favoritism, call it what you want, was alive and well when I started in with the *Transcript*. I needed a job and my father knew the managing editor from the Masonic Lodge. They had one opening. The competition was a boy my age with a degree in journalism, with high honors, from the university of Missouri, and four years on the paper there. Plus summer jobs at the *Athol Daily News*, where he was from. I had the degree in English literature from Wheaton, and no experience at all. But I submitted my application by the compass, by the square, by the all-seeing eye. He went in on merit. I got the job. He got the brush-off. 'Welcome to the real world, kiddo,' I said to myself, and went to work."

"My first assignment," Baldwin said, smiling, "was to the Waterford bureau. It was brand-new then, just opening up. It was sort of an experiment, part of one at least. The last of the three regional bureaus set up by the *Commoner*. The publishing implications of the exodus to the suburbs and the simultaneous decline of the railroads around the end of the Fifties had gradually begun to worry people like the Goulds. They were nowhere near as oblivious to worrisome developments and trends as their detractors sometimes claim. They may have been a little slow getting the point, but they didn't miss it entirely, and they decided they had two choices: either they could watch their PM readership decline and concentrate on the AM market and the city readership exclusively, or else they could spread out their operations and try to compete with the papers in the suburbs that were already there, and couldn't possibly match the *Commoner*'s State House and national coverage.

"I'm not sure they made the right choice, financially," he said. "It cost them a lot of money, and they still ended up losing the bulk of the PM market because they couldn't get the paper out to the sticks before the commuters got home. Not with no trains to ship it, and all those same commuters out on the highways in the late afternoons, blocking the *Commoner*'s trucks. True, they got a lock on the morning advertising, because there's still nothing out there that can go head-to-head with the AM *Commoner* and everybody knows it. But they had that anyway.

"Journalistically," he said, "there's no doubt in my mind. It was a wise and courageous decision. I'm not saying they invented the idea of well-staffed suburban bureaus and rigorous training programs. They had lots of models to study. I'm not even saying that they ran the operations that well, after they set them up. Administratively, the editorial decentralization of the paper created a lot of headaches that're still throbbing and are probably incurable. One of which, as a matter of fact," he said, "could very well turn out to be the cause of the events that you're investigating.

"The whole notion," he said, "was that the all-powerful lords in Boston could create three dukedoms strategically located in the geographical centers north, west and south of the city where the critical masses of the baby boom seemed likeliest to build their houses and make their homes. There was a lot of guesswork involved, and it guaranteed that mistakes would be made. Twenty-eight years after the decisions started to be made, it's pretty easy to say the one to put the northern bureau in Burlington was mediocre, and it should have been in Lawrence. If not in Salem, New

Hampshire. But back when the choice was made, nobody anticipated the draw that southern New Hampshire would have for State tax refugees, and Burlington looked like a good idea. Framingham was for the west. It was probably the best guess of the three that anyone made. And Waterford? A clear case of your classic compromise, embodying the worst features of the alternative proposals and gaining the best of neither.

"One faction in management," Baldwin said, "strongly argued that the southern bureau should be located in New Bedford. In the summer the reporters would be close to anything that happened on the Cape, and all year 'round they'd be within a thirty-, forty-minutes drive of anything that happened north of the Canal but more than half an hour or forty minutes south of Boston. The other faction said the only reason the paper needed a southern bureau was the fact that you can't get reporters or any other living thing out of Boston in the summer, or any other season of the year, in the afternoon. And that New Bedford, not at all fashionable then, was too far away from the obvious population center growing on the South Shore to be much use to anyone.

"So they compromised on Waterford," he said. "It was a bad choice. It's got Plymouth, a very long town, between it and the Canal. It's a long way from New Bedford and Fall River. And the areas further north — Braintree, Quincy, so forth — are now and were then covered by the *Quincy Patriot Ledger* well enough so the *Commoner* could never compete in the afternoons." He paused. "Lots of decisions in business get made because the people in charge of making them just get tired of arguing and accept something for the sake of peace and quiet. Waterford was one of those. Now it's a fairly sizeable place, around sixteen thousand population with another fifteen, sixteen, in the towns around it and a good thirty-three or so in Plymouth to the south. But then it was about seven, eight thousand people, a sleepy little summer resort that'd never quite made it in the Twenties, a small fishing industry and a lot of raw land. It was not a good place to set up a four-man bureau expected to cover everything that happened in Massachusetts between Neponset Circle and Provincetown, but that was what they did.

"Mel Shaw," he said, tapping the top folder, "was not a good choice as chief of that bureau. But the brass made that one, too. In other lines of work, they call it 'compounding a felony,' I think.

"Mel was sort of a conundrum to management," Baldwin said. "The Goulds, and the Puccis they picked to edit the paper, really didn't know what to do with Mel. They'd hired him as rookie staff in the Framingham bureau when it opened in Fifty-eight, one of the freshman class in this ambitious plan they had to develop their own team of reporters. The bureaus were supposed to provide minor league training for the recruits, give them experience, and provide a continuing supply of reliable staff for a constantly-expanding paper. Which of course had to keep on expanding to pay for the bureaus and stuff. Mel came into Framingham and made the ideas look good. Without the bureau program, he never would've been hired — there would've been no room for him. But with the program, there was room, and he came in and he did this bang-up job on a sensational murder case, got himself promoted to Boston, went from Boston to the Washington bureau, and there he fell apart.

"They didn't know what to make of him," Baldwin said. "You have to understand that the Goulds, with the best intentions in the world, were determined that none of their employees should fail. It was a rigidly-paternalistic system when they owned the paper, and it drove people nuts. But it also saved a good many who would otherwise have destroyed themselves, and you can't fault the Goulds for that. When Mel hit the skids in Washington, and ran up the white flag, they were badly disappointed. But they didn't give up on him. They brought him back to Boston, found a place for him on the desk, and then when Waterford opened up, put him in charge of it. He was in his middle thirties — he'd done four years in the Army out of college before J School, before he joined the paper — and he was getting a little long in the tooth for a boy wonder, but they still thought he could make it, and they gave him his own bureau. And they were wrong."

"What was the matter with him?" she said.

"Well," he said, "if we agree that it's generally much better that you form your own conclusions, and not just adopt my opinions, I'll tell you what I think."

"I didn't say I was going to accept what you say," she said. "I'd like to know what you think, though, before I see this guy cold for the first time."

"You know," Baldwin said, "I think you're going to work out just fine on this assignment."

"Thank you," she said.

"I also think it's about time for lunch," he said. "Does that interest you?"

"Very much," she said.

He punched the intercom. "Anne," he said, "call Bruno at Toby's Landfall and tell him we're coming down. And have Ben bring the car around, please?"

"Certainly, Mister Baldwin," she said. "And: *bon appetit.*"

Two minutes after Baldwin and Gates had left his office, the phone rang on Anne Leeds's desk. She picked it up. "He's taking her to lunch, Sylvia," she said. She paused. "To Toby's, naturally," she said. "Just like he always does." She listened. She sighed. "Sylvia," she said, "it's not like this is new. Not like the guy has changed. You knew what he was like, when you got involved with him."

15

Toby's Landfall on Northern Avenue was about a third of a two-story waterfront warehouse. The rest of the grey wooden building was still occupied by wholesale fish merchants whose trucks and employees kept the area in front of the restaurant crowded and noisy. Ben, a tall, thin, twenty-year-old with a crop of black hair and a bad case of staphylococcal acne disfiguring his face, eased the charcoal Lincoln Town Car in among the trucks and stopped it at the restaurant entrance. He got out of the driver's seat quickly, went around the car and opened the right rear door for Gates with her tape recorder and then Baldwin to get out.

Inside there was a circular bar with seats for twelve in the center of the room. There were three burly men with greying hair and deep suntans seated at it. Two were drinking pilsener glasses of beer. The third had a bloody mary. They wore short-sleeved polo shirts and the one nearest to Gates had a tattoo of a panther on his right forearm. He was hunched so that his face was nearly touching that of the man in the middle of the grouping, and the man on the left leaned in as well. They were discussing something but their voices were inaudible.

To the right of the bar there were nine tables grouped between the inside wall and the large glass windows overlooking the dock and the harbor; to the left two steps led down to a grouping of twenty more tables. Each of them was set with a long white tablecloth, tall crystal glasses and peaked white napkins.

"This is so lovely," she said, "and nobody's here." A bartender in a white jacket came out of the kitchen to their right as she spoke, and made his way down to the bar. He glanced at them when he reached the bar. He picked up a telephone from a wall cradle under the counter, punched one number, spoke into the phone, and hung it up again.

"It's not open for lunch," Baldwin said softly.

A short, thin man in a blue blazer and white shirt with no tie came out of the kitchen, wiping his hands on a small white towel. He had black hair, greying at the temples, and bushy black eyebrows. He wore a white apron over his jeans, and Gucci loafers. He smiled at Baldwin. "How's your back, my friend?" he said. "Can you make it upstairs, or would you like one of the places by the window?" He looked at Gates with interest.

"Bruno," Baldwin said, "this is Miss Gates. Just taken an assignment with one of our magazines. Miss Gates, this is Bruno. Good man to know."

Bruno and Gates said they were pleased to meet. Baldwin said he thought that if it wasn't too much trouble, a table on the first floor might be easier for him. Bruno said it was no trouble and took them to the front corner table to the left, the furthest in the restaurant from the three men at the bar. "Some wine?" he said, when they were seated. Baldwin said that sounded good. Bruno snapped his fingers once. The bartender looked up, nodded, opened a small ice chest below the counter, removed two frosted glasses and a bottle of wine, and began uncorking it.

"Mark, Miss Gates," Bruno said, leaning over slightly, "tonight we will be serving calamari, which I have not tried today but which looks very good. It is lightly breaded and quickly sautéed over very high heat so that it retains its natural juices. Most of our customers enjoy it very much.

"For your entrée, I recommend the scampi in a light garlic sauce which we make with wine and butter. But we have of course also the swordfish, which we do with an anchovy butter sauce with white wine, and the salmon we prepare in the same fashion. I would suggest *insalata verte* to complete your meal."

"Miss Gates?" Baldwin said. The bartender came to the table with the wine wrapped in a white napkin in his right hand and a pewter bucket of ice containing the two wine glasses in his left. He set everything on the table, removed the glasses from the bucket and put the bottle in, twirling it once. He set the cork on the table and stood the two glasses up in front of the bucket. "Thank you, Ray," Baldwin said. The bartender nodded and departed. Bruno took the wine out of the bucket. He sniffed it. He nodded. He poured a small amount in the glass nearest Baldwin. Baldwin pushed the glass to Gates. "You try it," he said.

"Thank you," she said. She sipped at the wine. "Very nice," she said. Bruno poured. "What is it?" she said.

"A Beringer Eighty-two Chardonnay," Bruno said. "Very fresh, I think, very spirited wine. Extremely good with the fish. Have you selected, Madame?"

"The swordfish, please," she said.

"Nothing to begin?" he said.

"Nothing, no, thank you," she said.

"Very good, Madame," he said, pouring Baldwin's wine. "And your selection, Mark?"

"The salmon, Bruno, thank you," he said. "And also, no first course."

Bruno bowed. "Enjoy your meal," he said, and left.

"This place is incredible," she said. "How many do you have to kill to get treated like this?"

"Well, Miss Gates," he said, smiling, drinking some of his wine, "actually . . . ."

"Can I stop you?" she said.

He looked mildly surprised. "Sure," he said, "but I thought . . . ."

"I wish you'd call me 'Connie' " she said.

"Thanks," he said, "I will. And you reciprocate. We're now on first name basis." They toasted the occasion. "Now," he said, "to answer your question: Bruno's from Milan. When he was about, oh, eighteen or so, he came through the tunnel at Menton with one suitcase of belongings and the absolute conviction that he was destined to become one of the great chefs of the world. And he apprenticed himself for the next six or seven years or so to several cooks aspiring to that class, and discovered he didn't like it a lot.

"When I met him," Baldwin said, "he was running the kitchen at the Restaurant au Porto in Monte Carlo, not taking any more abuse from autocratic superiors but not enjoying himself much, either."

"Was that when you were married?" she said.

"That was before I was married," he said. "As a matter of fact, I was there with Lucille, whom I had just met. The Grand Prix de Monaco was about a month away, and I had Cal, my younger brother, on the Team, just going over the route, nice and slow, taking his time, relaxing and resting. So it was a sort of semi-vacation. And Bruno came out of the kitchen and asked if we'd enjoyed our meal. Which was very ordinary stuff — a pasta, some cold *vitello tonnato*, nothing elaborate. It was lunch on a warm day in a slow season — that was all. And I don't know why I did it, but I said that, yes, we had enjoyed it, it was nice to have a simple meal. Which was not that easy a thing to do on the Riviera in those days. This was well before *nouvelle cuisine*. If the dish wasn't smothered in some rich sauce or other, it wasn't worth serving. Bruno's food was a nice change.

"He got all excited," Baldwin said. "By the time we got out of that place, it was the cocktail hour. And we'd heard Bruno's entire theory of successful fish cuisine, which not one of the *bâtards* he'd worked for would allow him to pursue, and now he was reduced to making spaghetti *bolognese* for fat rich men and their whores. It was absolutely heart-rending.

"So," Baldwin said, "without thinking much about it, I said something to the effect that Bruno was wasting his time on the Riviera, if that's what he wanted to do. I said he should come to Boston, where the fish was plentiful and fresh, and his style of cookery would be appreciated.

"Which he apparently interpreted as my undertaking to sponsor him if he decided to do that." Baldwin poured more wine. "So," he said, "two, no, three years ago, the housekeeper called me at work and said there was a Mister Bruno Dellorfano calling me collect from Nice, and should she tell him where to find me at my office? And it didn't register on me, but I figured it must be someone my ex-wife'd put on to me to keep my days from being dull, so I said: 'Sure,' and she did. And Bruno in due course got me at the office, and I accepted the charges, and he said: 'Mark Baldwin, of Team Lotus?' And I said to him: 'Good God, who is this? It's been over twenty years since that.' And he told me. 'Bruno from the Porto. I am ready.' 'Ready for what?' I said. 'To come to America,' he said. 'What should I do?'

"I didn't have the foggiest notion of what the hell he should do," Baldwin said. "But I figured it couldn't possibly be too difficult — look at all the dumb people who've done it. So I put him in touch with my lawyer, and my lawyer helped him, and Bruno came over and started this place. And he's gone hammer and tongs at it ever since. Does exactly what he wants to do, when he wants to do it. Food is, well, try it and see. I think it's spectacular.

"And that," he said, "to give you more answer than you wanted, is how you get to eat lunch at Toby's Landing, which does not open for lunch."

"Uh huh," she said. "Who is Toby?"

"Toby is Sam Toby," Baldwin said. "The guy that owns this warehouse and who rents Bruno the space."

"I see," she said. "So what you're telling me is that you own this restaurant. It belongs to you."

"I didn't say that," he said. "I've got some money in it, of course. I thought it would succeed. And I was right. It did."

"How much?" she said.

He worked his mouth. "Okay, okay," he said, "I'll concede. You really are good. But what I own and don't own isn't in your story, so I won't tell you, all right? I have a share of this place. That gives me privileges."

She was deliberating whether to respond to that when Bruno delivered the fish. She decided to keep still.

"If you start up that recorder," Baldwin said, cutting the salmon with the edge of his fork, "we can get a little work done between bites." She did as instructed.

"Mel Shaw," Baldwin said meditatively, "was the kind of man who looked a lot simpler and more ordinary than he actually was. I'm using the past tense here because it's been over twenty years since I've had any kind of regular, day-to-day contact with him, but people in their thirties generally have their characters pretty much set. If they change in later years, they get more so, not really different from what they used to be.

"He presented himself as a contented man," Baldwin said. "He said what he had gotten from the *Commoner* was exactly what he wanted: a secure billet in a nice town where he could raise his family in peace and go sailing in the summer without ever having to get on another airplane or pack another suitcase. He had three children, and one of those quiet, mousey wives. I don't recall any indication that he spent much time with any of them. He did spend every minute that he could sailing his boat, and he said on several occasions that none of his family liked the water. If he wanted to pretend he had renounced the fast lane for the sake of his family, what harm did it do?" He tilted his head and cut a piece of fish. "Quite a lot, it appears now," he said. "Mel was not always careful with the truth.

"Toward the end of that June," Baldwin said, "couple weeks after Mel and I opened the bureau, Didi Chenevert came aboard. She was about twenty-one, twenty-two, fresh out of Columbia J School.

Extremely fresh, in fact, and very ambitious. For the first year or so, she managed to keep her ambition pretty much in check, and her tongue mostly under control, probably for the same reason that Mel and I somehow managed to get along with her — we were all completely new to what we were doing, feeling our way along, learning the routines of new occupations, and not so incidentally, struggling to develop enough stories of reasonable importance from a geographical area, that didn't have that many of them, to convince Boston that the Waterford bureau was a valuable addition to the paper.

"Tell you the truth," he said, "I wasn't personally too concerned about the possibility that Boston might decide after a year or so that Waterford had been a mistake and correct the error by either closing the bureau or moving it somewhere else. Just between the fish and us, it didn't matter to me whether I worked there or in another town, and I knew very well that I had a job with the Goulds as long as I wanted one. Where I lived didn't matter to me, either. I was never the car freak that my brother was, but I had a Porsche Three-fifty-six that I loved to drive, and our summer place down at Cataumet was winterized — if the job remained in Waterford, I could commute in an hour or so, early in the morning, from my home in Boston, or in half that time from Cataumet any time of day. If on the other hand, the job moved somewhere else, I knew they wouldn't fire me, so what difference did it make? To me, absolutely none.

"I did my best to conceal that fact from Mel and Didi," Baldwin said. "Mel had committed himself entirely to Waterford. He'd bought more house than he probably could afford out on Atlantic Avenue. Ocean frontage, a nice new gambrel Cape. He had his boat, also brand-new. And he was boss in Waterford. If the bureau closed, or moved to New Bedford, he was in a bad position. He wouldn't lose his *Commoner* job, but he'd have to start all over somewhere else. And if the *Commoner* decided that a southern bureau wasn't needed, he'd be back up in Boston, answering to somebody else, doing as he was told. So Mel was under some pressure.

"Didi was under even more pressure," Baldwin said. "Most of it was of her own making — she was one of the most driven people I've ever seen. But some of it was real — rookies under the *Commoner*'s bureau program were probationary in every sense of the word, and the terms of probation were severe. She could lose her job for any reason for her first year on the paper. Not just for not doing it properly, being lazy, making mistakes, or something like that. No, she could be let go because the bureau closed and they didn't want her in a new one, or couldn't use her in Boston, or didn't like the way she powdered her nose.

"Didi didn't have much in her life but that job," he said, "which she was convinced was the first chapter in a journalism career that would make her famous. She was not attractive. She didn't have a social life. Her father had been killed in the war without ever seeing her. Her mother had raised her on Martha's Vineyard by teaching school, I guess. Didi'd made it through college on scholarships and desperately hard work. She was *summa cum laude* at Columbia, and I would guess if she'd been a little more polished, a little less abrasive, a little less obviously unhappy, she probably could have gotten something better somewhere else. Her explanation was that she had to be in Massachusetts to be near her mother, and the *Commoner* was the best paper in Massachusetts, so that's why she was there. Either way, she had a bigger investment in the success of the bureau than she really could afford, and a hell of a lot to lose if it folded.

"So," he said, working on his salmon, 'it was a fairly tense place that first year. And by May of the following year, which would have been the spring of Sixty-three, it was pretty obvious to each of us that if Boston was paying close attention, we were in bad shape. We had enough territory to cover, more than we could handle, actually. But there weren't enough people in it doing newsworthy things, and the result was that we spent large amounts of time riding around from one small story to the next, hitting a School Committee meeting in Marshfield and a Selectmen's meeting in Duxbury before a quick check of three speeding tickets and a driving-under charge on the Waterford police blotter let us close up for the night.

"What we didn't reckon on," Baldwin said, "was that an operation which made absolutely no sense from a news viewpoint had been oversold with enthusiasm by the advertising department, and the *Commoner* was committed to keeping Waterford open for at least two more years. It was a competitive marketing thing. The other Boston dailies didn't have a presence south of Boston. The *Commoner* did. In terms of news produced, it wasn't worth its upkeep, but in terms of lineage sold, it was a real bargain.

"Not knowing this, we were naturally surprised in June of Sixty-three when a bureau that didn't justify three people on board got expanded to four with the arrival of Joe Logan. Mel was overjoyed. He interpreted Joe's hiring as a permanent expansion of the bureau. He took Joe's assignment to mean Boston was delighted with the job he'd done, even though I'd stake my life on the position that until the day that Joe came in, Mel'd feared otherwise. I didn't give much of a hoot, for the reasons I've told you. Didi did, though — she immediately jumped to the conclusion that Joe coming in meant she was going out. On her good days, she thought she was going to be promoted, ahead of the training schedule that said you spent your first two years in the bureau. On her bad days, she thought she was getting canned. Before Joe got there, she was driven, as I've said. After he arrived, she was damned near frantic.

"The result was that when Mel started changing the routine in the bureau later that summer to give Joe his beats to cover, along with Didi's and mine, Didi became a basket case. Boston, the national desk, had decided that what the paper needed was a big, take-out series on the two-hundred-mile limit. The Coast Guard enforced the twelve-mile limit on foreign fishing fleets in those days, and the coastal States were hollering and yelling that it ought to be extended to protect our fisheries. The issue was heating up in Washington, and naturally it had always been a big topic in Rhode Island, Massachusetts and Maine. The *Journal* was on it down in Providence. The *Globe* and the *Herald Traveler* had people more or less following it, but waiting for something to happen. The *Commoner* therefore decided to grab the issue and run with it, maybe to a Pulitzer.

"The reason that they gave for picking me to do it was that I'd had the time at Fletcher and the experience with the State Department to make me the logical choice. Which was plausible but not the reason — the reason was that the Goulds had decided they wanted this story, and they wanted me to do it. But I didn't make a fuss. I'd learned the mechanics of reporting after a year — I don't say I was any whizbang at the trade, but I knew how it was done — and I was getting reasonably bored writing long Sunday pieces about whether the Waterford School Committee's indecision on a new central high school district incorporating four towns was shrewd politics or plain stupidity. The Law of the Sea is not a sexy subject, as sexy subjects go, but it was miles ahead of anything I saw happening in Waterford and I grabbed the assignment.

"The reasonable thing to have done," Baldwin said, "would have been to transfer me to Boston and turn me loose on the fisheries story. But the Goulds were not always reasonable, and they were very proud of their bureau training program. Everyone joining the paper without experience would, without exception, spend his or her first two years in a bureau. No allowances had been made for the possibility that the same people making the rules would want to flout them, as the Goulds did in my case, so when they did in fact break their own rules, they just pretended they had not. I was spending two thirds of my time in the bureau on the telephone to Washington and Boston, and one third of my time out of the bureau if not in one of those places, then in New York or Augusta, or some other place. Which made it awfully hard to maintain the pretense that I was still plugging along in the second year of my novitiate, just like everybody else.

"It also made it hard for me to cover the School Committee and so forth, as I was technically supposed to be doing. So Mel, going along with the gag, put up this schedule of beat assignments which made Didi my backup on the School Board and the Selectmen, and Joe my backup on Police and Fire, and there were a whole mess of other changes too.

"Didi blew her stack. She wanted Police. She felt she was senior to Joe, and she thought Police had a better chance of developing a breaking major story that would front-page all editions than the School Committee did. Which was of course correct. What was not correct, though, was Didi's claim that a year-plus on the job made her technically senior to Joe with two months — that was another one of the silly rules of the bureau program: all rookies are equal, no matter how long they've been at the paper. And what was also not correct was her opinion that since Police *might* break a big story, Schools, invariably long-winded and dull, was therefore less important. Schools was a sure thing, an ongoing story which really interested people who paid taxes and did or did not have kids. Mel needed a steady hand on that topic, and he had the right to put her there, no matter what she said.

"She said a lot," Baldwin said. "There was a real morale problem in that bureau, *before* Timmy Lavelle got his skull crushed with a blunt instrument in the woods off Route Four south of town in September of that year."

"And Logan got that story," Gates said. "Not Didi, who wanted it."

"Worse than that," Baldwin said. "Logan was on his day off when the body was found. Didi was out of the office doing some fool Sunday feature. Mel was sailing. I got the story for the first two days, when it was the hottest, which of course made Didi hate me as much as she hated Mel and Joe. It was really a mess."

Bruno approached the table with a portable telephone and set it in front of Baldwin. "Mark," he said, "sorry to disturb you, but you have a call."

"This had better be an emergency," Baldwin said, accepting the instrument. "Yes?" he said into the phone. He exhaled and frowned. "Anne," he said, "you're kidding." He paused. "There must be some mistake," he said. "They don't take people to the station house for that, for Christ's sakes. They take their names and tell them they're going to swear out complaints." He waited. "Well," he said, "what do they say it was? I mean what the hell's involved here, anyway? The Hope Diamond?" He waited again. "Oh my God," he said. He sighed. "Well, of course she's got to have a lawyer. Doesn't her husband know one?" He shook his head and smoothed the tablecloth with his right hand while he listened. "That doesn't make any sense either," he said. "She's not a celebrity, for God's sake. Her husband does pretty well, sure, but the public's never heard of him. Keeping it out of the papers is not an issue here." He listened again.

"Well, I realize that," he said. "Of course she's upset. She's also a little goofy, too, if you want my opinion. But the hell with it. Get on the phone to Roger Kidd and tell him to send some mouthpiece down to New Chardon Street and bring a bondsman with him and get her the hell out of there while we think of what comes next." He waited again. "Probably not," he said. "If she called you instead of her husband, it probably means she didn't want her husband to know." He paused. "I know, I know, Anne, she called me. Not you. But that changes nothing. She probably wants some time to think of how to break the news to Jason. If that's what she wants, let's give it to her." He waited. "Yes," he said, "that's what I said. And quit jawing with me here now, and get it done, all right?"

He hung up the phone. He sat there frowning and stared at the tablecloth, absently smoothing it.

"Trouble?" Gates said. She shut off the recorder.

He shook his head. "I don't know," he said. "I've been around for a long time and I've seen a lot of things. And then someone like this perfectly normal woman that's our receptionist, that I've known about four years, does something absolutely incomprehensible and I don't know anything."

"Is she the one at the front desk?" Gates said.

"That's the one," Baldwin said. "Her husband's got plenty of money. He runs an investment group. They don't have any children. About, well, about four years ago, I ran into him at the Brown game at the Stadium, and I knew him from some alumni business we were both involved in, very casual acquaintance, and I asked him how things were going, and one of the things he said was that his wife was bored and looking for a job. And I said: 'Well, what can she do?' And he said that was the problem. She didn't have any skills. And so one thing led to another, and I asked if she'd want to be a receptionist, and he said he would ask her, and he did, and she did, and we hired her. I suppose she's making twenty-three, twenty-four a year, strictly pocket money. Her husband's well-off, as I said, and now I get this call that the woman's been arrested for shoplifting eight bucks' worth of silk scarves from a shop in Quincy Market. Which had her arrested by the cops for doing it, for God's sake.

"Eight bucks' worth of silk scarves — can you beat it?" he said. "She and her husband must have a combined income of probably three hundred and eighty thousand dollars a year, and she steals eight bucks' worth of scarves? And they cart her off to the pokey? It makes no sense at all."

"Well," Gates said, emptying her wine glass, "does this mean that you have to go back?"

He was leaning forward to lift the bottle out of the bucket. He tilted the bottle and marked the level of the wine above the napkin. "Go back?" he said, refilling her glass first and then his own. "No, it does not mean that. What could I do, if I went back? Go to see her in her cell? Have some more wine, Connie," he said, putting the bottle back in the bucket and raising his glass. "Let me tell you about Joe."

16

Shortly before 10:00 P.M., naked except for white shorts at her desk in her bedroom, Gates felt her eyes tiring and pushed the Shaw file away. She stood up and stretched, extending her arms towards the ceiling. She shook her head several times. She went into the bathroom and moistened a washcloth in cold water. She used it to mop her face and massage the back of her neck. She rubbed her torso vigorously with it. She took a clean bath towel off the rack and patted her face. She rubbed the back of her neck and her chest roughly. She stared into the mirror and grimaced. She brushed her teeth and rinsed her mouth.

She went out into the living room and stood indecisively staring at the silent television. From Tina's apartment below her she could hear the steady murmur of conversation. That would be the sound track of the second of the two videotaped dirty movies that Leonard always brought with him when he visited on Monday and Wednesday nights. Gates knew from experience what the routine would bring next. She also knew because most of Tina's poetry was about that routine; one of the poems of which she was proudest was "Leonard's Double Features." Tina had not found it amusing when Gates had suggested she substitute "Creature" for "Leonard" in the title. Gates wiggled her toes in the rug nap and dreaded what would happen when the movie ended.

After the two hundred or so minutes of the two films had run, Leonard and Tina would attempt to duplicate on Tina's living room floor, on the furniture or in the shower what they had seen the actresses and actors doing on the screen. After lots of practice they had gotten good enough at it so that what they did to each other always made Tina scream several times in ecstasy. When she did it in the living room and reached that point early, the sound carried up through the floorboards of Gates's apartment and seriously compli-cated her ability to concentrate on the late news. When the night's movies called for bedroom work, Gates found it very hard to sleep or read in her bedroom above Tina's. When the two of them had seen the people in the movies doing things in their showers with soaps and oils and hydraulic appliances, Tina's screams reverberated off the Fibreglass tub enclosure and the glass doors enclosing it, so that no matter where Gates happened to be in her apartment when Tina reached orgasm, there was no way of avoiding her announcements, except by going out and remaining out until 12:15 A.M., when Leonard got tired and went home.

Gates stood on the rug and sighed. The murmur continued from Tina's apartment. She had asked Tina once, about a month after she moved in above her, if she should be worried and perhaps call the police when she heard the screams, thinking that might be a tactful way of getting her to quiet down. Tina had misinterpreted the question as Gates's bashful way of seeking an invitation to join in the fun. She had clapped her hands and said: "*Ohh*, me and Leonard, you know, we were wondering if you could hear us? And the other night he had one where there was two girls, you know? And one guy? And he was saying when I mentioned you, 'Well, she's good-looking, Tina. She has got a real nice bod. You wanna ask her to come down? I sure wouldn't mind.' And I said: 'Geez, Leonard, I don't know. I don't know her good enough. Lemme get to know her better, and then if she says something, well, I can ask her then.' So, you wanna? Leonard's got a humungous cock. I think you'd really like it. And me, I like you a lot, just from seeing you. We can get that flick again. It's really a good one. One of our favorites. We seen it lots of times, of course, but you would like it too."

Gates had had a hard time separating Tina from that idea without actually coming right out and telling her she did not engage in copulation with slimy-looking men who kept dumb bimbos in modest luxury and concluded from that that they were studs. "What I really wanted to say," she had told her lawyer, Linda, after a settlement conference producing more bad news, "was that I don't do windows, other broads or creeps. But I was well-behaved. I didn't."

"Well, glad to hear it," Linda had said. "But then, what do you do now? Where do you draw the line?"

"I don't know," Gates had said, "but somewhere this side of that. I'd rather sit by myself."

"I would rather not sit by myself," Gates said to the furniture in her apartment, "I'll go out and have a beer."

She went back into the bedroom and took off her shorts. She put on white Levi's and a rose-colored cotton fatigue sweater, pushing up the sleeves, and a pair of white Adidas sneakers. She fluffed her hair once and decided against lipstick, and left her apartment and the building as quietly as though she had broken in.

There were no lights on in the yachts in the marina except for those in the main cabin of the yawl *Mercator*. The owners were a couple in late middle-age who lived aboard year 'round, wintering in Florida waters and returning via the Inland Waterway to New England in May. Their names were Charles and Virginia Sampson. They walked her miniature white poodle, Delilah, on the dock each morning and each evening, were totally devoted to each other and the dog, and believed their choice of floating residence, lifelong belief in Christian Science, warm hospitality to "the nice people that we meet," and two circumnavigations of the globe combined to make them the natural conversational companions of all solitary persons they encountered. She avoided them for the same reason she avoided radishes: they left a taste in her mouth that she didn't like, and they made her stomach upset.

She went up the wharf to Commercial Street and crossed under the Central Artery, entirely secure among the pedestrians who had chosen to park their cars illegally under the elevated highway, maybe not getting an expensive ticket, in preference to parking their cars legally in the lots and garage near their destinations in the Quincy Market and surely incurring an expensive fee. She reached the foot of Batterymarch Street and went up half a block towards the financial district until she came to the dark-green door with the coach lamps on each side that opened into Gable's. She opened it and went in.

The light was dim and came from clear incandescent bulbs in brass fixtures with frosted glass shades that looked like inverted flowers. The oak bar ran to her left along the easterly side of the room. It had high-backed stools for thirty-two customers. At the far end was a door to the kitchen in the back. There was a mirror behind the shelves where the bottles stood. Next to the door there was a pass-through window with a counter. The kitchen was dark. The remaining space was large enough to hold forty booths, each big enough for four persons, and twelve tables for six persons each. At the back of the room in the center was a raised platform about nine by twelve feet square. There was an old baby grand piano with a straight chair at the end of it nearest the bar. Crowded onto the rest of it were two wooden chairs, a small table holding amplifying equipment, four microphones on stands and two large speakers. To the right of the platform was the corridor leading to the restrooms. The walls behind the platform and above the booths on the westerly side were occupied by eight large black and white blow-ups of Clark Cable in roles from *Red Dust* to *The Misfits*.

There were two couples in the booths near the center of the wall to her right. She did not recognize the woman she could see in the further booth, drawing with her forefinger in the condensation left on the oak table by her glass. The man in the tan suit in the nearer booth looked vaguely familiar, but he was talking softly and earnestly to the woman opposite him and Connie shifted her gaze before he had a chance to notice her. She turned toward the bar. As she went down the space between the five-foot partition that sheltered the easterly row of booths from the patrons of the bar, she saw that there were three young women drinking in the second from the door, and two more young couples seated further down. There were four solitary drinkers, all men, at the bar. She did not recognize any of them. The bartender was nowhere in sight. She took the third stool from the back wall. She rested her elbows on the bar and stared into the mirror.

After a while she saw in the mirror the bartender emerging from the restroom corridor. He was about forty, middle-aged man wearing a white apron and a blue shirt over dark trousers. He was wiping his hands on the apron. He opened the countertop where it was hinged at the end of the bar and approached her. "*Connie*," he said joyously. He offered his hand. "Howya doin' these days? I haven't seen you in what, years?"

She took his hand and smiled back. "Gene," she said, "I'm doin' all right. Just haven't been around." She paused. "Just made a deal for myself. I got to tell someone."

He grinned and shook his head. "*Hey*," he said, resting his hands on the bar, "nice to hear it, for a change." He jerked his head to indicate he was referring to the room. "Glad *some*body's doing good, at least, way things've been goin'."

"Well," she said, "sure, but after all, your crowd comes in at lunch. And then you get the cocktail crowd. I assume they're still around."

"Oh, yeah," he said, "all still around. The cheap lunch bunch comes in at noon, makes their noise and leaves. Not big tips, though, don't leave those. Or so the help tells me. And then the after-workers: they are still around, and they still do like a drink. Complaint with them's that they don't eat, but then you can't please help. Thank God for that group's what I say. Especially when the market's up, which it's been doing lately. But late at night, like this, it's dead. Could be that I should close."

"Ahh," she said, "this's summer. Almost summer, at least. I thought this happened every year, the late crowd disappears."

"It does," he said. "It always does. And I still don't like it. Six years now, I had this place. Happens every year and still I always get the jitters, you know? That they won't come back. And then they do, and I forget, after Labor Day. Until the winter ends, they leave, and I go nuts again. What's on your mind, kid? Like a drink?"

"I think I'll just have a beer," she said, "a nice cold Miller Lite."

He nodded and slid open the top of the refrigerator, taking out a frosted mug. "Maybe," she said, "maybe if you still had the band in the summer, then they'd keep coming in."

He shook his head, working the tap. "Nah," he said. "I tried that last year. Didn't work. Business still dropped off. The kids, you know, they're saving their drinking money for Hampton Beach or the Cape. Or their cottage rentals. And the older crowd that comes in in the winter later on at night after the kids've gone, they've got concerts that they go to or places on the Cape. The trade's just not around." He put a neat head on the mug and drained it on the grate under the tap. "All I end up with, with the band, is losing more this time of year'n I'd lose anyway." He set the beer in front of her and wiped his hands on the apron. "Jess still comes in, though," he said carefully. "No band suits Jess fine."

She drank some of the beer. "Ahh," she said, "that's good." She put the glass down and returned his gaze. "I'd imagine it would," she said. "How *is* Jess? Haven't seen him in months."

The bartender shrugged. "He's been better," he said. He avoided her gaze. He jerked his head toward the back wall. "I got him in the office, lying down right now." He read her expression of concern as one of accusation. "I don't mean he's drunk," he said hurriedly. "Jess's all right on that. But geez, you know? He don't look good. He don't look good at all."

"Do they know what it is this time?" she said, sipping beer.

"Oh, sure they do," he said. "Same thing it was before. The guy, I don't know how such a smart guy can be so unhappy as he is, and just not do anything about it, you know? I don't understand it, is all. He comes in in the morning and he spends the whole day telling other people how they're gonna get rich next, and they do what he tells them and they do get rich, and he makes nothing but money. And then the market closes, and he don't want to go home, so he comes in here. And maybe he eats and maybe he doesn't, and maybe he just forgets. And some nights he leaves, and some nights he don't, so those nights he just sleeps here."

"He give up his apartment?" she said.

"The one on Clarendon?" the bartender said. "Yeah, he gave that up. Joint went condo and he said it wasn't worth what they were asking. Which I said made absolutely no sense, all the money Jess's got, and he says it doesn't matter how much dough he's got, he's not gonna hand it over to some bandit that wants it without working. I think myself personally, you know, I think it's something else. I think it's that Jess, lately he don't want to own nothing, you know? Sold the Mercedes last year when he had some trouble with it, which he could've fixed. Gave up on the idea we had, ever since we was kids, that someday we would have a boat and go out sailing on it. He don't buy anything now that's gonna last beyond the end of next week. I tell him that and he says: 'Right. No green bananas.' And he laughs it off. But that is what I think. And I don't like it, either.

"But anyway," the bartender said, "he's got a new place that he rents now, over in Somerville, but that means he hasta take a cab if he's late, screw that damned subway at night unless you want your head beat in, so if he's in here playing and it gets late to closing time, he's just as liable as not to decide to sleep right here."

"Cripes," she said, "how's he go to work in the morning doing that? He can't go into Clark, Reach looking like he crashed in some doorway the night before. I don't care what a genius analyst he is — you've got to be an artist if you want to work like that."

"Oh, he doesn't," the bartender said. "When he wakes up in the morning he makes himself some coffee and lets himself out, I shown him how to work the alarm, and he grabs a cab, goes his apartment, and gets himself cleaned up. He's the only one that knows. Him and me, of course." He paused and frowned, pretending to notice something stuck to the surface of the bar which he could scrape off with his right thumbnail. He looked back at her abruptly. "Listen," he said, "whyncha go inna back and say hello to him, huh? It'd cheer him up, I think. He's kind of down inna dumps tonight, you know?"

"Oh, geez Gene," she said, "I don't want to do that. Not if he's sleeping and everything, wake him up like that. I just was working late, you know, and came in for a beer. I don't want to bother him. Leave the poor guy alone."

"He's not sleeping," the bartender said. "I was just in there and he isn't doing that. He's watching TV in there by himself. That's all he's really doing."

"Killing time," she said.

"Killing time," he said. "He's not enjoying it. Whyncha, whyncha go in there like you just found out, I just told you he was here, and tell him you want him to come out here and play something, all right? Cheer the guy up some. Make him feel as though there's still a couple people, give a shit he's on the earth."

She paused before she answered. "I don't know, Gene," she said. "I don't know if I'm ready for this. I don't know if he is, either. Seeing each other again."

"Well, shit, Connie," the bartender said, "I didn't mean you hadda *see* him for Christ sake. I know you two, that you had some problems. But you can go in there and talk to him, can't you, and pass the time of day? Just sort of remind him, you know, that he's not all alone inna world."

"I dunno, Gene," she said. "Does not sound good to me."

"Trust me," he said imploringly.

"Trust you," she said slowly.

"Yeah," he said. "Do like I said, what I just told you. I ever steer you wrong? You tell me that, just tell me that: I ever steer you wrong?"

"No," she said, "but then, you never steered me."

"Well," he said, straightening up, "this time, let me do it. Just trust what I say, all right? And do like I just said."

She nodded. "Okay," she said, "I'll do it. And if it blows up in my face, you're responsible."

"I'm responsible," he said. He grinned.

She knocked once on the hollow door to the office at the end of the corridor that gave off onto the restrooms, and heard a voice say:

"Min." She was unsure whether that meant to wait a minute or come in, and hesitated with her hand on the knob. "'S all right," the voice said, "come in."

She let herself into the office. It was a cubicle about ten by twelve with a desk made of a door and green metal file cabinets built along the far wall. There were two draftsman's lights on goosenecks over it. There was an adding machine on the right and on the left there was a typewriter. On the floor next to the northerly wall there was a small Mosler safe next to two three-drawer metal file cabinets. Stacked beside them were cases of liquor piled four high in five rows. There was a dirty orange shag rug in the middle of the room. On it there was a battered maple coffee table with a small Panasonic television set facing a foldaway double bed made up as a couch. Jesse Marcantonio sat hunched in the middle of it, holding a coffee cup in both hands over his lap. He wore a red and white striped shirt with a white collar and white french cuffs linked in gold, and a grey patterned tie pulled down from the neck. His trousers were grey and when he stood up she saw that he still wore black wingtipped shoes. His hair was mostly grey and looked damp. His face showed beads of sweat against a pallor. He was thirty-eight years old.

He stood up, a smile creasing his face. He put the coffee cup down on the table and extended his arms wide. "Connie," he said, but not loudly, "how the hell are you?"

She did not advance. "Pretty good, actually," she said. "How the hell're you?"

He let his arms drop slowly to his sides. He maintained the grin. He shrugged. "Oh, not bad, actually," he said. He nodded toward the television set. "Just catching up on *Saint Elsewhere* here, episode I missed. Not a bad show at all, you know? I must've been playing piano, night that it was on."

"Actually," she said, "Gene and I, I just dropped in tonight because I got myself a job today that kind of excited me, and I sort of feel like celebrating, you know? With some music, maybe? And the two of us were wondering, if maybe you would play."

"Congratulations," he said warily. "Good for you, Connie. Always knew you'd make it. What kind of job? Is this one permanent?"

"Oh, no," she said. "Not permanent. I haven't changed on that. I don't want one that's permanent. I like my freedom, still."

"Right," he said. He put his hands in his pockets.

"But," she said hurriedly, "it does pay well, and it'll keep me busy, and let me pay my bills, and looks really interesting." She took a breath. "So I'm excited about it. How 'bout playing me a song?"

"What does Teddy think of this?" he said.

She sighed. "Ted's long gone, Jess, and hard to find. I hope he stays that way."

He shook his head and looked sad. "I'm sorry to hear that, Connie," he said. "I truly, truly am."

"Thanks," she said. "Now, play a song?"

"I know," he said, "I know better probably'n anybody else, what hopes you had for that. For what you had with Ted. I wish it had worked out."

"So do I," she said. "But that's the way it is with hopes. They don't always work out. How about you coming out now and playing all the Chopin études for me? How 'bout doing that?"

He chuckled. "Chopin, Connie, cripes," he said. He nodded toward the front. "The folks that Gene's got here tonight, they would pay up and walk out. And there goes tonight's receipts, little as they are. Those folks were looking at me funny when I played 'Yesterday.' A group too dense for Beatles music? They won't like Chopin."

She went over to him and held out her hands. "Okay, then," she said as he took them, "play Floyd Kramer, then. Play Roger Williams's 'Falling Leaves.' Don't tell me it's not fall. Play any goddamned thing you like, but just come out and play." She began to pull him toward the bar, and when he stopped mildly resisting, released his left hand and towed him along by his right, going ahead of him. His hand was clammy to her touch. It felt like he was dead.

She got him out into the barroom and ushered him up to the piano and sat him down in the chair. "You want a drink?" she said.

He looked up at her with mild amusement. "You want to hear me play?" he said. "You know this performer's rules."

"Still Cutty Sark and water?" she said.

He nodded. "Cutty Sark and water," he said. "The more things change, the more they stay the same."

"I'll get it," she said, and stepped off the platform. He bent over the keyboard and began to play softly Floyd Kramer's "Last Dance." The other customers in the room did not pay any attention.

She nodded to Gene at the bar as he picked up the Cutty bottle and looked at her inquiringly. He poured a stiff shot into a six-ounce glass and added water, no ice. He pushed it toward her. "He shouldn't be doing this, you know," he said. "It isn't good for him." "Jesus," she said, reaching for it, "you're hard to please. First you tell me to get him out here, and then you nag me when I do."

"It's his belly," Gene said. "Doctor got him off it, after you two broke up. He's been drinking beer since then, and not too much of that."

"Hey," she said, taking it, "this is what the player wants, this is what he gets. This Florence Nightingale drill, Gene, this was your idea. It does something to him, friend, blame it on yourself."

She put the drink on the left corner of the piano. Jess nodded his thanks, segueing into a *largo* version of "Georgia." After that he played a medley of "Smoke Gets In Your Eyes" and "As Time Goes By" which took a very long time to finish. The man at the end of the bar closest to the door chugalugged the remainder of his drink and left at 10:50, followed within two minutes by the third man down from the door, and then by the man on the stool between theirs. Shortly before 11:00 the earnest, slightly-familiar looking man in the tan suit stood up with his companion and left Gable's silently. The party of young women in the booth close to the bar had one more round they did not finish before they too were gone. The woman and the man at the booth near the back were gone before 11:10, and the other couple in that row left at 11:15. Marcantonio signaled for another drink, which Gates brought him, and when she tried to speak he shook his head and put his right index finger to his lips. He began to play Chopin. She went back to the bar. The last man at the bar finished his drink and left.

"And he does all this by ear," she said to the bartender.

"Every bit of it," he said. "It's that same damned memory, you know? The one that makes him so good with the stocks. The guy forgets nothing. Nothing that he ever learns ever goes out of his head. When we were young, Ma used to tell me if I only studied like Jess did, I'd be a success too. I would get good marks in school, and I'd be a musician. And I used to try to tell her, you know, that when she thought he was studying, he wasn't doing that. He was reading something else, because what was supposed to take us all two hours only took him one. You know what his piano teacher finally told him? He told him he'd never be as good as he could be himself, because his goddamned memory made it so easy for him to be just as good, no better and absolutely no different, from the guy that played it the first time he heard it. He said it was Jess's curse. Maybe he was right."

Just before midnight, Marcantonio finished playing études and variations and went into a reflective version of "The Party's Over." It lasted a long time. When he had exhausted all the ideas he had for it, he let the last note linger on the pedal until it disappeared. Then he stood up and stretched. Gene and Connie clapped, their applause too scant for the room. Marcantonio bowed from the waist and stepped off the platform toward the bar. When he reached it he said in a husky voice: "Innkeeper. Oats for my horses and whiskey for myself."

The bartender poured a third Cutty Sark and water while Marcantonio studied Gates with a smile on his face. "Thanks, Connie," he said. "that was very good for me. It made me feel much better. Of course I still don't know whether Mrs. Hufnagel ever dies on *Saint Elsewhere*, but it'll probably be on again, and I can find out then."

"What comes around, goes around," she said. "Or is it the other way around?"

The bartender slammed the fresh drink down in front of Jess. He untied his apron string and wadded the garment on the bar. He opened the register and took out the drawer with the night's receipts. He took it down to the back end and opened a hinged counter with his left forearm. "I'm going in the back with this and then I'm locking up," he said. "You folks decide to leave before me, give out a yell, all right?"

"Will do," Jess said. He raised his glass. "Damned if I know," he said, looking at her. "It's true, though, either way." He toasted her and drank.

"How are you really feeling, Jess?" she said. "You don't look so hot, I think, if you want the truth."

"As a matter of fact," he said, setting the glass down, "I didn't want the truth. But since you gave it anyway, well," he made his right hand flutter, "*mezzo mezz*, you know; not so bad and not so good."

The bartender came out of the back without the cash drawer and went to the front of the bar. He locked the door and shot two deadbolts. He returned to the back.

"You get out at all?" she said. "Out of doors, I mean, in the sun and stuff?"

"Actually, no, I don't," he said. "I find it's too much trouble. At home it was convenient. In the backyard was the pool, and the sun shone down on it. But unless I am mistaken, good old Carol's out there in it, and I will take rat poison before I catch rays with her."

"You still haven't done anything about that," she said.

"Right again," he said. "That's exactly what I've done. Absolutely nothing. And that's what I'm going to keep on doing, since it seems to be working so well."

" 'Working so well'?" she said. "You look like pure hell, Jess."

"Well, yes," he said, "I do. But I figure, well, as I see it, there isn't much point, doing anything other than I'm doing now, and lots of reason not to. If I divorce the baggage, she'll get half my property, and I'll support the kids. Just as I am doing now. She'll get half of all my dough, and half of this place, too. Gene will have to sell it out, or else put up with her. Gene cannot put up with her. No human being could.

"But if I don't divorce her," he said, "well, she'll only get a third and the kids will get the rest. They'll get their share in trust, of course, and their share will include all of this. Gene can work with a trustee. They all will be all right."

"I'm not tracking you," she said.

He shrugged and had some of his drink. "My learned counsel tells me," he said, "that the widow's share's a third. The statutes of this Commonwealth provide that's what she gets, regardless of my will. If I divorce the wench, she will certainly get a half. But if I die still married to her, she will get a third. So, I drew up my will to say I'm giving her that third. That statutory third that she would get anyway. And all the rest goes to the kids, whom I actually like." He paused and finished his drink. He belched softly. "I'm going to trick that fucking bitch. I'm going to die on her."

Gates put her left hand on his left forearm. "Christ, Jess," she said, "don't say that. You're still a young man."

He snickered. "The man is young, but the body's old," he said. He turned to look at her directly. "I didn't mean I'm going to do it tonight, Connie. Or even next week. Or before Labor Day. Or that I want to do it. It's just something that's going to happen to me before it happens to most other people my age. I'm going to be one of those obituary page stories about a guy that died in his forties, the kind that makes me and all my friends shudder when we see them in the paper.

"That's a fact," he said, "like a balance sheet fact. Happy, sad, mood indigo; doesn't matter how you feel. Docs say that's the way it is. So make your plans on that. Make the best of bad things, that's what you have to do. I'm not looking forward to it, but since I know it's coming, I can at least go out having the last laugh. Some good will come of it."

She shivered. "Brrr," she said. "I don't like this talk at all."

He shrugged. "Hey," he said, "we aim to please. What kind you got in mind?"

She studied him. "This is probably not a good idea," she said.

"Let's hear what it is," he said. "My job's in counseling, after all. All kinds of investments, designed to meet all needs. Tell me your expectations, m'am, I'll tell you what I think."

"What I have in mind," she said, "is definitely not a long-term thing."

"So far, so good," he said. "The long-term stuff is risky unless you feel very sure."

"More along the lines of a, oh, I don't know," she said. "I guess what I mean is: you wanna fuck?"

He grinned at her. "What a nice idea," he said.

She nodded. "Well," she said, "I don't like to brag, but that's what I thought, too."

"There is one problem, though," he said.

"What is that?" she said.

"Since we parted company," he said, "I had a little fling with Diana. In Commodities?"

"The tall blonde bitch with the great big boobs?"

"That's the one," he said. "Turns out one of the commodities Diana had available was herpes. So I can now offer that along with my skilled techniques in bed. You want to take that chance?"

"Are you active now?" she said.

"I don't think so," he said. "I've got no visible lesions. But you never know with this stuff. I could wake up in the morning with bad news for both of us."

"Look," she said, "I don't mean to shock you, and I know how you feel about, well, barriers. But since you and I last saw each other, well, I don't know how to put this, but there's most of a package of Trojan Enz in my bathroom."

He laughed. "Good God, Connie," he said, "did Teddy have VD to go with everything else? You dumped me for a hitter and he had VD as well? That's not very flattering."

"Oh my God," she said. She sighed. "It wasn't Teddy that brought them, all right? It was another guy. That I picked up in a bar, after Teddy left, and he didn't believe *me* when I said I was all right. So he had these rubbers with him in his briefcase, and when he left in the morning, he left them behind."

"I see," Marcantonio said.

"He wasn't very good," she said. "I never saw him again."

"Not as good as me, you're saying?" he said.

She linked her left arm through his. "Come on, Jess," she said, "let me up. Get your coat and grab your hat. Leave your worries in Gene's office. Just direct your feet down to Five China Wharf, and we'll make slow gentle love, okay? Like we used to do?"

"For auld lang syne, my lads," he said, smiling on one side.

"For auld lang syne," she said.

17

Just before 10:45, Mark Baldwin and Msgr. Francis Claypool emerged from the threadbare gentility of the St. Botolph Club on Commonwealth Avenue into the cool, quiet dark and stood for a moment in the ring of light at the entrance to the club. Claypool had a habit of limbering himself after sitting a long time by interlacing his fingers below his groin, the palms of his hands downward, and stiffening his arm and shoulder muscles until his knuckles popped. Baldwin waited for him to do it and he did it, saying: "Ahh." Then he said: "Sure is a nice night, Mark."

Baldwin scanned the street before them, the man and the two women exercising and evacuating three dogs on the esplanade between the automobile lanes, each of them studiously maintaining distances between one another and their dogs, yet simultaneously remaining within hailing distance should some mugger approach any of them. There was a glow in the sky to the south beyond the buildings on the other side of the avenue, from the cafeterias and bars bordering the Prudential Center on Boylston Street west of Copley Square, and he could smell a faint odor of pizza.

"Late spring and early summer's the best time of the year in this town, Frank," Baldwin said, as though he had thought it over and decided the opinion safe enough to venture. "After it's been too cold and wet, before it gets too hot and dry, we get four or five weeks of splendid weather. And then the Red Sox begin to lose, and the temperatures get up into the nineties, and the humidity goes up, and after that the only thing you've got to look forward to's the fall, when its starts to get too cold and wet again."

Monsignor Claypool chuckled. "No one's ever going to accuse you of being a Pollyanna, Mark," he said. "No one who knows you, at least."

Baldwin gave him a raised eyebrow with a sidelong look. "Is that why I'm on this committee?" he said. "The dash of pessimism to moderate the hopes of the idealists involved?"

Claypool chuckled again. "Don't be too hard on Don Joyce now," he said. "He has a cause. He really believes in it. And if you had as much regular contact as I do with people who're generally on the same side he's on, you'd find him quite refreshing and realistic."

"Well," Baldwin said, "I agree he doesn't seem to be out bombing the clinics or picketing the Supreme Court, if that's what you mean. But at the same time, you know, I see him fairly regularly on business at Rand, Hayes, and he's a different man. Strictly business, *all* business, every single minute. Then I meet him at these things, and he becomes a raving ideologue — at least by my standards, anyway."

"Not ideology, Mark," Claypool said. " 'Faith' is what it's called. He's a believer. A sincere believer. And unlike most who think and believe as he does, he's willing to do something to demonstrate his commitment. He's put a lot more than rhetoric into this proposal of his, you know. He's put a lot more than money into it too, as far as that goes. And until such time as he and others can get the same sort of governmental support for adoption programs that now flows to abortion programs, he'll stay with it, whatever it costs. I admire him. His money and his time are where his mouth is. He's a man of principles."

Baldwin nodded. "He's that, all right," he said.

"But you don't think he's realistic," Claypool said.

Baldwin shrugged. "I suppose whether he's realistic doesn't matter a lot," he said. "If you put it in those terms that you've just used, then whether this notion he's got — underwriting unwanted pregnancies to term with preplanned adoptions — happens to be realistic is irrelevant. Doesn't matter whether it's got snowball's chance of taking place. It's something he has to do."

"That's exactly right," Claypool said with satisfaction. "I wish we had more like him."

"No doubt," Baldwin said. He could not keep the impatience out of his voice.

"You seemed a little off your feed tonight, Mark," Claypool said.

"Oh, I am, Frank," Baldwin said. "I've been back at my desk for less than two weeks, and every bit of the tension I went away to get rid of is right back on me. Six weeks to uncoil, ten days to get coiled up again. It's very discouraging.

"But the back isn't caused by this," he said. "Catholic Charities is about the only thing I do with my time that I don't have to do. I'm not Catholic, and if you ask my employees, they'll tell you I'm not charitable. So the very fact that this is strictly voluntary on my part makes it important to me. And makes me feel better about myself. Besides, it's the only organization I belong to that I wasn't hammered into joining because my father belonged. Man's entitled to at least one hashmark of his own identity."

Claypool laughed and clapped him on the shoulder. "Well," he said, "we appreciate it, Mark. And thank you for the dinner, on behalf of all of us. I'm sorry Don bored you."

Baldwin grinned. "He's not the first, and he won't be the last," he said. They started down the walk.

"Can I offer you a lift?" Claypool said. "I found a meter just down the street. Cabs're scarce this time of night."

"That's kind of you," Baldwin said, "but I think what I'll do is take a stroll for myself, at least down to the Garden. See if I can walk off my frustrations."

"Watch yourself," Claypool said. "Many victims of social oppression come out at night with knives and things. They don't always give uncharitable non-Catholics like yourself the respect you ought to have."

"I'll be all right," Baldwin said. They shook hands and said good night. Claypool, walking rapidly, turned west on the sidewalk and headed up toward Fairfield Street. Baldwin stood for a while in the rim of light and watched the priest walk into the dimness. Then he went out to the sidewalk and headed east. At the corner of Dartmouth and Commonwealth he turned left and walked north on Dartmouth, crossing Marlborough quickly as though fearing interception, making his way through the light from the streetlamps and the first floor apartments towards the river and its weedy summer smell. He turned left on Beacon, heading west, and crossed in the middle of the block almost furtively when he was opposite 160 Beacon. He had his keys out when he reached the front door and was inside with it shut behind him and the alarm reset in less than fifteen seconds. He went up to the apartment.

At first he thought she was not there, and he felt reprieved. The only light in the living room when he unlocked the door was the pale illumination from the lights along Storrow Drive and Cambridge, reflecting on the Charles. He had to switch on the overhead light to select the proper buttons to disarm and reactivate the alarm. While he waited the thirty seconds for it to recycle, he listened for evidence of her presence. He heard nothing. It occurred to him that there was another possibility besides her absence to account for the silence. He was unpleasantly surprised to find himself suddenly perspiring. He forced himself to keep his eyes on the dial of his watch until the cycling time had passed. Then he reset the alarm and turned around.

She was curled up in the Eames chair to the right of the picture window. She was wearing a red silk kimono robe and she had her feet tucked up under her. Her hair had been wet and had dried flat against her skull. Her face lacked make-up or lipstick. Her eyes were red and as he stared at her they began to fill up again. She gripped her right ankle with her right and left hands and tried to make herself smaller in the chair. When she tried to speak, her voice clogged up and she had to cough. She shook her hair impatiently and began again. "I wasn't sure you'd come," she said.

He stared at her. "Sylvia," he said, anger overtaking the mistaken fear and making his voice harden as he spoke, "what choice did I have, pray tell? How could I not come? What options did you leave me? You pulled that silly stunt. You got yourself arrested. You called the office for help. You called the office from the station after the cops let you go. You called the office after you got here and had hysterics on the phone with Anne because I wasn't back, to the point at which I thought Anne was going to have hysterics, when I did get back. You called the office three more times, after I got back. I told you each of those times I would come as soon as I got through with what I had to do. I asked you twice, during those calls, if you wanted me to cancel out the dinner with Monsignor Claypool, and run the risk of starting talk that I don't think you want, and I'm sure that I don't want, and each time that I asked you, you said that you did not. Now why the hell would I not come, after all that stuff and nonsense, going on all afternoon? What would you do if I didn't?"

She looked down miserably and looked down at her legs. She unclenched her left hand from her shin and picked with her nails at the hem of her robe. She shook her head twice. "I don't know," she said in a small voice. " I . . ., when I got here I got undressed and took a shower, and I lay down for a while and hoped you would come. After I talked to you, I mean. And I guess I fell asleep. And then I woke up and it was dark and you still weren't here." She paused while her voice filled up again and she swallowed to clear it.

"And then I came out here and I sat down and that was all I could think of. That suppose you didn't come. And I didn't know what I would do."

"But you didn't make any more calls, I hope," he said.

She shook her head. "No," she said. "No. After you left the office, no. I was just here, like I said." She looked up at him.

He knew she was lying. "You're sure of that, Sylvia," he said. She nibbled at her lower lip. She nodded twice, rapidly. "Uh uh," she said. "I really didn't."

"You didn't call Mrs. Han, and get her all upset," he said.

"Uh uh," she said and shook her head. "No, I really didn't." She watched him anxiously.

He expelled breath noisily. "Sylvia," he said, starting for the kitchen, "I don't know what the hell to do with you." In the kitchen he opened the refrigerator and took out a fresh bottle of Muscadet. He located the corkscrew and opened it. He poured a glass. "Do you want some wine?" he said.

She delayed her answer. "Uh," she said, "I don't know. Yeah, I guess so. Some wine would be nice."

He poured a second glass. He put the bottle back into the refrigerator and returned to the living room. He walked over to the window and handed her one of the glasses. She accepted it with both hands. He backed up and sat down on the grey tweed couch, facing her. He put his glass on the coffee table. He studied her. She lifted the glass with both hands to her mouth and drank deeply. She lowered it to her lap and raised her eyes, full of tears, to look at him. Her upper lip glistened from the wine and her cheeks shone from the tears.

He softened his voice. "Did you have anything to eat?" he said.

"No," she said. "I was going to. But then I looked in the fridge, you know, and there wasn't anything except some cheese and the rest of that old quiche I made about three months ago, and I threw that out."

"Isn't there some frozen stuff?" he said.

"I don't know," she said. "I didn't look. I wasn't really hungry, you know? My stomach was upset and I didn't feel like eating anyway. Like if I started heating something that the smell would make me sick. I didn't want to throw up." She took another drink of wine.

He picked up his glass and swirled it. The light from the overhead

fixture near the door was at the same time very harsh and insuffi-
cient. It made the wine look flat and yellow. He got up and turned on
the lamps at either end of the couch. He walked back to the door and
turned off the overhead. He returned to the couch and sat down. He
picked up the wine again and swirled it. Now it was a pale gold that
he liked better. He drank some of it. He put the glass down. He sat
back on the couch slowly, favoring his back. He put his left arm out
along the back of it and stared at her. "All right," he said, "tell me."

Her upper lip trembled. She shook her head again. "All right,"
she said. She looked down. "I did call your house." She looked up
pleadingly. "I didn't know where you were, Mark. All you told me
was you had this dinner meeting that you had to go to, and you
thought you should go. And then I went to sleep and I woke up and
it was dark and it was past nine, and I didn't know where you were.
And I got frightened that you weren't going to come. Like you said
you would. And I called up. But it was Mister Han, not Mrs. Han,
and I don't think he recognized my voice, and I didn't tell him who I
was or anything. I didn't give anything away."

"You just told him it was someone from the office," Baldwin said.

"That's right," she said eagerly. "Someone from the office."

"Which of course immediately threw him into a state of absolute
panic," Baldwin said, "because if my office doesn't know where I
am, and he doesn't know where I am, where the hell am I and what
has happened to me?"

"No," she said. "No, it didn't do that. It was all right. He didn't,
he didn't act like that."

Baldwin shook his head. "Sylvia," he said, "you don't understand. Victor and Mrs. Han are not Americans. They are refugees.
They don't make the same assumptions we do, when something like
this happens. They don't assume when someone's late and they don't
know where he is, that he's simply gotten tied up at a meeting or
stopped for a drink on his way home. They assume he's been
kidnapped, or arrested, or worse. What time did you make this
call?"

She shrugged. "Nine," she said, "nine-fifteen."

He exhaled again. "Shit," he said. "So they've been beside
themselves for almost two hours now. Go get me the phone."

"What?" she said. She looked up like a startled animal.

"Go into the bedroom and get me the goddamned telephone," he said, putting his head back on the couch and closing his eyes.

She got out of the chair fast, so that the robe came open. She started for the bedroom in an awkward slow trot, running on the balls of her feet, her breasts bouncing, her face contorted and her eyes screwed up against new tears. She came back with the handset to the Uniden portable phone and cautiously put it on the couch. She pushed it towards him with quick little movements, as though afraid he might snap at her. "Here," she said, straightening up quickly and backing away as he opened his eyes. She stood there in front of him, watching anxiously as he sat up.

"Thanks," he said. He turned on the phone and selected the number. He put the handset to his ear and waited. "Victor," he said, "Mister Baldwin. Any messages for me?" There was a high-pitched gabble. "No, no," Baldwin said heartily, "I'm perfectly all right. Just got tied up at another one of those damned dinner meetings that keep me out too late." He waited. "Sure, sure, perfectly all right. I'll be home later on. Don't wait up. Any messages that can't wait 'till morning?" He gazed ruefully at Francis while he listened. "Just someone from the office? Well, that can surely wait. Now, remember that Mister Kelleher from the BRA will be joining us for breakfast." He paused. "The usual, I think, Victor. Mister Kelleher's fond of your roast beef hash. Yes, that will be fine. Now, go to bed. I'll be home later on."

He switched off the phone and put it down on the coffee table. She gathered the robe about her and went back to her chair. She sat down and curled up again. "All right," he said, "let's talk about it."

"You can't stay all night?" she said. "I was hoping you could stay all night, and I could talk to you."

He sighed. "Sylvia," he said, "do we have to go through this every time we're both here and it's dark? Don't you understand by now why that's seldom possible?"

"You're not married," she said.

"You are, though," he said. "*And* you're an employee, *and* your husband knows me. How you work out your absences with him is none of my concern, so long as he's satisfied with your explanations, and so long as he doesn't know who the other man is. But if Jason finds out who it is, even if he doesn't do a thing, it could complicate our lives.

"I don't want that, Sylvia," he said. "We're sexual friends. That's all we've been 'till now and that's all we're going to be. Now, I'm willing to help you as much as I can in this mess you've gotten yourself into, and I hope you know that. It's why I'm here. But I'm not going to do anything that's going to end up turning our nice little arrangement into some damned public scandal that will embarrass Jason and embarrass me and make you look like a whore."

She was picking at the hem of her robe again. "Why not a whore?" she said mournfully. "That's what I am, isn't it?"

He snorted. He picked up his wineglass and drank. "No, it's not what you are," he said. "Stop dramatizing things for once, will you? For whatever reasons you've got, you need more sexual release than you're getting at home. I need more than there otherwise is in my life. There's nothing wrong with that, so long as nobody gets hurt. And so far, nobody has. Let's keep it that way. What the hell got into your head, to go down to Quincy Market today and steal two damned cheap scarves? Is this a hobby of yours, stealing things? Shoplifting? Is that what it is?"

She nibbled at her lip again. "It isn't that," she said. "I never stole before. And it wasn't in the Market. It was that bitch Michelle that runs the Gattopardo store in the Neilson Building across from the Market. That one that they rebuilt?"

"You know this person?" Baldwin said. "This Michelle, is she the one that had you arrested?"

"Uh huh," Francis said. She clasped her hands together over her right knee. "I know her. She's got this little shop that sells Italian silks to all the tourists that come to the Market. In the Neilson Building. And I went in there at lunch because I was sort of depressed, and I saw these two scarves that looked kind of pretty, so I took them. And she caught me, when I tried to leave. And she called the police and said she'd swear out a complaint. So they took me up to the station and booked me and I have to be in court next week."

"I don't get it," Baldwin said. "I didn't get it before, and I really don't get it now. Why did this woman that you say you know have you busted for swiping eight bucks' worth of scarves? Why didn't she just ask you for the money or something?"

"Because she hates me," Francis said. "She always didn't like me from the time that we first met. And I went in there and she saw me and this was her big chance."

"Why does she hate you?" Baldwin said. "What did you do to her?"

"Jason's company owns her building," Francis said. "She's a tenant of theirs. And she's very political. She's in that Gay Lesbian Caucus thing they've got, that're always saying homosexuals have rights, and all that stuff? She thinks everyone should get involved and do things, and that one of the reasons that the gays and the lesbians have so much trouble getting things, and being discriminated and stuff, is that people that really agree with them're too scared to come out in public and say that they agree."

"I still don't get it," Baldwin said.

She unclasped her hands and started to examine closely the stitching at the seams along the front of her robe. She pouted out her lower lip. "Well," she said, "when they had the grand opening of the building three years ago, I think it was, the ribbon cutting, you know? I went there with Jason naturally, because it was Appalachian that put it together. And she was there. And she came up to me and she said I should let Jason do what he really wants to do. That I am holding him back and making him pretend to be something that he isn't, and he's never going to realize his full human potential as long as I keep doing this. And she kept touching me. And I got mad. I was nineteen years old, when Jason and I met. I gave up my whole career, all the chances that I had, with the airline then. Jason wanted me around? I dropped it all for Jason. And I married him. And he belongs to me. And now she's saying this to me? It really ticked me off. And I said: 'Get your hands offa me, you dyke bitch. Jason does what he wants.' And ever since then, she doesn't like me."

"Whoa," Baldwin said. Francis smiled and continued to pick at her robe. "What the hell're you telling me here?"

She clasped her hands over her right knee again and looked Baldwin in the eye. The demure smile broadened on her face. "Michelle doesn't like me," she said, "because she thinks I'm the reason Jason's still in the closet, and not out on the street asking for stuff for gays."

"Jason's queer," Baldwin said.

She took her lower lip between her teeth and nodded. "Uh huh," she said. "So he tells me, now, at least."

"You told me it was medication," he said. "You said your sex life fell apart after your husband had those seizures, and they said he had to take those drugs that made him impotent."

"So I lied," she said. "I asked him what he wanted, after he was sick. We told people it was *petit mal, tic doloreux*, all those fancy names. Some kind of epilepsy. That was Jason's idea. Because of the people in his company, that he didn't want to find out. Because they would let him go, he thought, if they knew what he was. What it actually was, when he collapsed, he had a good old nervous breakdown, okay? It got to be too much for him, pretending, and he just popped his cork. And I said to him: 'Look, Jason, tell me what you want. Only, tell me now, all right? While I still got time enough to maybe do something about it. You're a nice guy. I don't want to hurt you. But it's not going to be enough for me, you know, just being your wife and everything while you're having affairs with guys.' And he said that was all right. That if I would just be careful and so forth, that so would he, and we could just go on and be married for a while longer and see what happened next. And that was when we decided, I would go back to work. Get myself a job and go out in the world and be someplace where I could maybe meet some men, all right?

"See, I didn't want to hurt the guy, Mark," she said. "He can't help the way he is. He says it's not me that's the reason, and I have to believe him, don't I? It's nothing that I did, made him this way. So I said: 'Well, all right, but I got to get out of the house here then, and start looking around.' And that was when I went to work for you."

"And he set it up," Baldwin said. "Son of a bitch."

"Oh, Jason is smart," she said. "He's a smart son of a bitch. He's as queer as green horses, but Jason ain't dumb. Jason's a regular fox."

"And you're imitating him, aren't you?" Baldwin said. "You did this thing today deliberately. You knew this woman, this Michelle, would arrest you, and start a big commotion. You did this on purpose."

She looked down at her lap and started fiddling with her robe again. She murmured something in a voice too soft for him to hear. "What?" he said. "Speak up. I can't hear you."

She looked up. "Sort of," she said. "Sort of, I did."

"Why?" he said.

" 'Why,' " she said musingly. She smiled at him wanly. "You're asking me 'why'?"

"Yes I am," Baldwin said.

She nodded. She got up from the chair very slowly. She let the robe fall off her shoulders and drop to the floor. She stood with her hands at her sides. "See?" she said. "This is all I am. There isn't any more to me. I don't paint. I don't collect art. I'm not a good cook. I don't like to read. I can't have children. I don't ride, I don't jog, I don't climb mountains and I don't like music. I'm forty-one years old and I've still got my figure and I like sex a lot. I'm married to a nice guy who turned out to be a queer. I sit at a desk and I answer the telephone and meet visitors to North American Group. And that's all I am." She started toward him across the carpet.

"I know what you are, Mark," she said, "to the world and the people you know. You're a lot more than I am. And that's all right. I like it. You're a powerful man. But all of them, those other people, they can get along without you, you know, and I'm different — I can't." She knelt in front of him and sat back on her legs. "North American could put somebody else in your job," she said. "All those other things you do, somebody else could do. But what you do for me, nobody else can do. So, I see someone like this Gates bitch come in, and I know what's going to happen, sooner or later. And it makes me desperate, you know? I know it shouldn't bother me. I know you've got your French lady, and the lady in New York, and the lady on the Cape and the one on Martha's Vineyard, and probably a hundred others that I've missed. And I know why you keep this place for us, and why I can't go to your home — I know all those things."

She reached forward deliberately and pulled down his zipper. "I know about them, Mark," she said, "but I don't like them. See?" She looked up at him and smiled brightly. "So, I did something foolish today." She used both hands to undo his belt and unfasten the top of his pants. She opened them and put her hands on the waistband of his shorts. She pulled them down, exposing his penis. She took his testicles in her right hand and his penis in her left. She watched it become fully erect. She looked up at him. "I've got an interest in this," she said. "It's mine. Now I'm going to put it in my mouth. Is that all right with you?" He nodded. "You're sure," she said. "I don't think you've been anywhere that you could've showered today. If you put this thing somewhere where it should-n't've been, I'll taste it and I'll know."

He had to clear his throat to say: "No."

She tightened her grip. "Good," she said, and leaned forward.

18

On the morning of the second Wednesday in July the sun came up flat and hot and early over Boston Harbor, baking the still air and liberating all the smells of iridescent oils that lay upon the water. In her bedroom at 5 China Wharf, Connie Gates awoke naked and perspiring to the sound of halyards slapping on masts of boats owned by careless yachtsmen as the currents in the Harbor moved the vessels around on their lines. There was also an undertone of cordial shouts exchanged. She sat up, groggy, and shook her head to clear it. She blinked several times and used her desk across the room as a focal point for her eyes. The three file folders were empty on the left side of the desk. The documents they had contained were piled up on the right.

She threw off the yellow sheet and started for the bathroom, lurching slightly as mild vertigo rebuked her for getting up too fast; she grabbed the bathroom doorframe to maintain her balance. She shuddered in the shower as the hot water hit her, hunching her shoulders under the spray. She set her teeth and racked the hot faucet shut, bracing herself for the unheated drenching that followed. She broke out in goose pimples and shampooed in the cold water, her teeth chattering. She shut off the water and got out of the shower shivering. She rubbed herself with a Turkish towel and then wrapped herself in it. She stamped her feet on the bathmat and shivered some more. The phone rang.

She went to the sink and stared at herself in the mirror. The phone rang again. She inspected her eyes and was satisfied. She brushed her teeth. The phone gave another abbreviated ring. She rinsed her mouth while the answering machine took the call. It said: "This is Connie Gates. If you have a message, please leave it with your name and number, at the beep. Don't be rude and hang up, so all I get when I get home's a dial tone recording. Leave your name and number. I will call you back." The machine beeped after making its speech. She heard the click of someone hanging up, and the dial tone coming on.

She went into the kitchen and put three scoops of Maxwell House coffee into the filtered basket of her coffee maker. She put four cups of water into the pot and poured it into the machine. She shivered again. She went out into the living room to the glass door overlooking the harbor and looked out. Six men from the Boston Police Department Scuba Team were practicing in the water at the marina. They wore black wet suits and yellow tanks of air and masks and flippers, and they were shouting at each other because they wore as well black sponge rubber hoods that covered their hair and ears. Two of them treaded water in an oil slick next to the dock, their face masks back on their foreheads and their faces shiny with oil. The other four stood like giant frogs on the dock, looking down at the men in the water. "I'm telling you guys," one of the swimmers said, rotating his arms in the water, "it's fuckin' beautiful today. You should all jump right in and get your arseholes wet. Just like swimming in the toilet, after it's been flushed. Nice and warm and mostly clean. Just keep your big mouth shut."

She stepped back from the glass door and closed it against the heat, already beginning to build at 8:10 A.M. She reached down to the controls of the air conditioner set into the wall and turned it to "high cool." She fluffed her hair as the unit came on. She went back into the kitchen as the coffee maker sizzled completing the brewing, and turned it back to "warm." She went back into the bedroom, fluffing her hair some more. The phone rang again.

She undid the towel and let it fall to the floor. She went to the bureau and opened the drawer containing her underwear. The phone rang again. She took out a blue bra and blue panties. She put on the panties. She got the bra over her shoulders as her recorded message finished. She was looking down to hook it when the caller began talking. "Connie," the voice said, "it's Ted. Are you there, or what?"

She said: "Shit." She went over to the desk and picked up the phone. She shut off the recorder and said: "Yeah, I'm here." She waited, cradling the phone between her left shoulder and her jaw, trying to fasten the bra while she listened. "I figured it was you," she said. "I was just waking up. I was too stupid to talk." She gave up fiddling with the bra clasp and stood with the garment open, holding the phone with her left hand and supporting her left elbow with her right hand. She put her right foot on top of her left foot and curled her toes. She made faces as he talked. She rolled her eyes and scowled. "Oh, I don't care," she said. "No," she said, "I really don't. Listen to me, will you please? I was silly last week. I shouldn't've called you. I did and I'm sorry, all right? You dusted me off. You were right.

"Now," she said, "you're the one that's being silly. You ought to cut it out." She let him object. "Yes, you are," she said. "Calling me up all those times last night, when I was trying to work. Really, Ted, heavy breathing? You're too old for that. *I'm* too old for that, for sure, even if you aren't. You and Donna've got a good thing going there, just like you told me last week. Stick with it and forget me." She paused.

"Well," she said, "I *assumed* you were drunk. Drunk or stoned, or maybe both. That goes without saying. But my God, Ted, you're a fairly young man. You've always liked to party, at least since I've known you. Does this mean for the rest of my life I can look forward to you calling me up six or seven times a night every time you get shitfaced? I'm going to move to Alaska and get an unlisted number, if that's what's going to happen."

She let him talk again. She dropped her right hand from her left elbow and moved her feet apart. She stood with her right hand clenched at her side and the knuckles on her left hand whitened as she gripped the phone. "Uh uh, Teddy," she said. She paused. "I said: 'Uh uh,' is what I said," she said. "What you're saying's not right. I've got my resources. I admit it — when I called you, I was desperate. I did not know what to do. But then you, well, you talked some sense, and I got myself shaped up." She paused. "Well, you're right," she said. "A good lay was exactly what I needed. And I got one, no thanks to you. So forget it, all right? Water under the bridge, over the dam, whatever you want to say." She waited. "Probably you do," she said. "You probably do know him. So what?" She waited. "So what if he is?" she said. "What do you care? What difference does it make to you, if that happens to be who it was? It's none of your business, Teddy, so long as it wasn't you." She laughed. "Well," she said, "I can tell you right now, that if that's what he is, he's not ready for the coroner yet. You should pray, or Donna should, that if you ever get that old and feel that sick, you perform as well." She giggled.

She tucked the handset tight against her ear. "What did you just say?" she said. "Say that again, you clown." She waited. She took a deep breath. "Don't be an asshole," she said. "Don't be a fucking asshole, Ted. Don't even say things like that, even for the effect. Talk like that's just stupid. Now you listen to me, and you listen up good. If you ever, *if you ever*, say that to me again, I'll call the police and report you." She waited. "Oh yes I will," she said. "I will call the police and the phone company and I'll turn your ass in. You know me, kiddo. I don't hack around. Now fuck off." She slammed the receiver down.

She stalked into the kitchen walking on her heels, the bra still open and her breasts jiggling. She went to the coffee maker and poured a cup. The phone rang again. She got milk out of the refrigerator and poured some into the coffee. The phone rang again. She remembered she had shut off the answering machine. "Shit," she said.

She went back into the bedroom at a dogtrot. She picked up the phone on the third ring. "Yeah?" she said fiercely. "Oh, Anne," she said, flustered. "no, it's all right. I thought you were someone else." She paused. "No," she said, "a former admirer with a roll of dimes, who won't take 'No' for an answer. Believe me, it's nothing serious. Yes, I will. Of course." She stood motionless for a moment and listened. "I'd love to, Mark," she said, "but I can't." She laughed. "No, I *really* can't. I've got this humpbuster of a job to do for this tyrant who won't wait, and I've got to go to New Bedford today. I can't have lunch with you, even though I'd rather." She let him talk and laughed again. Her face lighted up and she traced her cleavage with the tip of her right forefinger. "Oh, I'd love to," she said, "but I don't know when I'll be back." She paused. She giggled. "I gathered that from what you said," she said. "Don't worry. I'm a big girl. I can handle him." She giggled again. "I'll be late," she said warningly. "Call me around nine."

She hung up. She went back to the kitchen, fastening her bra and half-singing, half-humming *Satisfaction*. She boogied three steps putting the milk back into the refrigerator. She took her coffee back into the bedroom, sipping as she walked. She put the cup down on the bureau and looked at herself in the mirror. She rolled her lips together and turned to look at herself in profile. She smoothed the flesh over her rib cage. She faced the mirror again. Still looking at herself, she reached down and opened the drawer that contained her sweaters. She took out a white cotton, loosely knit, and held it up in front of her. It had a scoop neckline. She nodded. She put the sweater down on top of the bureau. She unhooked the bra and took it off. She put the sweater on over her head. She settled herself in the garment by moving her shoulders. She looked at herself critically in the mirror. She cocked her head to the left and to the right and shrugged to see whether her nipples protruded. They did not. She rubbed the cloth against them to gauge whether she would find the friction uncomfortable during a full, hot day. She decided that she would. She pulled the sweater off again and put the bra back on. She put the sweater on again. She studied herself in the mirror. She frowned. She went to the closet and took a yellow cotton skirt out of a cleaner's bag. She laid it on the bed and studied it. She went into the bathroom and began to use the hairdryer, fluffing her hair again. She decided to leave it loose. She put on her make-up and lipstick. She went back out into the bedroom and studied the skirt again. She took off her panties and put the skirt on, buttoning it at the waist. She inspected herself in the mirror. She shook her head. She picked up the panties and put them on again under her skirt, squatting and wiggling her behind to do it. She looked at herself ruefully in the mirror and waggled her forefinger at her image. "No no no," she said.

19

Constance Gates parked her BMW at a meter in front of a second-hand furniture store on Winter Street in New Bedford across from Number 208 and inserted enough change to pay for two hours. Carrying her attaché case in her left hand, she crossed the street to the two-story business block faced in brick tarpaper and entered it through the door between the discount drugstore and the submarine sandwich shop.

There was a sign to her right on the pea-green wall. It was made of Lucite etched and lettered in gold leaf that said: "Geoghegan & Ramos, Attorneys at Law," and included an arrow pointing diagonally up the stairs. She grabbed the cylindrical railing on the right wall and nearly pulled it away in her hand. She shifted her case to her right hand and tried the railing on the left. It was secure, and she climbed the stairs using it, the heels of her sandals scraping on the metal treads as she went up. At the top of the stairs was another Lucite sign, with another arrow pointing right — to her left there was a blank wall. She turned right and went down the narrow hallway, smelling oregano and onions and olive oil on the hot, still air and feeling a little sick. At the end of the corridor there was a walnut veneer door. There was another Lucite sign on it that identified it as the entrance to the offices of Geoghegan & Ramos. She opened it.

She was hit by a blast of frigid air and an uppercut of Bruce Springsteen's recording of "Born In The USA" playing at a level beyond her pain threshold. She blinked reflexively and shut the door behind her. She saw that the door and the wall around it were sheathed in acoustical tile. The floor was covered with aquamarine, three-inch shag carpeting. It was all matted down. She turned to face the room. She saw that the ceiling and the interior walls were paneled with acoustical tile.

There were four desks in the reception area, two along each wall. Each of them was occupied by a woman in her late 'teens or early twenties working intently at a word-processor. Each of the women wore a tank-top — lime, yellow, hot pink, neon blue. Each of the women had frosted hair and a very deep suntan. Three of the women were chewing gum, out of synch with one another; each of them wore earphones plugged into a portable tape deck on her desk. The fourth woman was smoking a cigarette, dangling it out of her mouth and squinting against the smoke as she typed. Her head bobbed in time to the Springsteen music, which was coming from a Panasonic ghetto-blaster on the sill of the two translucent safety-glassed windows at the other end of the room. None of the women appeared to notice that Gates had come in.

Gates took a deep breath and shouted: "Hey!" The smoking woman looked up with mild interest from her VDT terminal. She took the cigarette out of her mouth and turned in her swivel chair so that she was facing Gates. She gave Gates the up-and-down. She nodded. "Yeah?" she said.

"My name is Constance Gates," Gates said, "I . . . . "

"Downah hall," the woman said, jerking her left thumb to Gates's right. She put the cigarette back in her mouth and turned back to the word-processor.

"I'm sorry," Gates said, "but I'm not sure I'm in the right place. My appointment's with . . . . "

The smoking woman turned back toward Gates. The cigarette remained at the corner of her mouth, and she continued to squint. ". . . with the DA," she said companionably. The cigarette bobbed up and down as she talked. "That's who you come here to see, idnit? And that's what I told you. He's downah hall the end of it. All right? Just go downah hall 'till you come the end, and there's an office there. And you open the door and that's where he is. Down the endah the hall."

"I've never seen him," Gates said.

"You ain't missed anything," the woman said through the smoke.

"No," Gates said. "I mean: so I would know him if I saw him, and I was in the right office."

The woman grinned. "Honey," she said, "he's the only one in there. You'll know him right off. And he's expecting you. So go downah hall, and openah door, and that's where he is, big as life." She turned back to the word-processor.

Gates started down the hall. She passed three office doors on each side, the top panels made of frosted glass with the names of lawyers in black script — "Atty." followed by a surname — at the lower right hand corners. At the end, directly ahead of her there was a door lettered: "Mister Swain." She opened it and went in.

She found herself standing in the middle of a room about ten feet wide and thirty feet long, extending the width of the building. In front of her there was a glass dinner table set on chromium legs, large enough to seat eight or ten people. Behind it there was one executive chair, upholstered in mauve vinyl. Behind the chair there was a fireplace. Over the fireplace there was a large picture of a horse with a blue ribbon hanging around its neck, standing against a background of vaguely English countryside of an unhealthy shade of green. On the mantel under the picture there were seven small loving cups. The wall was paneled in cherry veneer. The lighting over the table was a large Tiffany lamp suspended on a thick gold chain; the lamp advertised Coca Cola. To her right there was a group of overstuffed leather chairs and a couch done in red leather and studded with brass. There were three more pictures of horses on the paneled walls near the grouping. To her left there was a daybed which had been made up hurriedly; the brown twill slipcover was rumpled and the pink sheet showed at the hem. The paneled wall over the daybed was crowded with four-by-five black and white glossy photographs, each of two or three people, including jockeys, standing and smiling next to the heads of horses; the photographs were captioned and the frames were black wood, and some of them had ribbons attached to them.

Beyond the daybed there was a small refrigerator next to a double stainless steel sink with gooseneck faucets. The opposite wall to the left of the fireplace was filled top and bottom with cupboards; one section of the counter was occupied by a four-burner electric stove top. One of the hanging counters supported a hanging Litton microwave oven. Stacked against the cupboards were nine metal folding chairs. At the left end of the room there was another grouping of red leather furniture arranged so that persons sitting on the couch would have their backs to the two safety-glass windows. Three chairs faced the couch and a rectangular oak coffee table. There was a thick manila envelope at one end of the table. There was a man in a blue blazer and tan chino pants standing in front of the chairs, his back to Gates; he had his hands in his pants pockets and seemed to be staring at the translucent glass.

Gates cleared her throat. "Mister Taves?" she said.

The District Attorney turned around. His face was mottled and his eyes were bloodshot. His grey hair was plastered against his forehead, blown dry and unruly over the rest of his skull. His jowls overspread the collar of his light blue silk shirt. He wore a textured silk tie with alternating jagged patterns of maroon and silver. His blazer buttons were monogrammed. He stared at her and said: "Constance Gates."

"Yes," she said.

He looked at his watch. "You're twenty minutes late," he said. "It's ten to ten. You were supposed to be here at nine-thirty." He gazed at her.

"I'm sorry," she said. "I drove down from Boston this morning. I'm not familiar with New Bedford. I thought, I assumed, that this must be somewhere near the courthouse. I was wrong. I'm sorry."

"You should've left earlier," he said.

"You're probably right," she said.

"Of course I'm right," he said. He gestured toward the chairs. "Have a seat," he said. He stepped around the coffee table and sat down on the couch, folding his hands at his waist, as she made her way across the room and took the chair to his left. She put her attaché case on the coffee table and opened it. She took out the tape recorder and put it on the table. She closed the case and sat back in the chair.

"Is that thing on now?" he said.

"No," she said. "I just thought I'd have it ready."

"Because I don't like those things," he said.

"You can check it for yourself, Mister Taves, if you want," she said. "It's not on. If I want to tape something, I'll ask you."

"Because they've got those things now," he said, "that they look like they're off but there's really another tiny little tape in there that's running, when the first big one that you can look at and see isn't."

"I'm not trying to trick you, Mister Taves," she said. "Besides, what would be the point? You know who I am. You know who I'm working for. If you don't want me to print something, don't say it."

"Who you're working for's what bothers me," Taves said. "I don't know you. All I know, you're perfectly all right. But you're working for that fuckin' Baldwin, and I don't trust that guy."

"Well, Mister Taves," she said, "that gives us something in

common, then. I'm not sure I trust him, either. But from what he tells me, you got this ball rolling by coming to see him. And I am here today because I went to see him. He didn't recruit you, and he didn't recruit me, and he probably doesn't trust either one of us too far, when you come down to it."

"So what's this crap with the magazine then?" Taves said. "I almost fell over, I heard you're writing this for *Journeyer*. You ever read that thing?"

"I've seen a few copies," she said. "I didn't go back and read every issue since it started publishing, if that's what you mean."

"What'd you think of it?" he said.

She shrugged. "Not much," she said. "From what I could see, Mister Baldwin's reason for hiring me, the reason he gave me, seemed plausible enough from the *Journeyers* I read. There isn't much to it. Some pretty explicit pictures, some articles that didn't interest me a lot — 'How To Live Without A Man Without Apologizing For It;' 'How To Live With Another Woman Without Apologizing For it;' that kind of thing. Since I'm not interested in doing either one, I thought they were dull. But that's what Mister Baldwin told me. That the magazine's dull, and it's not making any money, and he wants to see if some decent journalism can turn it around and broaden its audience." She stopped. "That was probably the wrong word."

Taves snickered. "Either that or the right one," he said. "I got to disagree with you about 'dull,' though. I thought it was pornography."

She nodded. "Could be," she said. "The issues I saw, I didn't think they were. But like I say, I've only seen a few, and nobody asked me to do a pornographic piece. What issues did you see?"

He frowned. "Well," he said, "lemme think. This was in my first term. So it would've been, what? Eighteen years ago, I guess. Yeah, eighteen years ago."

"Oh," she said. "well, that was before Baldwin's company owned it. They didn't buy it until recently. So I didn't see those issues that you saw."

"Oh," he said. He unclasped his hands. He undid the button of his blazer and relaxed his belly out over his belt. He spread his arms out along the back of the couch. He pondered for a while. He nodded three times. "Okay," he said. "I guess you're probably all right." He made a motion with his head to indicate he was referring to the tape recorder. "You want to turn on that thing there, or you just wanna talk first?"

"Let's leave it off for a minute," she said. "I've got some questions of my own that probably don't have anything to do with the story, and I'd feel more comfortable asking them off the recorder. As you might also feel, answering them."

He grinned and crossed his legs, showing white flesh above his anklet stockings. "Fine by me," he said.

"You're the District Attorney," she said. "I ask for an appointment and you make one for me here. Why here? The things I've got to ask you have to do with the District Attorney's office. Why am I in this office, with Mister Swain's name on the door?"

"You're in this office," he said, "because I didn't want you coming to the DA's office." He smiled.

"Want to tell me why?" she said.

"I don't mind at all," he said. "This is an election year for me. I got the *Standard Times* and the TV boys and the *Herald* in Fall River and Baldwin's fuckin' paper and a couple radio stations too, all watching my ass like a buncha hawks. And I got two, so far, opponents, with a third one getting warmed up, and they're all playin' grab-ass with the damned reporters, trying to embarrass me. So, I meet you inna public building, somebody's gonna, be sure to ask me why, and who the hell you are. And anything I tell them, gets me in the shit. I say you're a reporter for a magazine, they are gonna say: 'Which magazine?' And what do I tell them? Do I tell them '*Journeyer*'? It's a matter, public record, I am onna goddamned record when I first took office, saying it's obscene. Because I hadda, until Father Gomes kicked off. And they're gonna look that up and get this whole thing going about how when I want four terms, I'm talking to the dirty books, and what do I say to that? 'I changed my mind about split beavers'? 'Now I think they're cute'?" He smirked. "I don't think so," he said.

"Or," he said. "I can do the other thing, which is tell them you work for Baldwin and you're doing a story about the *Logan* case. That'd be bright, wouldn't it? They'd want to know what I'm telling you, I'm not telling them. And how *come* I'm not telling them. This here's a rough case I got on my hands here. That's why I get down on my hands and knees and drive up to see Baldwin. And you know which paper'd be hottest after my ass, they started thinking I was telling you things I'm not telling them?"

"The *Commoner*?" she said.

"That's right, little lady," Taves said, "*The Boston Commoner*. There's two things you should know about me and Mister Baldwin and his damned newspaper. I don't like either one of them, and both of them scare me. It doesn't matter what I do, good, bad or indifferent down here, right in this district; so long's the *Commoner* don't print it, I am in good shape. But the minute those bastards up in Waterford get ahold of something and it gets printed up in Boston, all of a sudden the locals're all up in arms and I got remote TV units from a hundred miles away, and CNN's calling me up, and God knows what's going on. The *Commoner* can drop it the next day, doesn't do a bit of good — for the next six weeks I'm gonna have reporters up the gump-stump that I never even heard of, bugging me with questions and making me and my supporters look like damned fools, coast to coast. And everyone who doesn't like me's telling *Time* and *Newsweek* what an alltime jerk I am."

"But you went to see Baldwin," she said.

"I certainly did," Taves said. "To see if maybe once in my life I can do something smart where that paper's concerned, and maybe save myself a lot of grief. I like to think sometimes that since I'm getting older, maybe I'm getting smarter. And maybe I can do some things to people before they do things to me. But I dunno if I succeeded, see? It's just possible by seeing Baldwin, I made myself more trouble'n I had before I did."

"And that's why I'm in the tack room," she said, "Mister Swain's name on the door."

He nodded. "You got it, little lady," he said. "I'm covering my own ass. You turn out to be a wrong one, well, I won't have to explain. Nobody sees you coming in, and no one, going out. Except the ladies at the front, and they don't talk a lot."

"Do they work for you?" she said.

"Indirectly," Taves said. "Indirectly, yeah. Me and Ward Keane, Plymouth DA, me and Keane own this. And me and Keane and other guys, these are our horses." He indicated the pictures of the horses by glancing around the room. "Mostly standardbreds, but we're moving up. We got ourselves three thoroughbreds, and we're not finished yet.

"Me and Ward, some years ago," he said with satisfaction, "when it was still legal, we had ourselves a damned good practice, and we saw what was coming so we made ourselves some plans. Started buying buildings up, and this was one of them. And Mister Swain, there on the door, he is our horse guy, takes care of all of them that we're invested in. He's down in New Jersey now, gettin' Sharpshooter ready for the Saratoga Meeting. Those ladies work for Geoghegan Ramos, which two people pay us rent for the front part of the office, and me and Ward keep this place private, have our meetings here."

"I think I see," she said.

"Sure," Taves said, "of course you do. I need my privacy like all guys. Politicians, too." He nodded toward the recorder again. "Turn that damned thing on," he said amiably. "You may have all day on this, but I got things to do."

20

"This here," Taves said, reaching forward to pat the bulky envelope on the coffee table, "this is video tapes. Which I assume you got one of those machines that can play them and you can see for yourself what I'm up against."

"I've got one of the VHS boxes," she said. "I can borrow a Beta, if that's what they are."

"I dunno about that," Taves said impatiently. He tapped the envelope three times. "All I know is I got one of these from the station, WSET, that they had and they made me a copy that I used for the first trial and everything, which was the Brutus case that was the accident. And the other ones, which there are two of them, those're tapes that we made down the office with Logan about the case we got now. Okay?"

"Okay," she said.

"Now," he said. He stood up suddenly and whipped his blazer off. He laid it on the couch and hitched up his slacks. He looked down at the tapes and scowled. "The tape the accident," he said, "that is pretty brutal. It don't show the actual accident, what started the whole thing off, because the TV truck didn't get there, you know, right when it first happened. But it was pretty soon after that, and the whole thing wasn't over, you know?" He looked at her anxiously.

"Miss Gates," he said, "I don't know you, all right? So I got to make it clear here, that I don't mean no offense. I know you're a reporter and everything, and you're used to things. Seeing things, I mean. But I got to warn you, okay? The tape the accident is awful. I mean it. People on the jury for that trial, that saw it, they got sick, you know? We had one woman on the jury there that actually fainted. And there was one older guy that we're a little bit concerned about, when we showed it. Had a heart condition, and he hadda take his nitro, when he watched the tape. And the TV station, when they showed it, they had all sorts of complaints. This kid that Logan had working for him — this cameraman he had? He was good. And he was close. And when you watch this thing, you know, you can see the faces of the people in the cars. Not all of them — just some of them. The ones that're going to die, especially, and there's no way nobody can get them out."

"I understand," she said.

He looked at her skeptically. "If you say so," he said. "I'm just trying tell you, this tape is no fun. What you see is, well, the TV truck gets there after the first car, which is Brutus, hits the Logan Jeep. The Jeep is coming south on Twenty-four, see?" He began to use his hands to show the directions of the vehicles. "And when you come off Twenty-four south onto One-ninety-five east, what you do is you come up this hill and on your right at the top is a whole buncha trees. And behind the trees is One-ninety-five east, up higher'n Twenty-four. And you're coming into the passing lane, the left of Twenty-four and also the left of One-ninety-five, and you're coming in blind. And because you're coming up the hill, up the ramp, behind the trees, even a sober guy in the passing lane on One-ninety-five can't see you until all of a sudden he's right fuckin' on top of you, get it?"

She nodded. "Which of course this Brutus guy wasn't," Taves said. "Sober, I mean. And he was in the passing lane on One-ninety-five, and the Jeep comes up the ramp, and the Logans can't see him and he can't see them, and he clobbers them. He's driving this old blue Valiant four-door, which is the second car you see when the tape starts. Before Silva got the camera going, as near as we can put it together, Brutus in the Valiant hits the Logan Jeep hard on the right rear quarter and slams it into the guard-rail. Then the Valiant, which is lighter, sort of caroms off the Jeep and out of the left lane so it slews up the road a hundred yards or so and ends up across the two center lanes of One-ninety-five, crossways. And the left front end's all bent out of shape. The hood's sticking up in the air and things're hanging off it and it's a sitting duck in across the center lanes. And you got to understand here, that the picture's shaky, because Silva's swinging it back and forth between the cars. And he goes back to the Jeep, which after it banged into the guard rail bounced off of it so it is also sort of crosswise in the left lane of One-ninety-five, and stopped. And it's sitting there. And this green Monarch sedan comes barrel-assing up the ramp from Twenty-four and slams into the passenger side the Logan Jeep and bounces off it into the middle of One-ninety-five.

"This Jeep tips over on its left side," Taves said, "so now you are looking at the undercarriage the Jeep, and Silva swings the camera back to the Monarch now, and you can see the Valiant up beyond it, and this fourth car comes up the third lane of One-ninety-five, and the driver sees the Monarch broadside in front of him — there's a guy and a woman in the fourth and it's a Skylark, and he rolls the wheel left, which was a bad mistake, and of course he hits the Logan Jeep, which is on its side, and that starts the fire in the Jeep. And the fourth car ends up facing westbound at the top of the ramp next to the Jeep, which is burning now and is about to explode. And this pick-up truck with two guys in it comes up the ramp Twenty-four, swerves around the Jeep and the Skylark into the middle lane, hits the Monarch broadside and rolls it two and a half times right down the highway like a bowling bowl. And the Jeep explodes."

Taves took a deep breath. He tapped the envelope again. "It's all in here on tape, Miss Gates," he said, "and you can see the faces of the victims and it's not pretty at all."

"I understand." she said again.

He began to count on his fingers. "The Logan kid was dead at the scene," he said. "Joe's wife, Rosemary, should've been, but she lasted until around nine-thirty that night. The woman in the Monarch that got rolled died in the ambulance. The guy in the Skylark lost his right leg and arm. His wife was in traction three months, and she hadda have plastic surgery that's still going on, I guess. Not that they'll ever make her right. The guys in the pick-up were all right, except for cuts and bruises and the truck was all banged up."

"What about the guy in the Valiant," she said. "This Brutus, that started it all."

"Bloody nose," Taves said.

"That was all?" she said.

"He hit loose," Taves said. "He was all full of booze and he got bounced around some in the car, and apparently he banged his beak on the steering wheel or something. But otherwise he was all right." He snorted. "Cops get there, he's totally out of it, sitting there grinding the ignition, steam and smoke and everything shooting out the hood, the Jeep's exploded and on fire behind him and the Monarch's been rolled to where it's about fifteen feet from his car on its side, and you know what he says to the cops? 'Won't start,' he says, 'won't start. Must be something wrong.' So they get him out and take him down the station and he takes the Breathalyzer and does all them other things, including blood test, and registers point-twenty-one, blood alcohol.''

"I thought point-ten was drunk," she said.

"It is," Taves said. "It is. What this guy scored is not quite dead, but certainly no small amount, a guy as old as he is."

He sighed. "Now that happened," he said, "that happened around noon, I forget the exact time, at the junction there, which is a terrible piece of engineering and everybody for years, including Joe Logan and all the rest the press and the cops and me and everybody has been howling that somebody's got to do something about that fucking intersection because it doesn't matter which way you're coming from, from Twenty-four or One-ninety-five, when you get to it you can't see what's coming from the other side. And too many people're getting hurt there. And we hollered and we yelled about doing something there, because sooner or later there's gonna be a real horror show, with people getting killed and all, and nobody did. And as a result, there was a big horror show, just like we said there'd be.

"So," Taves said, "naturally we arrest this guy Brutus that started the whole thing, and he is shitfaced. And we look him up and he's got eight priors for drunken driving. He's hit things and left the scene, and he's hurt people just a little, and he's driven up on people's lawns and hit light poles and all that shit. Eight times this guy's been grabbed. And every time before this, when he finally kills some people, every time before this the judges keep letting him go and suspending his license, see? They don't do anything to him. The guy's a fucking alcoholic and he can't drive when he's stiff, and nobody does anything about it, that this guy understands. And as a matter of fact, his license was suspended six months and he turned it in to court in Attleboro about two months before he did the Logan thing, all right? And before that, he had six suspensions going back to Nineteen-seventy-four. None of which did any good. Because suspending this old bastard's license doesn't mean a thing to him. Not a goddamned thing. What's he care about a license? He's got a car? He drives the car. If he's got his license, fine, and if he doesn't, also fine. Get in the car and drive it: that is what he does.

"So now," Taves said, "we got to try this guy for motor vehicle manslaughter. And of course we also throw in driving to endanger, and operating under, and operating after revocation, and speeding and defective equipment and everything under the damned sun, but basically the biggest poke we can take at him is the manslaughter charge. The other stuff's just window-dressing. And I put my best guy on the case, my very best assistant, which was Manny Ross at the time, and I tell Manny, all right? 'Go for the downs on this son of a bitch, Manny. Pull out all the stops here. No mercy, no bargains, no deals, no nothing. Because what we got here is he killed the wife and kid of a prominent citizen, the community, and you nail this guy.' "

Gates permitted herself a small smile. "That matters, huh?" she said.

"Turn that thing off," Taves said, gesturing toward the recorder. She reached forward and shut off the machine. "I thought you were on the level," he said.

"I am," she said.

"Then why the hell'd you ask that question?" he said.

"Just verifying suspicions," she said, feeling very uncomfortable.

"Oh bullshit," he said. "that was a crack. You weren't born yesterday, little lady. You know better'n ask some dumb question like that."

"Yes," she said, "I do. You're right."

He shook his head. "Bush league," he said, "bush league. You gonna do that again?"

"No," she said, "I won't."

He nodded. "Awright," he said, "I'll take your word. Turn it back on." She reached forward and restarted the machine.

"Manny did a bang-up job," Taves said. "Of course if he'd've lost that case, I would've cut his balls off and he would've let me, but the jury was out maybe half an hour and nailed the old drunk on all charges.

"Which," Taves said, "put the ball in Judge Melanson's court. And he gives Brutus two years for killing Ricky Logan; one to ten indeterminate at Concord for killing Mrs. Logan; two years concurrent for killing the lady in the Monarch; two years concurrent for every other major charge; one year concurrent for each minor charge, and a five-hundred-dollar fine. Oh, and loss of license, of course. Permanent loss of license."

"Which meant Brutus served two years," she said.

"Twenty months, actually," Taves said. "One year and eight months." He sat down suddenly on the couch, letting his hands flop into his crotch. He stared at her. "I couldn't do anything about that, Miss Gates," he said. "You understand that I hope. There was not a goddamned thing that me or Manny Ross or anybody else in this whole wide world could do about what Judge Melanson did. I could've jumped over the bench and bit him on the neck, and it would not've mattered in the slightest. He was the Judge. I was the DA. It was the Judge's call."

"Did Joe Logan understand that?" she said.

"Oh," Taves said, "yes indeed. Understood it perfectly. Right down to the ground. Liking it was a different matter. Very different matter."

21

"I knew Joe, I was in Plymouth," Taves said, backing up to the couch and sitting down again. "I also knew friend Baldwin there, and Mel Shaw and Ward Keane, and a whole bunch of people that I've also known since then. Sometimes I get the feeling that by the time you're thirty-five, you've met all the people that you're ever going to meet. After that it's just keeping up with them and using what you know about them so that they can't blindside you, the ones that you don't like, and taking care of the ones that like you, just like they take care of you." He paused and pondered. "I dunno about that, though," he said. "Maybe that's not right.

"Anyway," he said, "we didn't think so at the time, but the whole bunch of us was wet behind the ears. Well, maybe Baldwin was just damp, because he had been around. But the rest of us were wet, and that included my friend Ward, just starting his first term. Ward's three years older'n I am, but he did three years inna service and I only did the one, so we're together in law school and got to know each other. And we get out and I go home and I hang out my shingle just about two blocks from here, and Ward sets up in Brockton, and we both do just the same. Lousy. Couple wise-ass punks, trying, muscle in on all them shrewd old bastards that've got the banks locked up, and they do the divorces of which there weren't so many then, and we are scrambling and starving, me down here and Ward up there. So one day me and Ward have lunch, and he tells me the DA of Plymouth County, in which Brockton is, he's getting ready to retire and he is going to run. And I say: 'Ward, you're gonna lose. You don't know anyone.' 'I don't know no Republicans,' Ward says. 'You got me there. And the Republicans are sleeping, 'cause they think this one's locked up. But you look at the newcomers, you take a look at them. All them people out of Boston, moving the South Shore, they're all Democrats by nature at the north end of the district, and that's where I make my move. And I want you to help me, all right? Just come up and help me out.'

"Now, I got nothing to lose," Taves said. "All that I am doing with my time is starving to death slowly, and I don't like that much. So I start running up and down Ward's district, making speeches, eating chowder, wearing out my car. And damned if old Ward doesn't win, just like he said he would. So Ward then says to me, he says: 'Awright, Billy, want a job?' And naturally, I did. So I close up my office and I wrap up all my business here, which takes a half an hour, forty minutes, the outside, and me and Ward set up in Plymouth, down the street the courthouse. And we did all right. He was the DA, of course, and I was first assistant, and that might've had something to do with all the trade we got, but basically we're making money, having a good time. In those days Plymouth wasn't hard, not a tough county. Hell, no county was tough then, compared to today. And we're doing all right.

"As a matter of fact," Taves said, "we're doing so all right that after about two years or so, we start to think about the next thing we can do to make things better. And what me and Ward decide is we will open up a branch down in my home town. And after a little while, comes the next election, I will run down here. And that will give us two counties, and maybe we get rich.

"Now right inna middle this," Taves said, "this kid Lavalle gets killed." He sighed. He let his shoulders slump and his hands droop between his thighs. "I assume you're gonna," he said, "that you're gonna talk to Logan before you get finished here."

"Gee," Gates said, "I think I have to. Logan is the story."

Taves nodded and looked mournful. "Naturally," he said. "Well, Joe is gonna tell you, and in no uncertain terms, that Ward and me palmed that one off, the Tim Lavalle murder. And I am gonna level with you, but I don't want it printed. Ward and I did palm it off. It didn't seem important.

"The fact the matter was, Miss Gates, that Lavalle was a drifter, next thing to a derelict, all right? One of those people that today they are the homeless and everybody's always running around all over the place and saying we got to do things for them. And we don't. He'd just got out of Concord doing time for armed robbery. And that was not his first offense, although his priors were shit. He was twenty-two, maybe twenty-three, a shitbum out of Dorchester with a B and E background that tried to move up inna world and got grabbed with a gun on his first time out. So he does his time, and he gets out, big goddamned deal, right? Who cares about this punk?

"Well," Taves said, "Jay Quentin did. Jay was this fat guy that owned Quentin's Bar and Grille in Waterford in those days when it was a one-horse town and the center was on Union Street, just up from the river. Now you go to Waterford, and there's this goddamned Vegas strip, up and down Route Four, light industrial, a mall, strip of office buildings, couple auto dealerships, three or four big condo things, a whole bunch of stuff. But back then, Union Street was Waterford, and Jay was Union Street.

"Jay evidently had a brother, younger'n he was," Taves said, "I don't remember what the kid's name was, but he come to no good end. And Jay, when he starts making money, he makes up for that. What he does is take one kid that just got out of prison, teach him how to run a grille, give him a steady job. His theory being, naturally, that if his brother had a job, his brother would've lived. Jay is making up with these guys for the things his brother did, and the things Jay didn't do. Parole board loved Jay Quentin, boy. They thought he was great. Bring these scumbags in and hire them, get them off their hands. Parole board didn't give a shit, the problems these guys cause — take some outlaw out of Boston, still moldy from prison, slap him down in some small town and wait for new problems. Long as he was off their hands, that was all they cared. And I guess Tim Lavalle was probably fourth or fifth Jay had."

"What happened to the others?" Gates said.

"I dunno," Taves said. "What makes you ask that?"

"Well, all the problems that you mentioned," she said innocently. "I was curious."

He chuckled. "Miss Gates," he said, "Lavalle got himself murdered. One murder is enough problems for any four or five guys to cause, if you are the DA. And that is what Lavalle did — got clobbered on the head.

"I remember," he said, "that year, that it was a hot September. Eighty, ninety, every day, really brutal heat. This was the year, if you recall, that Kennedy got shot. It was still hot in November, was how hot it was. And one day me and Ward are over having lunch across the street, and we get this call down in Plymouth, cops've found a corpse.

"Well," Taves said, "we didn't need that. We were making plans, and we had other things in mind. But naturally we sent the cops, State cops up, with the cameras and stuff, and naturally Ward sent me up, just to show the flag. Murders were uncommon then. They were real events. DA had to show, he is on the job. So I went there and I saw him, just off of Route Four. Lying face down in a clearing of some pine trees off a turn-out just above the South River. And the medical examiner later says he's been there about four days. Which I had no trouble believing — like I say, it was hot that fall, and this one stunk like hell. So we pose for pictures that your friend Mark Baldwin takes, and I tell everybody that the DA's office will be working closely with Chief Deese to solve this thing, and then they cart the stiff away and I go back to Plymouth.

"Now let's be reasonable, all right?" Taves said, "This kid lived in Ma Doherty's rooming house. Had no car. Had no friends. No one called him up on Ma's phone and he had no phone himself. We talked to his family, up in Dorchester, and all they wanted was for us to leave them alone and let them sink this disgrace in a deep hole in the ground. We checked out all his sidekicks from when he was in Concord. We checked out all his bad companions from his burglary days. We — I'm including Deese in this, Deese and his detective, who is Dan Munroe, now chief — ran down every lead we had and some we didn't have. And every time we came up short. They didn't go nowhere. Let's face it, Miss Gates, all right? If you want to kill somebody for the hell of it, in the first place pick a drifter, 'cause nobody misses them. Don't use a goddamned pistol or some weapon we can trace — use some kind, blunt instrument, we'll probably never find, and if we do find it we won't know that it was what you used. And if you have to have a motive, something you can think about, try to pick some reason that nobody thinks of much.

"Which in Nineteen-sixty-three," Taves said, "was a love fight between queers. Nobody thought of that back then. It wasn't on the screen. If a guy was killed like Lavalle'd been, with a blow from a blunt instrument on the front of the head, then we thought someone was robbing him. Or it was thieves' revenge. Or he's screwed somebody's wife. We checked those things out with Lavalle, and we come up zero. He didn't have no money, so robbery was out. He'd been living in the town for just over a year, and no one ever saw him sneaking out to see some broad. No one ever noticed him, which was another thing, but if they had've noticed him, it would've meant nothing. The chances are that if they saw him, he was with a man, and no one thought too much about that, down in Waterford at least, back in Nineteen-sixty-three.

"So," Taves said, "we didn't solve it. Nothing complicated. Very simple case, in fact, easy as apple pie. A bum and someone he knew went into the woods on a warm Sunday night in September. The bum turned around when they got to this clearing and the guy that was following him — almost hadda be a man, from the force and direction of the blow — gave him the biggest and the last shock of his life. Banged him right on the forehead with a piece of metal, and crushed his goddamned skull. We assumed of course it was a strong man, because like I say, we were not thinking passion. But of course now I see that it could've been a weak man, or a woman, that was really pissed or really scared."

Taves stood up suddenly and hitched his pants again. "What Logan's gonna tell you," he said, "is: I should've seen it then. He's gonna say, as these tapes show, I didn't do my job. I did not do my job and Ward Keane did not do his. And therefore we made murder worse, if that is possible. We added in corruption and we helped guys steal the town. And we let Tim Lavalle's killer get rich and still go free." He shook his head. He stared down at the floor. "He's going to say this also," Taves said, "when his case comes up for trial. It won't help me, it won't help Ward, and it will not help him. I used to think I knew Joe Logan, not good but good enough. Now I wonder whether I know anyone that much."

22

"The truth the matter is," Taves said, "when Joe Logan comes down here I don't recognize the guy. Now, I haven't looked this up, all right? But this has got to be, say, Nineteen-sixty-nine or seventy, when he shows up here. And by now I'm not only DA, I'm seeking my second term. I'm a big man in this burg, here and in Fall River. People listen, what I say. I have got some clout. So all I'm really thinking about's, you know, the election. And also whether my suit fits right and I didn't spill food on it — and all that kind of crap.

"As far as I'm concerned," Taves said, "this new little TV station's a pain in the ass. We have already got one, right? And I know those guys. Now we're gonna have another one, WSET. The hell we need another one for? That's like having two sets of bedbugs, one for home and one for when you're out onna road. The only thing this means to me is that the new boys onna block come in and complicate my life."

"I don't see how that follows," Gates said, having flipped the tape. "What difference does it make to you, if something like that happens?"

"You've never been in politics," Taves said. "I can sure see that. The first thing you got to know in politics today, and believe me, I have talked with guys were running on the national level, right? The first thing you have got to know, in politics these days, is how the goddamned media works. Because otherwise, you die. And one the things I know, even 'way back then, is that those guys compete like we do, just exactly like we do. If one outfit likes a guy, paper, radio or pictures, then some outfit that's competing with them doesn't like that guy. You can gimme all the bullshit that you own and then give me some more, and when you get through giving it, I won't've changed my mind. Most times there's only one story, and that is not enough. So if there's two outfits working it, one will say you're great, and the other one'll get all over you like a rash or something. And that will make two stories, so the both of them have fun.

"Now," he said, "naturally these guys come in, Bill Glass and Jack Mahler. Who turn out to be nice guys too, but I don't know that then. And they address the Rotary, and all them other things. And what they're gonna do for us, they're gonna make their station into one topflight newsroom, all the latest stuff, all the smartest people, and all that hoo-de-doo. It makes my blood run cold. And pretty soon the big day comes, they open up their shop. And everybody shows up because they're afraid not to, and one the people we meet there is their new news director.

"I didn't recognize Joe Logan," Taves said sheepishly. "I didn't see him all that much, when I was down in Plymouth, and Joe back when I knew him first was ordinary goods. Had the lousy haircut so it stuck out over his ears. Dressed like a bum. Face was thinner'n a cat's, had some pimples, too. And this new guy I'm looking at, he doesn't look like that. I'm not gonna sit and tell you, he's a movie star. But this new news director was by then a full-grown man. And I get introduced to him, and I say: 'Pleased to meet you,' and Logan, confident as hell, says: 'Oh come off it, Bill. You know me from Waterford.' As of course I did. And as, of course, I didn't.

"Well," Taves said, "I cover myself best I can, and of course I say: 'Of course.' And all the time I'm wondering: 'Did I piss this guy off, back then?' 'Is there some way, if I did, I can fix things up?' 'Cause I do not want this guy doing numbers on my office every night at six o'clock with an election coming up. I'm going to treat him with kid gloves. I'm going to be careful."

"Did he mention the Lavalle killing to you then?" she said.

"Not a peep," Taves said. "Not once did he bring it up. Not until this year. We get together and sit down, catch up on where we been. I've been running for election, then running the office. He left Waterford for Worcester — went to the AP. Made himself a big name there, big enough, at least. Comes to the attention of these two guys, Glass and Mahler, and they offer him this job. Takes it, reasonably enough, thinking of his family as well thinking for himself. And here he is in New Bedford, thirty-one or so, running his own operation, making dough at it." Taves paused and looked at Gates. "I know my own weaknesses, and that is one of them. Guy that comes up off the floor, now he's doing all right and he treats me equally? Got to like a guy like that. Got to like him lots.

"He did a great job here," Taves said, "and that's not just me talking. I never saw enough of him in Waterford to know if that was where he picked it up, or if he got it somewhere else. But by the time he got here, boy, he had the drill down pat. He was also a pretty fair pol in his own right. Had more moves'n Allied Vans. I don't mean he was running for anything, least I knew about. But he was visible, you know? And not just on the news. The people saw him on the box, well, all they had to do was ask him and he came to their church breakfasts, made himself a little speech about this great community, this wonderful vacation region, all that good old stuff. Visited the schools, you know? Spoke the Holy Names. Kiwanis in Rehoboth wanted someone next Wednesday? Joe Logan would be there, and he'd make a big hit, too. Every night at six, he's on. Every night, eleven. I'll tell you something, and I mean it: I was glad he didn't run. That glib bastard'd been a lawyer, with his recognition, I would've been a sitting duck. He was too much for me.

"And then Tom Brutus hits his car," Taves said grimly, "and that ended that." He paused and shook his head. "I have seen a lot of people get destroyed by tragedy. I never saw one get slugged quite as hard as Logan did."

"What'd he do?" Gates said.

Taves frowned. "At the beginning, not much. Not much that you could see," he said. "Seemed to be taking it all right, if you looked at him. Easy thing to do now of course is look back and say it was shock. Which it could've been. I'm not denying that. But maybe it wasn't shock. Maybe it was booze. Maybe he was already doing it, and, well, that stuff takes some time. What he was doing was drinking, is what I mean to say. What I'm trying to say is that I don't know when he started to do it. Whether it was before Brutus got sentenced and he was just mourning his wife and kid, or after Brutus got sentenced and he was drinking mad," Taves shrugged, "I got no way of knowing. either. Joe was in good shape, before the accident. He could've abused himself for quite a while before the trial was over and nobody would've known it. But I don't think he did."

Taves sighed. "Not that it really matters. Point is that Brutus got the two years less time served awaiting trial, which was far as Joe was concerned meant Brutus got twenty months for killing Rosemary and Rick. And he didn't think it was enough. Which it wasn't, but there wasn't anything I could do about it. And I guess Joe realized that, you know, that it was hopeless. So gradually you begin to see this guy is going downhill.

"First," Taves said, "he's got these bags under his eyes when you're watching the news. His color's good enough at first — it was summer when things went to hell, and he was out in the sun, I suppose, sitting in his backyard, maybe in his boat. But then around Thanksgiving, you know, the tan sort of fades away, and he's got rum blossoms. Which I guess somebody told him about, so he starts using all this make-up. And by the end of the next winter, he looked like a fuckin' corpse, on the camera. But everybody's still pulling for him, you know how it is, and the cops see him driving in the Porsche when he shouldnt've been doing it, well, they gave him a few breaks and we all looked the other way. Ellie down the Captain's Table, she's the hostess there? She was like his mother and like everybody else in all the other bars in town, and all the liquor stores and packies, far as that's concerned. When Joe came in to any place, whoever happened to be running it would try to get him out. And of course in the restaurants, and so forth, when he started getting stiff, most the time they'd try to get him to at least take a cab. And most the time, of course, he'd pay no attention and he would drive himself home.

"And at the TV station," Taves said, "they were patient too. Everybody was. But I guess it was about a year after the accident, you know, they hadda go to him and say: 'Hey, Joe, all right? You need a rest. You got to take things easy. Whyncha leave the kids eleven? You can just do six.' See, they're hoping they can get him out the place, and maybe he'll go home. Start sleeping some instead of staying out till midnight boozing.

"Well," Taves said, "Like they all do, he kicked like a steer. Nothing wrong with him at all. He's as fine as he can be. No need to be doing this. Work is all he's got. But they don't listen to him, and he stops doing the eleven, and he don't get no better — he gets worse'n he was before. Now when he's through at seven, he can go out and get it in pails. Doesn't have to worry about slurring words on camera, or falling off the chair, or collapsing on the weatherman or anything like that. And we go into the second fall of him being alone, and things're getting worse and worse. Now he's not pacing himself during the day like he did before, so that even though you can tell he's had something to drink before he came on, he's still perfectly all right. Now there're nights when he screws up the stories, introduces the sports when he means the weather, shows you pictures of a fishing boat and reads a story about a bank. So they go to him again, Bill and Jack do, and they say: 'Joe, all right? You need a vacation. You got to take some rest. Now here's a nice cruise that we've got planned for you.' And they give him tickets to the *QE-Two* or something, and tell him he's taking some time off and he rips them up on the floor and says his friends're all trying to kill him, and why won't they leave him alone.

"So," Taves said sadly, "in January of this year, they took him off the air and told him he could not go back until he got shaped up. He could still do the work behind the scenes and everything, or pretend he was doing it, at least, while the other folks covered for him, but until he got straightened out, no more on-air stuff. And he got even worse. So, around the beginning of March they put him on paid leave and said he hadda see a doctor. And he didn't do it. And about a month or six weeks later, he's coming home one night dead drunk, and he misses his driveway and puts that little Porsche right into the boulders, the end of his street, where the harbor is.

"He was all banged up," Taves said. "He was in intensive care for two or three weeks, and then when he got out of that they shipped him off to Finisterre. You know where that is?"

"No," she said.

"It's a drying-out place in Rhode Island," Taves said. "Over in Barrington. Very fancy joint. Alla best drunks go there when their livers turn to concrete but their wallets are still thick. Glass and Mahler put him in there. Perfect place for him, they said, fix him up real fast. And they also got physical therapy and other stuff he needed — he's got two or three pins in him in various places, I guess, from the accident. But mostly what they do at Finnisterre, where they made their reputation, they have got their own variety of counseling there which they claim can reach any drunk that God ever put on earth. Something like a ninety-percent cure rate, I think is what they claim, and this is *permanent* cures I'm talking about, not just guys that dried out. And that's why Joe went there. Not that he was in any condition to decide for himself when he went there, of course, but that's another thing."

"Is there anything to it, the cure rate?" she said. "That does seem awfully high."

"Search me," Taves said. "All I know's what I hear. Doesn't matter anyway, not where he's concerned. Doctor over there, guy that runs the place, he told me Joe Logan was the most difficult patient he's ever seen, bar none. What was it he called him? 'The most resistant subject I've encountered yet.' And this is a guy that's had rock stars and judges and God knows what kind of folks in his pokey, coming down off of stuff guys fly into cornfields in light planes in the middle of the night."

"Did he say what the problem was?" Gates said.

"Doctor Gibbs?" Taves said. "No, he didn't. Not to me, at least. Of course I didn't ask him. He might've if I had. The only thing that interested me was whether Logan was okay in his gourd when he left the place first week in May. Right from wrong, up from down, in from out — does he think he's Napoleon sometimes, or has he got all his marbles. And as far as the doctor could tell, goddamnit, he was perfectly all right. 'Stubborn as hell, and very depressed, but perfectly, legally sane.'

"You can see where that left me," Taves said morosely. "The guy is legally sane. Or was legally sane, so far as Gibbs knows, five weeks before he killed Thomas Brutus. Pretty unlikely he went soft in that amount of time, once they let him out. Here I am for once, *trying* to find some cheap hook to hang a quick plea on and blow out a bastardly case, and I can't even do it with a good old marble counter. Jesus, what a mess."

"Temporary insanity?" she said.

"I thought of that," Taves said. "I sat down with my present first assistant, Dave Viola, and we talked about it, and it just won't fly. Now, keeping in mind most the work we generally do on the defense side is sitting down and trying to figure out how the other guys're gonna try and bamboozle us, we're maybe not too good at this. But just looking at it, you know, the temporary insanity thing, it just won't fly at all. Either one of us could knock that down in a minute. You look at Logan's record in the hospital, for Christ sake, and it's loaded with premeditation from the first day they took notes. The son of a bitch was thinking about killing Thomas Brutus. Maybe hadn't decided, but he's thinking about it. Now if the doctor says he was sane when he was talking like that, how the hell'm I gonna stand up on my hind legs and say that when he did it in June, he was suddenly insane? I'd get laughed out of court."

"Did he actually say that?" she said. "Did he use those words? Did he say that as soon as he got out, 'I am going to kill Thomas Brutus'?"

The DA shook his head. "No," he said, "not in those precise words. That got written down, at least. But if you read what he said carefully, it was pretty clear — hell, it was unmistakable — that the way Joe Logan looked at it, a bunch of people that he hadn't asked had meddled in his life and stopped him from killing himself, and therefore he was going to pay them back by killing Brutus. And pay Brutus back as well. And that is what he did."

"Let me ask you something," Gates said, "How does he connect killing Brutus with the Lavalle murder? The two things seem so different. So far apart, you know?"

The DA nodded solemnly. "To you, they do," he said, "and also to me. But he does it very simply. Gives him no trouble at all. He says this old faggot Shaw got away with murder because the law didn't work, and Thomas Brutus would've too, for the same basic reason. Nobody cared enough. In other words, he saw society ignore the death of Tim Lavalle, and then he saw society pretty much ignore the deaths of Rosemary Logan and Rick, and he recognized what was going on for what it was and he did something about it. Basically what he comes down to is that if somebody hurts you, the people who love you are the only ones who will take care of you. And that includes revenge."

23

At 6:15 in the soft humid evening the only people in the stands below the luxury boxes at Fenway Park were stray ushers and security guards sitting in the field boxes behind the dugouts with their feet up on the rails, or leaning on them on their forearms, watching batting practice. The Royals had finished taking BP and had left the field. The Red Sox in team pants and sweatshirts with the sleeves ripped off were taking turns in the cage, slapping hard grounders back at the protective screen in front of the non-roster pitcher in full uniform and complaining he was trying to throw curves. In the outfield, four pitchers jogged along the warning track, starting from the field access gate near the right field foul pole and trotting through the remaining direct sunlight in deep right field into the shadows that began in center at the end of the bullpens and deepened progressively into the left field corner. One of the Sox who played shortstop did birdcalls skillfully as he worked taking grounders from the dirt, and the sound of his whistling carried in the park so that the fitfully-wheeling small flock of pigeons in the rafters of the stands seemed to have better songs than their own.

Mark Baldwin had left his blazer on the couch in the glassed-in parlor of the rooftop luxury box behind him and gone out and down into the seats at the front, overlooking third base. He chose the one nearest the aisle and slid into it so that he sat on the base of his spine with his black loafers cocked on the rail in front. He had a plastic cup logoed "Red Sox" containing Budweiser in his hand, and from time to time he sipped at it reflectively. In the cage down on the field one of the players connected cleanly with a fat pitch and sent it arching into the net above the wall in left field. He stepped out of the cage, spraddled his legs before his teammates, and used his right hand to demonstrate his view that this act took balls. His teammates jeered at him and made sounds of flatulence, and he went back into the cage, swaggering. Baldwin's expression did not change.

Richard Pond in a khaki suit, blue shirt and maroon challis tie emerged from the suite and came down into the seats. He carried a bloody mary. He stood next to Baldwin for the moment and then cleared his throat. "Pay no attention, Mark," he said, "he's just showing off."

Baldwin looked up at Pond. "Beg pardon, Richard?" he said.

Pond used his head to indicate the batting cage down on the field. "That young show-off," he said, exaggerating petulance. "They always promise so much more than they can possibly deliver."

Baldwin laughed. He took his feet down from the rail and made room for Pond to enter the row. "Always in there scouting, Richard," he said. "Got to hand it to you."

"No one has to hand it to me, Mark," Pond said, entering and sitting down. "I have no trouble whatsoever getting everything I want."

"That's the only way to be," Baldwin said.

"You ought to know," Pond said.

"That's certainly true," Baldwin said. "Everybody should."

Pond sighed. "Oh goodness," he said, "now I hope I haven't ruined everything, and such a lovely evening."

"Well," Baldwin said, "you haven't for me, certainly. I can't speak for anyone else."

"That's true, isn't it," Pond said. "You never did like baseball. That's the strangest thing, the kind of stud you are. I would think you'd love the sport, absolutely love it, and invite all your coarse friends and fellow womanizers out to every game."

Baldwin did not respond. He sipped reflectively on his beer. The Red Sox finished batting practice and straggled back into the clubhouse as the field attendants lowered the wheels of the batting cage and began to roll it away. Another crew of groundskeepers carried a large rolled mat onto the field from the access gate near the right field foul pole. They took it to the first base line, unrolled it, and began to drag it over the dirt. Another groundskeeper came out and connected a hose to an underground silcock. He sprayed the infield dirt behind the men with the mat. In the outfield the pitchers began a last lap out of the deep shade in the left field corner, heading for the right field line.

"Now you're angry," Pond said accusingly.

Baldwin sighed. "Not angry as much as puzzled," he said.

"Puzzled," Pond said.

"I don't know what I'm doing here," Baldwin said. "What's this urgency of yours?"

Pond sighed again. "Jason is lamentably late," he said. "He told me he would be here from the hospital at six, and here it is almost seven and he isn't here. It's inexcusable, Mark, and you're quite right to be annoyed. I will speak to him."

"Jason would be Jason Francis," Baldwin said.

"Yes," Pond said, "correct."

"And the hospital," Baldwin said, "would be the Teal Retreat where Mrs. Francis is recuperating from her recent episode."

"That's also correct," Pond said.

Baldwin took his feet down off the rail and planted them on the floor. He set his beer down on the floor next to his right foot. He hunched his shoulders over and rested his elbows on the arms of his chair, loosely clasping his hands in front of him. "Richard," he said, looking down, "every time I see you, after a long silence, I am again reminded that you do have a deplorable tendency toward mendacity."

"Mark," Pond said, "you must listen to me."

"In a minute," Baldwin said. "When you called me up today, you told me you had just acquired an important new client, one that could mean a lot of money, to you and your firm. Stupidly, I failed to ask you at the time for the name of this new client. You asked me, as a personal favor, to come to the ballpark tonight and have a meeting with you. You said it would carry a lot of weight with your new client.

"I came here on that understanding," Baldwin said.

"If you will listen to me," Pond said, "I can . . . . "

"I will listen to you when I've finished talking," Baldwin said. "I will listen carefully, too, but not until that time. For reasons I am not prepared or willing to discuss with you now, I have no desire to have a conversation with Jason Francis, at this point in time. If you had told me you were asking me to come to the ballpark to watch a bunch of young gorillas scratch their nuts and yell, and then to talk to Jason Francis, I would have told you that I wouldn't do it." He looked up and stared at Pond. "Those are not precisely the words I would have used, Richard," he said, "but the meaning would've been clear."

"I understand," Pond said.

"You didn't tell me that was the purpose of this excursion,"

Baldwin said, leaning back in the chair. "I call that 'deceit'."

"I know," Pond said, looking contrite.

"Sheepishness won't do it," Baldwin said, "meaning no offense. You'll have to come up with something better. Otherwise, I leave."

Pond worked himself around in the seat so that he could lean on the armrest with his right elbow and face Baldwin up close. He used his left forefinger to tick off points on the fingers of his upraised right hand. "Jason's hospital visit," he said, tapping his right forefinger, "is coincidentally the cause of this delay. Coincidence, that's all. He went to Everett to the hospital tonight because the doctor in charge of his wife's therapy asked him to confer. That's the only reason. Apparently this analyst, or whatever he is, needs some further information from Jason about whether Sylvia may have had physical problems that contributed to her reaction to the drugs she took, and Sylvia's not talking. That's the only reason Jason went there. He is not there to acquire ammunition to shoot at you."

Pond tapped his right middle finger. "Jason has no interest in discussing your affair with his wife," Pond said. "He will if you bring it up, and he will be civilized about it. But that is not why he wanted this meeting. Therefore it is not why I wanted this meeting. I did not lie to you."

Pond tapped his right ring finger. "Jason's company has substantial investments in Waterford. Owns a good part of the town, if capital investment is the index of ownership, as I for one think it is."

Pond tapped his right little finger. "Day before yesterday, a reporter showed up at the police station in Waterford and started sweet-talking the police chief into showing her around. That was apparently quite easy for her to do. This police chief's wife left him some time ago, from what I understand, and he's a sucker for women. She's apparently still there, and as you might expect in a small town that doesn't have much going on, there's talk around that he's sleeping with her. Whether that's true, I don't know. What I do know is that he took her on a airplane ride, showed her how the town has grown. He told her all kinds of things about its history. He knows a lot of town history. He's a history buff. His name is Dan Munroe, I'm told, and he says he knows you." He paused. "If my information is correct," Pond said, "Munroe whether rightly or wrongly also believes that some of what he knows about you isn't flattering. Can you think what that might be?"

"Not offhand," Baldwin said.

Pond nodded. "Well, whatever," he said. He tapped his right thumb. "Jason thinks, and so do I, that it is not a good idea from his point of view, and that of his investors, who are now my clients too, for this reporter to be snooping into Waterford affairs. Regardless of what she may have picked up incidentally about yours. Or starting one of her own, as far as that goes — goodness, these bloody women. So promiscuous. But that doesn't matter, I suppose. The point is that I don't know what went on, many years ago, and Jason doesn't know what went on, many years ago. But neither of us thinks that finding out might be great fun. It could be expensive. It could ruin everything."

Pond dropped his right hand and his left hand over it. "That reporter works for you, Mark. If it doesn't concern you that she's prying into your personal past along with whatever else you hired her to do, it certainly doesn't concern me. The same applies to this little arrangement that you have with Jason's wife. If you want to discuss that matter with Jason, and he wants to discuss it with you, I'll leave you two to that. It is none of my concern. But first, if we can, let's we talk about real money."

24

Shortly after seven, two Fenway Park stewards in white jackets delivered lobster salad and chilled Pouilly Fumé to the Appalachian Investors' luxury box, and set the circular white table in the parlor for dinner for three. Jason Francis, looking harassed and sweaty in a dark blue lightweight suit and blue and red striped tie, arrived before the stewards had finished. He did not pause at the bar but went out to the rooftop seats at once and apologized to Baldwin. "It's so frustrating, dealing with those guys," he said. "The first time that you meet them, they come on all confident and sure of themselves. Oh, they don't say they're going to cure anyone, but they give you the impression that the situation's well in hand. All you have to do is cooperate with them, and pay them a bundle, of course, and if you're patient and you don't make waves, in a while you will see progress.

"And you don't," he said. "You go to the meetings and you have the consultations, and the bills keep coming in while the checks keep going out, and they keep on patting you on the back and telling you everything will be all right, stiff upper lip and all that stuff. And nothing ever happens."

"Jason," Pond said warningly, "why don't you have a drink. Take your jacket off. Relax. Mark and I have plenty of time. Let yourself unwind."

Baldwin glanced at Pond. He looked back up at Francis. "Jason," he said, "I don't mind if you don't. It's perfectly all right. I've been through with other people exactly what you're going through now. If you want to talk about it, I won't be offended."

Francis looked down at him without expression. He exhaled. He nodded. "I'll take both pieces of advice," he said, pulling off his jacket and loosening his tie. He slung the jacket over his shoulder. "Let's go in and eat, before everything gets warm."

They sat at the white table with the sliding glass doors to the rooftop seats closed as about twenty-three thousand people assembled below them in the evening to watch the baseball game. The ballpark lights came on, pale in the early evening. The air conditioning in the parlor hissed lightly in the vents. Somewhere in what seemed like the middle distance, Sherm Feller began to read the starting lineups for the game. Over the center field bleachers the giant television screen delivered the same information against the rose sky as it gradually deepened to dark blue. Feller asked everyone to stand and join in singing the national anthem, as played by John Kiley at the organ.

"The woman will not talk," Francis said, cracking a lobster claw with the shellfish pliers. A small amount of white gelatinous material and cold water ran out of the broken shell. He extracted the meat and sprayed it with lemon juice. He put it in his mouth. He chewed and swallowed hastily, and drank some white wine. His face contorted and he tensed the muscles in his throat. Pond stood up fast, knocking his chair backward. Francis shook his head, his eyes watering, and held up his right hand. He swallowed hard. He exhaled. He nodded. He motioned Pond to sit down. "It wasn't caught," he said in a husky voice. "Just stuck." He drank some more wine. Pond pulled his chair back and sat down again, redraping his napkin over his lap. Francis smiled at him. "You react fast, Richard," he said.

"Huh," Pond said, selecting a piece of lobster, "ever since Paul Porter celebrated his faultless physical with a lobster at The Palm in Washington and choked to death, people in my line of work have been ever vigilant."

Francis grinned. "And much more so, no doubt," he said, "when it's not another lawyer, but a client in distress."

"Well," Pond said, "I wouldn't go that far. It would depend on the client. Some of mine I'd cheerfully watch strangle, without lifting a hand."

"You're a hard man, Richard," Francis said. "I'm glad you're not her doctor."

"I take it they're baffled," Baldwin said. He speared lobster and dipped it in mustard mayonnaise.

"That's my impression,' Francis said, "that's not what they say to me, that they don't know what to do. But from what they do say to me, I don't see how a reasonable person could form a different impression. See, their whole theory is interactive. The doctors make themselves available. The patient talks. The doctors examine what the patient says, and try to persuade the patient to look at things differently from the way she did in the past. I guess it works all right when they have a suggestible patient, someone who's troubled by the conclusions that she reaches and wants to reach different ones. But Sylvia apparently doesn't. She told them when she was admitted out of Newton-Wellesley Hospital what she'd done and why she'd done it. It wasn't particularly complicated. It wasn't particularly cheery, either, the story that she told, but it wasn't complicated. She'd taken an inventory of her life, and where it was heading, and the results depressed her. She concluded that she didn't wish to live it any more. Therefore she took all the pills she could find in the cabinet."

"Tell Mark what she said," Pond said, cracking a lobster claw.

Francis glanced at Pond and then at Baldwin. "I don't know," he said.

"Oh, go ahead, Jason," Pond said impatiently. "You know you're going to in the end anyway. Why waste all this time being coy?"

"It's all right," Baldwin said, glancing at Pond with distaste. "I said I don't mind and I don't."

"This isn't why I wanted you to come here tonight, Mark," Francis said.

"I said it doesn't matter," Baldwin said. "Go ahead and tell it. We're not going to get any rest from Richard until you do, you know."

Pond kept his eyes on his lobster, picking small bits of meat out of the cracked shell and putting them delicately in his mouth. Francis studied him for a minute, frowning. "She said," he said, looking back at Baldwin, "she said when she came out of the stomach pump and all the other business and they'd gotten her revived, that she's married to a faggot and her lover doesn't love her and she doesn't think they'll change, so she doesn't want to live. That's the substance of it. They told her that she could have a full life even if all that was so, and she said that might be right, but not one that she wanted."

"So basically then," Baldwin said, "the problem they've got with her now is that they can't find a way to make her agree with them, so they're grasping at straws, calling you."

"That's what it amounts to," Francis said. "They want me to tell them that she's always had a dependency on drugs and alcohol, and that accounts for this chronic depression they see. But I don't think it does. I never saw anything like that in Sylvia, and we've been married a long time, over fifteen years. We were together before that, when I was struggling. I don't think she's depressed because she took drugs. I think she took drugs because she was depressed. I think when she says she was depressed because of me, and depressed because of you, she's telling the truth accurately. I can't argue with her position that I'm not likely to change. I didn't know if it would matter much to her if I did. And I certainly can't argue to her that you're going to change. How the heck would I know?"

"Well, I'm not," Baldwin said. He drank some wine.

"Of course not," Francis said. "And if either of us tried it, tried to argue with her, she would laugh right in our faces." He picked up his wine goblet in both hands. From outside the sound of the crowd cheering was softly audible. "This latest shoplifting disaster," he said, "the one in Bloomingdale's, fighting with the security people and generally making a scene — if that doesn't suggest her state of mind to you, there's something wrong with you. Thirty dollars' worth of Givenchy perfume? She doesn't even like Givenchy perfume. The only fragrance she's ever worn since I've known her is Guerlain."

"Let me ask you something," Baldwin said. "This shoplifting business — how long has it been going on?"

Francis looked uncomfortable. "Oh, not that long, actually," he said. He toyed with the silverware.

"I'm going to press you, Jason," Baldwin said. "That little adventure down by Quincy Market came as a distinct shock to me. It didn't make any sense at all, and the explanation for it, well, I thought it was farfetched, but with a little counseling, some tender loving care, it might just be an aberration. Something she just did, on impulse. But then she came back to work, and everything seemed reasonably all right, I thought, and the next thing I know, I get back from Montreal, and she's tried to kill herself after first getting herself arrested at Bloomingdale's. And I thought: 'Well, this is obviously a helluva lot more complicated than I thought it was. But what the hell is it?' And I still don't know."

Francis sighed. He swirled the wine. His face showed more fatigue. Outside the sliding doors the crowd erupted again. "Little less than five years ago, Mark," he said, "as Richard here can tell you, I had one of those personal crises that are so popular with men in their mid to late thirties. And I came to grips with a number of

facts about myself, some of which kind of frightened me. Scared the
hell out of me. And the stress was too much for me, and I collapsed.

"Now," Francis said, "I'm not particularly proud of that, but it
happened and I have to deal with it. And one of the things I did to
deal with it was tell Sylvia that in one respect at least our marriage
was over. You probably knew this."

"Jason," Baldwin said, "until six weeks ago, I did not know what
was going on in your marriage. Nor did I want to. It was none of my
business. Obviously something was wrong, but what it was was none
of my business. As I saw it at least. Then, after the first incident, she
told me. And I was stunned. But that was my first information."

"Mark," Pond said, leaning back and gazing at them, "that was
not the first incident."

"It wasn't?' Baldwin said.

Francis shook his head. "Uh uh," he said. "I'm not really sure
what the first incident was, since Sylvia's become a rather capable
liar in the past few years. To protect me, of course, but not only for
that. It's very hard now when she says something to be confident
she's telling the truth. Impossible, in fact. So all I can tell you for
certain is that the first theft I know about was after she started
working for you. She got caught lifting one of those Colibri butane
lighters that look like Dunhills but cost nine bucks in the newsstand
in your building. And she doesn't even smoke."

"You're kidding me," Baldwin said. "I heard nothing about that.
What the hell did she do with it?"

"She gave it away," Francis said, "That's what she told me, at
least — she gave it away. To someone she trusts."

"You heard nothing about it, Mark," Pond said, "because the
manager of the store is my friend. And once he found out who she
was, and where she was working, he called me up right off.
Fortunately, I happened to be in my office. And I told him not to
prosecute. I said Jason would make it good, knowing that he would,
and he did."

"This was about two months after she first went back to work,"
Francis said.

"Oh, for heaven's sake, Jason," Pond said, "let's stop beating
around the bush here. It was right after she started having her affair
with Mark, and we both know it. She started stealing from stores
when she started cheating on you."

Francis looked pained. "Mark," he said, "look. Sylvia cheating on me is an idea that exists only in Sylvia's head. Please don't get the idea that I've been questioning her, or bothering her, or anything like that. I know she has to have a life. If you want to know the truth, I was glad when she got involved with you. That wasn't my expectation when I more or less asked you to give her a job, but I have to admit, after I realized what had happened, I wasn't unhappy about it. I was delighted."

"Even knowing me," Baldwin said.

"Especially knowing you," Francis said. "Knowing your reputation as a ladies' man, I was selfishly delighted. Does that satisfy you? My board is very straitlaced. It's important to them, and therefore important to me, that my private life remain strictly private. No unseemly scandals. If she was involved with you, I thought, she would be contented and, well, tolerant. And that nothing would come out.

"When Richard called me about the lighter," he said, "just like you, when she stole the scarves, I thought it was an aberration. And I said well, of course I would pay for it. And made up my mind, when she got home that night, to give her what-for about the whole embarrassing business.

"But she didn't come home that night," Francis said. "In retrospect of course there was no reason why she should. I had told her the day before I was going to New York overnight and she had no way of knowing I'd canceled my trip when she got caught. Or even of knowing that I knew, that she had gotten caught. So I imagine what she did was spend the night at your place, as of course she has done since. And I woke up the next morning, and she wasn't there, and I began to see that perhaps this whole business was a little more complex than I had thought at first.

"So," he said, "I didn't say anything. I didn't even tell her that I hadn't gone to New York, that I had waited up for her, and that I knew she hadn't come home. Which was probably a mistake, from any point of view. What I did was face up to the fact that perhaps this strange new behavior of hers was connected in some way to my strange new behavior. And, believing that I was doing the right thing, and that she'd stick to one place for her commercial adventures, I made arrangements through Richard with his friend, Dexter, so that no complaints would be made when she stole from the newsstand. And that's being going on now for more than four years."

"I'm astonished," Baldwin said.

"Fifty bucks or so a month, Mark," Pond said. "Fifty bucks a month. That was how she got her thrills. Stealing stuff she didn't need and could easily afford, on her way to see you for still more illicit thrills."

"You're enjoying this, you bastard," Baldwin said to Pond. "You've enjoyed it all along."

Pond shrugged. "I don't enjoy seeing people hurt themselves or each other, Mark," he said. "If you think that, you're wrong. If you think I'm fascinated, when they do that kind of thing, well, you're right, of course." He leaned forward and patted Baldwin twice on the left wrist. "You've always fascinated me, Mark," he said. "Like the cobra does the mongoose, you have fascinated me." Outside the glass, the crowd cheered again in the brilliant darkness.

"I don't have to take this shit," Baldwin said, half-rising.

"Yes, you do, Mark," Pond said, his eyes glittering. "Oh, my, yes you do."

25

The Fenway Park stewards came in and cleared away the dinner dishes. They brought a tray of coffee and offered pastries from a tray. Each of the men at the table accepted coffee and declined dessert. The crowd booed outside the glass doors and began stamping feet. The stewards departed and the air conditioning hissed through the vents.

Francis coughed twice. He stirred cream and one Sweet'n Low into his coffee. He slumped down far in his chair. "This was not what I meant to happen," he said.

Pond snickered. "What you mean to happen, Jason," he said, "and what generally happens, seldom bear much resemblance to each other."

Francis looked at Baldwin. He raised his eyebrows. "Can you believe," he said, "I actually hired this guy as my lawyer yesterday? Knowing him all these years? Knowing what a diplomat he is? There any doubt in your mind I'm at the end of my rope?"

Baldwin considered his coffee. He stirred it. "No," he said.

"So what do I do now?" Francis said, looking at Baldwin.

"Well, Jason," Pond said, "for openers you could try telling him what you had me drag him here tonight to listen to you say. That would be a good beginning."

"See what I mean?" Francis said.

"Incredible," Baldwin said.

"Horsepucky," Pond said. They looked at him, startled. "It's a Wyoming term," Pond said. "A friend of mine used it the other night, and I asked him what it meant, and he told me. It means: 'Horseshit.' "

"Oh," Francis said.

"Why don't you try him out?" Baldwin said. He drank some coffee.

"What?" Francis said.

"Do what he says," Baldwin said. "What did you want to tell me?" The stamping in the grandstands outside stopped abruptly. There was an instant of silence. Then a great roar went up.

"Oh," Francis said, "yes. The reason that I wanted to see you was because you've got a reporter down in Waterford, it seems, and she's asking a lot of questions. And my people are getting nervous about it."

"So far, so good," Baldwin said.

"Well," Francis said, "have you?"

"Yes," Baldwin said.

"Go on, Jason," Pond said irritably. "You're not going to get anywhere sitting there staring at me."

"Yes," Francis said. "Well, I understand she's been going around all over town and asking all sorts of questions. And looking up records, too."

"Probably," Baldwin said.

Francis looked at Pond. Pond shrugged. "Well," Francis said, "there could be a problem there."

The crowd groaned outside the windows.

"How?" Baldwin said.

Francis swallowed. "We're a young company, comparatively speaking," he said. "Appalachian's only been in existence for a little over eleven years. It was one of the latecomers to the big tax-shelter boom that started in the early Seventies, basically formed by a bunch of extremely conservative, cautious people whose idea of a major gamble up until then was buying common stock in the telephone company instead of Treasury notes and Fannie Mae mortgages. The motive was self-defense, not innovation. You had the confiscatory upper tax brackets still in force then, and these people were getting murdered on ordinary income taxes. So their theory was to set up what amounted to a venture capital trust that would shift some of their earnings into long-term capital gains. These were not speculators, running around all over the country buying up oil leases and financing offshore drilling platforms. These were old-line families making discreet efforts to hedge their bets by buying into something that would show growth by appreciation. Along with returning a modest rate of interest."

"He's trying to say they were chicken," Pond said.

"That's about it," Francis said. "No glamour was involved and no wild risks were taken. When these people bought something, it was something they could see and touch and go and inspect if they felt like it. Tangible investments in existing properties.

"One of our acquisitions," Francis said, "was a very large parcel of undeveloped land assembled down in Waterford by some local people. People who could see what was happening to the South Shore and had the foresight to start buying up woodlots and fallow farms before word got around about the possibilities being opened up by the construction of Route Three. You were down there, Mark, so you know what I mean."

"Doctor Penn and Doctor Foster," Baldwin said. "Ah, yes, I remember them well. Two old dentists sitting in their tiny little offices over Quentin's Bar and Grille, no patients to speak of all day, looking out their windows at Route Four and watching the traffic build up."

"Uh huh," Francis said, "and taking turns serving on the Selectmen, term for term, with Richard Badger, the town counsel, and whoever else happened to be interested in the job in any given year."

"Which meant that they controlled the Zoning Board of Appeals when the Selectmen met as that," Pond said.

"I used to cover them," Baldwin said. "I remember it well. Seldom been so bored in my life."

"But of course there wasn't much going on then, when you were down there," Francis said, "It was Nineteen-sixty-nine, Nineteen-seventy, when they really got rolling. And all of a sudden this quiet little program that they'd had of buying up land came to fruition and woke everybody up to the fact that six or seven perfectly ordinary people in the town had turned themselves into potential millionaires, those that weren't already. They'd cornered all the real estate that didn't have buildings on it, as well as a fair amount that did, and what wasn't zoned for mixed commercial and multiple-unit residential use before they got it, well, it was soon afterwards.

"They set up Waterford Associates," Francis said, "and by using all sorts of complicated transactions back and forth, they amalgamated all their holdings into close to nine thousand acres on both sides of Route Four. Now they needed capital infusion, because of course they'd pretty much depleted all of their own personal assets acquiring the naked land. One of my customers, and a pretty good one, too, at Clark, Reach was Dorcas Munroe."

"The mother of the guy who's the chief now," Baldwin said.

"That's the one," Francis said. "And she was one shrewd trader. She came to me with Oscar Deese, who was then still the chief, and either Penn or Foster, I forget which one of them, and they asked me for advice on how to get capital participation. I knew Jim Avery had put together Appalachian with a group of his friends, and he'd told me they were on the lookout for investments, so I put them together. Everything looked pretty good, but Jim and his co-venturers had some reservations about their ability to oversee a project of that size, what with all their other interests, so they asked me to come aboard as a full-time director of Appalachian. Which, since I was clearing about twenty-three thousand a year in salary and commissions busting my hump for Clark, Reach while the big money went to the bosses, I was only too happy to do."

"So far, so good," Francis said. "My oversight consisted mostly of riding herd on architects and site planners, checking out subcontractors, showing up at hearings and town meetings in Waterford to reassure the townspeople that we were not a bunch of pirates out to loot their heritage. I suppose you could say I deliberately preserved my ignorance of any shenanigans that preceded our involvement in the project, but in my own defense I'd argue that what was done before I got there, after all, was done. I couldn't change it. If Penn and Foster and Deese and Badger, and gimlet-eyed Dorcas Munroe had pillaged the countryside like a bunch of Cossacks before Honest-as-the-day-is-long Jim Avery and his pals arrived, what was that to me?"

"So long as you and Jim and those folks profited from it too," Pond said dryly.

"That's right, Richard," Francis said. "Jim and the rest of my people were in it to make money. They never made any secret of that then, and they don't today. Furthermore, and this is a matter of public record, they did in fact make money. Just as they had hoped. Lots and lots of money. And so did Penn and so did Foster, Oscar Deese and Dorcas, and Dick Badger, too. And me.

"I was a smart kid myself, Mark," Francis said. "When Jim hired me away from Clark, Reach, he and the others gave me the choice of forty-five thousand a year in salary or thirty thousand plus twenty-five thou in participations in the corpus of the trust. Which, when you figure what inflation and increasing land values have done to their basic investment of a little over two million dollars in the past ten years or so, is a very tidy estate for a man of my former means."

"What do you figure, Jason?" Pond said. "Nine hundred percent, somewhere in that neighborhood?"

Francis snickered. "Couple weeks ago," he said, "fellow from Ronald and Devoe in Chicago dropped by to see me with a proposal for a big project they're planning in Indiana. Trying to set up a consortium. Looking for, oh, call it eighty million, ninety million, from maybe ten partners. And I gave him my standard routine, which is that Appalachian likes to stick close to home where we can watch what's going on, and finished it with my clincher, when I want to say: 'No,' without hurting any feelings, by saying that anyway we're all tied up in Waterford. Most of our money's there. And he came right back at me like a slingshot letting go and said he'd anticipated that argument, and Devoe would loan us forty million against our Waterford holdings anytime we asked. For the Indiana project, or anything else we might come up with on our own."

"Wow," Pond said.

"Well," Francis said, "that's 'way too high, of course, Devoe's notorious for overvaluing assets for purposes of making bigger loans to smaller groups than those groups can afford. And then gobbling up the smaller groups when they head for default. But it's not more than double what our interest is worth. It's probably only about thirty, thirty-five percent over actual market value.

"But," Francis said, "and here's the point, that still means we've got somewhere in the neighborhood of thirty, thirty-two million dollars exposed in Waterford. A scandal's not going to wipe that property off the face of the earth, of course, no matter how much trickery those upright townsfolk used on each other twenty years ago. But if some of the people that they took advantage of decide to get up a nasty class action lawsuit, our dentists and our former town counsel and the present chief's mummy and the former chief's widow are liable to get hit with a big verdict down the line. One which they will not be able to meet without selling off their interest in the property.

"I don't know whether Appalachian can raise enough cash to exercise the mutual buy-out provisions in our agreements with Waterford Associates, if that should come to pass," Francis said. "More to the point, I don't know if Appalachian would want to, or whether I would advise them to do it if they could but didn't want to.

If Appalachian has a weakness right now, and I'd argue that point very strenuously with you, it's that our portfolio's top-heavy with the Waterford holdings. So long as the other parties involved are the original packagers, I don't have a problem with it. Whatever their cleverness may have been in putting the tracts together, they've been straightforward and above-board in their dealings with us. We're comfortable with them.

"Take them out of the equation," he said, "substitute some cash-rich, leveraged raider like Devoe in their place, and I begin to have misgivings about our situation. I wouldn't want to wake up some morning and discover that Devoe has mortgaged Jim Avery's biggest asset, not to mention mine, to the Bank of Tokyo for a big participation in a North Slope drilling deal. And make no mistake about it: if Waterford Associates gets stripped in a legal fight, someone like Devoe will be their only recourse to raise the cash they'll need. Either they'll cut the deal themselves, or we'll have to cut it for them to protect our own assets.

"Now," Francis said, "I know the dentists are old now. Ye gods, they must be eighty. And I know old folks get nervous sometimes, when there isn't any need to be. But Arthur Penn told me yesterday that this lady reporter, what's her name, Constance Gates?"

"Connie Gates," Baldwin said, "That's the lady's name." Pond's face was expressionless.

"Constance Gates," Francis said, "well, he got that right, so he isn't senile yet. Arthur told me she's been spending too much time with Chief Munroe. 'And you know Dan Munroe,' Arthur says to me. 'Dan got his brains from his father, who did not know how to swim. Not from his mother. Dorcas wouldn't take a fishing boat out with a nor'easter coming, looking to drown herself. But Dan's father would, and did, and so would his damned kid. Here he is, his wife's left him, and this tart comes to town and starts to drain his brains. He's telling her everything he knows, damnit, and as long as she keeps jumping into bed with him, he'll continue to do so. Sooner or later she's going to get something out of him. He's too stupid to stop her. And when she does, there will be trouble. Mark my words: big, nasty trouble.' " He paused. He studied Baldwin's face. "He also said, and I don't know quite how to put this, but he said what he especially can't understand is why you, 'of all people' would want the past raked up in Waterford. I don't know what he meant."

Baldwin shrugged. "Neither do I," he said. "My guess is he thinks the paper won't look too good if she finds out and prints it that the bureau chief was in cahoots with the speculators, but it could be anything."

Francis nodded. "Just repeating what he told me," he said. "Like the rest of it."

"So," Baldwin said, "what is it you want me to do? Supervise the personal life of one of my reporters? I don't want to shock you gentlemen, but we don't have a morals clause in our staff contracts. I might like it better personally if she weren't contributing to the local gossip in the town she's studying, but so long as she does her job for me during working hours, what she does after sundown is her personal affair. Literally."

"Oh, Mark, for heaven's sake," Pond said, "will you please stop this *shit*? We didn't ask you here to hear a speech about the Bill of Rights. Jason wants you to take her off the assignment and stop her from printing anything that she's found out so far. What reason you give her's none of his concern. Don't give her any reason. Just tell her you changed your mind, and get her off the case."

Baldwin looked at Pond incredulously. "You must be joking, Richard," he said. "That's the worst thing I could possibly do. If there is a scandal down there, and she's onto it, and I yank her off the assignment, all it'll do is make her more determined to get to the bottom of it and then print it somewhere else. And if she doesn't suspect there's a scandal there, yet, my taking her off it will convince her there is. Let's face reality here, Richard. I'm sorry if there seems to be some potential danger to Appalachian in this story, if it comes out, which it never may. But the machinery's in motion. I can't stop it now."

Pond sighed. "Mark," he said, "you disappoint me. You really, truly do. You know just as well as I do that none of this stuff came out at the time it was going on because the *Commoner*'s man in Waterford made sure that it did not. Now the *Commoner*'s man in Waterford is a woman. Not working for the same legal entity; perhaps, some magazine instead. But still responsible to, and responsive to, the man who runs the operation. Which is you, Mark Baldwin. You know you can put the kibosh to this assignment if you wish. All you have to do is tell her she's paid off and off the case. That is all you have to do. She's working for you as a writer-for-hire.

You own what she's done so far, and you can suppress it if you wish."

Baldwin stared at him. "How do you know that?" he said.

Pond sighed again and shook his head. "Mark," he said, "all your life you've been underestimating me. You think since I'm a sissy I'm also a silly boy. Some day, maybe, you'll wake up. I hope I'm still alive."

26

Jay Quentin was in the middle of recalling his service in World War Two when Joe Castiglione's voice reported the end of the sixth inning from the GE clock radio lodged between the sash and sill of the kitchen window to the right just behind Quentin's porch chair. As he had done at the end of each of the previous innings, Quentin paused in mid-sentence and listened attentively. Inside the darkened white wooden frame house behind them, a woman coughed convulsively, phlegm nearly gagging her. Castiglione said that the Red Sox and the White Sox remained tied at 5, the White Sox getting their runs on a first inning grand slam and a third inning solo home run by former Red Sox catcher Carlton Fisk, the Red Sox scoring on two-run homers by Tony Armas and Rich Gedman, and a triple by Wade Boggs who had then scored on a passed ball. Gates started to speak, but Quentin held up his hand. Castiglione said the White Sox had left three runners on base "while the Red Sox have stranded seven." Quentin shook his head sorrowfully. "Wasting their chances," he said.

"You follow baseball, do you?" she said. On the two-lane blacktop road down the hill below the house a blue and silver Ford Bronco with a Waterford Police shield painted on the door headed slowly east toward Route Four two miles away.

"Chief Munroe again," Quentin said, nodding toward the Bronco. "That's twice he's been by here tonight, more'n he usually gets out here in a year."

"I said I'd meet him for a late dinner, after I finished here," she said. "I didn't say what time."

"Dan must've thought it'd be earlier," Quentin said. She could not tell in the deepening dusk whether he was smiling. "Dan's always been the nervous type. Never could sit down. Even when he was just a kid, always on the go. Thought when he got married, older, became the chief and all, that might slow him down. Let him take things easier. Didn't, though. He's probably gotten worse now, since his wife left and all." He paused. "I was lucky in that, at least. Never had that happen." He thought about that. "She's awful sick, of course," he said. "Has been, good many years. Don't suppose she could've gone anywhere, if she'd wanted to." He lapsed into reflective silence. She could hear him rocking in the green chair with the wicker seat and back.

"You were talking about baseball," she said. About two acres of the woods to the west of the house had been cut some years ago on both sides of the small stream that ran through the declivity. Underbrush about six feet high had grown in place of the trees and there were crickets in it chirping as the dark came on. He had told her he had had the trees cut about four years earlier, when "it seemed Cheryl at least, and probably Patty, 'd be coming back to live. But then neither one of them did, and I didn't see much sense, going on, you know. Assuming I could've got the money, which don't seem likely now."

"Baseball," he said quizzically. "I was? Talking baseball?"

"Well," she said, the tape recorder running on the small nail keg that stood between the two rockers, "no, actually, you weren't. I asked you if you followed it. Followed the teams, I mean."

"Oh," he said. He thought about it. "Not anymore," he said. "I, ah, oh, I guess I used to. Back in the old days. Sonny, one of my bartenders, and a few of the regulars that was red-hot fans, you know, every year they'd get up a charter bus and go up to see the games. And I liked to see that kind of thing going on. Good for business, you know? Course all it was was a couple afternoons or nights a year when they got drunk on a bus instead of in my place, and we always found we had to throw in a keg at cost, keg of beer, I mean. But lots of those guys, you know, my place was like home to them. Fishermen. Laborers, all kinds of people, really, and my place was where they came afternoons, they got through work. Stay until closing time. So you liked to see them getting together to do something in a group, you know? Few years, long time ago, we also had a bowling team, candlepins in Marshfield, Brant Rock. A Christmas party, of course, every year. You didn't, people didn't stay home as much those days, after they got through work. It wasn't, the television didn't have the hold it does today. Lots of them didn't even have one, where they lived. They wanted to see one, watch a ballgame or something, they had to come to us." He subsided. "It wasn't a bad thing, that way," he said. "Not a bad thing at all. People was more in touch with each other then, you know? And I don't think the way folks do it now, I don't think they drink any less, watching TV at home." He paused. "It's not like it's healthier."

"They ate there too, did they?" she said. "Their evening meals, I mean?"

"Oh, sure," he said. "You mean their suppers, yeah. They ate suppers with me. I was a pretty fair cook in my day, you know. Course, that's another thing that's changed. Back then, well, even back then, most of our trade was at lunch. And breakfast too, of course. We had quite a few at breakfast, sitting in the grille, having their coffee and eggs. Didn't have those drive-in places all over the place like you've got these days. Not for that at least. But back then, you know, most of our trade for supper'd be getting off work around four-thirty, quarter-five, and they'd probably've been on the job since six-thirty, seven that morning, down the landing and the fish plant and so forth. So when it comes five or so, maybe five-fifteen, those fellows were hungry. Ready to eat. I generally had them all fed, all the ones that came in, by six o'clock or so, and Marie'd have them all served and cleaned up after by six-thirty, the latest. Then they'd just go in the bar and we'd finish cleaning up, get ready for another day. Just like the one we'd had." He paused.

"Six days a week in the grille," he said, "seven a week in the bar. It was a regular life, you know? Doing the same things every day, right in the same place. It had sort of a routine to it." He paused. "I don't know's Marie liked it quite the way I did, getting used to living that way after so many years. But I did like it. I did."

"Because it was regular," she said.

"Sure," he said. "Because of that. You've got to keep in mind, I went in the service in Nineteen-forty-two, seventeen years old, lied about my age, didn't know blessed a thing. And they launched the *Jackson* up there in the Fore River shipyard that's all gone to the devil these days, and we crewed her up and took her around to San Diego and reprovisioned there, and we put out to sea. And for the next three years, you know, we didn't step ashore again. All we did was fight Japs. And when we'd take a hit — two kamikazes got us toward the end of the war, and we took a lot of bombs before that —

well, they'd just bring us alongside a repair ship and do what needed doing and then off we'd go again. Supplies, ammunition, everything — all of it came to us. And eating your meals, or cooking them like I did when we weren't in an actual battle, or trying to sleep or anything, in the middle of a war, well, when that's over and it's all you've had for three years, it doesn't look so bad. A regular life on land."

"I suppose not," she said.

He shifted in his chair. "I don't know," he said. "I thought I was pretty smart, back in those days. I never had much education, only had two years of high school and I didn't like it much, but I guess I figured if I was smart enough, outlast the Japs, I'd probably do all right, myself, if I could just set down somewhere and do what I learned to do. I knew how to cook, see? I figured that if I could cook when the Japs were dropping bombs on me, I could do it in peace and quiet too, and maybe do all right. And I had all my service pay. After all, there wasn't much chance, spend it, out the middle the Pacific, unless you were a gambler, which I never was. So I come home, like I said, and Marie'd waited like she promised and also saved her pay, and we set down together in her father's house in Chelsea and planned how we would do it.

"And see what we decided," Quentin said, stirring in the chair as more coughing in the house seemed to break his train of thought, "well, what I decided, and she backed me all the way, that what we wanted to do was get ourselves set up someplace where you didn't already have a lot of competition. Because anywhere we opened naturally was going to be the newest place in town, and you didn't want to have to take trade away from somebody that'd always had it in order to make your pile. And in the service one of the men I knew, one of the officers, was this Lieutenant Richard Badger, one of the fliers, and he was already telling everybody on the *Jackson* about this great town he came from, and that soon's the war ended, he was going back to stay. After he did law school of course, but you know what I mean. And so I heard so much about it, you know, that before I even saw it, I knew that I wanted to. And I come down here and looked up Richard, and he shown me around and gave me some information about what was available here and how the town was sure to grow once everybody got back on their feet after the war and all.

"Well," Quentin said, "I looked it over and Marie saw it and liked it, and we decided to come down here and this was where we'd live. Richard helped me with the bank, getting me the loan, and of course I was a veteran and that didn't hurt, back then, and both of us were young, Marie and me, and we went right to work. You said Dan showed you my old place?"

"Yesterday morning," she said.

"That's a good building," he said. "I don't know how much you know about building, but that one's a good one. Cinder block, brick face, good solid hardwood, plumbing's real brass pipe — the best materials, you know? The very best there was. That place'll stand forever, likely." He paused. "Wish I still owned it," he said. "Broke my heart to sell. I didn't like it, you know, when I had to start selling off all the land I bought, over all those years. But selling my own place like that, well, that hurt quite a lot."

"Then you hadn't planned to retire out here," she said.

"Oh," he said, "no. Not here at all. This place, rundown old house probably built in Eighteen-forty, maybe even before that, never kept up right, we've got a beam down in the cellar I'd pull out and replace if I didn't think it might last longer than the two of us, and that's really a toss-up — darned thing's loaded with dry rot. No, what I had a mind for this place, well, I bought it for the land that went with it, you know? Never much good for what the people who owned it used it for — the Breens was all farmers. Trees for lumber out that side, some crops out in the back. But except for that little creek down there, it's all good dry land and she'll drain good too, you know? Eighteen acres when I bought it. I was planning to build houses. Tear this place down and put up maybe, twenty with three bedrooms each, on poured concrete slab. Good, inexpensive housing that young families could afford when they were just starting out."

"But you never got to it," she said.

"Put it this way," he said, "Other things got to me first. All those years we just scraped by, saving every dime we got, putting it all by, using it for down payments when I saw a piece of land? All of it just went to the devil, started to go about fifteen years ago.

"Everything used to be all right," he said. "Before Cheryl's kid got sick, when her and Patty was still married, with their husbands, before everything just started to go downhill like it did, well, I owned over nine hundred acres in various places here in Waterford. And most of it was prime land. I don't mean it was on the highway, don't mean that at all. That stuff, even then that stuff, the commercial property, was mostly out of my reach. What I could afford. All I had down in the center, or what used to be the center, was my own building and its lot, and the lot out back of it. Which come to only about two acres, more or less. But this undeveloped property, this kind of land out here, this was woodlots and old pasturage you could pick up in those days for a hundred bucks an acre, less, and when you started talking those prices, you were in my league.

"When I sold off the eight, nine acres out in back where the Giddings put their big house and their stables and their paddock and their swimming pool and all, tennis court, I guess, when I sold that to them in Nineteen-sixty-nine, they paid two thousand bucks an acre for the property. House changed hands again last year — you know what they got?"

"The way you describe it," she said, "I would say: a lot."

"Three hundred twenty thousand dollars," he said in the darkness. "Isn't that something? Property that I bought total for less than a thousand dollars, course it didn't have improvements then, that big house and all, but property I bought for less than a thousand dollars over thirty years ago, and sold for almost twenty about sixteen years ago, that same piece of land last year went for three hundred thousand more.

"So," he said, "you ask me if I expected, me and Marie'd be living here, after we retired, and I have got to tell you, m'am, we certainly did not. I figured this place to be knocked down and a new ranch house sitting on the lot with some up-and-coming young fellow and his wife raising their kids in it. And me and Marie'd be living in our own place down in Delray, winters, and I was going to build a nice Cape for us out on a dead end that runs off Atlantic Road, up above the beach, and you can see the river some, where it bends beyond the cove. That's what I expected."

"And instead," she said, "your friends cheated you."

"I don't know if you could say that," Quentin said. "They sure took advantage of the things that happened to me. They did that all right. But you got to keep in mind that it was me that asked them to, asked them to step in. I started all the deals myself, that helped make those people rich."

"Well," she said, "but you more or less had to, didn't you? Your back was to the wall."

"Yeah," he said. "It was and is. But they didn't put in there. It's like I told you. First it was the girls, them deciding they'd run off and get married and leave home. Get away from me. And especially Patty, when she brought home that coon, you know, I didn't treat her right." There was a long spell of coughing inside the house. He went on as though it made no impression on him. "For a good many years there, when Marie wanted us to take a vacation, you know, and go out there to see them, I wouldn't do it. I said, well, I said that I would do it, I always said I would. But then the time would come, and I wouldn't do it. Why should I spend my money and give up two weeks of my business, go all the way out to California there to see a kid, two kids, really, that didn't want nothing to do with me at all anymore? I'd get to thinking about it and I would end up saying to myself: 'Hey, I didn't run away from them — they ran away from me.'

"And that made Marie feel bad, you know," he said. "And then when the kid got sick, and there was all this medical to think about, that's when we find out that Patty and the coon aren't married anymore, and furthermore, neither's Cheryl — her guy took off too, and she don't know where he went. And they're both on the welfare, and what're they going to do? So we end up, instead of saving our money and waiting, the land prices go up, all of a sudden we're using our savings, giving them to them, and that don't take long because most of what we got to show is all tied up in land, and then we have to start selling off the land after I can't borrow no more from banks and can't pay the loans we got.

"So, yeah, maybe Dorcas Munrow didn't give me what the land I had out on Margin Street was actually worth when I hadda raise the money there to pay for Mexico. But it wasn't her idea that Patty got that stuff they made from peachpits or whatever the heck it was, that Laetrile flimflam? That was Patty's whole idea. That this's gonna fix what the kid had that the American doctors in San Diego didn't seem to be able to cure. Wasn't Dorcas, you know, was the one that thought that up. Only thing that Dorcas did was first lend me some money, and then say she'd take the land for it when I couldn't pay her back. Which made me some relieved, you know. I wasn't after charity, when the bank turned me down."

"But the lot behind your restaurant," Gates said. "Now that was an example."

"Yeah," he said, "you could say that. That was pretty sneaky, them taking that when my taxes come due. Helen Deese, there wasn't any damned need Oscar'n her pulling that stunt on me. And acting so foxy afterwards, like they didn't know what they done, and nobody ever told them if they got that piece with what Dorcas had, the abutting lots, the bunch of them'd have that whole strip going north on the east side of Route Four. For which I think I heard they got about a million and a half from the outfits that come in. Nothing compared, of course, to the bundle that they must've got for what's on the west side, but still, you know, it was good money. Very good money. Better'n I saw.

"But then," he said, "when you say that, you also got to say at the same time, you know: I didn't pay the taxes. I didn't have the dough. I lost a lousy piece of land because I didn't have, I guess, about a hundred twenty bucks. And if I'd've known they posted it, if someone'd told me, and that someone was looking to snap it up, I probably would've paid the dough and kept it for myself. Because I would've figured, something was up, even if I didn't know exactly what it was. But I didn't know Dorcas had the connecting parcel, see? I didn't know that at the time, until afterwards. So if I had've known it, I don't know, you know, what difference it would've made."

"Don't you think," she said, "don't you think that Mel Shaw helped them to cheat you? Cheat you and the other people who sold land to them, when the paper wasn't printing all that was going on?"

He waited for a while before he answered. "Mrs. Gates," he said, "I don't know what was in people's minds and in their souls when they did the things they did. All I can tell you is what I did, what I had in mind. All my life I tried to be a good man and live like I was supposed to.

"Mel Shaw," he said. "You know, I never knew him good. I was out in the back of the place most of the time. It was Marie that saw the customers out front and Sonny in the bar, so if Mel was tied up with Oscar and Dorcas and the doctors and them, well, he probably knew them better. And he could've just figured, you know, that if they were asking him if he would like, get in on things with them, well, did I ever ask him? No, I never did. Which if I had've, maybe he would've had the money that I needed when I did, and maybe then I'd still have some of the stuff that I sold."

"Mister Quentin," she said, "there have been some reports, you know, that Shaw killed Tim Lavalle."

He cleared his throat. "I heard some of that stuff a while ago," he said.

"What did you think of it?" she said. "Think there's any truth in it?"

His voice become gruff. "Mrs. Gates," he said, "I never, I learned a long time ago, when I was in the Navy, that there's always somebody roaming around with a dirty story full of dirty language to tell on somebody else. And I learned never to pay no attention to that garbage, any of that kind of stuff, because you generally can't tell, you know, if it's true or not. And all it does is sit there on your mind when you see that person it's about, and it dirties your thinking about him."

"But suppose it was true," she said.

"Well," he said, "that's what I would have to do, isn't it? Suppose that it is true? I'm not on earth to do that, to suppose that stuff, you know. I didn't know Timmy too good. I brought him down here because he was one of the fellows that I was trying to do something for on account of the way my brother's life went, but I didn't know him real good. And if that's what he was doing, if he was doing the kind of thing they say he was doing with Shaw, well, I didn't know he was doing that, and I would've fired him if I had, not because I was judging him but because I wouldn't want no one like that, that was doing those things, handling food in my place of business that I had. But I didn't. I didn't know that. And I still don't. All I know is someone says he was. If Timmy was doing that and Mel Shaw was doing that, what they are saying now, well him and Timmy'll both have to answer for it some day, if Tim hasn't already. I believe a person has to take responsibility for their own acts, for what they did." He paused. "I believe," he said. "I believe there is forgiveness, if you ask for it. And I hope I am right, you know, because I'm going to have to ask."

"I see," she said.

27

The original design of the Waterford Mall on the west side of Route 4 called for a three-story main atrium with a thirty-foot waterfall falling through a rough stone grotto and feeding into a shallow pool. The pool was irregularly shaped, roughly ten by twenty feet, bordered with large rocks, rimmed by lily pads and housing Japanese carp averaging about four pounds each. The fish and the aquatic plants in the daytime were lighted naturally through the peaked glass roof and at night by the blue and red lights housed in the border of the pool. The concept in execution proved more spare than the designers had intended. Vines with broad green leaves were therefore added to the grotto, and twelve tall fica trees were located around its base.

From the central atrium, the designers had planned for three one-story main spokes extending in the northerly, westerly and southerly directions, each with shops on either side of its four-hundred-foot extension and a three-story department store at the end of the spoke. At first the shops in the arcades were accessible both to pedestrian shoppers inside the corridors and to those just arriving by car in the broad parking lots outside. Within a year, all of the arcade shops had secured the exterior doors leading to the parking lots, their merchants' association explaining at a press conference that the decision had been taken reluctantly in order to curtail shoplifting by thieves using the outside doors to make quick getaways.

"Which was about a third the story," Dan Munroe told Connie Gates in The Caballero after ordering a pitcher of margaritas. "They were having trouble with boosters, but no more'n they expected. It was just that until they actually opened for business it didn't occur to them that what all of them want is for every one the shoppers that comes here for one item have to march his sad ass all over the whole damned lot, and look in all their windows before they get out again. And also, they didn't think about the heating bills in the winter and the air conditioning, the summer, when they put in those outside doors. So they sealed them all up tight, and now the only thing you hope is that if there ever is a fire in this monster, everybody in it can get out without being trampled to death. Which Dominick Leonard the fire chief says they got ample exits and there is no problem there, and I sure hope he's right."

Profiting from the experience they gained in the first years of operation, as well as from the rent increases they were able to command from envious applications for space, Waterford Associates directed the design team in charge of planning expansions to arrange the southeasterly arcade leading four hundred feet into the two-story, ten-screen movie complex, and the northeasterly spoke leading four hundred feet into the two-story dining and amusement complex so that the exterior walls of the arcades were solid brick, interrupted only by steel fire doors as required by code. Their intention was to require visitors to enter either through the central atrium, or through the doors leading from the terminal complexes into the parking lots.

"Which their idea was," Munroe said, "what my mother said at least, their idea was that the people coming in for movies, they're probably not gonna shop much anyway, and it's all right if they come in and go out without looking in the stores. And the people coming in to eat, and the damned kids playing the video games and that crap on the first level, the thing to do with them is pack them all together and make sure they smell food all the time, because that's the only other thing they spend their money on anyway, unless you count clothes, which they'll go looking for, and grass, which they get delivered.

"And which," he said in The Caballero, "explains why when you're in the Messkin restaurant, you also get a good whiff of the pizza parlor, *and* the Chink joint, *and* the fried dough cart, the burger palace, the cookie shop, the coffee shop, fried chicken and the seafood. Nice, isn't it?"

"Compared to what," she said, "a locker room, a stable, or a low tide at Revere Beach?"

The pitcher of margaritas arrived. It held about a quart and a half of green frothy liquid. The two six-ounce glasses were upside down on the plate of salt. "Ye gods," she said, "this much? You'll carry me out of here, you know, I drink my share of that."

He poured for each of them. "No sweat," he said. "Inna first place, I got a folding gurney in the back of my Bronco. And inna second place, you're gonna find that this here margarita here's a little short, tequila, and there's not a lot of triple sec involved in it either."

"Well," she said, "what is it then? Straight lime juice or water?"

"My guess is mostly water," he said. "They advertise it, 'frozen margarita,' you notice, which means they chop up a lotta ice inna blender when they make the things. It isn't bad to drink. It's just not an actual drink."

She sipped. "It's pleasant enough," she said, setting the glass down. "At least it cuts the dust."

"Sure," he said, "harmless. Just like everything in here. Kind of a fake, you know? Not what it's supposed to be, what the menu says, but nothing very dangerous that'll injure you at all."

"Do I take that to mean," she said, "I can sit here and stuff myself with frijoles, and enchiladas, and refried beans and nacho stuff with plenty of what looks like hot sauce, and I won't long for death before morning?"

He grinned. His round fat face, capped by a tonsure fringe of black hair cut short on the sides and front, changed remarkably. His teeth were heavily tobacco-stained and his skin was oily enough so that it shone in the orange light. His nose had been flattened. He had a dark beard which by evening had produced a noticeable stubble, and his brown eyes were small, set in pouchy flesh under untrimmed brows, but when he grinned it was as though he had been letting out a person whom he guarded closely and seldom exercised. "You'll be all right. You're in good hands. I'm your friendly policeman."

He gestured to call her attention to the restaurant decor. "Just look around," he said. "What you see's what you don't get. The bullfighters," he said indicating the false arched windows over each of the booths along the walls, every third one displaying a backlighted transparency of a matador completing a *media veronica* to a bull bowed down by *banderillas*, hooves tramping up the dust. "The cowboys," he said, calling her attention to the second in the repeating series, each of them in gaucho garb astride a prancing black horse saddled in heavily-silvered tack. "The *señoritas*," he said, referring to the third variety of subjects, each of them the same dark-eyed beauty peeking over a large rose from under her black *mantilla*. "Look at the tables," he said, "every one with the same planks, exactly the same knotholes, all of them turned out in some factory somewhere. Listen to the music, all right? Just try listening to that."

She strained to hear the background music over the conversations of the other diners. "It doesn't sound too bad," she said. "What is it, anyway, Herb Alpert and the Tijuana Brass?"

"That's who it is," he said, "and any time you come here, whether it is day or night, you will hear one of his tapes, or one that's so much like it that it won't matter at all. Always mariachi music, day and goddamned night."

"Let me ask you something," she said. "If this place bothers you like this, why come here at all?"

"Simple," he said. "It's this or one of the other joints. Captain Billy's Whalespout. Papa Mia's Pizza. Sun's Chinese Pavilion. Burger Palace — that is it. It's nine-thirty at night, Connie. This town don't stay up late. Dave's Eighteen-fourteen House is nice. The food is pretty good. But Dave's serving the desserts right now. Dave's kitchen is closed. Besides, he can't compete with these folks, these joints in the mall. Dave wants to sell a full dinner, few drinks and all that stuff. People out to eat this late, down this way at least, they're all pooped from shopping or they've just come from the movies and the reason that they come in here is because it's where they are. And that's why you and I are here, because this is all there is." He grinned again.

She drank some more of her margarita. She put the glass down. She studied him, the pudgy neck constricted by the collar of his blue button-down shirt, bulging his jowls out further, the broad shoulders in the tan corduroy sport coat, the maroon knitted necktie in the clumsy knot. "You know," she said, "I thought of this day before yesterday, when we were up in the plane there and you were telling me how smart you were talking Doctor Fellows into buying it and then talking the Selectmen into letting you rent it for aerial surveys of the town. And you were so pleased with yourself you started grinning like you are now. I should've told you then, and if not then then yesterday at lunch. When you started telling me about your mother and her white Cadillac, terrorizing every other driver that she meets, and you did the same thing. I should have told you then."

"Told me what," he said suspiciously, the grin fading away.

" 'Munroe, you big asshole, you think you're a little kid?' "

"*No*," she said laughing, "not like that at all. You're very attractive when you let yourself do that. Show that you're feeling happy. Having a good time. You should do it more often. You're really a nice guy."

He blushed. "Oh, come on," he said.

"I mean it," she said. "Eve, when I called Eve and asked her about staying with her, and she said she'd be away, one of the things she told me was that I should call you. As I did. 'Not only does he know a lot,' she said, 'but Dan is a nice guy. Don't get put off by what you hear, by what some people say. Dan's really a nice guy. Just give him a chance.' And she was exactly right. Why do you come on all the time the way you do, like you're pissed off at the world?"

"Well, for one thing," he said, as the food arrived, "most of the time, I am. I'm a police officer. The only time I see most people is when they've got some problem, which they'd like to blame on me. So, either I'm pissed off, or I'm getting set to be, or I'm afraid I'm going to be in a minute and that idea all by itself, that pisses me off."

"And for another thing," she said, "you're afraid not to be."

"That's probably true," he said. He was eating a chili taco, having trouble keeping the contents from dropping between the cylinder and his mouth.

She began on her enchilada. She sighed. "I don't know anything about men," she said.

"Whaddaya mean?" he said with his mouth full. 'Jeffrey rides again,' she thought. 'I wonder if this guy changes shirts before they catch on fire.' "You, you act to me as though you do all right, I'd think."

She drank the rest of her first margarita and poured another for herself and him as well. "Oh," she said, "I didn't mean, I don't know *any*thing. Of course I do. Even if what I do know's mostly things to avoid, if I spot them again. No, what I mean is, I just spent the better part of two hours with your friend, Jay Quentin. I went in thinking I had a pretty decent idea of what kind of man he was, and I came out thinking I don't know beans about him."

"Jay's not exactly my buddy," Munroe said. "I've known the guy a long time, ever since I can remember. He's always been around. And I like him all right. I get along with him. But I wouldn't say, you know, that old Jay is my friend. He's just somebody that I know."

"Okay," she said, "but that's what I mean. I don't know what to make of him. I approached him thinking: 'Here's a guy that got taken all right? He's going to be mad at the people who took advantage of him. Where he used to run a barroom, there's an auto parts store. Where he used to run a restaurant, there's a discount drugstore. Where he used to live upstairs, and had tenant offices, you've now got a bunch of yuppies doing aerobic dance. His wife's really sick. He doesn't look too good himself. He's broke. All he has to do is look around him to see other people making even more money buying and selling land he used to own. This is going to be good. This is going to be hot stuff.'

"And what do I get?" She took another drink of margarita. "I get an old man who tells me that he doesn't judge people. That most of the bad things that've happened to him and his wife've probably been mostly his fault. Except for her emphysema, which he thinks is hers. That he believes in forgiveness, and if people did cheat him, or lie to him, well that's not for him to say.

"What's with this guy?" she said. "Is he for real? Is this what he really thinks? Is he stupid, maybe, or maybe covering up something that's even worse than what I'm trying to find out? Is somebody blackmailing this old guy, got something on him so he doesn't dare to talk? What the hell is going on?" She dug into her refried beans.

"Probably nothing," Munroe said, helping himself to an enchilada. "What you say sounds like Jay. I don't mean he went around preaching to people, telling them how they should live, but he always was pretty religious. Him and Marie both. He told my mother once, after she bailed him out of a money jam, and he was slower paying her back'n he intended to be, he told her he was praying for her. She thought he meant it too. That he probably was. Never saw where it did much good, but the thought was there.

"And that program he had with the ex-cons," Munroe said, "that was another thing he did. No fanfare or anything. And the same thing with, he had a couple, maybe half a dozen customers of his in the saloon, you know? That couldn't handle the stuff. And he took care of them. There was one of them, guy by the name of Bob Grover. Him and his wife, wife's name was Julia, they ran this real estate office on the front the second floor Jay's building. And Bob, he'd come down the lunchroom at noon every day and pick up a couple sandwiches to go, and a couple cups of coffee, or tonic in the summer. And a good many the other people in there having lunch, well, everybody liked Bob. Nice guy. And they'd be having beers with their lunch. Nothing heavy, just a couple dimie drafts with their pot roast or whatever, maybe chicken pie. And they'd invite him, you know, sit down with them and shoot the breeze. And he would always tell them, No, he couldn't, because he was an alcoholic and he shouldn't even be sitting at the same table with the stuff. And then every night at five-thirty, he would come downstairs into the saloon and prove it. Two beers, three at the outside, Bob is shitfaced by seven. And by then Jay is out of the kitchen and into the bar, and he calls up Julia upstairs and tells her Bob's ready, and she closes up the office and comes down and Jay helps Bob out the door and gets him loaded in the car, and Julia takes him home.

"Now," Munroe said, "you would think, you know, that he'd get sick of this. Even if the guy was a tenant of his. But he didn't. Just went right along, taking care of Bob, and that was the way he lived. That's the way he's always lived.

"Is he for real when he does this?" Munroe said. "I'll be damned if I know." He took a large bite of enchilada, and with some of the food still chipmunked in his cheeks said: "Which doesn't mean he doesn't know stuff. Don't mean that at all. This is a small town, even if it's gotten pretty big. Jay's lived here since right after the war. His place was the clearing house for all the gossip in town. Oscar did more talking in the grille'n he did in the police station. Shaw and Baldwin and Logan, and all the other people, Didi Chenevert, from the *Commoner*, the first thing they did after they wrote their stories for the paper was come over to Jay's and blat what they knew all over the place." He swallowed the last of the food. "So," he said, "what I'm saying is, I guess, is that Jay probably means all that ragtime he gives out about not spreading gossip, but that don't mean he doesn't know it, know it word for word."

"He's just not telling," she said. She speared the last of her enchilada with her fork and raised it toward her mouth.

"Basically, that's it," Munroe said. He lifted another large piece of enchilada.

"Damn," she said, and put the food into her mouth. The two of them sat there with their cheeks bulging, chewing and swallowing. "This is really gross," she said, getting down the last of it. She picked up her margarita glass and drained it. She put it down and refilled it.

"Sitting here eating like pigs. Here I am on the shag end of a day, I should be back in Eve's apartment thinking up some way to get what I didn't get, and instead I'm sitting here with you, packing my face with immigrant food and filling my liver with booze."

"Well," he said, swallowing, picking up his glass, "maybe I can help you. Just what did you expect from Jay?" He emptied the glass, set it down, refilled it from the pitcher, put both hands on the table and belched silently.

She peered at him over the rim of her glass. "You've already told me a lot," she said. "Giving me the aerial tour, driving me around, introducing me to the assessors — all that kind of stuff. I hate to impose on you more'n I have. And besides, you have to live here, after I've left. I don't particularly want this story coming out and you getting blamed for it all over the place."

He took a drink of margarita. "Ahh," he said, putting it down, "don't let that bother you. Inna first place, half the town's already decided that we're sleeping together." He kept his gaze on her. "You staying in Eve's condo and all, they just assume since I do some nights, when Eve is in town, I must be staying there these nights, while Eve's off in Spain. So, doesn't matter what you write, as far as I'm concerned. Long's my name's not on it, that's all matters to me."

She did not say anything.

"Inna second place," he said, "when I talked to you before, on those other times, keep in mind I didn't know, what you were looking for. Wasn't my fault, exactly — you didn't tell me much. All's I know from talking you, is: Joe Logan's story, which the big part of it didn't happen back when Joe was here. And also that Joe Logan thinks Mel Shaw killed Tim Lavalle." He shrugged. "Frankly, Connie," he said, "I don't see how Jay Quentin, what he knows, could've helped you much in that line, but apparently I'm wrong. So, chances are I know what he knows, most of it at least. And chances are, if you ask me, I won't mind telling you. Most of it, at least."

"Okay," she said, emptying the pitcher equally into their glasses, "that's nice of you. That's very nice of you. Here's what bothers me.

"First," she said, raising her glass, "first what I've decided that I really need to know, just for background, not for print, is what else'd gone on around here before the real estate started changing hands. Before Lavalle's murder, in fact.

"This Taves guy," she said, "I do believe him. I think he's telling me the truth. Just not all of it. What's he got on the guy that hired me, got *him* involved in Taves's mess? Mark Baldwin was here when that kid got killed. He must've had some suspicion. And then after the Goulds sold out, and Baldwin was running the paper, why didn't he watch this guy Shaw, maybe get rid of him? And what's with your predecessor there, Oscar Deese? First he treats the Lavalle murder pretty casually, seems like. Then he gets involved with his wife in the land deals that go down. Now Logan says that Deese bagged the Lavalle case — well, is that why Shaw helped him get away with the real estate deals? Did Shaw do that because Deese did what Logan says he did?"

"Lemme get us another pitcher here," Munroe said, raising his hand to summon a waiter. "I don't know all the answers to the questions that you're asking, and the ones that I do know, well, they're strictly FYI. This is just hearsay, okay? Hearsay and suspicions." He leaned back in the booth. "But it's good hearsay, I think, even though you can't print it."

"I'm all ears," she said.

He nodded. "Okay," he said, after the waiter had taken the order and removed the soiled dishes, "the first thing you probably should know is that Mark Baldwin came about this far," he held his right thumb and forefinger about one inch apart and squinted at them, "from a statutory rape charge that he would've lost in court."

She sat back in the booth. "Well," she said, "that's interesting. Very interesting. Was that while he was working here?"

"Uh huh," Munroe said. "Old Mark picked up a teenager one night in the coffee shop at the gas station just this side the Sagamore Bridge, took her down to his cottage and fucked her. Now I'm not saying he forced her, and I'm not saying he broke her in. All I'm saying is that far's the law's concerned, if the kid's fifteen years old, or whatever this one was, doesn't matter if she's hot, got big tits and puts out. All the law says is: 'Don't do it. You will go to jail.' Baldwin did it. Her father found out, and he did not like the news. Went to Ward Keane and tells him he's filing a complaint.

"Now Ward," Munroe said, as the waiter brought the fresh pitcher of drinks, "Ward likes the news about as much as he'd like a poke in the eye. First thing he thinks of doing is, he's gonna bump this case off onto Bristol. Because Baldwin's house is in Cataumet, and this is before they chop the Cape and Islands District off the Bristol one, and Ward can get rid of it because that's where the rape occurs. But Billy Taves, who's his assistant, he don't like that idea. Because he's thinking of running in Bristol, and no matter what happens if Baldwin gets tried there, it isn't good for Billy. Baldwin gets convicted, the *Commoner*'ll be mad at not only Barlow down in Bristol but also Billy because the case got bumped down. Baldwin gets acquitted, *Commoner*'ll still be mad because the case went down. And that won't help Ward, either, when he comes up again." He poured each of them a margarita.

"So, Billy talks to Oscar," Munroe said. "And Oscar was always thinking, and he says: 'Keep that case here. And tell the parents, all right? That they have to talk to me.' And they do that, and Oscar gives them this big song and dance, all of which is true, about what a hell of a time the girl's going to have in court when she testifies.

"It doesn't work," Munroe said. "Billy comes back to Oscar and tells him they're going forward, going to file the damned complaint. Oscar says: 'Now lemme think. Got to be some way.' And pretty soon he thinks of one. He has Mel Shaw call up. Shaw calls up the parents and says he's a reporter for the *Barnstable Record*, and he's heard that their daughter got raped by this fellow that works for the *Commoner*. Have they got a recent picture? Can he interview the kid?

"And that did it," Munroe said. "Bobo Rivera and his wife don't file charges against Mark. They put the little honey in the convent, I think, and it's possible they called Mark up and told him that they reconsidered what he offered, damages."

"He paid them off?" she said.

"I don't know that," Munroe said. "I know, I know before all the other stuff started going on, I know he offered them ten thousand dollars to drop the case. I assume when they called him up again, he probably didn't go any higher, and he might've told them to go jump. But I know he made the first offer, and I know they dropped the case, and I know they called him afterwards, when they decided to do that." He swigged from his glass. She did the same.

"Now, Oscar," he said. "Oscar didn't get anywhere near as much credit's he deserved for the land deals that went on. He didn't have much money and he didn't spot the trends, but when the whole thing was just about ready, he was a big factor. According to my mother,

Oscar was indispensable when that all came together and the deal was shaping up." He drank again.

"Do you know what he did?" she said.

He put the glass down. He belched silently. He nodded. "Yep," he said, refilling the glass, "I know most of it. And most of what I know, you'll find, I am not telling you."

"Oh, what is this?" she said. "Are you teasing me?"

"No," he said, "not at all. There are some things that I won't tell you. But quite a few, I will." He raised his glass and twinkled his eyes at her over its rim. "Oscar couldn't prove it," he said, "and he never even tried. But Oscar knew in Sixty-four that Mel Shaw killed Lavalle."

28

The floor-to-ceiling windows of Eva Dean's two-bedroom condo on the fourth floor of the Waterford Estates South Towers faced the west. Six of the eighteen outdoor Hartru tennis courts grouped around the three buildings were under those windows; the outdoor Olympic-sized pool with thirty-foot diving platform was just to the north of the courts. Beyond the pool and the courts the nine-hole "executive" par three golf course extended compactly over the knolls above the South River marshes, the short fairways richly green around the perfectly-white sand traps and the little man-made brooks with their wooden bridges.

Early in the morning, before the July sun got high, the tennis players and the swimmers and the joggers and the golfers who were serious about their play went out in their togs with their equipment and their Thermos jugs of orange juice chilled by flaked ice from the refrigerators standard in the units and their Thermos jugs of decaffeinated, freshly-ground coffee and their little wicker baskets of microwaved Sara Lee chocolate croissants wrapped in red-and-white checked napkins.

The tennis players put their breakfasts on the white metal tables under the yellow-and-white striped umbrellas on the patios around the courts. The swimmers took their breakfasts to the white metal tables under the blue-and-white striped umbrellas on the patios around the pool. The golfers put their breakfasts on the white metal tables next to the small rustic cabin labeled "Pro Shop."

At 6:30 in the morning, Constance Gates awoke sluggishly and grudgingly to the conversations and the noises that accompanied the sports beneath Eva Dean's windows. She was lying on her left side, so that she faced the outer wall of the bedroom, and the early sunlight insinuated itself around the edges of the light-blue drapes, illuminating the noise. She resisted waking up. She shifted position slightly, straightening her legs and rolling onto her back. Almost immediately she felt stubby fingers sliding over the right side of her pelvis and stealing into her pubic hair.

She sighed and murmured: "Aww." She shook her head and tasted in her mouth the gluey residue of enchiladas, refried beans and margaritas from the Caballero. The fingers crept into her. She smelled the loamy odor of a man who perspired freely and tried to cope with it by using roll-on Old Spice deodorant profusely, did not clean himself thoroughly, and smoked two packs of unfiltered Luckies every day. She opened her eyes suddenly and sat up, pushing his fingers away.

"I got to brush my teeth," she said. She threw off the sheet. She forced herself to sit on the edge of the bed for a moment, to avoid vertigo. Then she made her way unsteadily to the bathroom.

When she returned to the bedroom, Dan Munroe was sitting up in the bed, smoking a Lucky. "Put it out," she said. He stubbed the butt in the Aztec clay ashtray on the night-table next to him. "Jesus," she said, getting back into the bed, "it's bad enough you smoke those killers all day long, but do you have to light the damned things up in the bedroom, man?" She lay on her back with her legs spread and her hands at her crotch.

He rested on his left elbow and grinned down at her. His teeth were very yellow in the ruddy and stubbled skin of his face. His remaining black hair sprouted away from his scalp above his ears. His eyes were slightly bloodshot. Naked he was obviously about twenty pounds overweight, more than he seemed with his clothes on; the jowls only hinted at the paunch below. "I already told you," he said, "if you drink, you have to smoke. The nicotine cancels out the alcohol in your system. Stops you from getting sick."

She shook her head. "You must be out of your mind," she said. "I must be out of *my* mind, come to think of it, hanging around with you."

He laughed. She rubbed her crotch. She smiled at him. "Well?" she said. "You started something. Aren't you going to finish it?"

He put his right hand down between her legs and gripped her buttocks with his fingers. He put his thumb against her labia and began to knead her. She opened her eyes wide and her mouth as well, wetting her lips and staring at him. She changed her position slightly to improve his access. She reached down into his crotch and manipulated his testicles. He moved so that he could suck her left nipple. she began to breathe through her mouth. She could feel herself lubricating.

"Now," she said, pulling his penis, "put it in me now." He mounted her and started thrusting, holding his weight off her with his fists pressed into the mattress. She wrapped her legs around him and pulled him down further into her. She had three orgasms before his, and lay panting under him with her eyes closed when he had finished. She opened her eyes and studied him. He grinned at her and rolled off. She felt the fluids running out of her. "Heavenly days," she said. "My mother always told me the policeman was my friend, but she never gave me details." She patted his penis. "You're a hard man, Dan Munroe, a hard man indeed."

He flopped back on the bed, puffing slightly. He coughed twice. "Well," he said, "yeah, but it'll take five minutes." He put his right hand over hers on his penis and rubbed.

"Nope," she said, taking her hand away and sitting up.

"Hey," he said, grabbing at her and missing.

"Got to call my place," she said, standing up and fluffing her hair. "I've been misbehaving all over with you, hacking around, staying out late, drinking too much and getting it on. I've been neglecting my responsibilities here. I've got to shape up."

"Like what?" he said. He lay on the bed like a beached white mammal with a red face. "You've been working."

"Right," she said. She went to the bureau and opened her purse. She took out an oblong black plastic device and a small spiral notebook and a ballpoint pen. She went out of the bedroom into the living room. On her way she said: "I haven't called my machine in three days. My kids could've been calling me. My employer could be calling me. My bill collectors almost certainly have been calling me. Nobody's hearing from me, back. Enough of this delinquency. I'm going to get straight here while I've still got some time."

She paused at the bathroom and grabbed a beige handtowel off the rack. She went out into the living room, which was done in lavender and tan, spread the towel on the cushion of the flowered overstuffed chair, took the phone off the counter dividing the kitchen from the living room, put it on the coffee table in front of the couch, sat down on the chair and dialed her own number in Boston. She held the black device in her right hand. When her answering machine took the call, she held the device against the mouthpiece of the phone and pressed its button, emitting a steady tone. She sat naked on the towel, frowning as she listened, writing things down. She was on the phone for nineteen minutes. When she hung up she had two pages of neat notes on the pad. She looked at them and frowned again.

Munroe naked had come out into the kitchen while she was on the phone. He had coffee making by the time that she hung up. He planted his fists on the counter and arched his back while he spoke. "Something wrong?" he said.

She said "What?" like someone coming out of a reverie.

"The kids or something?" he said. "You looked like something's wrong."

"The kids," she said. She snorted. "The kids need me about as much as they need athlete's foot. The only time they call me is when it's become inconvenient for them to come and visit me. Which only happens when the sun goes behind a cloud, or there's some other catastrophe like that. Nah, the kids're all right. Estelle wants ninety-dollar jeans that her father won't buy for her, reasonable man, so she thought she'd try me out on the deal. But that was three nights ago. Night before last, she got impatient with the tape and chewed me out on it. Last night she didn't call. So either her daddy bought the jeans or now she wants a trip to France, or some other bribe."

"So," he said, "why the expression? Why the gloomy look and all? Has to be some reason."

She snapped the spiral pad shut. "Oh," she said, "it's probably nothing."

"What's probably nothing?" he said.

"Baldwin wants to see me," she said. "This very morning, he wants to see me. Office called me up last night. Said it's very important that I get in touch with him today."

"So, call him up," Munroe said, moving away from the counter to the coffee maker as the percolation ended.

"At seven-ten in the morning?" she said. "I tend to doubt he'd be in just yet."

"Call him at home," Munroe said.

"I don't have his home phone," she said. "What're you, kidding me?"

"Could ask you the same question," Munroe said, pouring two

mugs of coffee. "Woman can do what you do in bed, and you don't have Baldwin's home phone? You've got to be shitting me."

"I think I'm being insulted," she said.

"You're not being insulted," Munroe said, bringing the coffee into the living room, his penis bobbing as he walked. "You're being complimented. Baldwin's well-known for his appreciation of fine women. You're an extremely good woman." He put the coffee down on the coffee table and lowered himself onto the rug in the lotus postion. "I assumed when Eva briefed me and said I would like you, I assumed when she said you were working for Baldwin that if we ever did get together, I'd be sticking my wick into one of his lamps the first time we did it."

"You son of a bitch," she said, picking up one mug of coffee and drinking from it gingerly.

He looked genuinely startled. "What's the matter with that?" he said. "Why wouldn't I think that? You're a friend of Eva's. She tells me you're lots alike, now that you're divorced. You're staying here. She's on one of her trips for seventeen full days, and she tells me Mark Baldwin's writer that she knows from college, she tells me you are coming down and we would like each other. I meet you and we do, just like Eva says. What would you make of it all? What the hell else am I supposed to think?"

"Dan," she said wearily, "you don't just tell somebody that you spent the night with that you assume that person got her job by putting out. Even if you do think it, you don't say it. You're a son of a bitch, telling me that. You're still a son of a bitch."

"Nothing of the kind," Munroe said. "You still didn't tell me what else I'm supposed to think. You come down here and you know Eva, and you're working for Baldwin. Eva tells me she's going to Madrid and all those other places, and she's letting this friend of hers use her apartment while she's gone, and I should be nice to her. I trust Eva, you know? Eva and me get along. I don't give Eva any trouble about the travel agency, and the high rollers always coming in and booking junkets here. Eva and I see each other, couple times a week. Eva tells me, her old classmate's coming in to visit, I should be nice to classmate — what should I do? Complain? Bullshit on that." Munroe sipped coffee. He put the cup down on the table and began to rise to his feet. "Got to get my cigarettes," he said, standing erect. "What's insulting about that? Want to tell me that? All I did was assume that if Eva's old pal and me hit it off, which we did, unless I miss my guess, at least two people out of three involved in the discussion wouldn't be as lonely as they might've been with Eva gone. I think I was right." He padded off toward the master bedroom.

She sat there on her towel and regarded his sagging behind as he left the living room. She looked down at the coffee table and slipped open the spiral notebook to the first page. She punched in the numbers for Mark Baldwin's office in Boston. She said, "Switchboard?" when the female voice answered "North American." She said, "Message for Mister Baldwin. Tell him Constance Gates will be in at ten o'clock."

When Munroe returned from the bedroom he was wearing a yellow silk robe with white piping and unwrapping a fresh pack of Luckies. He stood at the edge of the living room rug and squinted down at her. "You know you," he said with narrowed eyes, "and this is another thing, you and me, we both know after all I said last night and then we end up here in bed, this ain't coincidence."

"I don't understand," she said, keeping her face expressionless, wishing she had clothes on.

He nodded twice. He tapped a cigarette out, stuck it between his lips, drew a pack of matches from the pocket of his robe, struck one, lit the cigarette, waved the match out and tossed on it the counter surface. He exhaled smoke and removed the Lucky from his lips, spitting small bits of tobacco from his lower one. "Yes you do," he said. "You just don't think I do. Which I think is kind of insulting, but never mind that for right now. You struck out with Jay Quentin before you came to eat with me. Myself, I got to wonder, you even would've shown up, he'd told you what you wanted, lots of which he didn't know, if it's my guess you want. But you did show up. And all of a sudden, after this day that you've had not getting what you need, there you are getting sloshed with me and telling me I'm cute.

"Now that was pretty sudden," he said. "You didn't tell me that the first day, when we're up in the plane. You didn't tell me that until the end the second day, when you've been out all day and all that you come back with is an empty tank. And I," he said, shrugging, "I figured from what you said and the way that you were acting, that something'd changed fast in a day, that before you could take me or leave me alone, and you're too tired to have me come up, and now all of a sudden you're coming on to me. And I didn't have much trouble thinking just what that might be. I may not be brilliant but when someone's making me a deal, and it's something that I want, at a price I don't mind paying, well, you don't have to be a genius to decide just what to do. And that is what I did."

"Tell me more," she said.

He shrugged again. "Isn't any more," he said. "That covers it, I think. I just don't like you swearing at me for being the same exact thing you are, all right? We made a trade. What you wanted for what I wanted. No need to call each other names, after we're satisfied. That's no way to do business. That's no way at all." He dangled the cigarette from his mouth and looked at her through the smoke. "I'm going in and take a quick shower and shave and get dressed," he said. "I'll be outta here in five minutes, and I won't come here again while you're here unless you ask me, all right?"

"Fair enough," she said dully.

"But if you do that," he said, turning toward the bedroom, "or even if you don't, no more of this pretending that you're better'n I am. We're just the same, Lady Gates. We're identically the same."

29

The brick-walled yard behind the Baldwin townhouse on Chestnut Street on Beacon Hill was almost exactly twenty feet square. It received sufficient sunlight to enable Victor Han to cultivate eighteen bushes of tea roses along its easterly and southerly walls, with vines of white morning glories climbing the bricks behind them. Ivy blanketed the westerly wall behind the white wrought-iron table and four chairs arranged in front of it. Songbirds came in the morning to the birdbath in the center of the lawn and sang outside the house.

In fine weather, Victor Han opened the French doors of the first floor parlor and turned on the underground sprinkler system to a fine, low mist before serving breakfast on the oak table that faced the yard, so that the odor of the flowers and the freshened lawn entered the room before Mark Baldwin did each day. Roger Kidd spread Trappist strawberry preserves on a hand-cut thick slice of whole wheat bread and said the room was his favorite place for breakfast in the world. "Except for the fact, of course," he said, "that the only time I ever have it here is when you're in some kind of scrape."

Baldwin poured mocha chocolate coffee into the Wedgwood cup and stirred it with a demitasse spoon. "My father," he said, "used to play golf with an undertaker who had the same sort of complaint. Stan used to say he never saw, professionally, anybody in a good mood. He used it to excuse his habit of getting drunk every time he came here. Good old Stan. When he kicked off, his son buried him in the cheapest wooden casket they had in basement stock." He drank some of the coffee. "Then he sold the business to his father's biggest competitor and took off for Santa Barbara to become a fisherman."

"That what you've got in mind?" Kidd said.

Baldwin smiled. "Actually, no," he said, "I was thinking more of France. Surprising how the Riviera becomes even more appealing when a few nuisances like this crop up. Trouble is, I've got a strong impression running wouldn't make these go away. I think at least one of them would follow me, and probably get worse."

"Do they have a firm diagnosis yet?" Kidd said. "One they're comfortable with, I mean, that they think might hold up?"

"Sure," Baldwin said. " 'Chronic depression.' Which is likely to get worse in a few years if she has the same severe experience with menopause that her mother had. Apparently her mother was near impossible for about two years when she went through it."

"Well," Kidd said, "but they can control that with hormones, of course, if they know what to expect and're alert for when it happens."

"They can," Baldwin said, "but keep in mind that treating Sylvia with hormones isn't quite the same kind of automatic pharmacology you can use on someone who has no history of instability. The hormones have their side effects too, not necessarily all good."

"Which means, what? Therapy?" Kidd said. "I've never seen that work. Not with the chronic cases, at least. Neurotics, people who're just unhappy now and then — with them I've seen it work. But when they get to the point of going into hospital, I've never seen it work."

"Neither have I," Baldwin said. "Neither has Richard, who of course has pretty much the same family experience with it that I've had, and who seems to be advising Jason very persuasively in this mess. I don't make a habit of agreeing with what Richard says, but that doesn't mean I just ignore it, either. And this time I think Richard's correct when he says the only possibility of Sylvia's recovery is by drastically changing her life."

"And that's where you come in," Kidd said.

"Well," Baldwin said, "that's where she'd like me to come in, obviously. And where Jason certainly wouldn't object to me coming in, not at all — it'd make his life much simpler, even if it did initially jolt his principals a little. And of course Richard would just *love* it. That'd mean that Jason could sashay out of the closet and give Richard another brilliant convert to his small salon."

"You really dislike Richard, don't you?" Kidd said.

"Richard is mean," Baldwin said. "Over the years, since child-hood, really, I've made determined efforts to get so I like Richard. He's smart and he's funny and he's very hard-working, and he certainly knows a lot. And let's face it, Roger, his persuasion does give him access to sources of information that people like us lack. There's an underground of those people, mutually protective, a very efficient subterranean network where they've hidden, reasonably enough, all these years, taking care of each other as best they can. I don't have any ambitions to join it, but it could be useful to have a pipeline into what's going on in there that might affect my business. Personal or otherwise. So, just for selfish reasons, I'd like to be able to let bygones be bygones and get along with Richard.

"But every time it seems as though I'm on the brink of being able to," he said, "every time I seem to be on the verge of being able to spend an evening in his company without grinding my teeth, he pulls some tricky business that reminds me I hate him.

"It's never anything major," Baldwin said. "Not in recent years, at least. Not since my brother died. Richard's gotten neater, become more surgical. Nobody's ever left bleeding to death on the floor with a dagger in his chest. Not anymore. Now it's just the nasty, petty, little things, that Richard does to people. And for no apparent reason, except to make them look small and him look big.

"Connie Gates, for example — Richard won her confidence easily enough. Her ex-husband's in Richard's firm. He asked Richard to look over her contract with *Journeyer*. Richard gave her sound legal advice, for which he didn't charge her. So far, he looks good. But then he betrayed her confidence, using what she told him so that he could advise her in order to whipsaw me into doing something that Jason wants. Because Jason is paying him money. See what I mean?"

"Well," Kidd said, "if the Gates woman didn't pay him, I mean, technically . . . . "

"Oh horseshit, Roger," Baldwin said. "It's unethical. You know it's unethical. Would you do a thing like that?"

"No," Kidd said.

"Neither would I," Baldwin said. "We're not talking here about some X-ten-B-five situation on Wall Street that you can't police, somebody using inside information that he obtained by chance in order to make a market killing off a bunch of strangers. We're talking about someone deriving information from a vulnerable woman, and using it to advance his own goals with a vulnerable man, at the possible further expense of an even more vulnerable woman who's tried to kill herself."

"If Sylvia in fact was trying to kill herself," Kidd said. "People who take pills and pass out, knowing they'll be found, well, they're not always serious. I agree it's a pretty extreme variety of showing off, but it is a proven attention-getter."

"People that desperate for attention," Baldwin said, "in my experience, at least, are always serious."

"Yes," Kidd said, "that's true."

"Sylvia was serious," Baldwin said. "Maybe not about wanting to kill herself. But as far as making some sort of statement about her life in general, she was serious. Very serious."

"Yes," Kidd said, helping himself to coffee. "Well, obviously the marriage has to end."

"There's a consensus on that," Baldwin said. "One that includes Sylvia. There are, as a matter of fact, no dissenters — that I know about, at least."

"Which leaves you — where?" Kidd said.

"That's part of the reason you're having breakfast here this morning," Baldwin said. "To answer that question for me."

"Will she be satisfied," Kidd said, "with something short of marriage? I assume you're not prepared to go that far."

"A safe assumption," Baldwin said. "A very safe assumption. I presume she would be, if she had assurances that in everything but name the deal would be the same. At least for the time being."

"Yes," Kidd said. " 'The time being' being that period of whatever duration before she again becomes discontented with her lot in life and brings another 'accident' upon herself to dramatize her discontent."

"People who've done it once and failed," Baldwin said, "usually do it again. In my experience, that is."

"And we know," Kidd said, "that she has a tendency to take what she wants, regardless of risks. And regardless of scandals."

"Yes, we do," Baldwin said.

"Yes," Kidd said. He sipped at his coffee and mused. "It's an interesting situation, I'd say."

"Isn't it," Baldwin said.

"Suppose," Kidd said, gazing at Baldwin over his coffee cup, "just supposing, now, but suppose that someone knowing everything she wanted, and that she'll stop at nothing to get it, suppose that person categorically refused to grant her any of it? What would happen then?"

"That's a good question," Baldwin said. "I may have come at the answer to it by asking a different one. Suppose the person knowing what it is that Sylvia wants, ultimately, and knowing also what most repels her, and being not inclined to give her what she wants — suppose that person deliberately confronted her with her worst fears realized."

"What would happen then?" Kidd said.

"Exactly," Baldwin said.

"So," Kidd said, "the real question is not whether Sylvia gets any part of what she wants, since she isn't going to get all of it and nothing less will please her. The real question is whether to give her the bad news now, or wait until later."

"That was my thinking," Baldwin said. "Obviously what was between the two of us is finished, over now. The kind of relationship that I had with Sylvia can't continue with any person who's unstable, especially one as unstable as she is. If she recovers fully tomorrow, that won't change a thing. Not as far as I'm concerned. Sooner or later, one way or the other, I've got to get rid of her."

"That sounds so harsh," Kidd said.

"Pity," Baldwin said. "It sounds true to me, the only thing to do."

"Just thinking out loud now," Kidd said. "If you give Sylvia some sop now, she'll get better. She'll divorce Jason and she'll be your regular consort."

"That's what she'll expect," Baldwin said.

"I'm just thinking out loud, Mark," Kidd said. "The next thing will be that she'll want to move in here."

"Probably," Baldwin said.

"You're not going to allow that," Kidd said.

"That's correct," Baldwin said.

"So, sooner or later," Kidd said, "that or something else will provoke a crisis, and Sylvia will do something that will make the police blotter."

"I think so," Baldwin said.

"If she does it sooner," Kidd said, "the officers responding will identify the victim as Mrs Jason Francis."

"Yes," Baldwin said.

"If she does it later," Kidd said, "she will find a way to do it here, perhaps in this very room. And the officers will identify her as the former Sylvia Francis, found at the Beacon Hill residence of Mark Baldwin, chief executive officer of North American Group."

"That's what I would do," Baldwin said. "If I were those officers."

"Therefore," Kidd said, "from your point of view, sooner is better than later."

"Precisely," Baldwin said.

"Continuing this speculation," Kidd said, as birds sang in the garden, "what in your estimation would be likely to precipitate this inevitable crisis to occur at the more, as opposed to less, favorable time to you?"

"That brings us," Baldwin said, "to the second leg of Richard's two-legged stool. Constance Gates."

"Ah," Kidd said. "Proceed."

"Miz. Gates, or Mrs. Gates, makes Jason Francis nervous," Baldwin said. "Not as nervous as she makes Mrs Francis, though. For some reason or other, Sylvia hated her on sight. Jason wants Miz. Gates silenced on the story that I put her on, on your advice. Sylvia wants Miz. Gates off the screen completely. Suppose I grant both of their wishes? What do I gain?"

"Time to prepare for the inevitable catastrophe," Kidd said.

"But now suppose I deny both their wishes," Baldwin said, "Suppose instead of calling Connie in today to fire her, as Richard and Jason tried to muscle me into doing, I sit her down and have a nice chat and bolster her confidence so she goes out more eager than before? And suppose Sylvia, one way or the other, finds out what has happened? Then what do I gain?"

"Immunity from responsibility for the inevitable catastrophe," Kidd said, "plus more time to think about whether in fact you will leave Gates on the job permanently."

"Exactly," Baldwin said.

"You know," Kidd said, "I'm extremely glad that you never practiced law."

"Well, I didn't," Baldwin said, "and that's why you're having breakfast. To tell me if you see a hole in what I've said."

"No, I don't," Kidd said, "and that's why I'm glad."

30

"Meat tenderizer," Baldwin said, leaning back in his chair with his hands clasped at his belt and arching his back. He waggled his head on his neck and grinned. "See?" he said to Constance Gates. "Everything works fine. This friend of mine — well, friend of a friend, actually — heard about the agony I was going through and called me up out of the blue and said: 'Go to Montreal. See Doctor Lavasseur. He works on weekends. Fix you up in a jiffy.' And I did, and he did, and I'm fine."

"Remarkable," Gates said.

"Well, it is," Baldwin said. "If you've had this kind of trouble on and off all your life, as I have, and you're truly afraid of surgeons, as I am, you'd listen if a fellow in a grass skirt and a voodoo mask said he could fix you up. Somebody who claims he can cure it with a horse hypodermic needle and a jug of what amounts to a high-falutin' variant of, say Adolph's Meat Tenderizer, doesn't seem like a quack at all. You go into the office and take off your shirt and lie down on the table, and he looks at your X-rays while your belly gets cold and he makes little noises that end in 'Uh huh,' and then he rigs up his needle and picks his spot and shoots the juice into you. And it hurts like hell, and you know you're going to be paralyzed thereafter, and you have to lie still for a little bit so you can reflect on what on earth possessed you to make this particular mistake. And then he takes some more pictures, and then he says: 'You can get up. I wouldn't do any weight-lifting for a while, but you should be noticing gradual improvement in about ten days.'

"And you don't," Baldwin said, "notice any improvement at all for about a week. What you do notice is that the place where he stuck in the shooter's all inflamed, and it is sore, and the trouble you had finding a comfortable position in the airplane seat going up was nowhere near as big as the trouble you have finding a comfortable position in the airplane seat going back.

"Then a funny thing happens," Baldwin said. "It starts to get better. The soreness disappears and the inflammation goes down and when it starts to disappear, there's nothing behind it. Nothing. The place that hurt in your back is still there, but it doesn't hurt anymore. And you start to try these little experiments, very carefully, of course. And usually in the shower, where the hot water's handy if something kinks up. And nothing does. That extra tissue or whatever it was that was clamping you up is all gone. You can move. It doesn't hurt. You're flexible.

"It's wonderful," he said. "it's like being a kid again."

"Congratulations," she said. "if I liked my ex-husband better, I'd tell him about it."

"Well," Baldwin said, "you're in a sour mood."

"I don't know why I'm here," she said. "I was out doing my job, what I thought was my job, at least, and I called my machine this morning and got a peremptory message from some night operator telling me to get back to Boston and see you. I was supposed to see some people that probably don't matter much down in Waterford this morning. Then, this afternoon, I was going down to New Bedford, to WSET. Instead, here I am, sitting here. Are you pulling me off this assignment?"

"No," he said.

"Then what's going on?" she said.

"You haven't shipped in any tapes," he said.

"No," she said, "I haven't."

"Why not?" he said.

"Because I didn't want to," she said. "I don't know how to work that way, people I don't even know getting between me and the basis of my work. I know what's on those tapes. I'm the one who needs to know. I don't need that intervention."

"I see," Baldwin said. He frowned. He picked up a pencil and toyed with it, turning it end for end. "Don't you think," he said, "my interest in the project is legitimate? That I have a right to wonder, after over a month, how it's coming along?"

She exhaled. "Yes," she said, "I do."

"And since I don't know," he said, "and I do wonder, I am asking."

She slid down in the chair. "I've read all the files," she said. "It was like you said: boring work. But I did it. Then I started in on the bureaucracies. I got the census figures from Nineteen-sixty, Seventy and Eighty from the Town of Waterford. They were also just like you said. The population went from forty-four hundred and eighty-two in Nineteen-sixty to just under seven thousand in Nineteen-seventy, to almost seventeen thousand in Nineteen-eighty. Taxable residential properties were assessed at a total of about six and a half million twenty-five years ago, twenty-three million in Seventy, and now they're over a hundred-twenty million. Commercial real estate assessments were under eight hundred thousand in Nineteen-sixty, and most of that was the fish processing complex on the South River. Even by Seventy, commercial real estate was only assessed at about three million, three-point-five, and most of that was raw land. But by Eighty, commercial was over ninety-three million, and that was two years or so before the Mall was finished and the condo complexes were ready and offices were up, and three years before the two industrial parks were open. I haven't checked all the current billings at the Town Assessors' office," she said, "but Dan Munroe says he thinks the total — industrial, commercial, residential — must be close to half a billion by now. That hideous damned mall alone, and the condo complex with the office space, where I have been staying, that stuff has got to be worth a whole damned bunch of money. The development hasn't exactly ground to a halt. It's still going on, in spades. And naturally, every time you open up a new commercial or industrial plant there, you drive up the value of the residential real estate, and that's still going on.

"So," she said, "what you told me about how the town's exploded in the past twenty, thirty years, that's certainly how it looks. I know all the towns've gone to a hundred percent evaluation now, and I know that probably exaggerates the increase. But I also know that most of the stuff that's in that town is pretty nearly new. Munroe took me on an airplane ride over it, day before yesterday, and sure, there's still a lot of green space down there, and it doesn't look like Worcester yet. But it's not a sleepy little town on the water any more. There's a lot of money being made in Waterford today.

"From what the District Attorney told me, this Mister Taves in Bristol? From what he told me," she said, "what Logan is supposed to be planning to say about the law ignoring what went on during all this growth is pretty much true.

"I have to give the guy credit," she said. "He didn't try to blow smoke at me. He said when he was still an assistant DA in Plymouth, under his pal, Keane, and the Lavalle murder happened, they didn't take it very seriously. Which of course is what Logan says on the video tapes Taves loaned me. Furthermore, Taves makes no bones about both Keane and himself not caring much today about whether any corners were cut and money changed hands under tables back when it was going on."

"Statutes of limitations've probably run anyway," Baldwin said. "Wouldn't make much difference if they did care."

"Yeah," she said, "but he didn't hide behind that. And neither did Munroe. Both of them seemed to feel that any way you look at it, Waterford's a hell of a lot more prosperous town today than it was back when you and Logan were down there, and if somebody got screwed or a body got buried in the process of making those improvements, well, somebody gets hurt in every kind of progress and that doesn't make the progress bad."

She laughed. "These are very practical people you've been sending me to see," she said. "They're not what I'd call a bunch of starry-eyed romantics, you know? Not like that at all."

"Have you seen Mel Shaw?" he said.

"I have laid eyes on him," she said. "Munroe pointed him out to me, coming out of Waterford Associates. The condo unit I'm using down there, belongs to a friend of mine? It's right next to the Waterford Professional complex on Route Four south of Union Street, and I saw Shaw leaving his office for lunch the other day. He's a dapper little devil, isn't he, this publicity director? Looks like a little banty rooster, strutting to his Lincoln in his preppy clothes."

"That's recent," Baldwin said. "Of course the money's recent, too. But Mel used to look pretty threadbare, back when he was a humble newspaperman."

"Well," she said, "he doesn't now. But what he's got to say for himself, if anything, I don't know yet. I called his office for an appointment, but his secretary said he was out and he'd get back to me. Which he hasn't done. And which, since I assume it's all over town by now that I'm doing a story, and what I'm doing it about, it wouldn't surprise me too much if he didn't."

"But you'll make another try, I assume," Baldwin said.

"Oh," she said, "several. And if the phone calls don't work, I'll stake the joint out and wait 'till I see him go in, and then march right in and try in person. But don't be surprised if I don't get to talk to him. I wouldn't talk, if I were Shaw."

"Neither would I," Baldwin said. He sat back and thought for a while. He leaned forward again. "Well," he said, "it sounds to me like you're doing all right. Making very good progress, in fact. Have you contacted Logan, made arrangements to see him?"

She nodded. "Uh huh," she said. "Next Monday at his home. Which was my convenience, more than anything else — he was eager to talk. But that left me today to wrap up in Waterford, and this afternoon at the TV station in New Bedford. Then tomorrow and however much of Friday it takes to get everything out of the doctor at Finisterre as he's got to contribute. Which I know I'm going to get all of because Taves said he'd call him and tell him to release any law enforcement stuff he's got, and Logan volunteered he'd call him up and tell him to come clean with me. Then the weekend to get my ducks more or less in a row, watch the damned tapes, again, and sift through all the stuff I've collected so far and lay out some of the things I want to ask Logan. And after I see him, start writing. You said time was important." She exhaled.

"Great," Baldwin said. He studied her. "So why are you so jumpy?"

She looked startled. "I don't know," she said.

"Are you sure?" he said.

She lifted her hands and let them drop. She shook her head. "I don't know," she said. "I just don't know any more. It seems as though, whatever I try to do, it doesn't turn out right.

"I think I'm in control," she said, "or ought to be, at least. But then, when I look at the way I'm living, I'm not in control at all. On the surface it seems like I'm doing perfectly normal things. Living in my tiny little apartment, driving around in my neat little German car, supporting myself and not leeching off of my ex-husband. Being available to my children I unselfishly gave up because I agreed with their father he's a better parent than I am, and can give them nicer stuff than I ever could. And I look at myself and say: 'Well, you're being a responsible adult citizen and you should be kind of pleased with yourself.'

"But I'm not," she said. "I'm not pleased with myself because nobody else I run into seems pleased with me at all. Instead of at least giving me my due for being fair-minded about the kids and not fighting him for them, my ex-husband feels nothing but contempt for me. And he doesn't bother to conceal it, either. Not from me, and not from the kids. And naturally, since they live with him and his new wife, he's been able to train them to think the same way.

"It's very easy for him, too," she said. "To turn them against me. I'm supposed to see them on alternate weekends and for a month every summer, and at Christmas and things like that. But I don't. I almost never see both of them together, and when I do, only one of them stays with me, because Jeffrey's got them brainwashed into thinking that a boy and girl not even teenagers yet are too big already to be sleeping in the same bed, and there isn't room in my place for a bed for each of them. So one weekend I see Estelle, and when the next weekend rolls around, Jeffy calls me up and asks me very nicely if he can postpone his visit because his father's gotten tickets to the baseball game or something, and I know he wants to go to that, so of course I say: 'Okay, kid, next week.' But next week comes and there's something else, and I'm lucky if I wind up seeing him twice in seven weeks.

"It's the same thing with my work," she said. "I've done a lot of stuff for Terry Gleason, and I know he respects my ability. But for some reason or another, his secretary hates me. Or I go out on this assignment for you, and I have to practically arm-wrestle that District Attorney before he'll be civil to me. I get down to Waterford there to interview that yokel police chief, and before I know what I'm doing, I've gotten drunk with him on margaritas and I'm in bed with the big jerk, acting like a cheap piece of ass and doing it just for good measure in my friend's bed. Which he's familiar with because he's been in it so many times with her."

"Your personal life's your own business, Connie," Baldwin said. "Very few people I know could tell me, so that I'd believe it, that they handle such matters well."

"You heard," she said.

"I heard you jumped into bed with him the first day you hit town," he said. "Notice what I said. I didn't say I believed it. I said I heard it. I know Waterford pretty well. I know Munroe's wife left him. I can easily imagine how your proximity to him would start a lot of talk. I wasn't worried about it when I heard it. I'm not disturbed about it now, when you tell me it's true. I don't think I would've recommended it, but I'm not disturbed."

"Well," she said. "it isn't true."

He stared at her. "I thought you just told me," he said. "I thought you just said . . . ."

"What I told you's worse than what you heard," she said. "But what you heard isn't true, all right? I didn't go gaga over the jerk and jump into the sack with him on my first night in town. What I did was stand him off, say to myself: 'No way.' Until I started to wonder if maybe fucking him was the only way I was going to get the information I needed. And then, that was when I did it. That was when I came across. Straight player deal, no cash involved. He got what he wanted, which was a large piece of my ass. I got what I wanted, which was most of what he knew." She chuckled ruefully. "Not all, though," she said. "Or at least that's what he claims. He left out stuff about his mother — he admitted that. And I'm sure without him saying that he left out other stuff. Dan Munroe is a damned clod, but Dan Munroe's not dumb. He knows who I'm looking for. He covered his own ass, while he was getting mine. If I took him, and I sure did, well, he took me as well."

"I see," Baldwin said. He cleared his throat. He rearranged papers on his desk, frowning as he did it. "Well," he said, "tell you the truth, I don't know what to say. Ordinary policy's that we discourage our reporters from, uh, fraternizing, say? But in this instance at least, so far as I'm aware, nobody encouraged you. You did it on your own." He paused. "So," he said, "I really don't know what to tell you. I'm sorry you feel badly. I wish you didn't. But what to say to you exactly, that I do not know." He looked at her directly. "What do you want me to say to you, Connie? Can you tell me that?"

"Yeah," she said, "I can. Why am I acting like this? I never used to do these things. A jerk like Munroe I would've brushed off in a minute, when I was just a college kid and didn't know a thing. I would've had nothing to do with him. Now, I'm supposedly mature. I have an afternoon's conversation with him. He takes me on a plane ride. I go to dinner with him. I decide I need something that I can't get anywhere else, and I think I know how to get it. I deliberately get plastered and jump into bed with him.

"He got it right, Mark," she said. "He gave me all the dirt on the folks in Waterford, all the dirt I need at least, in exchange for an all-nighter, which is what he had in mind. I got briefed and I got laid, no bad bargain for me. But I can't call it, you know, anything but bargaining." She shuddered. "I don't like myself like this. I feel uncomfortable. I sort of despise myself. I want to go home to my apartment and take a hot bath and get clean.

"Before I got divorced," she said, "I didn't act like this. Jeff had an affair — he had a couple of them. Women from his office, which Andrea was. Secretaries, paralegals, you name it. That I knew about, I mean. He probably had more. One-night stands and stuff like that. And I was always amazed. And I felt superior. Amazed that any woman would find Jeff wildly attractive. Superior because I thought he'd lost his mind.

"Then we got divorced," she said. "Free lady, all of that. The first thing that I did was get involved with a guy who wants to kill himself. I decide: This will not work. I horse around. Then I go for a young guy, hardly more than a juvenile, who decided after he moved in with me that I was not only supposed to support him, and tell him he was a great artist, and screw him upon order, but also that when things got frustrating in his life, to let him beat me up. So, I came to my senses after a while, and I got rid of him. And now what do I do when *I* get frustrated? Fool around some more. Then call him up, of course, and let him mess with my head on the phone. Tell me that he's coming over to slap me around and get me shaped up again, because I need discipline to feel good about myself. And then what do I do? Go back to the self-destructive guy. And then to Munroe.

"I get discouraged," she said. "I have to ask myself: What is the matter with me? It's not just lovers. It's everyone. Why do I always encounter this sort of undifferentiated hostility, you know? Antagonism. And not just from total strangers. People I don't even know, who may have something wrong with them that I don't know about. No, when I run into someone I've known for a long time, the same thing seems to happen. It almost has to be me that's the reason. Has to be, doesn't it? Other people don't seem to have this problem. What is wrong with me? And then I get depressed.

"Why do I let everything and everyone *get* to me like this," she said. "I'm an intelligent woman — at least I think I am. Why do I always feel like I'm on the edge of losing complete control and just flying all to pieces like a window with a rock through it? *Is* there something wrong with me?"

He nodded. "Probably," he said. "But I doubt it's permanent.

More like a run of bad luck. Plus fatigue, too, I would guess. What you need some R and R, a day or two of rest and relaxation. You'll be as good as new."

"I thought time was a factor in this job," she said.

"It is," he said. "but you're not going to save any time working yourself into a state that prevents you from functioning — wouldn't you agree?"

"Don't have much choice," she said. "So what do I do?"

He looked at her appraisingly. "Feel like taking a chance on another man?" he said.

She returned the level gaze. "Well," she said. "it's not as though I had a lot left to lose."

31

Following instructions, Constance Gates pulled into the Gulf station at the southern end of the Bourne Bridge at 6:30 in the evening, and parked next to the ice machine. She shut off the BMW and thought about what she would do if Mark Baldwin didn't show.

At 6:35, Mark Baldwin in a metallic maroon Porsche 911 Carrera pulled in to the gas station and made a "follow me" gesture. She started the BMW and trailed him west on the two-lane blacktop through the dunes and scrub pines onto County Road in Cataumet, never less nor more than ten miles over the thirty-mile-per-hour speed limit.

The Baldwin house at Cataumet was old from the front. Set about two hundred feet back on its circular drive from the western edge of County Road, it was two stories of silvered cedar shingles over an underground three-car garage, framed in white boards at the corners and the eaves and sheltered behind a low stone wall among maples and oaks on a knoll. She followed him into the circular white gravel drive and noticed the post lights come on. She waited behind the Porsche while the doors of the garage opened under the northerly side of the house. She followed when he stuck his left hand up through the sunroof on the Porsche and beckoned her off the gravel and onto the macadam incline. When the cars were in the garage, the door shut behind them. They shut off the engines and got out.

"That's unexpected," she said, gesturing toward the Porsche as she yanked her overnight bag from the back seat of her car. "I was expecting Ben, and the block-long pimpmobile."

Baldwin shook his head. "Private business," he said. "Private car."

He escorted her to the door into the house. He used a key to deactivate the alarm system and another to open the door. Ahead of them there was a flight of six stairs leading to another door. He locked the door behind them and ushered her up the stairs. The door at the top opened into a wide foyer with an Oriental carpet. An electrified anchor light glowed in the arched entry. To the right there was a room of billowy white couches and chairs and a grand piano glowing orange in the sunset light coming through the tall glass windows at the western end of the room. The front door was to the left. Ahead of them was a corridor into the kitchen; she could see copper-bottomed pots suspended from ceiling racks. Beyond that there was a formal dining room, also orange in the sunset.

"Bedrooms're upstairs," Baldwin said, gesturing vaguely over his left shoulder at the spiral staircase. "Leave your bag here and I'll show you the rest of what's down here." She did as she was told.

From the back the house was new, a broad expanse of glass opening on a tri-level, cedar-planked deck overlooking a trapezoidal lawn expanding and sloping gradually toward the edge of a sand cliff. Sailboats far off on Buzzards Bay displayed sails translucent against the sunset.

"There's a beach down there," Baldwin said, squinting toward the far edge of the lawn and pointing. "You can see the railing of the stairs. It's about forty feet down. The stairs are steep and the water's colder than a lawyer's heart. But it's there."

The lawn was flanked on the northerly and southerly edges by densely-overgrown hemlocks about fourteen feet tall.

"I assume you can see the decks for yourself," he said, gripping her arm. "That's where most of the sunning gets done."

The first and highest level of the deck was shaded by a blue and green striped awning. Under it were white wicker chairs, settees, and three tables. The second level, open to the sky, was furnished with blue and green chaises longues grouped in a semi-circle around a spa bath set into the platform. The tub was bubbling.

The third and lowest level, two steps down from the first, surrounded an octagonal swimming pool thirty feet across at its widest points and five feet deep at its center. It was bubbling at its corners.

"Salt water," he said, gesturing toward the pool. "Only difference between it and what's at the foot of the cliff is that it's heated to a temperature mammals can enjoy, and it's filtered and you don't have to climb stairs to use it."

"Mark," she said, turning her head to look at him, "is somebody else here?"

He grinned. "Not to my knowledge," he said.

"Does everything come on when you arrive?" she said.

"Usually," he said. "When things are working right, yes, every-thing comes on. When there's an electrical storm in Bourne, or Roger Kidd's secretary forgets to pay the light bill, or the couple that comes in here twice a week and looks after the place omits to leave the switches set in the proper sequence, then absolutely nothing works. Place seals up like Pharaoh's tomb and I have to jimmy my way in and explain to the police why the bells and whistles are resounding."

She sighed. "Good domestics are so hard to find these days," she said.

"Oh, shut up," he said. He steered her back toward the interior of the house. In the foyer he released her arm and picked up her overnight bag. He walked toward the foot of the curving stairs. "Coming?" he said. She followed him up the staircase on the Oriental runner. There were four sconces, smaller versions of the anchor light hanging in the hall, mounted at eight-foot intervals seven feet above the steps. Between them were ordinary water-colors of ocean and dune scenes matted in white behind glassed frames.

He stopped on the open landing at the top of the stairs and directed her to the right down a short hallway opening onto a large bedroom to the left and a smaller one to the right. He paused in front of the door to the smaller room and allowed her to precede him into the larger one. There was a king-sized bed spread with a yellow-and-white Lily Pulitzer-designed comforter against the wall nearest the door. There was a large white-and-gilt make-up table against the opposite wall, with a white-and-gilt chair upholstered in matching Pulitzer fabric in front of it, and a white negligée over the back of the chair. Flanking the table were two chests of drawers, also white and gilt. At the far end of the room there was a chaise longue done in the same fabric, and two chairs in plain yellow silk with a white wicker coffee table between them. Beyond the furniture yellow linen drapes hung beside the two French doors opening onto a balcony with a white wooden railing and a view of the Bay. "Bath's to the left beyond the bed," he said. He set her bag on the spread. "I think you'll find everything you need, but if there's something missing, holler."

She took a deep breath. "Okay," she said, "thank you. I'm sure I'll be all right. This is magnificent."

He smiled at her. "Don't be too hasty," he said. "Danny and Agnes McGee are good-hearted, well-intentioned, and not always reliable. If they've stocked the refrigerator and done the other chores I asked them, *and* if Mort's Fish Market did have a fresh catch in, then after we've had dinner I will accept 'magnificent.' But not until then." He started out of the room.

"Before you go," she said, "are we having dinner now?"

He stopped at the door. "If you're hungry, we can," he said. "I was thinking, though, if you're not, we might have some wine and a swim first, take the first layer of city grit off, at least, and then eat around nine. What's your pleasure?"

She stretched and sat down on the bed. "So far today," she said, "by following your lead I've made about a hundred-eighty-degree improvement over the way I felt this morning. I'm not about to start bickering now." She flopped back on the bed. "I'll be down in a little while for the wine and the swim."

"There's a robe in the bath, or should be," he said. "I'll see you outside." He shut the door behind him.

She lay still for a few moments after he was gone, stretching and relaxing her muscles. Then she sat up and began to undress, piling her soiled clothes on the bed. Nude, she opened her overnight bag and fished out a white maillot swimsuit. She carried it into the bathroom with her, debating whether to shower before putting it on. In a distant part of the house she heard water start running. She put the swimsuit on the vanity and stepped into the shower.

She did not see him as she went down the stairs and out through the music room doors onto the deck, but she heard him moving around in the kitchen. There was a southwest evening breeze off the water by then, and she was glad of the heavy white terry-cloth robe over her swimsuit. She went over to the spa tub and dipped her hand in; the water was fairly hot. Her test of the swimming pool on the next level persuaded her that it was heated also, to perhaps eighty degrees. She was standing beside the pool, hands jammed into the pockets of her robe, when he came out with a tray that he brought to the grouping of chaises longues beside the tub and set down on one of the tables. He was wearing one of the heavy white robes. His hair was wet.

"Wine?" he said, holding up a green bottle. "I can make you a kir if you like."

"Oh," she said, "no. I mean: Yes, wine will be fine. Don't bother with the kir."

He brought two glasses of wine down to the edge of the pool and handed one to her. "Thanks for coming," he said. He touched her glass with his.

"Well," she said, grinning, "it's a dirty job, I know, but somebody's got to do it. Thanks for asking me."

They stood there for a while, watching the last few sailboats head for harbors in the blue evening, and she leaned back against him. "Tell me something," she said. "I suppose it's lots different in the winter. Hell, I grew up on the water. I *know* it's lots different in the winter."

"Actually," he said, "it isn't all that bad. There's nobody around. Sometimes solitude is nice. But not as a steady diet. It can get pretty bleak when the snow comes down from Canada and starts blowing across the bay. Shallow water, you know? The waves really build up and they smash against the rocks below the cliff here hard enough so that spray comes up onto the lawn. It's all eroded down there from it. They tell me that in a hundred years or so, this pool is going to topple right into the sea. But I don't worry too much about that. I figure the chances of my being here to watch it then are pretty slim, and if the Archdiocese of Boston doesn't have brains enough to sell it before then to some wealthy fellow with more cash than brains, well, that'll be their problem."

"The Catholic Archdiocese owns the pool?" she said.

"The Archdiocese owns the whole layout," he said.

"I thought it was your family's," she said. "I thought this was your place."

"It was," he said. "But I'm all that's left of the family, unless you count certain cousins I dislike. I'm fifty-three years old, and I'm unlikely to have children now. Leaving aside the question of whether I really ever wanted to have any in the first place. So my lawyer suggested to me one day, in his gentle fashion, that perhaps instead of leaving my executor with the work of converting this property into cash in order to discharge the charitable bequests I've made in my will, I might prefer to save myself a tidy sum in taxes by disposing of it myself."

"You're a Catholic?" she said.

"Oh, no," he said. "I'm not much of anything. But you don't have to be Catholic to want to save money on taxes, and the Archdiocese does some charitable work that I'm interested in, sort of a private welfare scheme which I personally knew to do a lot of good, and which could use the kind of money that this place represents. So I deeded it over to the Archdiocese and reserved a life estate to myself. Which means I get to use the place as I like for as long as I live, and I save on the taxes right now, and my prick of a cousin doesn't get a chance at it, and the Archdiocese gets it after I'm dead. But for tax purposes, back when I did it some years ago, the gift took effect immediately. I probably saved as much in taxes as I could have gotten selling the place to someone who wouldn't let me use it for the rest of my life."

She sighed. "Lawyers are wonderful," she said.

"Clever," he said. "Cleverness is really all that most of us claim to have."

"Yeah," she said. "I should get some of that."

"Oh," he said, rubbing her waist through the robe and the swimsuit, "you seem sharp enough."

She laughed. "My father used to say I was shrewd," she said. "After the way I behaved, ending my marriage and then afterwards, I think he may've retracted that, but he used to say I was."

"Are your parents still alive?" he said.

"My father is," she said. "Says he's retired now, but I notice whenever the weather's even halfway decent, he's still out in his boat pulling traps. My mother died four years ago. For which my father partly blamed me. For acting like I did with Jeffrey and the kids; he made it pretty clear that he thought I broke her heart. I don't see the old man much. It's awkward when I do."

"That's too bad," he said.

"Well," she said, "it is. But I was suffocating in that marriage. And if it was selfish for me to want to get out of it, at any cost, which I'm willing to concede it may have been, then: okay, that's what it was. But what I asked him, when he laid that trip on me, was: 'Isn't it even more selfish of you to tell me I should've stayed married to Jeffrey, when I was miserable, for your sake and Mom's? You weren't the ones who were putting up with him, taking his sneers and feeling like you were good for nothing. How do you know so much?'

And he couldn't answer that. So he just got mad instead, and stayed that way. Fishermen're good at getting into moods and staying in them — all that time out on the ocean by themselves. They're all brooders, every one. And after a while, I got sick of banging my head against his attitudes, and more or less stopped seeing him."

"It's still tough, though," he said.

She straightened up. "That's all right," she said. "I'm a tough kid, too. I can take it." She turned and faced him. "Are we going to swim or what, here?"

He bent and set his wine glass down on the apron of the pool. He unknotted the belt of his robe. "Swim it is," he said. "I ought to warn you, though. This is a lawyer's pool. No diving boards for people to jump off and break their necks and sue me. The deepest part's in the middle, and you can stand up there. Shallow dives only."

She watched as his robe fell open on light blue cotton boxer trunks, then started to undo her own. She let it drop on the apron of the pool. "Look," he said, "if you're self-conscious about this, it's perfectly okay. But my own preference in the swimwear-optional policy at this establishment is to go without. Will that bother you?"

"Watch," she said. She did a shallow dive into the pool, her momentum carrying her almost to the middle. She stood up and shook the water out of her eyes. She started walking up the incline, the water running off her body and the white swimsuit, which had turned transparent and plainly displayed her aureoles and pubic hair.

"I guess it won't," he said. He reached into the waistband of his trunks and pulled out the drawstring, which he untied.

She stood in the water up to her thighs and stripped off the wet suit, tossing it onto the apron. She kept her gaze focused on his crotch as he dropped his trunks. "You don't seem too surprised," he said. He was tumescent. He sat down on the apron of the pool with his legs in the water.

"I'm not," she said. She nodded toward the line of trees at the northerly edge of the lawn. "When I saw those trees," she said, "I figured maybe they were a windbreak along with being a privacy screen, but even if they weren't, they'd still thwart those prying eyes." She shivered, and ducked down in the water so that only her head was above the surface. "I don't see how you can stand it, sitting there in that breeze, though. Aren't you coming in?"

He eased himself into the water slowly.

"Back hurt again?" she said solicitously.

"Nope," he said, shaking his head, "but the memory lingers on, and I'm not about to do anything that might make it happen again." Immersed, he began a deliberate Australian crawl stroke that took him slowly across the pool to the opposite angle where he did a dive turn and swam back. She watched him until he got halfway across, then launched herself into a faster crawl that brought her to the opposite side just behind him. They maintained his pace for nine laps each. On the closing leg of the tenth lap, she increased her pace and reached the wall first, standing up as he came in and gripped the edge of the apron.

She shivered again, folding her arms under her breasts. "That's enough for me for now," she said. He helped her out of the pool. She grabbed her robe and wrapped it around her as she stood up. "You staying in?" she said.

"What I recommend," he said, standing up in the shallows and displaying a full erection, "is more wine and the hot tub."

"The hot tub, huh?" she said, gazing at his penis.

He looked down. "Well," he said, "there are two things I can say about that. The first one is that one of the reasons I prefer to swim nude is because it makes me feel good. Like this. And the other is that you've got a nice body, and seeing it naked arouses me." He looked up at her. "Both of those things are true. Either one offend you?"

She hunkered down on the pool apron so that their eyes were on a level. "Mark," she said, "the only complaint I've got is that I'm chilly. If you say the hot tub will help, I'm willing to give it a try. And as far as erections are concerned, I've got an open mind. It all depends on the man it belongs to. Yours looks fine to me."

32

She dozed off after they made love again very early in the morning, and awoke alone in his big bed when the phone rang on the night table just after nine-fifteen. Drowsily she lay there, expecting someone to answer it elsewhere in the house. When it reached the fifth ring, she said: "Oh, shit," and sat up and answered it. She told Sylvia Francis she did not know where Baldwin was, but assumed he was somewhere in the house, and that when she located him she would have him call the office. Francis said that would not be necessary, that the call wasn't urgent, that she wasn't at the office, and that she would try to reach him later on.

Gates got out of bed and put on the white robe. Barefoot, she descended the stairs in the silent house, hearing only songbirds joyous in the sunlight out of doors. She padded up behind Baldwin and kissed the back of his neck. When he looked up at her and smiled, she rubbed the place she had kissed. "Thought you'd deserted me," she said. " 'Seduced and abandoned,' I thought. 'Should've listened to my mother.' " She sat down opposite him at the table. He picked up the empty goblet and said: "Mimosa?"

"Well, that would be decadent," she said. "Champagne before ten A.M. But then again," she said, stretching, "this whole interlude is decadent. So, why not?"

He mixed the wine and the orange juice and handed it to her. "I take it you slept well," he said.

She drank the fizzy liquid. She nodded. "I certainly did," she said. "I'd probably still be at it if the phone hadn't rung."

He looked puzzled. He gestured toward the portable on the table. "The phone?" he said. "The phone hasn't rung."

She shook her head and drank some more of the mimosa. "Yes it did," she said. "Around nine-fifteen. I was having a perfectly nice nap for myself, gathering my strength, and the phone rang next to your bed."

"Goddamnit," he said, picking up the portable. "This damned thing doesn't work at all." He slapped it down on the table. "Did you answer it?"

"Not right off," she said. "I more or less assumed it wasn't for me, since I haven't given out this address. But then when no one else seemed about to do it, I picked it up."

"Who was it?" he said.

"That woman from your office, the receptionist? The one who steals from stores." she said. "Is Francis her name?"

He looked glum. "Sylvia Francis," he said. "Sylvia called here this morning?"

"That's who she said she was," Gates said, sipping at her drink.

"What'd she have on her mind?" he said.

"That she didn't say," Gates said. "I said — I assumed she was at the office — I said I'd have you call in as soon as I found you, and she said she wasn't at the office, and she would call you back."

He slumped in the chair. "Oh, dear," he said.

"Does that mean I did wrong?" she said. "I'm sorry if I did."

He waved dismissively. "No, no," he said. "What you did was harmless enough. It's what the phone call means. She wants to come back to work."

"Has she been sick?" Gates said.

He nodded. "That would be a mild way of putting it," he said. "Apparently the shoplifting that day we were at Bruno's was just the tip of an iceberg. She's got all kinds of problems. She got arrested again, at Bloomingdale's. Then she overdosed on Seconal or something and had to be rushed to the hospital. Then it came out that her marriage is sham. Her husband's decided he's a homosexual, and it seems as though she blames herself in some way for that. She was in the hospital until yesterday, all that therapy routine. He decided it was useless, and checked her out. So now she's home. Oh, dear." He sighed. "She's really all screwed up."

"That's too bad," Gates said.

"Well," he said, "it is. But that doesn't mean anybody at North American can do anything to correct it, make things so that she'll be happy. Which is what I suspect she's got in mind for us to do."

"You could let her go," Gates said. "I don't mean to sound hardhearted, but couldn't you do that?"

He sighed. He shook his head. "No," he said, "I can't. I can't do that for the same reason that those two guys who own SET couldn't let Joe Logan go when he started to break up. And for the same reason, as far as that goes, why the Goulds didn't just fire Mel Shaw when he came apart in Washington. It's hard to draw a precise line that's clear and bright in all cases, but there's a distinction between conduct that's appropriate when you know that nothing you do will help, and conduct that's inappropriate because it'll make things worse."

The portable phone chirped on the table. He glanced at it with impatience. The phone chirped again. He looked at it with mild annoyance. "Come on, Anne," he said. "After coffee break. 'Way too soon for lunch." The phone uttered another half-chirp. It stopped abruptly.

"You shouldn't've answered that?" she said.

"No," he said, smiling, "of course I shouldn't. It's supposed to ring twice here, and then if I don't answer it, the automatic switching equipment puts it onto Anne's desk in Boston. She picks it up and takes the message, and when I'm ready to think about work, I buzz her and get the news. The only reason I bring it out here is in case *I* want to make a call. Same attitude's the old Vermont storekeeper, let the phone ring all the time. 'I got that thing for my convenience, not for every other dumb bastard that wants to call me up.' And that's the way I use it."

"Yeah," she said. She drank some of her mimosa. "Can I ask you something?"

"Sure," he said pleasantly, reaching for the champagne. "Fire away."

"I've heard a lot of stories about you," she said. "Since you hired me for this assignment, and I've gotten into it, I have heard a lot more of them."

He smiled. He poured champagne into his glass and then into hers. He put the bottle down and picked up the pitcher of juice. He topped off each of the glasses. He chuckled. "I bet you have," he said. "Ah, to be eighteen, and have my teeth again." He set the pitcher down and beamed at her. "And you want to know if they're true."

She swirled her mimosa with her right forefinger, sipped at it and put it down. She folded her hands in her lap and studied him. "No," she said, "not that. Not actually. My guess is that most of them are, and the ones that aren't, should be."

He had picked up his glass. He held it in front of his face. He looked quizzical. "I'm not sure how to take that," he said.

"Well," she said, "I guess what I'm saying is: Never mind whether what I'm hearing about you up in Waterford is true, is it going to be a problem for you if this Logan says it, when I talk to him?"

"I don't see how," Baldwin said. He drank deeply from the glass. He put it down. "Let's be realistic here. You and I both know I'm not going to publish anything you might write that might harm my reputation. And both of us also know that you're not going to write anything that might have that effect, so the question won't ever come up. So what's the problem here?"

"You mean," she said, "because we slept together, those things will not happen?"

He laughed. "No," he said, "I don't mean that. And you know I don't. Our going to bed had nothing to do with this assignment that you're on. We slept together because both of us wanted to do it the first time we saw each other, and the time was finally propitious. So we did it. Both of us're adults. We've both done it before. We will both do it again. That's the way it is."

"But," she said, "will we do it with each other?"

"Possibly," he said. "Very possibly."

33

On Monday afternoon, the sky over Mattapoisett had turned slate-blue by two o'clock and there was nothing moving on the grey waters of the harbor. The air was still and muggy. Connie Gates turned the BMW onto Coffin Street and headed down toward the water and the three big white boulders at the end of the street. The houses on both sides were small and low to the ground, shingled Capes sheltered by pine trees and oaks, with front yards carpeted by pine needles behind split rail fences. On the right at the edge of the end of the street there was a black and yellow metal sign that said "Barry Painting Contractors" and gave a license number and an assurance of union contract. It was next to a split rail fence that enclosed a front yard of pines and oaks. Visible behind the trees was a two-story Cape, shingled in cedar shakes and trimmed in barn red, with an extended wing to the south. Beyond it was a small red barn trimmed in white. She pulled into the white gravel driveway behind a black and yellow Chevy van with a rack on the roof. To her right, three men in jeans and painters' caps were descending two ladders from a scaffold made of boards. Off to their left, a man in chino pants and a blue oxford cloth shirt stood with his hands in his pockets, looking on.

She got out of the car. One of the painters noticed her and shouted. "You wanna save yourself some trouble, lady," he said, "you'll back that bucket up and let us outta here. Have to do it anyway, soon as we get down."

The man in the blue shirt turned towards her when the painter yelled. He shook his head and started towards her car. He removed his right hand from his pocket and offered it to her. "Constance Gates?" he said. He grinned. "Joe Logan." She took his hand, registering quickly everything she could. He was in his middle forties. He was about five-ten. She guessed his weight at around one-sixty. His hair was receding and he had not combed it forward.

He was deeply tanned. "Nice to see you," she said. "I didn't mean to raise a fuss."

'They're mad at me," he said. "There's a squall line coming through. They're using oil-based stain, as we agreed. I won't let them put it on when there's rain coming. They're on contract, not hourly. They want to finish this and get on to the next job. I want the job they do here to last more than one winter. So we've just had a battle, which I won, and they're taking it out on you. Back your car out of the driveway and park it beside the fence. We'll go in the house and let'em steam."

She did as he instructed, leaving her car off the edge of the pavement, taking her attaché case out and walking up the driveway. The painters were slamming their gear into the back of the van, muttering and cursing. Logan was waiting at the southwest corner of the house. He escorted her up onto the broad redwood deck to the back door. It led into the kitchen. To her right there was a counter and a sink under a casement window overlooking the deck and the back lawn and Mattapoisett harbor at the foot of it. The refrigerator and the cooking units along the adjoining wall were framed by maple cabinets. There was a butcher block island unit in the center of the work space. To her left there was a dining area with a circular butcher block table and four Breuer chairs. It faced a sliding glass door which opened onto the deck.

It was cool in the house. She put her case on the counter. "Whew," she said, "I'm not used to this strenuous life."

"Where have you been?" he said.

"Oh," she said, "this morning to Finisterre. Then to New Bedford. And now, if you don't mind, to the bathroom."

"Right in there," he said, gesturing to his right toward the hallway from the kitchen. "First door on the right."

When she came out he was pouring dark liquid from a large plastic pitcher into a tall glass filled with ice. "Iced coffee," he said. "I also have beer, wine, tonic, iced tea, various juices and lemonade. I think. Name your preference."

"What you're having," she said. She heard the engine of the Chevy van outside start with a roar. "They're not happy," she said.

"Life is hard," he said, handing her the iced coffee he had poured and selecting another tall glass from the cupboard over the sink. "Milk, cream, in the fridge. Simple syrup here." He indicated a small pewter pitcher on the counter.

"Black is fine," she said. She drank half the contents of the glass.

He finished pouring his own glass. "First, the tour," he said, taking her left arm. "Get that over with, as though it mattered. Then we can sit down and talk."

She resisted slightly. "You don't have to show me your house," she said.

"Of course I do," he said. "In the first place, if you're any good, you already know what everybody else in Christendom thinks of me, and what I've done, and what the explanation is. So it's to my advantage to be perfectly open with you. If they've told you I'm crazy, as most of them probably have, my normal behavior may cause you to hesitate before you print those opinions. If they've told you I'm sane, well, my normal behavior will convince you that against all odds, I am. Which is what I want.

"In the second place," he said, "you may have enough money hidden somewhere to buy this place from me, and if I can show you what a lovely house it is, you might make me an offer good enough so I can avoid placing it with a real estate agent. Which would save me a hefty commission. Every penny counts."

"You're selling it?" she said, ceasing her resistance.

He led her into the hallway. "I don't have much choice," he said, "with what's in front of me. I've got to put my affairs in order. This property is my only tangible asset. I've got savings, of course, and guaranteed retirement benefits, but if what I expect to happen, happens, I'll be crowding sixty when I get out. Pretty unlikely I'm going to get a job at that age, especially as a convicted murderer. Pretty likely also that inflation will have continued while I'm in the can. I'll need every cent I can get, just to live out my life. I can't wait to sell the house then. Even if I rent it, lease it out while I'm away, it'll be close to worthless when I come out. I used to be a tenant — tenants don't take care of things, no matter what they promise. Hell, I spent the last two years here in this house myself, goofing off and generally making a big fool of myself, not paying attention to anything going on around me. And the place went right to hell. Dining room," he said, pointing into the room beyond the bath-room, at the front of the house. He steered her left down the hall.

"Now," he said, "come August or September, whenever the Honorable Taves decides the trial does him least damage, I'm going to get myself at least a guarantee of fourteen, fifteen years of residence as a guest of the government. If the roof started leaking and the yard got overgrown, and the outside of the building started to deteriorate in two years while I was here, although not taking care of things and keeping the place up, can you imagine the condition the joint's going to be in at the turn of the century? When I haven't been around at all?"

"So, why do it?" she said. "Why face the risk you're facing?"

To the left of the hallway there were two doors, both open. He paused at the first one, inviting her to look in. "Greenhouse," he said. "Used to be the kitchen, before we added on." She peered in and saw a sloping wall of glass built out from the house. There were wooden shelves, empty except for dirt, under the windows, and several tall, dead trees in green plastic buckets on the dirty, carpeted floor, their branches drooping leafless in the diminishing light. "Hasn't had much use in the past couple years," he said. "Caretaker got herself killed. Poor judgment on her part."

"You didn't answer my question," she said.

"I'm doing it," he said, "because I have no reason not to. That mundane enough for you? Chances are I'm going to live another thirty years, now that I've been forcibly prevented from checking out early. What am I going to do with them? I'm forty-four. The first two dozen years of my life I spent virtually alone. The next eighteen years I was happy, successful and proud. And that all got wiped out in one instant. There's no way I can rebuild it, replace what I had. The people who made it possible, and important, are dead. On my own I wrecked the little that outlasted them. And nobody gave a good shit. Nobody at all."

"You're feeling sorry for yourself," she said.

"Goddamned right I am," he said, pausing at the next door on the left. "Guest bedroom. Used to be the dining room, before we added on. Theory was, Rosemary's theory, Bomber and his wife could come down, spend weekends with us. Bomber's my brother-in-law. Not what you'd call a cultivated fellow, Bomber, but a very decent guy. Bomber's his bowling name. Great candlepin bowler. One-thirty-one league average, which is very good. Absolutely will not try to get on the TV shows. Not a cultured fellow, Bomber, but a smart one, nonetheless."

He turned her around toward the door on the right and ushered her through it. "Living room," he said. He gestured to his right toward the flight of stairs and the front door visible at the south end of the room. "Stairs go up to bedrooms," he said. "Master and the bath with it, right up over our heads. Hallway and two others at the end over the dining room. Ricky's was the one on the front. He hasn't used it for two years. Being dead and all." He released her arm. "Go in and sit down," he said, his voice thickening. "I got to take a leak." He walked rapidly away from her, back toward the kitchen.

She went into the living room. There was a bow-front mullioned window with a green cushioned seat at the center of the front of the room. In the middle there was a three-cushion tan couch opposite a three-cushion maroon couch, with a cobbler's bench coffee table between them. To her extreme left there was a glass-fronted brick fireplace, and beyond it a doorway. There were two barrel chairs upholstered in peach crushed velvet arranged to face the fireplace. The walls of the room were painted cream. They were crowded with photographs.

Most of the pictures were in color. They showed a woman and a boy and Logan. The woman was alone in one picture; she wore blue shorts and a yellow tank top and she was working a winch handle on a small sailboat. Her arm muscles were taut. In another, the boy had the autumn ocean behind him; he was holding up three ducks by their feet; he was wearing a canvas jacket with shotgun shells in loops at his left breast, and holding a Mossberg pump-action shotgun in his other hand. Logan in one picture was at the tiller of a small sailboat, his left foot on a cockpit cushion, his upper body relaxed but his right arm braced with his left hand on the wrist; there was a foaming wake behind him, and the boat was heeled. The black and white pictures showed Logan with senators, governors and other politicians. Gates sat down on the tan couch and put her glass on the cobbler's bench. She heard the toilet flush at the other end of the hall.

Logan came back into the living room, carrying his glass. He set it on the cobbler's bench and sat down on the maroon couch. "Tell me about yourself," he said.

"I'm not the story," she said. "And there isn't much to tell."

"Sure there is," he said. "Nobody I talked to after you called knows who you are. And to be perfectly frank with you, *Journeyer*'s not the sort of magazine I'd expect to be interested in a vigilante story. I may be unfrocked now, but I was a reporter for half of my life. You can't expect me to shake my habits of curiosity now. Who am I talking to? Why is she interested? What gives here, anyway?"

"I suppose that's reasonable," she said. She summarized her career for him. "Mark said when he offered me the job that he wants to do something to improve the magazine. He thinks your story is a step in that direction. I have to take that at face value, especially since the face value of the money he offered me was so attractive. If there's some other reason behind the assignment, I don't know what it is."

"Neither do I," Logan said, "but I'm sure there is one, somewhere. What he's paying you's about seven times what an experienced, name, magazine writer could possibly hope to get from a publication *Journeyer*'s size. Which, if you will forgive me for saying, you're not. I'm not saying what he told you isn't true; I'm saying that it's almost certainly not the whole truth. Unless Mark's had a lobotomy or something that nobody's heard about, gone through some massive change, he's still a cagey rascal. He never did things for just one reason back when I knew him well, and I doubt he's started now."

"You got me," she said. "I've told you what he told me. That is all I know." She paused. "Confrontational, aren't you, Mister Logan?"

He ignored the question. "You called him 'Mark,' " he said. "Had you known him before this assignment?"

She hesitated. "No," she said, "I didn't."

"But you know him pretty well now, don't you?" he said. He was smiling.

"Cut it out," she said. "This kind of coy little junior-high game bores me. Don't sit there and make insinuations. You want to know something, just ask me. If it's whether I've slept with him, the answer's Yes. I have. I've slept with several men since I got divorced, and he's one of the most attractive. But it was long after he hired me. I didn't come across for the job."

"My," he said. "Sensitive, aren't you?"

"I get irritated when I'm pushed," she said. "If that's what you mean by sensitive. If you only talk to virgins, I don't qualify. I was married for several years to a man whose many faults did not include impotence. That was one of the main reasons I married him in the first place — Jeffrey can be a major league stinker, but he was good in bed. After we split up, I missed it. I missed having sex on a regular basis. I still do. I'm a healthy adult woman. When I've gone without for a while, I get distracted from my work and everything else I try to do. So I look around to see who's available that might help me out." She shook her head. "And I've picked a few beauts, doing that, I must admit, but it's better than celibacy. Celibacy stinks, once you've had the other thing."

"You're telling me," he said, grinning now. "My wife's been dead for two years."

"I shouldn't've left my tape recorder in the kitchen," she said. "I should be getting this down."

"I'll repeat it if you forget," he said. "I'm not saying I don't miss the companionship and the sharing and just having her around. I do. Terribly. Hourly. But to a degree, at least now, those things I can control. The sex part I cannot. I wake up in the middle of the night and I'm on her side of the bed, practically falling out on the floor. Hunting for her. Hard as a rock. And then I lie there with my erection, which at least distracts me from crying, I suppose, telling myself that men my age don't beat their meat. And then of course I do it."

"Beat your meat," she said.

"That's what I said," he said. "It's either do that or lie awake for the rest of my life, feeling sorry for myself. I do enough of that during the day as it is. If I don't get some sleep, I go nuts."

"That's awful," she said.

He shrugged. "It's embarrassing," he said. "It makes me feel childish and silly, and vulnerable, I guess. But I've learned a lot these past two years about what happens to animals who lose their mates. It's not just the loss of the company that makes you pine, having to remind yourself not to put two plates out for dinner, night after night, and then doing it anyway and seeing what you've done and just breaking down. It's a lot more basic than just that." His voice clogged up. His eyes filled. He shook his head. "Oh, Jesus," he said. He stood up and walked out of the room through the doorway near the fireplace. She heard him in the other room, blowing his nose.

"Don't . . . ," she called out, "don't feel that way. It's all right. I didn't mean it, what I said about the recorder. I won't do that to you."

He came back into the living room. "I'm really sorry," he said, collapsing into a sitting position on the maroon couch. His shoulders slumped and he rested his forearms on his thighs, dangling his hands between his knees. "Ever since it happened, everything's just been so close to the surface with me, you know? I can't keep anything to myself, it seems like. Keep things bottled up. There's too much pressure, of all kinds. I go along trying to act like a normal person, and then it's like a geyser going off. Everything just blows, and I break down again." He mused. "It was easier with the booze, when I was on the sauce," he said reflectively. "It was definitely much easier to handle when I could just get plastered, and come home and pass out. It was turning my liver to concrete, maybe, and rotting my brain cells away, but it's an anodyne just the same. Don't let anyone tell you different. It has its useful features."

"You can't drink any more?" she said.

He shrugged again. "I don't," he said. "Doctor Gibbs at Finisterre — I assume you talked to him?"

"This morning," she said. "Thanks for calling him. He was very helpful."

Logan laughed. "I'll bet he was," he said. "That goddamned charlatan."

" 'Charlatan'?" she said. "What makes you say that?"

"Oh," he said, "I shouldn't. He's probably a very fine man. But we had and still have a strong difference of opinion about why people — this people at least — drink too much. He thinks everybody with 'a substance problem,' as he prefers to call it, no matter what's involved, starts with a physiological problem and that creates the psychological problems. He thinks alcoholism is a form of allergy. The victim can't metabolize alcohol, or narcotics if that's what he happens to like, but he uses those 'substances' anyway, and that screws up his mind. So in my case, if you listen to him, I couldn't come to terms with my loss because I was drinking. And I did not agree with that. I said I was drinking too much because of my grief, not grieving because I was drinking.

"I suppose it's academic, though," he said. "Probably doesn't matter. Either way, I don't know if I *can* drink because I *don't* drink. My reason's fairly simple: the Massachusetts Correctional Institution at Cedar Junction has a very limited wine list, no happy hours, and serves very little beer. So why resume a pleasant habit now that I'm going to have to give up soon for a very long time?

"Same thing with intercourse," he said. "I've thought about one of those out-call services they advertise in the *Phoenix*. Go up to Boston, take a room in one of the less inquisitive hotels, have a whore sent over, on my Mastercard. But Taves's office might get it into their heads to subpoena my records for some plausible reason or other, or just put a tail on me, and then when I took the stand and began telling how much I miss my wife, I might have some trouble explaining a paid encounter.

"So," he said, "heterosexual entertainment being another item not included on the MCI program, I may as well get in training right now. Don't drink, and: masturbate. Provide, provide. Prepare for what's in store."

"Cripes," she aid, "you are low. Are you sure you're up to this?"

He sat back and straightened his shoulders. "Oh yeah," he said, "I am. Hell, this is a piece of cake. At least I'll have the consolation of knowing that even if nobody covers the trial, none of the networks and none of the papers, I mean, at least what I've got to say will come out somewhere, and somebody will know."

"You think that's likely?" she said. "That it'll be ignored? Because I sure don't; Taves doesn't; and neither does Doctor Gibbs. Doctor Gibbs is very worried about what you're going to say."

"I'll bet he is," Logan said with satisfaction. "I just bet he is. He called me up a couple days after I settled my score with Mister Brutus and started giving me his patented razzmatazz, feeling me out about something I'd said to one of the reporters that mentioned Finisterre. And he was beating around the bush and making these veiled threats that basically amounted to warning me I'd better not disparage him and Finisterre, or I might find myself getting sued for defamation. And I said: 'Doctor, in the first place, a libel case really doesn't frighten a murder defendant a whole lot. And in the second place, what should worry you is not that I'll tell lies about you — it's that I'm going to tell the truth."

"Which is?" she said.

"That he and his whole breed are milking rich, weak people out of piles of money," Logan said. "And for what? For replacing one dependency — on booze or drugs or both — with another one: dependency on them and their soothing noises."

"He claims it works," she said. "He said it gets them cured."

Logan snorted. "*Post hoc, propter hoc*," he said. " 'After,' therefore 'because.' I don't buy it. He knows that. That's why he's worried."

She gazed at him for a few moments. "You know," she said, "for what it's worth, I think you are going to be a formidable witness."

He chuckled. "If I can keep my dauber up, as the ballplayers say," he said. "If I can keep my mind on what I'm doing, and not let one of Billy Taves's two-bit Darrows turn me into a blubbering idiot, when I take the stand."

"I think you'll be able to do that," she said, standing up. "I think I'd better get my machine now, so we can get to work."

34

They were sitting at the kitchen table with the tape recorder operating between them when the squall line came through Mattapoisett from the west. A dark barrier of cumulonimbus clouds formed over the western shore of the harbor and formed a hammer and anvil, spreading like an umbrella over the water and darkening the eastern littoral. The water turned black and whitecaps came up. The first fat drops of rain slapped against the glass door; the downpour followed almost at once, sheeting down the glass. In the distance there was a rumble of thunder, preceded by brief flickers of lightning. She shivered.

"Are you afraid of electrical storms?" he said.

"I used to be," she said. "Not because I was afraid of getting hit. My father was a fisherman. Still is, as far as that goes. When I was young and he was out, and one of these things came up, I used to think I'd never see him again. You get a different conception of nature when people in your family make their living out at sea. I see things in the paper now about people who went out in pleasure boats and got into big trouble, when everything the sky told them said they shouldn't do it, and they didn't *have* to do it, and it makes me angry, you know? That they could be so stupid. What do they think those guys in the Coast Guard are for? To risk their lives saving people whose own stupidity got them into the messes they were in?"

"You're close to your father," he said.

"I used to be," she said. "I'm not anymore."

"Why is that?" he said.

"He disapproved of something I did," she said. "Why do you ask?"

"Because I'm interested," he said calmly. "I hated mine. Not that I knew that much about him. But what I knew, I sure did hate."

"You're not going to leave it there," she said. "I'm not going to let you."

"My mother was a liar," he said. "Her motives were good. Her procedure was wrong. Nick was a union organizer. Nick was my father. His territory was everything from Boston harbor to Cleveland. South to Philadelphia. North to the border. That was what he said, anyway. He was a liar, too. Except his motives weren't so good. He wasn't home much. He made a fair living, and spent it on himself. He'd come home in a new suit, fresh haircut, shined shoes, and tell her that he had to look presentable. 'I can't be meeting with the brass, and looking like a bum,' he'd say. Then he'd stand and preen for her, the selfish old bum. Like a fool, she'd admire him. And like a little jerk, I'd go out in the neighborhood and brag to all my friends. My father in the union, what a damned big job he had, and how it kept him awful busy so the only times I saw the Red Sox were when one of their dads took me.

"I didn't go to Northeastern because I chose it from a list," he said. "I went there because it had the cooperative plan. Kids like me who didn't have the money for college could alternate school and low-paying jobs, all year 'round. We weren't the wild-ass college boys who got in scuffles with the Fort Lauderdale cops in the spring. We were the greasy grinds. Five exhausting years of penury and struggle, pinched and fatigued, with nothing on our minds but success, success, success. Making money. Lots of money. So that we would never have to scrape and grind again, and so that no kids that we ever had would ever have to, either.

"Nick came to my graduation," Logan said. "It was in Boston Garden, in June, and it was hotter'n the hinges of Hell. It was a real surprise. I hadn't sent him tickets. I didn't want him there. Son of a bitch'd done nothing to contribute to the occasion. His sister, Sandra, raised me, after my mother died. And here is my dear Dad, with some blown-out, bleached-blonde floozy clinging to his arm, crushing the sleeve of his new suit, and him with a lovely tan. Countess Mara tie. Bally tasseled loafers. Shoes alone cost more'n the biggest check he ever sent Sandra, when she was raising me. He had this silvery grey hair by then, styled, naturally. Manicured nails. Sticks out his hand and shows me the caps on his teeth. 'Congratulations, son,' he said. 'You've worked hard for this.' And the tramp beams on her man, who's so proud of his son.

" 'Fuck you, Daddy,' I said. 'You're not just coming in for the good parts, you miserable son of a bitch.' And I left his hand out there. Haven't seen him since that day, and I am satisfied. I don't think the old bastard's dead, but he may be. More likely he's in Florida, or Arizona, maybe, another retired old roué making big eyes on his pension to sweet old widow ladies with blue hair and hidden yearnings, pushing seventy and hiding early prostate troubles that he courted all his life."

"Goodness," Gates said. "You don't like your sire."

"I really don't," he said. "His sister didn't, either. 'Joe,' she said to me, 'look out if you get married. Both of us grew up with Nick, and that oughta be enough to make any person wise. But I went and married Rafe.' Which was how Ralph, who was Welsh and in a British army hospital when she met him during World War Two, pronounced his name. At least to female American Red Cross workers who looked like free tickets to the USA. After he found out the streets weren't paved with gold, he packed up his kit and went home. Leaving behind two small children, that she had to raise. Along with me. 'An imported Nick's what he was,' she said. 'And don't think you're safe from doing the same thing, because you're a man. There're women like those two, my brother and my husband. Rotters wearing skirts. Watch your ass if you get married. Don't pick up another one.'

"I didn't," he said. The rain streamed down the glass door and poured off the roof. The thunder rolled and lightning illuminated the dark sky. "I got a perfect one." He paused. "Then look what happened," he said. "There're times, you know? Times when I wonder if I was better off. If Rosemary'd been a toad like my father was, and she'd gotten wiped out just the same, I might've handled the loss a lot better."

"How long were the two of you happy?" Gates said. "Eighteen years, did you say?"

"Almost that," he said, reaching behind him and turning on the light over the table. "She got killed in early June. I met her late in June, in Nineteen-sixty-four. Almost eighteen years."

"And you're bitching about that?" she said. "Eighteen years is more than most people get. Lots more."

"More than you, for example," he said.

"Absolutely, more than me," she said. "More than I, I mean."

"Very good," he said. "Got to watch the grammar there. The kids that I used to hire at SET, they drove me nuts with that stuff. I'd tell them over and over again: 'It's not "between you and I." Not if you're on the air, at least, at a station where I decide who gets to go on the air. If you don't know the difference in cases, learn it. Or resign yourself to a career in production.' "

"You were a martinet," she said.

"I think so," he said. "I tried to be, at least. 'Lots of people in New Bedford speak Portuguese. I'm not one of them. I speak English. I'm the fellow you have to satisfy. Don't tell me the viewers don't notice. You've only got one viewer. You're looking at him. Please me and you become rich and famous. Make me wince when I'm watching your tapes, and you become out of work.' "

"And did they become rich and famous?" she said. "The ones who obeyed the tyrant?"

"They certainly did," he said. "Do you watch the evening news on NBC, by chance?"

"I've been known to," she said.

"Then you know Don Cressey's name," he said.

"White House correspondent," she said. "Very slick fellow. Appallingly young. I hate people like that."

"Don's one of my alumni," he said. "You're right to envy him. Should've seen him when I hired him, fresh out of the University of New Hampshire. Looked like one of the kids in the Salvation Army's ads for the fresh-air camps. Raw as uncooked meat. But smart, boy, very smart. He came in April of Nineteen-seventy-eight, looking for a job. 'What do you want to do in TV news?' I said. 'Replace Walter Cronkite, make the world forget Chet Huntley? Something along that line?'

" 'Find out whether I can make a living at it,' he said. 'That shouldn't take too long. I'm twenty-two years old. I can afford to spend two years finding out. If I'm not making progress by then, I'm gone. You won't have to throw me out. My father raised the three of us on sergeant's pay in the State Police. I can do the same.'

"So I hired him," Logan said. "And after he'd been there for about six months, it dawned on me I had another autodidact on my hands. Here was this kid who'd floundered around his whole four years at UNH, trying to figure out what the hell was going on, and what he should be doing. Mediocre grades, in everything but history where he'd managed to get Bs, and no activities to speak of, except what you'd expect — the campus radio station where he didn't really shine. But the kid was a dynamo at SET. Put him on a story about, oh, public education, and within a couple of weeks he'd know more about enrollment patterns, racial problems, curriculum disputes, test results and job actions than the head of the NEA. Breathtaking powers of absorption. So I went to him after about the third one of those performances and said: 'All right, come clean with me. How the hell did you manage to get through four years of college without showing a damned thing to anybody? What were you doing? Playing possum?'

" 'Simple,' he said. 'I never got around to finishing the assigned reading.' He'd start off all right at the beginning of the term, go like everything. 'In Shakespeare,' he said, 'I was doing fine until about the second week. Then the assignment sent me off looking up Christopher Marlowe, and I got interested in Marlowe. Which led to another tangent, of course, and by exam time I knew quite a lot about theater design in seventeenth-century England, and David Garrick's place in nineteenth-century society, and how much the weather had to do with victory over the Armada. But I still hadn't read *Richard the Third*, which the professor picked as the subject of one of the three essay questions on the final. I did all right, I guess, under the circumstances — I got a C-plus, faking it. But my grades would've been better in everything if I hadn't kept doing that, skipping the stuff I was supposed to do and spending my time on what I liked.'

" 'Which means,' I said, 'you like this stuff.'

" 'Uh huh,' he said, 'I do.' " Logan shook his head. "I tell you," he said, "if you could find a way to identify people like that when they're very young, and just select them out of the mainstream and let them go do what they want, from the day they turn three years old, you could rule the world."

"Geniuses," she said.

"I suppose so," he said, nodding. "Something like that, anyway. Not being one myself, I really don't know what they are. Wizards, maybe? But whatever they are, Don is one of them." He sighed. "I wish I could watch him now."

"Why can't you?" she said.

"The day Rosemary and Rick were killed," he said, "Don was the one that gave me the news. About the accident. It's almost as though I blame him for it, you know? For what happened to them? I see him and I hear him and the association starts, and I go through it all again." He paused. He stood up fast and faced the glass door, turning his back to her and staring out into the rain.

"Tell me about it," she said.

"That's what that fool Leland Gibbs used to say," Logan said. " 'Tell me what happens, Joe,' he would say. 'Ventilate your feelings.' "

"And did you?" she said.

"Oh, yeah," he said. "Sure I did. Time and time again. But it didn't help. The verb is wrong. 'Ventilate' is not something you can do with something that's not gas. What's wrong inside of me is bone. Solid everlasting bone. It's there, you know? You can't let it out. All you can do is cut down to it and expose it. But that doesn't accomplish anything except fresh bleeding. And why the hell did you do it, anyway? You grab your arm, or someone else's, and just squeeze it, you know there's bone in it. The poor bastard doesn't have to slice through the flesh to prove it to you. You know it's there."

"Do it anyway," she said. "Do it anyway."

35

"Hyman Rickover was coming to Newport," he said slowly, still staring out the window with his back to her. "Down at the Naval War College there. Every so often the public information officers'd schedule a lunch for 'public opinion makers,' as they respectfully called the media to our faces, and invite some big shot in to make a speech. Which was always for some reason or other about the Navy's vital need for more money from Congress. And how crucial it was for the national interest to entertain the sons of Arabian kings and Greek prime ministers for a year or two of cushy 'training' on Newport's lovely waters. It was nothing but stroking, of course, the service flacks laying on the cocktails and the wines and the fresh swordfish for the freeloading press, contriving an event to retail propaganda at appropriations time.

"And we all knew that," he said. "But we also knew it was June. There wasn't a whole lot of competing, actual news, unless you counted graduations and the annual optimistic predictions of summer tourist business. Besides, anybody who doesn't like free swordfish and California rieslings has got something wrong with him. So most of us always went."

He turned around and sat down at the table again. "I had a policy," he said, "of rotating assignments so that everybody in News got roughly the same ratio of nifty, pleasant stuff to rotten, grubby stuff. And I applied it to myself. You couldn't do that with a big operation, of course, but there were only six of us involved. It gave me a staff of relatively-happy generalists, instead of one with a couple of happy stars and a bunch of disgruntled malcontents grumbling behind my back.

"That was a reaction to working for Mel Shaw in Waterford," Logan said. "He enforced a rigid system of beats. We had a woman in the bureau, Didi Chenevert, who bitched endlessly about whatever he had her doing, always mad about something — a great big pain in the ass. But in addition to being a nuisance, she did have a point. She was right when she said he discriminated against her, wouldn't let her cover the cops because she was a woman. Later on, of course, she got even by marrying the chief of police, which turned her off not only cops, but the entire male sex."

"Who'd you hear that from?" she said. "Dan Munroe?"

"Uh huh," he said. "He came all the way over here for the funeral, just because the two of us used to drink some beer together and he felt sorry for me. Nice fellow, basically. Once you get used to the fact that he's not the smartest item that ever showed up on the screen, pleasant company. At least I don't *think* he ever did anything that justified what she did to him, but I could be wrong."

"You mean, leaving him," she said.

"Oh, hell," Logan said, "leaving him was all right. It was the way she did it. If a woman in her forties wants to wake up in the morning some day and announce to her husband that she's always been a lesbian and she's going home to be with the woman that she loves, fine and good. Let her go and do that. But I don't think it was absolutely necessary for her to bring her lover to Waterford to help her pack her belongings, and incidentally parade her around all over town while Dan was away, so everyone would know. That was just gratuitous cruelty, doing that to him."

"I don't see why," Gates said. "What difference did it make, why she was leaving him? For another man, another woman, or maybe just to be by herself. The effect's the same."

"Not to him, it wasn't," Logan said. "Dan's a cop, for heaven's sakes. Macho man in that position, and he can't even compete with another woman sexually? If you don't like the way your marriage turns out, fine. End it. But at least show a little respect for the other party. And she didn't do that. She humiliated him. It wasn't necessary."

"Okay," she said. "I don't agree with you, but go on anyway."

"Well," he said, "if you don't think ethics have anything to do with the way you behave sexually, I'm not sure there's much point in going on."

"You getting mad at me?" she said, with surprise in her voice.

"No," he said. "Just making a point. I don't mean to shock you, but one of the things I've learned about myself, one of the pleasanter things, is that I really don't approve of people who use sex as a weapon. And a lot of people seem to do that. They may say they're doing something else, 'being honest about feelings' or some crap like that, but what they're really doing when they act like Didi did is intentionally hurting other people, and then copping out.

"Everything's on one string, you know," he said. "I don't think you can isolate how you treat people that you do business with from how you treat people that you sleep with, and say what's dishonorable professional conduct — lying to people, cheating on them, going back on your word — is perfectly okay to do to people that you go to bed with."

"You don't," she said.

"I really don't," he said. "And if you don't understand that position, if it doesn't make any sense to you, then you're not going to understand a damned thing I say to you. I'm not condemning you, understand, if you don't agree with me. Lots of people don't. I'm no authority on morality. Hell, I killed a man. Am I going to tell somebody else how he should behave? I doubt anyone would listen. But if you want to know why I did what I did, and do what I do, you at least have to understand how I think. Why I react the way I do."

"I'll do my best," she said.

"You think I'm strange," he said, smiling.

"Well," she said, "you're unusual. I never met anyone before who was accused of homicide. But be patient; I think I can deal with it."

He drew a deep breath. "All right," he said, "Rickover. The Navy's event for June of Eighty-two at Newport was his speech on the importance of a well-equipped nuclear submarine fleet. Probably of very little actual interest to the average SET viewer, but plausibly worth coverage. It was my turn for a soft assignment, and it was not one which would make the rest of the staff really envious. So I scheduled myself the week before June tenth as the staffer covering the Rickover luncheon at the Newport Naval War College, and assigned a cameraman.

"Tommy Silva read his schedule on the ninth. He was furious. We were short-staffed on the technical side that week, one cameraman out sick, another one on her honeymoon, and we had one opening unfilled. So the mobile unit, which Tommy operated, was very mobile that week. At ten-thirty on the morning of the tenth, he had to tape a press conference of Bristol County mayors and selectmen on a joint sewer study Laura Charles was covering. Then he had to go back to New Bedford to tape a noon speech by the Governor at a Rotary meeting, which Carl Fast was covering. After which he had to hightail it to Newport, to take my picture on the lawn of the Naval College with the Jamestown Bridge behind me, doing my stand-up, on-scene report of what former President Jimmy Carter's favorite admiral had told the multitude.

"Tommy was pissed," Logan said. "He came stomping into my office and told me there was no real journalistic reason for him to go to Newport. 'What I should do this after,' he told me on the ninth, 'is go over there now and take ten seconds of the truck with the bridge behind it there, and then tomorrow you get some Navy bozo to take pictures of you talking and we splice it up back here.'

" 'What you should do, Tommy,' I said, even though he was logically correct, 'is keep in mind that until we got that van, Tommy Silva had no job. That's what you should do.' All I ever hoped to do with Tommy was keep him performing. He's a very capable camera-man, but difficult to work with. Sullen but disciplined: that was my goal with him, and I thought when I left work that night I'd achieved it again.

"I got back here after the eleven o'clock news on the ninth, and everyone was up, full of the old harry. I say that because it was unusual. Rosemary was a charge nurse on the day shift at New Bedford General. She had to be at work at eight A.M. Rick had a summer job driving a truck for Coca-Cola in New Bedford. It paid well, but it wore him out. And in order to get to it by eight-thirty, when he had to report, he had to leave when his mother left at seven-fifteen. Which meant both of them had to get out of the sack by six-forty-five, and that in turn meant that I seldom saw him when I got home around midnight, and she was dozing on the couch.

"But not that night," Logan said. "On her lunch break, Rose-mary'd seen an ad in the paper for Avis rental cars for sale in Brockton. Now, another thing you have to understand about this family that I used to have is that we were open to charges of materialism. We liked nice things, and we indulged ourselves as much as we possibly could. Rosemary grew up in a longshoreman's family in Somerville. I told you how I grew up. Her first husband, in addition to his other excellent qualities, was a classic bum on the job. When the two of us reached the point where we had the money to buy things we'd always wanted, we bought them. This house. My

Porsche. Her Wagoneer. The Whaler at the dock behind the barn. When Rick's grades were good enough to let him choose between UMass-Amherst and Colby College, and he liked Colby better, that was where he went, regardless of the fact that it cost a lot more.

"Rick was not a student," he said. "He was a hard worker, he applied himself, and he was a wonderful kid to be with. But school was not something he liked. It was something he had to get through. He came out of his freshman year with a C-plus average. The argument he made to us was that on his record, it wasn't likely he'd do much better, and not likely either that he'd do much worse. Colby, just as he said, is 'way the hell up in the Maine woods in Waterville there, difficult to reach by public transportation. He needed his own car. In addition to wanting one, of course, like every kid does.

"We agreed with him. We didn't give him everything he had in mind, of course, that being either my Nine-eleven or Rosemary's Jeep, but we did decide to get him a fairly recent used car. Rosemary saw the Avis ad for Eighty-one Oldsmobiles and Buick Regals for about five grand, showed it to him when she collected him from work, and they went up to Brockton to check them out. The deal made sense. The cars were low-mileage, good condition, guaranteed for a year. They had one he liked, a tan Cutlass hardtop, so they bought it on the spot.

"He was so excited when I got home that night he was ready to be wrapped in a wet sheet. He'd already called his boss at home and gotten the next day off. If the Registry'd been open at night, they would've rousted our insurance man from his dinner and most likely the car would've been sitting in the driveway when I got back from work. As it was, though, the fastest he could possibly get his hands on it was by noon the next day. And in order to do that, one of us had to drive him up to Brockton, deliver the checks, pick up the title, drive back to New Bedford, get the registration stamped by the insurance people, pick up the plates at the Registry, and then drive him back to Brockton to pick up the car.

" 'Which,' Rosemary said, 'since I drove up today, we thought you might like to do.'

" 'Hyman Rickover,' I said.

" 'Can't Carl or Laura do it?' she said.

" 'Navy regulations,' I said. 'Navy has to have the name of the person assigned a week before the event. Make sure he's not from

SMERSH or something. Mine's the one I gave them. Therefore I have to go.'

" 'I had this feeling,' she said. 'Coming home tonight, I had this strong suspicion I was going to take a personal day from work tomorrow. Just a hunch, but I knew. Knew it in my bones. Three trips to Brockton in twenty-four hours. Where did I go wrong, Lord? Where did I go wrong?' "

"So," he said, "when I got up in the morning at my usual time, around eight-thirty, they'd already left. For all practical purposes, I'd seen the two of them alive for the last time before I went to bed, and I didn't even know it. Followed my usual routine. Made coffee, read the papers, went into the study and looked over the tapes of the six and eleven news, made a few notes, comments for the staff, rewound the tapes, reset the timers on the VCRs, and around ten, went to the station. Everything seemed to be going all right there. By eleven I was on the road to Newport. Beautiful day with the sunroof open, little Mozart on the tape deck — nice to be alive.

"Lunch was top chow," Logan said. "Clam chowder, grey sole, a grey riesling. The Admiral spoke well and briefly about the need to attract and keep educated officers and enlisted men as career personnel. I came out of the Officers' Mess around one-fifteen, comfortably well-fed and mellow, and the mobile wasn't there. I was furious. I stood there with two or three of the other freeloaders, thinking about Tommy Silva goofing off at some McDonald's with three cheeseburgs and a Coke, and what I was going to do to him when he did show up. This young ensign came up to me, tapped me on the shoulder, said I had a call inside.

"I turned to go with him, thinking it was Tommy with some cock-and-bull excuse for why he wasn't there, hoping the other reporters thought I was actually going in for a private interview with Rickover. In the parking lot I saw Ron Seevers from PRI in Providence come out of his mobile unit and start waving to me. He yelled something, but I couldn't hear it. I went with the officer.

"The call was from Don Cressey at the station," Logan said. "The reason that Tommy hadn't shown up was that on his trip from the Fall River mayor's press conference to the New Bedford speech by the governor, breaking the speed limit on One-ninety-five, he'd witnessed a very bad accident at the junction with Twenty-four, a chain collision, and stopped to take pictures of it.

"We'd been hammering the issue of that damned intersection for over two years," Logan said. " 'Son of a gun,' I said. 'Tommy's off the hook. I was going to brain him for standing me up. Very good judgment on his part. That's just what he should've done. Pull Carl off the governor and have him start calling every cop and highway person he can think of. We'll lead at six with this.'

"Don didn't say anything," Logan said. "He was still on the line. I knew he was there. But I finished talking and he didn't start. 'You with me, Don?' I said.

" 'Joe,' Don said, 'I don't know how to tell you this. The lead car. The one that got hit first. It was Rosemary's Jeep.'

"All the air went out of the world," Logan said. "The room tilted on its axis so I lost my balance and fell against the desk. I grabbed the edge of it to stay on my feet, couldn't hold on, and sat down on the rug. I must've made some noise, because the ensign who'd brought me in came back into the room and yelled something. They got a medic in and made me lie down on the rug and elevated my feet and gave me smelling salts and put ice on my forehead and loosened my tie and kept me pretty much conscious so I wouldn't miss a single minute of what was happening to me.

"Which is why, to this day," Logan said, "hearing Don Cressey's voice makes me cringe."

36

The trailing edge of the squall line blew through Mattapoisett. The sky lightened to whitish grey. The western shore of the harbor became indistinct. "Fog's coming in," she said, nodding toward the window. "Bad thick stuff too, by the look of it."

He twisted around in the chair. "Uh huh," he said. "Soup. Cops'll have some fun tonight, with the Jaws of Life. That fog'll just settle in the hollows on the roads and stick there until morning."

"You think so?" she said. "It's only four-fifteen. Ought to be enough sun left to thin it out pretty well."

"Not down here," he said. "You're used to the exposed coast. This harbor here's really sheltered, facing south, not east. We get fog in here and it lies in the lowlands for at least overnight." He turned back to her. "I'm not throwing you out," he said. "I know we haven't finished. But if you've got plans to be back in Boston tonight, the smart thing to do would be to leave now. Another forty minutes and you won't be able to see beyond the hood badge on your car out on the road."

She shut off the tape recorder. She frowned and gnawed at her lower lip. "I really want to get this done," she said. "I've been digging into your life for quite a while now, and if you want God's honest truth, I'm anxious to get finished."

He chuckled. "That's pretty much the way I feel about it too," he said. "I wish I had your option."

"Look," she said, "I don't mean to be forward or anything, and I'm not going to get mad at you if you say I'm out of line. But would you be shocked if I asked you if I could use that guest room tonight if you're right about the fog? Because I sure don't want to drive in it. And I do want to get this done."

"Wouldn't bother me in the slightest," he said. "I'd like the company."

"That'd help a lot," she said, turning the recorder on again.

"You'd just finished telling me why you can't watch Don Cressey."

"Right," he said. "The day of the accident, after I got the word, I went sort of numb, I guess, and the numbness lasted for a while. Nature dulling the nerves, I guess. Like a robot, you know? I left Newport on autopilot and went to New Bedford General. Got there and the first thing they do is sit me down before they tell me the glad tidings. Rick was DOA. Keep in mind I hadn't seen the tapes then. All I actually knew was that it was a bad accident, that it probably happened at pretty high speed because those roads are super-highways and it didn't matter whether Rick or my wife'd been driving the Jeep — they both had heavy feet. So whoever hit them must've been really traveling, just to get close enough to them to clout them. So I'd already sort of braced myself for very bad news. And they sat me down and said he was dead. And I asked about her, and they said she was critical. They hadn't reached the point of really detailed diagnosis, being mostly concerned with just keeping her alive and stabilizing her, but she had severe internal injuries, they knew, and bad head injuries as well.

"What they told me, in other words," he said, "was that she was still breathing, with a lot of help, and they thought they might have an outside chance of keeping her alive until morning. When, if they could do that, if she made it that long, they'd feel a lot better about her chances of surviving for a while.

"So I sat there," he said, "from about two, two-fifteen in the afternoon until about ten past nine that night, and then they came up to me and told me I could see her. And like a fool, I thought at first that was good news. I went into the IC unit, intensive care, and the instant I walked in that door, I knew it was not good news at all. It was very bad news. Her breathing was shallow and labored, even with the respirator, and I got to her bed and the rattles had begun. And I looked at the doctor, you know? Wanting him to say something that would make it so I wasn't hearing what I was hearing, and he just shook his head. She was drowning in her own blood. And I took her hand, her right hand, and it was cold, and I held it tight, and I tried to say her name and call her back, and I couldn't, and she died." He coughed.

"And that was it," he said. "Nine-twelve P.M., Nineteen-eighty-two. Severe internal injuries. Massive internal hemorrhaging. Compound cranial fractures. Fracture of the spine. 'Joe,' the doctor said, forgetting that I didn't know him from seeing him every night in his living room, where he'd been seeing me, 'believe me, it's better this way. She was very badly hurt. The pain would've been terrible, and whatever recovery she finally made would have taken months and certainly been incomplete.'

"I kept what grip I had," Logan said. " 'No, it isn't better,' I said. And it wasn't, either. Nor has it become better since then. She was forty-four years old. She should've had at least thirty, thirty-five more years, and I should've had them too. Instead she's lying there dead in a bed where she tended people herself for a while, and it was not better at all.

"That natural numbness carried me through, oh, probably the next two weeks," he said. "Don and Laura got me out of the hospital after she died. Wouldn't let me drive. Don drove me in my car and Laura followed us in his. I got the keys away from him when he stopped in the garage and made it first into the house. Which neither of them wanted me to do, of course, because they knew about my habit of taping our news and they didn't want me to see Tommy Silva's film from the six o'clock broadcast. I went into the den and pulled out that tape, and Don followed me in and said: 'Boss, that is not a good idea. What you should do is put that cassette right back in there and rewind it and tape "Dynasty" over what's on it now. You should not watch that tape.'

"I told him of course I was going to," Logan said. "I said I had to, and I was going to retape it anyway when they showed it on eleven. And he said: 'We're not showing it at eleven.' And I said: 'It's that bad, huh?' And he said Yes, that it was. And like I say, I was still sort of numb. And I said: 'Look, if it's that bad, then you should be showing it, and I'm ordering you to show it, because showing that's what happens at that junction's the only way we're ever going to get anybody stirred up enough about that damned situation so they'll do something about it.' And he just stood there and shook his head and said he didn't care what I thought for once, the tape was not going to run again. So I snapped off the tab on the cassette which means you can't erase what's on it by taping over it, and said: 'So much the more reason for me to save this one. Now let's all have a drink.' They had several of them, and I had twice as many, and then they put me to bed and stayed overnight in case I went batty or something. Which I didn't. Not right then. Not for quite a while.

"The advantage of coming from a small family," Logan said, "is that if you're lucky it's not until you're middle-aged that you have to deal personally with the barbaric treatment personally-unaffected people give to the bereaved. My devoted father donated my mother's remains to the Harvard Medical School, after a funeral home service Sandra arranged, and took off as usual for parts unknown, so he didn't suffer much. But he wouldn't've anyway, not giving a shit whether she lived or died. I on the other hand had to fight a pitched battle with Milton Sousa at the funeral home, Milton seeing me as a prime sales prospect for the two solid bronze caskets in his basement that no other stricken pigeon had bought from him in three years. Then there was the Reverend Henry Bowles, who was certain that since no one had ever seen me or Rosemary going to any church, we were obviously devout Congregationalists and I was in dire need of his pastoral counseling at this troubled time in my life. I think both of them were very startled to find out just how forceful and disagreeable the affable anchorman could be on the first day of his bereavement, on nothing more than his grief, his massive hangover, about a quart of coffee and four good-sized screwdrivers.

"But I did it," Logan said. "I got my way. Rick and Rosemary got plain wooden boxes, were placed in them without embalming, cremated that same day, and that evening at sunset I scattered their ashes on the harbor. The staff from the station came, but no camera crews as I ordered, and Jack Mahler and Bill Glass, and Dan Munroe and my aunt, Sandra, who looked like hell herself. And Bomber and Jill, of course. Then we came back into the house, and after a while everyone but Sandra left and the two of us got drunk. Which was when she told me what she had — cancer — and that she'd appreciate it if I made sure she got the same treatment when she died. I said that I would do that, and she died a year later; her kids naturally took complete control of the whole thing, so I was powerless, and Sandra had a funeral that would've made Barnum blush.

"Rosemary's parents boycotted my pagan ceremonies," he said. "Fair is fair, though. If they wanted to give me another shot at my worst possible time, by staying away, then I would hurt them as much as I could by attending the show they staged."

"You didn't get along?" Gates said.

"They did not like me at all," he said. "They're devout Catholics.

She'd been married and divorced when I met her — Rick was her son by her first husband. They didn't know the facts, what had made her leave that bastard, and I don't think it would've mattered in the slightest if they had. Very doctrinaire. If the Pope says you can't do it, then you'd better not do it, or you'll burn in the fires of Gehenna, for all eternity. Rosemary became an adulteress by marrying me before a JP. I was the serpent that led her into mortal sin.

"It was quite a performance," Logan said. "The pastor seemed pretty optimistic about Rick's whereabouts. He'd been waved through the Pearly Gates without showing his credentials because at eighteen and a half he was still a holy innocent. I had the strong impression that implied the good father believed Rick'd retained his virginity. Which I sort of doubted, but he seemed confident. Rosemary was a different matter. He was pessimistic about her reception at the Throne of Heaven. She'd started off well, obedient daughter, good student a Saint Joseph's parochial school, but he seemed to think she'd gone astray at some point later on. He said God'd been known to commute the sentences of those who died in a state of sin, and he certainly hoped that had happened in her case. He did not look optimistic. He said we should pray for her a lot. All during this I got hard looks from her mother, me being the architect of her state of sin and also at fault, I suppose, for not having a priest on hand in the Jeep to hear her confession before the lights went out. I did not go back to the Feeley homestead after the service, as Bomber and Jill had requested. I went home by myself and got drunk.

"That was precisely a week after the committal here," he said. "The natural sedation was wearing off, and I was starting to develop bad habits."

"You mean drinking," she said. The tape ran out and the machine clicked. She changed tapes and motioned him on.

"That was one of them," he said. "Tell me something: when you talked to Doctor Gibbs, how did he describe what I did, before my accident?"

"He said you went into a fugue state," she said promptly. "I'd never heard that one before, except when someone was talking about music, and I asked him what it meant."

"Neither'd I, when he used it to me," Logan said. "Then he explained it. That I excused myself from reality, from facing things, by devising this elaborate, repetitive behavior pattern, and then just staying in it. Like a record stuck in a groove."

"And you disagreed with him," she said.

"Oh, no," Logan said. "Not at all. That's exactly what I did. I didn't know I was doing that, of course, but that was what I did.

"One of the things that strikes you," he said, "after working for the paper, working for the wires, working in television, is that many of the people out there, the civilians, have got a little warp in their boards. The harmless ones are the people who get peeved when you don't show up and take pictures of their fifteen-pound zucchini squash. Or do a story about the speech some African exchange student made in halting English to the Rotary. Or give two minutes on-air, minimum, to the Thanksgiving Day high school football game when the local team went into it with a chance of finishing six wins, four losses, on the season, and ended up five-and-five.

"When you first encounter it," he said, "you tend to brush it off. It's just ego on their part. Ordinary, garden-variety solipsism, perfectly harmless, you know? And then after you've run into a lot of it, year after year after year, it begins to dawn on you that these people are slightly deranged. Not dangerously so, but still, a little out of whack. They are not satisfied that an event is real unless they see it on television and then read about it again in the paper the next day. They've seen so many instant replays in their lives that they don't think the forward pass occurs until it's shown the second time. And until it's described in detail in the morning paper. They have to validate their lives from the public record. They confirm that their own lives have taken place each day by watching and reading accounts of the other events that happened simultaneously in the world around them. And when their own lives chance to include some event out of the ordinary for them, they want ratification of their personal belief that a big thing in the major scheme of things has actually occurred.

"What I did," he said, "what I did was carry that little, and very common, weakness to a mildly pathological extreme. I didn't mean to do it, and I didn't know I was doing it, but what I tried to do was stop the pain from really ever hurting by stopping time in its tracks. You follow me?"

"I'm trying," she said.

"Look," he said, "I wasn't clinically crazy. I was trying to *avoid* becoming clinically crazy. Gibbs got frustrated with me one day and started yelling all I was doing was practicing massive denial, refusing to admit to myself what'd happened. That my family was dead. And I yelled right back at him. I wasn't doing any such thing. Without any conscious reflection, I had figured out that as long as the initial shock of it had lasted, improved by lots of booze taken while I was alone here, I handled the loss pretty well. I could function, in other words. People complimented me on my courage in the face of the awful blow. I made self-deprecating remarks about getting on with my life and facing up to things, and I came home every night and got plastered and watched Tommy Silva's tape again. Over and over again. But I wasn't doing it so I could pretend what was on it never happened. I was doing it to keep myself in the state of suspended animation I'd been in right afterwards.

"It worked beautifully," he said. "The only trouble with it was, my body couldn't stand it. The routine was: get up in the morning very early with hangover. Brush teeth and shower while stomach rumbles. Get dressed and make coffee. Fetch paper from driveway and place on counter. Mix phlegm-cutter."

" 'Phlegm-cutter,' " she said. "Define."

"Into an eight-ounce glass," he said, "put two or three ice cubes. Add generous dollop of vodka. Fill to brim with orange juice. Ingest while coffee brews."

"Thank you," she said.

"To avoid dangerous addiction to sunrise screwdrivers," he said, "alternate with bloody marys, substituting tomato juice for orange. For a nice change of pace, grapefruit juice and vodka makes a salty dog. Cranberry? A Cape Codder. If you forget to shop, as you may when living alone and on this regimen, things have a way of slipping your mind, the juice from a can of pineapple sections may be employed to the same end."

"My," she said.

"Yes indeed," he said, nodding. "I have also used iced tea, Coca-Cola, beef broth, and on one desperate morning, tap water. The orange juice was best, I'd say, ranking the beverages, but the tomato was close. The grapefruit was too sour. Made my lips pucker up."

"But you never ran out of vodka," she said. "You always remembered that."

"On the contrary," he said, "two or three times I forgot. Fortunately I had adequate supplies of my nighttime refreshments. Scotch, bourbon, gin, cognac: I can't say any one of them makes a particularly tasty waker-upper, but they're better than suffering."

"How long did you do this?" she said. "It's a wonder you aren't dead."

"Well," he said, "looking back on it, that was my purpose. To get dead, I mean. But it wasn't apparent to me at the time, at least at the beginning, that that's what I was doing. They don't call it 'slow poison' for nothing. It's progressive. If you're in physically good health, as I was, and you pace yourself, as I did at first, you can do it for quite a long time.

"How long, exactly," he said, "I don't know. Because I gradually increased the rate. That July, when I really got into the drill, I was getting up at six or so, which left me four hours of solitude before I had to get ready to drive to work. By the time I shaved, my hand was steady. When I left around ten-thirty, I was nicely set up. A little subdued, perhaps, and smelling quite strongly of shaving lotion, toothpaste and mouthwash, not to mention the odor of twelve or fourteen cigarettes."

"You also smoked," she said.

"I've always smoked," he said. "I've never been a smoker. For some reason or other, I never got hooked. Which used to infuriate Rosemary, who was a total addict. I can smoke one, five, thirty or none. Doesn't matter to me in the slightest. I smoked then because I knew how the smell covers other indiscretions. When you're running on ethyl like I was, you get crafty.

"I had no trouble getting through the hour or two before lunch," Logan said. "This was partly because lunch invariably included two vodka martinis before the food arrived, a beer or two with the meal. That kept me on an even keel through the afternoon. Between lunch and the cocktail hour, I had nothing interesting to drink. No jug in the bottom drawer, no beers in my office fridge.

"Then I started to make small changes," he said. "The lunch hours arrived sooner. So did the cocktail hours. Both of them started sooner and got longer. It became hard to tell where lunch ended and the cocktail hour began — you had to watch closely. Oddly enough, that change roughly coincided with the sentence imposed on Thomas Brutus in Bristol Superior Court." He paused. He gazed at her. "I thought that sentence was too light for what he'd done."

"So I've heard," she said.

"You've probably also heard," he said, "the eventual results of my self-inflicted therapy."

"You know I have," she said.

"I became a fucking drunk," he said.

"That's what I heard," she said.

"I'm not particularly proud of that," he said. "I know it's part of the story, and that you have to tell it, but since you already know it, I wonder if I could be excused from telling it."

"Certainly," she said. "Talk about something else. Tell me how you met your wife."

37

"I met her by being in the right place at the right time for the wrong reason," Logan said. "When I got out of college at the age of twenty-two, I behaved like a prime exemplar of the nasty irony of life, which is that you get all your options, and have to choose among them, about twenty years before you develop the judgment to make wise choices, when the options have expired. I wanted to work in Boston. The job was in Waterford. If I survived the first three months of probation, I would spend at least twenty-one more months right there, working in Waterford. If all went well for the full two years, and I graduated to senior staff, I might still be assigned to Waterford, shifted to another satellite bureau, or sent to Washington.

"All of this I knew," Logan said. "Therefore, with impeccable logic, I signed a three-year lease on an apartment in Quincy, at a rent I couldn't afford. And why on earth did I do that? Because I entertained the illusion that all rules and regulations to the contrary, I would be promoted from Waterford to Boston within a year or so. Quincy, a good thirty miles from Waterford but right on the Boston line, was consequently a shrewd compromise. And of course the commuting distance to Waterford, sixty miles a day, round-trip, had the additional attractiveness of justifying the purchase of a car I also couldn't afford. If I was going to make that trip five times a week, I needed a good car."

"What was it?" Gates said.

"Sixty-two Buick Skylark convertible," he said. "Fire engine red, white vinyl seats, whitewalls and a white top."

"Those were neat cars," she said. "My mother had one of the Pontiacs, the LeMans hardtop? Hers was white, with red inside. I really liked that car."

"Oh," he said. "I tell you, I was hot stuff in that car. The owner of the dealership'd gotten it for his wife, so it'd been kept up and she hadn't driven it much. It was a sharp little buggy when I got it. Not a ding on it. When I took that car off the lot, I figured I had it made. Driving this thing, I thought, I'm irresistible.

"Another miscalculation," he said. "I was just as resistible in a shiny red convertible, with my own apartment, as I'd been taking the train back and forth to school and living with my aunt in Stoughton, looking worried all the time about whether I had enough cash on me to pay the check out on a date. You're not that much younger'n I am," he said. "When you were in college, what was the word for clumsy, awkward, embarrassingly horny guys who had no social smarts at all?"

She giggled. " 'Geeks,' " she said. "I think we also called them 'nerds,' back then."

"That's what I was," he said, "a geek. I knew absolutely nothing about getting a girl's pants off, including how to conceal the fact that my central purpose in life at that time was to get a girl's pants off. Any girl's pants off — didn't matter to me. I was paralyzed by horniness. It was as though erection for me made my whole body rigid and my brain concrete as well. And, since I had lots of erections in those youthful days, that meant I spent a lot of my time almost speechless."

She was laughing. "Oh, sure," he said with mock bitterness, "all very well for you to laugh. What were you, about sixteen, when I was twenty-three?"

"Somewhere in there, I suppose," she said. "Oh hell, why lie? I'm nine years younger than you are. I would've been fourteen."

"Well," he said, "then that's a good thing for me. Because if you'd been twenty, twenty-one, nineteen even, and I'd run into you in some bar or something, I would've tried to pick you up, and you would've laughed at me to my face."

"I would not," she said.

"Well," he said, "maybe not to my face. After you'd gone to the ladies room and not come back. Ditched me and gone home. *Then* you would've laughed."

"I was always very kind to my escorts, and men who tried to pick me up," she said. "I would've done no such thing."

"*Were* you?" he said. "Really? Very kind? Gee, maybe I should've met you."

"That's not what I meant," she said. "Besides, fourteen's against the law. You would've gone to jail, if you'd met someone like that."

"I suppose so," he said. "Mark Baldwin didn't, when he met one and picked her off, but most likely I would have. I never had Mark's smarts. Or his money, either." He looked rueful. "It's best to have one or the other, if they offer you a choice."

"I heard something about that from Munroe," she said. "That Baldwin got into a bad scrape with a teenaged girl."

Logan nodded. "Happened before I got there," he said. "The actual humping, I mean. But there was still sort of a low-level, rumbling flap going on about it after I showed up. I guess it was pretty messy."

"I heard people got paid off," she said. "Anything to that?"

"I'd assume they did," he said, "given the situation. Mark's next stop was going to be the penitentiary, if something didn't get done. His natural inclination would've been to fall back on all that money and try to buy his way out. You generally can, if you've got enough and there aren't too many bodies lying in the street. And he didn't get prosecuted. So, two and two together, all that kind of thing, I'd have to assume that he probably greased a couple palms to get the thing blown out."

"Billy Taves?" she said.

"Possibly," Logan said. "The Plymouth DA, Ward Keane. Maybe the odd cop here and there. But the family would've been the most important thing. And if they chose to drop the case, well, nobody else involved in it would've been obstructing justice, because there wasn't any to obstruct. So if Mark wanted to distribute generous tips, well, what the hell? No harm in being friendly."

"You were envious of him," she said.

"Hell, I'm still am," he said. "There I was in the same office day after day with a guy who's been everywhere, seen everything, pockets full of money, smooth as he can be, and I know he's getting more ass than a toilet seat. And opposed to him I've got Dan Munroe, still a detective then, rougher'n a cob and living with his mother, and what he tells me to do is join him in his weekly trip to the whorehouse down in Plymouth.

"Now you've got to keep something in mind," Logan said. "In addition to harboring these ambitions of rapine, I was also a complete prig."

"A bundle of contradictions," she said.

"Well, I was," he said. "I associated whoring with what my father did. I hated him. I certainly didn't want to be like him. So when Dan told me to stop griping about not getting any, and come to Plymouth with him, I was actually shocked. And I showed it. 'You go to whorehouses?' I said.

" 'Well,' he said, practical man, 'what the hell else'm I supposed to do? I'm twenty-five years old. I live with my mother, so I can't bring girls home, and anyway, I don't know any girls I'd want to bring home. I used to know some, but while I was flunking out of college and doing my army, you know, they either got married or moved away. So, that leaves the kind of girls I can get to know fast, in joints and bars, and I'd better not try that. They all know I'm a cop. They're either going to think if they come across for me, they've got a license to do business with no trouble from the law, or else that I'm setting them up for an arrest for solicitation. That isn't going to work, and Chief Deese'd suspend my ass if he found out, bring me up on charges. Besides, I'm unlucky. If I tried it, and did get away with it, I'd probably catch a dose. My dick starts dripping and I have to get medicine for it, and where do I keep that? I'd have to keep it at home, and Dorcas'd find out. She's like a hawk, my mother. I ever got the clap, boy, her finding out'd be worse'n the Chief.

" 'So,' Daniel said, 'I go the cathouse on Thursday nights, and get my ashes hauled. It's twenty bucks. The girls're clean. It's not in my jurisdiction, so if Margie's paying someone off, or giving out free blow jobs so her house don't get raided, it's got nothing to do with me. I'm not married, so my wife's not gonna find out and blow the whistle on me. And I walk around comfortable as a result.

" 'You got to treat a stiff prick with respect,' Dan said. 'There's only three things you can do with it, and only one of them's really fun. You can walk around with your legs crooked until it goes down. You can jack off. Or you can get laid. You can't bargain with it. You can't say to it, "Well, look, all right? I haven't got nothing for you right now, but come back in six months or so, I may have something then." It's not gonna do that. You either use it for what it's supposed to be for, and get some fun outta life, or you don't. And you don't. It's that simple. You should come with me.'

"And I didn't," Logan said.

"What did you tell him?" she said. "He must've wanted a reason."

"I told him," Logan said, "that while Margie's wasn't in his jurisdiction as a cop in Waterford, it was in mine as a reporter. And if some cop who didn't know about or approve of arrangements raided the place some night when I was in it, I would lose my job."

"And he believed that?" she said.

"Of course he didn't," Logan said. "But like I say, Dan's a clod, but basically a nice guy. He pretended to, and he didn't razz me too much, and I walked around with my legs crooked all the time, feeling uncomfortable.

"I had Tuesdays and Wednesdays off when I worked in Waterford, which is the kind of treatment the newspaper business and the television business and every other outfit that works every day gives to the rookies to teach them some manners, respect for their elders. So on the third Monday in June of Nineteen-sixty-four, I drove home in my snazzy red convertible to my apartment full of rented furniture to start my riotous bachelor weekend: no particular place to go, no one to go there with, and no real prospects of improving matters, either. You know how depressing that is, when you're twenty-three years old?"

"No, I don't," she said. "I was going with Jeffrey then. But I know how it is when you're thirty-five. I have one of those weekends most weeks. They're downright horrible."

"They certainly are," he said, "but at least the desperation's less. At least if you've had someone for a while, you don't have to think you never will. Which my uninterrupted string of strikeouts by then had pretty nearly convinced me was never going to change.

"When I got back to my apartment that night, there was a U-Haul truck in my parking place. Now that was a serious breach of tenant etiquette. The building fronted on Hancock Street, which is a main drag. No parking allowed on the street, and if it had been, I wouldn't've left my lovely red car out there anyway.

"It was hotter'n hell that night," Logan said. "I sat there stewing in my car for about five minutes, planning all sorts of mayhem on the body of the son of a bitch who'd parked there. Until the son of a bitch came out of the building. Then I started feeling much more peaceable toward my fellow man.

"Bomber Feeley was about thirty. He was wearing this grey USMC tee-shirt with the sleeves ripped off, most likely after his biceps had burst through, as his pectoral muscles were threatening to do to the body of the shirt. I'd guess he weighed about one-ninety, a good two or three pounds of it, at the most, fat that he couldn't make into muscle. He had hands on him that looked like the buckets on a clamshell dredge. He spotted me. He came over to my car. He put those paws on the door and said: 'That your place we're blocking?'

"Knowing that this might get me killed, I admitted that it was. 'Shit,' he said. 'I was hoping this wouldn't happen. I said to Rosie when we pulled in: "I hope this guy works late." And she says: 'What choice've we got? It's the only place here." So, we blocked it.'

"Bomber blinks a iot," Logan said. "It's a tic. It doesn't seem to bother him, and once you've known him for a while and he seems to've taken a liking to you, it doesn't bother you. But when you don't know him, when there's still a possibility that he might take a dislike to you and remodel your face, it's very disconcerting to have his jaw about a foot from yours and watch his eyes maybe signaling he's about to run amok and attack. 'Can I ask you a favor?' he said.

"Of course he could ask me a favor," Logan said. "He could've asked me if I'd mind giving my car to him in return for letting me live. I would've given it serious consideration. Sweat's running down his noble brow, and he's looking worried, which makes me concerned as well. 'Ask ahead,' I said, trying not to squeal.

" 'Rosie's upstairs with the kid, giving him his dinner,' Bomber said. 'We're hoping we could finish getting the stuff in before he starts to yell, but we didn't make it. We only got three things left, two chairs and the desk and chair. I can get the chairs up myself. I could get the desk up, too, if there was room enough in the door so I could get my arms around it, but there isn't. So as a result I need Rosie, take the other end. She'll be down inna minute. So, I could ask you to just sit there a little longer, all right? And I'll take the chairs up, and then when Rosie's down, she'll help with the desk, and we'll get outta here.'

" 'Look,' I said, 'my name's Joe. Don't worry about it.' This makes the bruiser smile. He sticks out his paw. He isn't going to murder me. We're going to be friends. 'Bomber Feeley,' he says. 'Pleased to meet you, Joe. Name's actually Mike, but Bomber's what everybody calls me.'

"That comforts me so much I get out of my car," Logan said. " 'Give you a hand,' I say to Bomber, just as the lady comes out of the door. 'And this here is Rosie, I was telling you about,' he says.

"She looked precisely the way any reasonable man would've expected this warrior's wife to look. She was all hot and harried, hair stuck to her face and this long palomino ponytail plastered to her neck. She was wearing this light blue halter top she had sweated to her body, and dirty white gym shorts that stuck to her rear end.

"I was immediately consumed with lust," Logan said. "Lust of course was a fairly constant element of my thinking in those days, but when I saw a cupcake like that, soaked down to the point where she might as well have been nude, her clothes a mere technicality, well . . . ."

" . . . you became a raging beast," Gates said.

"Well, no," he said, laughing. "Not with this monster that I thought was her husband standing right beside me. No, I managed to control myself. But I was glad Bomber's talents didn't include mind reading, or I would've gotten croaked."

"Hers did, though, of course," Gates said.

He looked mildly surprised. "You think so?" he said.

"From what you've already told me," Gates said, "I'm absolutely sure she knew what you were thinking. Most women I know, the normal ones, at least, all of us can tell right off whether any man we meet has got the hots for us. It's how we usually decide whether a man's straight or gay. If there isn't that little zing when we meet one, we tab him 'queer' right off."

"Yeah," Logan said, "but suppose the guy's straight but just doesn't happen to be interested in you?"

"Same thing," she said. "Doesn't matter. If he's not interested in me, then he's as good as a queer. He goes into my fag book, and he stays in it forever. You think you men have a monopoly on sexual egotism? Isn't true, my friend. After all the time and money and effort we spend on dressing and primping to excite you guys sexually, if you don't get excited, we write you off. At once. Otherwise we'd have to consider the possibility that we're not attractive after all, which would be humiliating. The first thing I look at when I meet a man is his crotch. And if there's a noticeable change there after a few minutes, well, that's the nicest compliment I could get."

"Amazing," he said.

"Didn't she tell you that?" Gates said. "Your wife, I mean?"

He frowned. "Well," he said, "sure. I mean, she told me a lot later she knew right off when we met that I was going to be interesting company, if her brother would ever clear out, and she was pretty sure she'd go to bed with me before I said a word. But she never mentioned anything about checking out all the other men she met."

"Two questions," Gates said. "When she was still alive, and you met other women, regardless of whether you had any intention of being unfaithful to her, did you fantasize about going to bed with the ones you liked? Yes or No."

"Yes," he said. "I never did it, and I never would've done it, but I sure thought about it."

"Sure," Gates said, "because you're not a fag, and you are alive. Second question: Did she keep her shape?"

"Certainly did," he said. "Far as I know, the only thing besides occasional smoking that I did that tacked her off was eating as much of anything I liked without gaining weight. She was on a perpetual diet."

"Then why do you find it so incredible," Gates said, "when I tell you that this healthy woman who took care of herself and was interested in sex checked out the boys just the same as you checked out the girls?"

He shrugged. "I guess I don't, actually," he said. "I just never thought about it before. Not in those terms, at least. As far as I was concerned, I'd come home on a hot night, met this woman and this man and this infant I assumed was theirs, discovered them moving stuff into the apartment across the hall from mine, invited them in for a beer after we emptied the truck, sat there for about an hour fantasizing about how some day there might be a hurricane or something that'd have him working as an emergency lineman for the phone company in Maine for a couple weeks or so, so I could make a pass at her in her loneliness, and then found out he was her brother and she wasn't married to anybody. And she obviously liked me. A week after she moved in, the kid's crib was in my bedroom and the two of us were sleeping, when we slept at all, on the sofabed in my living room. It was magical. I didn't try to explain it, analyze it or understand it, what had happened to put us together."

"You were a lucky man," she said.

"I was," he said. "I was."

"And she was lucky, too," Gates said. "You shouldn't leave that out."

38

Shortly after six, when the second side of the second tape ran out, the fog had enclosed Logan's house so that everything beyond the deck outside the glass door was hidden from their sight. He stood up and stretched when she removed the tape from the recorder and said: "I know you want to finish, but I could use a break."

She nodded. "So could I," she said.

"Furthermore," he said, "you really ought to get your car in off the street. I know a guy who came down it in a fog of his own making one clear night, and hit the boulders at the end. Somebody cold sober could total your wheels in this stuff, and you might not like that."

"I would not," she said. She got up and dug her keys out of her bag.

"What I could do," he said, "since we're obviously operating on Plan B now, and you're staying over, I could forage the refrigerator for dinner. If you like." He looked anxious.

"That would be nice," she said. "You're going to a lot of trouble. I appreciate it."

"Ahh," he said, waving that aside, "I planned to eat anyway. I made a quahaug chowder last night. Without any damned flour. Should be right fine by now."

She returned to the kitchen after moving her car in behind the barn. She was carrying her overnight bag. "That's a new Corvette in there?" she said, shutting the kitchen door. She sat down at the table again.

He was at the counter, chopping a cabbage with a long knife and periodically scraping the slivers into a brown china bowl. There was a blue double boiler heating on the stove top. "Yeah," he said. "Embarrassing, isn't it?"

"Not if you like it," she said.

"Oh," he said, "it'd be even more embarrassing if I liked it. Man

of my advanced years roaring around in one of those plastic pigs.
I know it's fast, and I know they've cleaned up the handling, and
I know it's the best buy in town when it comes to getting something that'll triple the speed limit. But my God, when I'm driving
it, I always feel like I should get a bottle of Grecian Formula and
some Italian silk shirts and a couple gold chains to wear around my
neck."

"Why'd you buy it, then?" she said.

"I didn't," he said. "That's why I'm stuck with it. When I got out
of Finisterre, Jack Mahler picked me up in it. And naturally I
thought it was his. White Corvette, for God's sake? Had to be
Jack's. I mean, up 'till then he'd always driven Cadillacs, Eldo
convertibles, but Jack's getting along in years and I figured, you
know, he's recapturing his lost youth. Getting softer in the head, in
other words. Jack's a wonderful man. He loves his wife, Ellie, and
it's not a good idea to ask him about his kids, because the boasting
lasts for hours, complete with pictures he just happens to have in his
wallet. But he does like the Armani suits, and the Italian loafers, and
he's got the forty-foot Chris Craft and the condo in Saint Thomas, so
Jack in a Corvette, at fifty-five or six, well, it didn't surprise me.

"What did surprise me," he said, spooning mayonnaise into the
bowl on top of the chopped cabbage, "was when we drove in the
yard here, he put it in the barn. Now keep in mind that the barn was
empty. In better days it held my Nine-eleven and Rosemary's Jeep.
Then when the bad times began, just my Nine-eleven. But I was
from Finisterre by way of New Bedford General, by way of the rocks
at the end of the street, which I'd tried to jump while wearing the
Porsche. So when Jack drove me home in the 'Vette, there wasn't
any car in the barn.

" 'Here,' he says, taking the keys out of the ignition and handing
them to me, 'Welcome home.' Then his eyes teared up. And while
I'm trying to think of something to say, Bill Glass and Laura Charles
pull in behind us in Bill's Cadillac. He's going back with them.

" 'Jack,' I said, 'for God's sake. You guys paid for the treatment,
which had to cost a bundle. You were kind to me for much longer'n
almost anybody would've been. I can't let you do this.'

"He shook his head. Guy's having trouble talking, and I'm making
him talk, knowing how emotional he is. He takes my hand in both of
his. 'Joe,' he says, 'you're like my son. Bill loves you too. We all do.

What you went through, all right? We know. And now you're going to be okay. You take your time. You think about things. You decide what you want to do. And whatever it is, Joe,' he says, practically crushing my knuckles, and Jack is not a bodybuilder, 'whatever it is, anything on this earth, from just being a reporter to coming back as news director, soon as you decide, my friend, you come back and let us know, and you have got that job. And you get back on your feet, you know, get some meat on your bones and you're feeling all right, you want to go back on the air, well, that is open, too.' "

"Jesus," she said, "that's a friend."

He was squeezing lemon juice into the china bowl. "He's a friend, all right," he said. "We started this place with you, Joe,' he said. 'Things went good for a long time. They can go good again. We know that already. We want you to know that, too. Now, you always liked the sports cars. I'm not gonna spend my money, give you one them German things that the people who make them're making ovens, forty-five years ago. Even though I know you like them. There are things I will not do. But this here's a good American car, and Bill and me want you to have it as our gift on your recovery, and so you will have something you can come by and see us in. In a few weeks, when you got your bearings back. 'Kay?'

"So," Logan said, stirring the mixture in the bowl, "what could I do, huh? Turn the thing down?"

"Only," she said, "if you're the worst piece of shit in Christendom."

"That's what I thought," he said. "So I didn't. But just between us and the slaw, I feel awful silly driving it. I feel like a fool." He sampled the contents of the bowl. He pondered. "Needs more pepper," he said, sprinkling some in. "Also more lemon juice." He squeezed the fruit over the bowl. He looked up at her and smirked. "My idea of slaw," he said, "is the runny stuff you get at the cheaper beachfront restaurants where they give you the fried clams and the scallops in cardboard boats, and the french fries heaped up on paper plates, and the slaw in the big pleated paper cups."

"Right," she said. "The tartar sauce and the ketchup in little pleated cups, and they're all runny too. But's okay if the clams and the fries come in those cardboard cartons like the Chinese restaurants use for chop suey. Maybe even better. With little packets of salt, and a two-pronged wooden fork."

"You got it," he said, wiping his hands on a paper towel. "Clam chowder in a Styrofoam cup, and you eat it with a white plastic spoon. You sit outside at a picnic table and behind you at the next table there's a family of seven, five screaming kids, one in a car seat propped up on the floor, wants his bottle, and all his mother'll give him's a damned pacifier. That's my idea of cole slaw, by God, and that's what I try to make."

"No carrot filings?" she said.

"Well," he said, "no, actually. But not on principle. I just didn't happen to have any. Usually I do, and I put them in. How about a drink?"

She hesitated.

"Oh come on," he said. "Don't hurt me like that. I told you when you came in, I keep booze in the house. I'm not afraid of the stuff. It never once attacked me, you know. When I was drinking, the bottles didn't sneak into my room at night, pin me, and empty their contents down my throat."

"But watching somebody else drink?" she said.

"I visit the real world from time to time," he said. "It's dawned on me that not everyone quit having a cocktail the day after I got drydocked. At first I thought it was a little disrespectful of them, but then I thought: What the hell — like to see the young people enjoying themselves. So, what'll you have?"

"White wine?" she said.

He nodded. "Should've figured. BMW, attaché case, woman-on-the-move. Had to be white wine."

"Oh," she said, "well, if what I order's symbolic in some way, got any Pabst Blue Ribbon?"

He laughed. "No," he said. He went to the refrigerator. He brought out a small jug of Taylor California Chablis. He held it up. "Not exactly *premier crû*," he said, "but potable, I'm told."

She nodded. "Fine," she said, as he poured a glass. "Who told you, if I may ask?"

"You mean: 'How come I've got an open jug of white wine in the icebox if I don't drink it?' " he said. He put the jug back in the refrigerator. He took out a bottle of Canada Dry seltzer and poured a glass of that, dropping in a wedge of lime. He brought both glasses over to the table and sat down.

"If you like," she said, taking the wine and sipping it.

"Laura Charles," he said. "She comes over from time to time, and she likes a glass of wine."

"She's very nice," Gates said. "I met her at the station. Very pretty, too."

"Yes, she is," he said.

"You having an affair with her?" Gates said.

"This off the record?" he said.

"Machine's not running," she said. "I won't print it if you say so."

"I say so," he said. "Not because I'm having an affair with her. I'm not. She was having one with Don. Don Cressey, I mean. For quite a long time, too. Then he went to the network, and she didn't, and her career sort of stalled, and it's still stalled, and for a couple years they took a lot of airplanes. Then he got assigned to the White House, and that sort of thing ended it. So she's still here while he flies around the world with the President of the United States. Reasonably enough, considering the difference in our ages, she regards me as father figure, I guess, and I try to be one to her. Makes me feel useful, you know?"

"If that's true," she said, "why don't you want me to print it?"

"Because it would embarrass her and Don," he said. "What she tells me is confidential. I want to keep it that way."

"She misses him," Gates said.

"Simply put," he said, "yes. That sums it up all right. A large part of it, anyway. The other part is that she's crowding thirty in a field where that's not a smart move for an ambitious woman. She's been at SET for going on eight years and she really hasn't gotten a lot of tempting offers to move up in the world. She doesn't know why, and I don't, either. The camera likes her. She's very competent. She doesn't have an obtrusive accent. She's easy to work with. But she's also apparently one of those people who hit all the marks you're supposed to hit to go far, and nothing seems to happen. It's very frustrating. I think she believes," he said, "deep down inside, that where she really went wrong was falling in love with Don. That when there was a potential for competition between the two of them for something that would lead to advancement, she consciously or unconsciously deferred to him. So he ended up getting the prize, and he became a star, and she got left behind with nothing but the feeling she'd been made into a sucker. She's never come right out and said that, not to me, at least, but I think that's what it is."

"Is she right?" Gates said.

"Actually, no," he said. "She's a talented person. But Don's an exceptionally-talented person. If she'd gone nose-to-nose with him, bidding for assignments, any news director would've chosen Don. He's better than she is.

"Look," he said, "you know and I know the Rolling Stones were right: You can't always get what you want. It often doesn't matter how badly you want it, doesn't matter at all. I did pretty well, but no objective judge could look at the job I had and rank me among the most influential people in my profession. SET is a great place to work, and I had a happy life, but it's still a small station in a small market, and I was small potatoes by the standards of my trade. The networks did not blandish me to reform their news divisions. I wasn't prominently mentioned as Brinkley's replacement when he left NBC.

"It would've been the same if I'd stayed with the *Commoner*," he said, "until it was sold by the Goulds. North American would not've picked me over Mark Baldwin to run the operation. I probably would've made it to assistant managing editor by now, if I'd wanted to be an editor, or had my choice of comfortable assignments at the State House or in Washington if I'd wanted to keep writing. But I never would've made it to the top of anything."

"Well," she said, "but Mark Baldwin had a lot of advantages, starting out."

"Sure he did," Logan said. "And one of them was superior ability. If you'd taken away all the other advantages, the education he'd had, the travel, all the polish he'd acquired before he even began doing something serious, just started him and Mel and Didi and me off with the same native talents that we had, and nothing else, at the same age, my guess is each of us today would be in pretty much the same position we reached without the equal start. Mark was the first person I'd met — Don was maybe the third or fourth, at the most — who could take hold of something that literally *nobody* else understood, figure it out and master it, and do it in record time. It's more than raw intelligence that those freaks have, and it's more than just their powers of retention, too. They have this amazing power to synthesize, like angels or something. They operate in a different dimension. We ordinary mortals can't compete with them."

"Yeah, but are they happy?" she said sardonically. "You bet your ass they are."

"Oh," Logan said, "I wouldn't go that far. I'd lean the other way, in fact. I'd say they mostly aren't. They don't really have anyone to talk to. They spend most of their time holding themselves at idle speed, drumming their fingers and humming distractedly, while the rest of us huff and puff, trying to catch up. Can you imagine how it'd be to spend your whole life explaining things to a bunch of dummies? Who probably won't get more'n a third of it anyway, after you've laid it all out? Maddening. But that's what they have to do — there aren't enough of them to form their own complete society, so they have to associate with the rest of us. Besides, why would you need two of them in any operation anyway? The second one would be redundant.

"That's where things even out for the rest of us," Logan said. "Rosemary, for example — Mark wouldn't've looked twice at her. Well, that's wrong — he would've looked and he would've tried to get her into bed. And be probably would've succeeded."

"I'm surprised to hear you say that," she said.

"Why?" he said. "He's just what you said: an extremely attractive man. Rosemary was a very good-looking woman. Her first husband's idea of changing from a swinging bachelor into a dutiful husband happened to include a lot of sadism that she didn't go for a lot, bondage and all that crap, but as bad as her experience was with him, it didn't convince her sex in general was something she ought to avoid. Just the opposite. When I met her she was starved for a man. She told me so, in very plain terms. She was twenty-six years old and she'd been married for about three years, and she liked intercourse. She told me many times that she was lucky I turned out to be the first man who showed up with an erection when she moved to Quincy, because she'd been hunting for one and she was beginning to wonder if maybe she was being just a little too selective.

"Now," he said, "you come in here and you tell me she probably had fantasies about other men. And you tell me that you do, which probably explains why you could figure that out about her without ever meeting her. And you tell me you found Mark a satisfactory partner. So, what's so surprising? I don't think she would've cheated on me. I'm not saying that. I do think if Mark'd met her before she got involved with me, he would've had her in bed pretty fast, without too much trouble at all.

"But once he'd accomplished that," Logan said, "he would've washed his hands and dropped her. 'That's done. On to the next thing.' I was different. I was a one-woman dog. I got a little sappy, as you might also expect, after she became my lover. Everybody in the first bloom of love thinks it's the first time in the history of the world that it's happened. I was no exception, as far as that went. Only difference was, I guess, I seem to've stayed that way. Long, long afterwards."

"That's not so bad," she said. She put a new cassette in the tape recorder and clicked it on. "Don't be ashamed of that."

39

In Boston the squall line had been followed by low-lying clouds and a fine mist that blanked out the difference between late afternoon and evening. In Richard Pond's town-house on the eastern side of Beaver Street north of the Public Garden, lights were necessary in the gloom when Jason Francis arrived at six forty-five. Pond, in rumpled white linen slacks and a plum-and-white-striped cotton sweater admitted him to the foyer through the double oak doors with frosted glass panes. Pond was barefoot and his hair was slicked back, wet. "We'll have cocktails in the front parlor, Jason," he said, leading the way down the narrow hallway past the umbrella stand and the highboy with the silver salver on the top, underneath the pier glass. The hallway was papered in gold peacocks against an asparagus background. The stairs to the second floor on the left were illuminated by sconces with fluted glass shades and chain switches.

The small front parlor looked out on Beaver Street through three tall windows arranged in a bay. They were heavily draped in emerald green velvet, with thick gold-braided tasseling. At the center of the windows there was a Sheraton table with a lamp based on a red Chinese vase. In front of the table was a Victorian loveseat done in jade green velvet. There was a massive low oak table in front of the loveseat, faced by three Queen Anne chairs upholstered in light green velvet. There was a small silver bell on the table. The carpet was a green Oriental. The fireplace was framed in mahogany and there was a spray of red gladioli in a basket on the hearth. Above the fireplace was an oil portrait; it showed Richard Pond's face as he had looked at thirty-five, grafted onto a reproduction of a body of Gainsborough's "Blue Boy." Pond took the chair in front of the fireplace. He gestured toward the loveseat. "Please have a seat, dear boy," he said.

Francis sat down on the loveseat. He clasped his hands between his legs and surveyed the room. He shook his head. "Why don't I smell any incense? he said. "Everything else is in place."

Pond smiled delightedly. "This is my home, Jason," he said. "No reason to pretend in my own home."

"Do you bring people here," Francis said.

"Of *course* not," Pond said. "Have you gone mad? Dexter lives with me here." He picked up the bell from the table and tinkled it. "He'd be very upset if I did that."

"I didn't mean that," Francis said. "I didn't mean people that you'd cruised. I meant business friends. People like that."

"Of course not," Pond said. "I'm not out of my mind, you know."

Dexter Finny in a white caftan entered the room through the dining room on the other side of the archway. He sashayed as he passed the oval oak dining room table and the highbacked oak chairs. He was about thirty-two years old. He had shiny black hair, wet and slicked back. He was barefoot. He was carrying a silver tray of hors d'oeuvres — small shrimp on toothpicks, cubes of cheese, bite-sized crackers, short celery sticks, slices of cucumber, a bowl of seafood relish and a bowl of hummus. He placed the tray on the table between them. He stepped back one pace. He locked his hands under his sternum and bowed. "Yes, Master?" he said.

"Oh, for Christ's sake," Francis said. "Will you two please cut it out? I came here to talk serious business. I've got a dying woman on my hands. Quit all this horsing around."

"Just showing you what you're missing, Jason," Pond said. "Yes, Dexter, if you would. I would like a daiquiri. Straight up. Jason?"

"Ginger ale," Francis said curtly. "On the rocks."

"*Jason*," Pond said. "There's no need to be *rude*."

"We don't have any ginger ale, I'm afraid, Mister Francis," Finney said. "I can offer you white Dubonnet, vermouth, vermouth cassis, a kir, perhaps a glass of white wine or root beer?"

"Root beer?" Francis said.

"Dexter's nephews were here last weekend," Pond said. "They're absolutely addicted to root beer."

"White wine," Francis said.

Finney bowed again. He remained bowed until Pond said: "Thank you, Dexter." Then he turned and went back to the kitchen.

"Is this vaudeville necessary, Richard?" Francis said. "Haven't we been through this whole tour about a hundred times or so?"

"*You're* a narcissist," Pond said. "I must say, I'm surprised. Just what makes you think all this is being staged for your benefit? You are in my home. This is how I live. I'm not at the office now. I've been there all day. Dexter's not at the newsstand now. He's been there all day. He doesn't have a problem. I don't have a problem. You're the one with the problem. You call me up at five-thirty and say you have to see me. I generously invite you to meet me at my home, after Dexter and I have freshened up, and you come to it and *bitch*? Who the hell do you think you are?"

Francis gaped. Finney flounced through the dining room again, carrying another silver tray with the drinks. He entered the front parlor. He set the tray on the table and hunkered down on his haunches. He fixed a doglike gaze on Pond's face. Pond picked up the daiquiri and sipped. He savored. He nodded appreciatively. "Very good, Dexter," he said. "I think we've finally got the right pulp mixture. Very good job." Dexter beamed. He did not change his position. He shifted his imploring gaze to Francis. "He wants you to try your wine," Pond said in a bored voice.

Francis tasted his wine. He nodded and put the glass down. "Very good, Dexter," he said. "Entirely satisfactory."

Dexter beamed. He shifted his gaze back to Pond. He put an inquiring look on his face. "I don't know, Dexter," Pond said. "Let me ask Jason. Jason, can Dexter stay to hear what you came to talk about?"

Francis looked at Pond. Then he looked at Finney. Then he looked back at Pond, and back at Finney again. "Sure," he said. "Sure he can. Provided: he gets a drink and he gets up off the floor and he sits in a chair and behaves like a normal human being, for Christ sakes. I don't give a shit if he hears what I've got to say, but I'm damned if I'm going to sit here like Mister Victor's Victrola and him playing the dog while I talk. Could you guys at least *pretend* to be normal, for a little while at least?"

Finney looked at Pond. "Do as our guest says, please, Dexter," he said. Dexter got to his feet. "And no mincing, Dexter, please. I've told you how clients are: picky, picky, picky."

Finney left the room. "You know, Jason," Pond said, "for someone who's depended on Dexter for quite a long time to keep his cock out of his zipper for him, you're very mean. You asked me to intercede for you, with him, to protect your wife. And he did it. He did it for a long time. Now you come here, as a guest in his home, and you sneer at him. I don't think that's fair."

Finney returned, carrying a glass mug of root beer. He sat down on the Queen Anne chair opposite Pond's. He put the mug on the table and crossed his legs. He looked at Francis with interest. "Nice to meet you, at long last," he said. "Wondered what you looked like. Could've asked for better circumstances, but what the hey, huh? Right? What'd she take?"

"They don't know," Francis said. "Well, they know, but they don't know exactly how much of what. Mellaril, some other stuff. She'd been saving it up. Washed it down with a bottle of Zeller Schwarzerkatz Moselle."

"Not a bad wine," Finney said, looking at Pond.

"Dexter," Pond said, "I'm warning you."

"Well, it's not," Finney said. "How's she doing?" he said to Francis.

Francis motioned with his right hand. "Wobbly," he said. "Fifty-fifty if she makes it."

"Respirator?" Pond said.

"Oh yeah," Francis said. "They've got all the stops pulled out."

"What's your question?" Pond said. "Why'd you call me up?"

Francis drank some of his wine. "To ask you what to do," he said. "You're my lawyer, right? I've got to make a decision. Or I'm going to, pretty soon. What do I do then?"

Pond looked at Finney. Finney raised his eyebrows and drank root beer. Pond nodded. Pond looked back at Francis. "What're your choices going to be?" he said.

Finney put the mug down while Francis was thinking. "Step on the hose," Finney said.

"I'm sorry?" Francis said.

Finney folded his hands in his lap. He swung his left foot as he talked. "Step on the fucking *hose*," he said. "Cut off her fucking oxygen. Let the woman die. Help her along if you have to. That's what she wants to do. Put a pillow over her face. Smother the poor bitch. But let her out of her agony. She's been in Hell too long. It's not fair to torment a person like what she's been going through."

Francis stared at Pond. "What do you want me to say?" Pond said. "I agree with him. I would've put it differently, but he was perfectly content to kneel before us and let me save your feelings. As confused as they must be. You're the one that wanted him to join in the discussion. And he knows her better than I do. I think he's probably right."

Francis cleared his throat. "Richard," he said. He croaked. He shook his head and cleared his throat again.

"Are you all right?" Pond said solicitously, leaning forward. "Did you aspirate your wine?" He touched Francis on the right arm.

Francis pulled his arm away. He shook his head again. "No," he said, "no, I'm all right. Let me just, listen to me for a minute, all right? I didn't come here to ask you if it's all right for me to murder Sylvia."

"No one's mentioned murder, Jason," Pond said. "All Dexter was suggesting, all I was recommending, was that if you, as her spouse, are faced with a decision of whether to authorize heroic measures, you should in both her and your best interests order them withheld. That's a perfectly proper course of action for a man in your position to take. She's a very unhappy woman, poor thing. She's been out of the hospital barely a week. This is the second time she's tried to make away with herself. This attempt appears to have been more serious than the last one. There's no longer any doubt that she's serious. There's no longer any substantial possibility that any form or amount of therapy will change her mind or her intentions, or her determination to carry them out, if she recovers this time. She rejected those efforts during her last recuperation. There is, on the other hand, a strong possibility, as I understand it, that she may not completely recover physically from this episode, even if she lives. Isn't that so, Jason?"

Francis sighed. "She may have some brain damage," he said. "They don't really know how long she was unconscious before the housekeeper came in and found her. It could've been as little as fifteen minutes, or it could've been as much as four or five hours. Unfortunately Mrs. Hendricks, tidy person that she is, put the rest of the wine back in the refrigerator right after she called the police, so we couldn't tell from that being warm or still cold about how long it'd been since she took it out."

"And if it was several hours," Pond said, "that increases the chances that she's brain-damaged now."

"Yes," Francis said. "That's what they called me about, just before I called you this afternoon. To ask me whether I want her transferred to the coma unit at New England Medical Center. And I didn't know what that was, whether it's a place where they ware-house people who aren't going to come out of it, or a place where they have specialists in bringing people out.

"I asked them which it was," he said, "and they weren't very forthcoming. Not very helpful, I guess I mean. They said to a degree it's both. They also couldn't tell me whether moving her at this stage might not do some more damage. Because, as I said, they don't really know how long it is that she's been unconscious. Apparently the longer they're out before they get supplemental oxygen and the drugs're pumped out of their system, the less likely the chances they'll make it all the way back. Also, on whether she's still in real danger of a sudden cardiac arrest. Which they'd have a lot better chance of pulling her out of in the hospital than in an ambulance taking her to another one. So, depending on how long she's been unconscious, it could either be dangerous to move her, or not dangerous at all. And the same applies as to whether the coma unit can actually do anything dramatic for her — the way I get it, at least, their success pretty much depends on how soon they begin whatever the procedures are that make them specialists."

"Leave her where she is," Pond said.

"You think so," Francis said.

"It's the safest decision, from every point of view," Pond said. "Any other decision you make now has to be based in part on guesswork. You know she's getting adequate care. You don't know whether the alternative treatment, given the risks of securing it, would really improve her chances. And for obvious and sundry reasons, you don't know either whether you want them improved."

"Richard," Francis said warningly.

"Jason," Pond said. "Listen to me. You came here for my advice. Leave aside the selfish question of whether your life would be better if she died. The only thing you have left to consider is whether her life will improve if she's kept around to live more of it. On balance, dear boy, you have to say that it will not. Either she'll be a helpless vegetable, of no use to anyone including herself, dependent on feeding tubes and catheters to put food in and take waste out, being turned like a leg of lamb on a spit every two hours to stop bedsores, or else she'll recover completely, get her wits back, and use them again as she has twice now to conclude that she'd rather be dead. And try it again. She's a chronic suicide, Jason. It no longer matters what her motives are, who's to blame, who benefits if she succeeds, or whether you feel guilty for your own feelings. It's the same thing now as the sun coming up in the morning — you can feel guilty about the sunrise, if you want, but it's still going to happen, no matter what you do."

"You're right," Francis said.

"Of course I'm right," Pond said.

"Of course he is," Finney said.

Francis glanced at Finney. "Jason," Pond said, "remember now, this is Dexter's home too. Surely more than once you must have been in the home of a heterosexual couple, one of whom annoyed you, and who disliked you as well. When you were, you behaved yourself. You have to do the same thing in this house, I'm afraid. Mind your manners."

Francis looked back at Pond. He stood up. "I've got to go," he said.

"It's down the hall on the left," Finney said, exaggerating a simper.

"Be still, Dexter," Pond said, also standing up. "Make the call, Jason," he said. He offered his hand. Francis accepted it and shook it. "Leave her where she is, and hope that's where it ends."

Pond escorted Francis to the door and ushered him out of the house. He returned to the parlor. "Dexter," he said severely, "you were a naughty boy. A very naughty boy. I ought to stop spanking you, if that's the way you're going to behave when we have guests."

Finney stood up fast. He wheeled so that the caftan billowed around him and knocked Pond's daiquiri glass off the table onto the rug. He put his hands on his hips. He pouted. "He didn't like me, Richard," he said. "That man did not like me. And after all I've done for him, and for his silly wife. And what's with this 'normal' stuff he's putting on us here? Is he kidding me?"

"He's kidding himself," Pond said. He went to Finney and placed his hands on Finney's shoulders. He spoke softly. "He doesn't like what he is, so he doesn't like seeing what we are, because we're the same as he is."

"That's very silly," Finney said. "That's a silly way to act."

Pond sighed. "I know it is," he said. He drew Finney into his arms.

40

Logan and Gates sat facing each other across the empty chowder bowls and the small plates with bits of slaw adrift in white dressing, the tape recorder operating between them. From a distance came the faint sound of a foghorn.

"Either I simply wasn't experienced enough, or I wasn't alert enough," Logan said. "Either Mark didn't notice, or he didn't wish to notice, or he simply didn't care. I don't know why Didi didn't smoke Mel out. Naïveté, maybe? It sure wasn't any desire to protect him. She hated his guts. But the upshot of it was that the obvious explanation for several odd events didn't seem to occur to any of us."

"Munroe says it did," she said. "He says he thinks it did, at least. He says Chief Deese figured out what Shaw'd done and deliberately sat on what he knew because by the time he worked it out, he couldn't prove it."

"Dan says that now," Logan said. "Oscar's safely dead. Dan's mother's made her pile in the land deals and it's probably too late for anybody to turn those around. Dan can say anything he wants about things that happened twenty years ago, before he was chief. It's cheap talk."

"You knew about this?" she said.

He shrugged. "I'm not really impressed," he said, "when somebody who had no responsibility at the time, and therefore has none now, starts telling people that he knew what was going on in the minds of people who came to room temperature years before he decided to talk. It's too easy. I know Dan and I like him, and I'm glad he made chief. But he was a blowhard in Nineteen-sixty-three, and I have no reason to believe he's not a blowhard today. Suppose Oscar did figure it out that Mel killed Tim Lavelle, a year or so after it happened, and that he didn't tell anybody? Could he prove it? If he couldn't, what difference does it make if he did keep still?

"Dan, anyone who runs his mouth on that stuff now: they're all dealing in minutiae. That's what I don't seem to be able to make Billy Taves understand. The reason I did what I did is precisely because the system didn't work when it was called upon to deal with Thomas Brutus. Long before, and many times, before he finally killed my wife. Now Dan says it didn't work when it was called upon to deal with Mel Shaw? I agree with him. I don't argue with him. I don't doubt it for a minute. That's what I am saying, that the system doesn't work. But I don't think the breakdown with Thomas Brutus was the fault of Billy Taves, and I don't think the breakdown with Mel Shaw was the fault of Oscar Deese. Whatever their motives might have been. What I'm saying is the outcome would've been the same, no matter what those motives were."

"But," she said, "when Dan says the police weren't all that interested in Lavalle, isn't he right?"

He got up. He began to clear away the dishes. "Oh, sure he is," he said. "They weren't. They went through the motions and performed their civic function. I don't mean they reached an obvious decision to sit out the case, just bag it. No, what they did was lollygag around with it, take the normal, perfunctory steps: check out former associates; make a desultory investigation of who might've had a motive to kill this Timmy Lavalle. And then when nothing much turned up, let the matter die of inertia. That happens a lot, in every area of government, much more than people think, things just sort of expiring if no one's flogging them. It's not really noticeable, either, because it's so commonplace.

"But in this case," he said, "it should've been. Because Oscar Deese and the dentists and the other speculators had something to gain from the police not being all that interested in pursuing the case, and Oscar was chief of police. He was a tyrant, too, a regular bastard to work for. If he wanted something to happen in that department, that thing damned well happened. And if he didn't want something to happen, well, it didn't happen. Dan used to tell me how Oscar'd ream out the patrolmen for the fun of it, and at first I'd pooh-pooh him. I knew Oscar, after all. Not too bright a fellow, but affable enough. Never gave me any crap."

" 'Oh, sure he doesn't,' Dan would say. 'He's scared out his mind of the press.' "

"I didn't believe that," Logan said. "I'd already met a fairly large number of people who knew I was a reporter and'd made it plain enough for me that they thought the next lowest form of life was a water snake. But of course I was reckoning without information that Dan had, from his loving mother."

"Who was one of the investors in Waterford Associates," Gates said.

"Right, along with Oscar," he said. "Hiding behind his wife, and all those other thoughtful folks, buying up the land. When Dan took you on his tour, did he take you up Union Street?"

"Uh huh," she said. "Flew over it, then drove me up, and we got out and walked."

"Not much there today," he said. "Everything's moved over to Route Four."

"Well," she said, "it's not exactly a wasteland, I mean. There's stuff going on there, people around."

"Sure," he said, "there's stuff going on. But nothing that really matters. Jay Quentin's building, for example — that used to be the hub of Waterford. And what's in there now, may I ask?"

"An auto-parts store and a discount druggist on the first floor," she said. "An aerobics dance studio in the front half of the second floor. There may be a couple apartments in the back. The old *Commoner* office is a real estate agency. The block of stores it was in on the south side of the street is gone, but it's not a blasted heath, you know. The back part of Waterford Village Estates, their tennis courts are there. And the north side of the street, that block of stores is still there. There's a laundromat and a Seven-Eleven variety and a cleaner's and a small liquor store. There's traffic through the area, in other words. It's not as though it's been wiped out by what's along Route Four."

He was measuring coffee into the filtered holder for the maker. "No," he said, "I didn't mean that. But the old Town Hall, for example, across from the *Commoner* office?"

"It's gone," she said. "Dan said the town had an architect come in, and he looked it over and said it'd been built in Eighteen-ninety-one or something, and rewiring it and putting in new beams and doing everything they'd have to do to make it energy-efficient now, it made more sense for the town financially to sell off the land and put up a new building. They sold it to someone who demolished it, and the word is now, according to Dan, it's going to be one of those automated car wash places that sells gasoline as well."

"Which architect," Logan said, "was retained by a Board of

Selectmen dominated by people like Doctor Penn and Doctor Foster, who owned the acreage where the new Town Hall would go. And who wanted it to anchor the office complex they had in mind for Route Four. And who were in cahoots with the lady who owned the land behind Jay Quentin's establishment, which they'd gotten when he couldn't meet his taxes on it. And who wanted that piece to complete the strip they had on the eastern side of Route Four, where the McDonald's and the Sears store and the computer store and the boutique food store are today."

"I see," she said.

"And which facts," Logan said, "were not reported to readers of *The Boston Commoner* while Mel Shaw was chief of its Waterford bureau. The same Mel Shaw who later resigned that position to become director of public relations for Waterford Associates, when Deese and Dorcas Munroe and Doctors Penn and Foster and the Badgers and all those other sterling citizens finally went public. Do you begin to see a pattern here?"

"Cosiness," she said. "That is what I see. But I can't say it shocks me. It happens all the time. People look ahead and see if they avoid making enemies now, they might make some money later. So Shaw didn't print stories about land transactions that might've disrupted the acquisitions. And then he went to work for the buyers. Shouldn't've acted that way, I admit, but this is felony?"

"The question isn't what he did," Logan said, pouring water into the coffee maker and turning it on. He came back to the table. "More wine?" he said, gesturing toward her glass.

"Sure," she said. "It's been a long day. A third glass can only help."

"The question's why he did it," Logan said, going to the refrigerator. "Mel was a bear for probing stories, when I first got here. *Why* the School Committee wasn't facing up to the obvious need for a regional high school. *Why* the Board of Selectmen hadn't recommended to Town Meeting that the town buy a Navy surplus DUKW, when the Police obviously needed it for coastal rescue work. *Why* the State Waterways Department hadn't dredged the river up to Dyson's Landing, to keep the fishing going. *Why* the local State Rep hadn't pushed for State funding for emergency medical technicians and equipment the police and the hospital were certainly going to need when Route Three to the Cape opened up, and people started getting creamed. The mark of a good newsman isn't whether he happens to be standing there when the passenger jet goes down; it's whether he can see things coming and prepare himself to explain them to his readers when they come to pass. Mel Shaw was a good newsman. He was hard to get along with. He had something wrong with him. But he could see the importance of things that looked trivial. I didn't like him, boy, but I learned from him.

"Now," he said, returning to the table and setting the wine down, "now the biggest issue in the history of the town comes up. Not whether it's going to expand, but how it's going to expand, and who's getting rich off of it. And all of a sudden, Mel isn't curious anymore. All of a sudden, lassitude becomes the order of the day. Why is that?"

She shrugged. "Maybe he didn't know about it," she said. She sipped her wine.

"Bullshit," Logan said. "He did know about it. We had a policy in the bureau. The bureau, hell — it was *Commoner* policy. A lot of the nice homes out on Atlantic Avenue, the beachfront places, were owned by people who lived elsewhere. Wintered in Palm Beach, summered in Waterford. Old places owned by old families with old money. And their financial affairs'd be handled by their trust officers in New York, or Hartford, or Providence or Boston. Absent landlords. Clerks who make mistakes. They overlook bills, or the bills get sent to the wrong address, or some other oversight happens. So in the normal course of things, every year a certain number of tax bills didn't get paid, went into delinquency, and by the time the tax collectors caught up with it, a year and a half'd gone by. And they'd put the property up for sale for non-payment of real estate taxes.

"Now that's embarrassing," Logan said. "You're a bloody millionaire, and you're relaxing by your pool in Palm Beach, and you open your *New York Times* and see a small wire service item about your house in Waterford's on the block because you didn't pay two grand in real estate taxes. And you're furious. You call up your trust officer in Hartford, or New York, or wherever, and you manage, over the phone, to eat a large piece of rug in his office. And he pays your goddamned taxes, like he should've in the first place, and you lie back on your chaise longue and go to sleep again. Knowing you're going to get your chain jerked several times the next time you go to the club. 'Deadbeat.'

"The Goulds knew all those people. When one of them got humiliated in the papers, the Goulds heard about it, in no uncertain terms. The Goulds were sympathetic, as people often are to their friends. They did not wish their paper to be printing those embarrassing notices that the wire services pick up for republication in Palm Beach. So, when we meticulous reporters went to the tax collector's office in the Town Hall, and found somebody — anybody — posted for non-payment of real estate taxes, we were supposed to go back to the office, tell Mel, and sit on the story for three weeks.

"What Mel was supposed to do," Logan said, "was get in touch, one way or the other, directly or indirectly, with the person who owned the house, and let him or her know that an embarrassment had taken place in Waterford."

"How considerate," she said.

"Oh," Logan said, "it made a lot of sense. If I ran the paper, I'd do the same thing. If I ran a restaurant where people clamored to get in, I'd let my friends in ahead of everybody else. The stories we held would've been shams if we'd printed them. Those people weren't going to default on their taxes. Protecting them was right.

"But," he said, "when it was Jay Quentin who needed the protection, Mel didn't give it to him. I came back from the collector's office with the list of names, and Jay's was on it for the parcel behind his building, and I showed it to Mel. And Mel said, sure, he'd let Jay know. And he didn't do it. And a week or so went by, maybe two, and I came back with another list, and Jay's name was still on it, and I asked Mel if he'd told him. And Mel said he had, but he'd mention it again. And more time went by, and another list came out, and Jay's name was still on it, and I asked Mel again, had he told Jay? And Mel said he had, but Jay was evidently strapped for cash and having trouble raising the money. But he'd remind him.

"And finally," Logan said, "a list was posted that the land in back of Jay's place'd been sold for back taxes, and who bought it? Helen Deese. And I was livid. And I said to Mel, how could he do that? How could he let that happen? And Mel got all stern with me. 'Look, kid,' he said, 'you may not realize this, but there are lots of people in this world that don't have your advantages. That can't raise a sum of money on short notice.'

"I blew up," Logan said. " 'A hundred and thirty-five bucks?' I said. 'You're sitting there and telling me a guy who owns a restaurant and a bar, that has tenants, that works his ass off every day in the week — you're telling me a guy like Jay can't raise a hundred and thirty-five bucks? Good Christ, man, he's got that in the register after lunch every day. I would've loaned him a hundred and thirty-five bucks, for that matter.' And I start out the door. 'In fact,' I said, 'I'm going over there now and loan him what he needs to reclaim that piece of land before the tax title becomes final.' Which of course I didn't have. I was going to kite a check.

"And Mel said: 'No, you're not. That man's got his pride. I offered to stake him myself, and he turned me down flat. Said he'd work it out himself. You go over there now, he's going to know I broke his confidence. His pride's more important than a damned piece of land. Leave him that, at least.' Which was a damned lie, of course. But I believed the guy.

"There must've been dozens of those deceptions," Logan said. "Hundreds, probably. Mark was gone from the bureau a year and a half after I got there, after his big series on the two-hundred-mile limit. I went to the AP less'n a year after that. Didi got her wish and moved up to Boston. Our replacements didn't notice anything out of place — Mel could see to that very easily. If the three of us who were there when the finagling began couldn't spot what was going on, how could people coming in with no history of the matter, not knowing to look for it, see what was going on?

"And, more to the point," he said, "see *why* it was going on. They couldn't. Here was this aggressive bureau chief ignoring all these land transactions, and why was he doing it, all right? What was his motive?

"A year after they found Lavalle's body," Logan said, "for my Sunday feature I did a piece on the status of the investigation. The usual anniversary story: what have the police done? Why hasn't it worked? What do they plan to do next?

"Now," he said, "this was an enterprise piece. Mel didn't assign it to me, and I didn't get it approved before I started on it. The rules said I had to turn in a Sunday feature every week, and for once it wasn't going to be one of those idiotic little 'brights' about some widow lady who made afghans out of feedbags or had a collection of trivets from thirteen different countries. This was going to be a genuinely interesting story. I interviewed Dan, who was running the investigation, and I looked up the old clips, and I wrote a nice piece, if I do say so myself. I was proud of it. Slugged it: 'Who Killed Tim Lavalle?' and left it on Mel's desk when I closed the bureau up the first night of my weekend.

"I came back on Thursday morning," he said, "and it's sitting on my desk with a black grease-pencil note: 'See me.' That was on the top. There was a big black arrow down the margin leading to a big black circle drawn around the lead to the fourth graf. Which was: 'After interviewing more than forty witnesses in the case, Detective Sergeant Dan Munroe ruefully admits he's no closer to solving the case than he was a year ago.'

"I was sitting there trying to figure out what the hell was wrong with that," Logan said, "when Mel came in. 'I don't get it,' I said.

" 'This I knew,' Mel said, in that sarcastic voice he had.

" 'So, what's the matter with it?' I said.

" 'Have I got to lead you by the hand on this?' Mel said. 'You've been in this job for quite a while. Should be past the point where I draw you pictures. Either you've got a very big story there, or else you don't know English well enough to do this job, and ought to get booted out.'

"I read the sentence again," Logan said. "Damned if I could see what was wrong with it. 'This is right,' I said. 'Dan did say he's talked to forty witnesses, more than forty people.'

" ' "People" I believe,' Mel said. ' "Witnesses" I don't. If Dan and Deese and the DA've got forty witnesses, why the hell haven't they saddled up the grand jury and indicted the killer, huh? Because those "people" that they interviewed weren't "witnesses," that's why, and the cops who talked to them found that out when they asked.'

"Now, I was feeling pretty sheepish by then," Logan said. "I've been humiliated. I don't have a comeback. I'd been careless, and I'd gotten caught. Mel'd made his point. I shut my mouth and put a fresh sheet of paper in the old Royal and started to retype the first page."

" 'Now what're you doing?' Mel said.

" 'Retyping the first page,' I said. 'Changing all those "witnesses" to plain old "people." Isn't that what you want?'

"The guy snarled at me," Logan said. "Keep in mind that Mark and Didi were in by then, watching this whole performance. 'Look, Joe,' he said, this weary tone of voice, 'don't be any more of an asshole than you can possibly help, all right? The story's not running, all right? It isn't any good. It's a non-item. You're a sloppy writer. You're in your second year in this place, and you're still making half-assed mistakes that a moron would've learned in a month to avoid. The only goddamned thing that story's good for is to promote your drinking buddy Munroe in the public eye. Good old Sergeant Munroe. Comes off in that thing like he's solved the goddamned case, not like the jerk he is for spending a year on it and still he's on Square One. The *Commoner*'s not a flack for promotion-minded cops, Joe, no matter what you think. And it's not turning into one, at least not in Waterford, as long as I run the show.'

"I sat there staring at him," Logan said. "I'd seen him ride Didi like that, and he'd ridden me like that. Never got on Mark's ass, though. He was afraid of Mark. I knew that was coming next."

"And what was that?" Gates said.

"Sexual innuendo," he said. "Whenever Mel caught me or Didi in some trivial error, and felt like blowing it all out of proportion and taking a power trip, he'd start jeering at your sex life. Something happened to his eyes. You could see the excitement in them. And then he'd erupt.

"Didi made the mistake of saying one night in Quentin's, after a few beers, that not one of the men she knew ever made a pass at her. 'I know twenty-seven men,' she said. 'Twenty-four besides you guys. And not one of them has ever made a move on me. Single guys don't. Married guys that fool around, they don't, either. And I know why it is, too. It's because I've got small tits.' She was a little drunk. She'd had about two and a half beers, drinking with the boys, and that was enough to get her mildly squiffed. 'All you guys ever think about's what's in a woman's blouse.'

"Mel was all right about it when she did it," Logan said. "But the next time he felt like going on a tear, and Didi made some petty mistake, he went up the front and down the back, his clincher was: 'Your chances of getting to Washington are no better'n your chances of getting laid, Chenevert,' he said. 'Your brain's as small as your tits.' "

"On second thought," Gates said, "maybe you should've shot him instead of Brutus."

"Oversight on my part," Logan said. "I didn't think of it before I got Brutus, and then when the thought did cross my mind, the cops had Rick's shotgun and it was too late.

"The day Mel roughed me up," he said, "the pattern was the

same. I told you I got goofy when Rosemary came into my life. Mel said to me: 'You first come in here, Logan, I thought you had some talent. I still think you might. But then you started guzzling the beers with Munroe every night, and your work started downhill. And then you meet the divorcée, and since then you've been useless. You know what's the matter with you, lover boy? All you can think about is cunt. Hot, wet cunt.' "

"This is your boss?" she said.

"This is my boss," he said. "In front of the other people in the office. My boss who holds the power of life and death over my career. My boss that I outweigh by probably no more than ten pounds, but I'm younger and I'm madder and I can probably beat the shit out of him if I go after him. Which will be the end of my career, no matter how good it feels doing it.

" 'Used goods,' Mel said. 'With another guy's kid. Spreads her legs. Your cock gets hard and your brain goes soft. What a jerk you are.' "

"What did you do?" Gates said.

"Same thing Didi did when he worked that act on her," he said. "Only without the tears. I got out of the office, went across the street, sat down in Quentin's and calmed down. I didn't hit him. I didn't stay and take it. And by that time I got back to the office, he'd left for the day. Which was another thing he always did. After he got through abusing one of us, he always fled. He was never there when you got back. A coward, in other words. Next morning when you saw him, he was perfectly nice. Nothing'd happened, as far as he was concerned. Everything was fine."

"The man is nuts," she said.

"Yes indeed," Logan said. "Crazy, and corrupt, and a killer, as well. I can't make him sane, or retroactively honest, or put him in prison for killing Lavalle. But I can do something to get even with him, as I head off to jail. I can ruin him."

41

"Oscar Deese got the medical examiner's report on Lavalle on the Friday after the body was found," Logan said. "Oscar being Oscar, and Waterford being Waterford, he didn't sit down in his office and study it. He grabbed his hat and brought the news down to Quentin's, to share it with all the regulars having halibut for lunch. Marie and Jay were devout and traditional Catholics. On Fridays, if you wanted the eighty-five-cent luncheon special, you were going to eat halibut with creole sauce. Catholic, Protestant, Jew, agnostic: didn't matter to Jay and Marie. On Fridays the luncheon was fish.

"Mark and Mel and I were in our regular booth, third on the left as you went in, Mel with his back to the street, facing me and Mark. The counter stools were filled. Marie was waiting table. The new grille man was Ted Corey. Jay was in the kitchen, doing the cooking. Doctor Penn and Doctor Foster and Evelyn — Evelyn was the electrolysis lady, with the office across from Arthur Penn's on Jay's second floor. She obviously didn't trust her own skill; she preserved her own mustache. And she certainly couldn't've done enough business with the people who did go to her to meet the rent Jay charged her for her office. What she did do, and you could hear it happening any time you went up to the second floor, was spend most of her day taking calls. The phone rang in her place all the time. Continuously. All three lines, I mean. Evelyn was a bookie.

"Not that this made her morally inferior to the dentists," Logan said. "They didn't fill any more teeth than she killed follicles. They sat in their offices and played the stock market by phone with their brokers in Boston. And when the market was closed, or they'd finished their trading for the day, they either came down to the grille for coffee, or down to the bar for beer. And when they didn't care to do either, they looked out their windows and figured out what the increasing traffic on Route Four was going to mean to the town, and how to capitalize on that. At the expense of people like Jay. What they were doing was legally better than what Evelyn was doing with the ponies and the ball games, but not morally. Morally it might've been worse.

"Anyway," Logan said, "they were in the booth behind us. Dick Badger, the town counsel and general authority on being rich, and Jim Slack from the hardware store, and probably somebody else, too, were in the booth in front of us.

"Deese charges in, all out of breath, waving the report. 'Here it is,' he said, 'autopsy on Lavalle.' And it was like one of those E.F. Hutton ads, you know? Everything came to a screeching halt. Marie stopped wiping her hands on her apron. The Corey kid at the grille pushed whatever he was cooking off onto the cool edge. The people at the counter put their sandwiches down. The mashed potatoes with melted butter that came with the halibut started to get cold.

"Deese wedged his big belly into the seat beside Mel. The people at the counter turned around on their stools. Mark and I both took out our notebooks. Mel shook his head and pointed at me. 'Joe's story,' he said. Mark put his book away. I remember having this quick thought that Mel's eyes looked funny.

" 'Now,' Deese says, 'I'm not gonna read all of this, but: "This well-nourished white male, twenty-two years old, height approximately seventy-one inches, weight one-fifty-one, died result massive subdural hematoma, hemorrhaging, caused results a single heavy blow, front cranial area. Large blunt instrument. Depressed fracture of the skull." And it gives some more measurements. And Doctor Colt goes on in his report here,' and he's running his finger down the page, looking for the good parts, and Mel in the meantime's reading right along with him, ' " . . . facing his assailant." See? When Timmy got walloped there, he was facing the guy hitting him. Looking right at him. Which to me says that he knew him. In the pine grove and everything, right? Just the two of them? They hadda know each other. *Timmy was looking right at the guy when he got hit.*'

"He turned to Mel," Logan said. " 'Am I right on that, Mel, huh?'

"Mel had this strange look on his face. He sort of smirked a little. It was almost a form of glee. He shook his head. 'Don't see how you could think anything else, Oscar. You're absolutely right.' He's being sarcastic, you know? Riding Oscar just a little, not so much that Oscar's going to see it and get mad, but still, you know, taking a risk. 'They were facing each other at the time, I don't see how it could mean anything else but that Timmy was looking at him.'

"Oscar gives him this suspicious look," Logan said. "He was smarter than Mel thought he was, but not much, or he would've seen Mel was making fun of him. And probably wondered why, just as I did. The man was positively elated. He was enjoying this. 'Right,' Deese says, and clears his throat, and goes back to the report. 'Now,' he says, 'where is it here, yeah. Right here. Colt goes on to say here . . . . '

"Mel interrupts him. 'Does he actually say anything about the assailant, Chief?' he said. He was really pushing his luck.

"Deese glares at him. 'Damnit, Mel,' he says. 'I'm just getting to that, you give me half a chance here.' And he flips the page. 'The answer to your question, Mel — if you'll just leave me alone here a minute 'till I find it, I'll read it to you. What he says about the assailant is: "The attacker was probably a male, at least seventy-two inches in height, in good physical condition, and right-handed." ' And he gives Mel another look. 'Which I can't tell you, you know, how much that helps us out. That could be practically anybody in this town, for Christ sake.'

" 'I see your point,' Mel said.

" 'Good,' Oscar says. 'Now, if you'll let me get on the important part here, where he gives us something we can work with, maybe, it's in here someplace, I know. Yeah, here it is: "The depth of the wound, its width, the damage to the bone and soft tissue structures in the area of actual impact, and the distribution of bone fragments viewed both in gross and microscopically throughout the surrounding tissue, and collected from hair and epidermis in the area of the wound, and sifted from dirt and debris collected from the soil around the place where the body was located, indicate that the blow was administered with a heavy cylindrical or oval object, probably of solid metal, approximately one inch in width or diameter, with a projection at the end furthest from the striking hand, and was at least eighteen inches long." '

" 'Piece of pipe,' Mel says.

"Oscar shook his head," Logan said. " 'I dunno about that, Mel,' he said, 'it could be, I guess, but it doesn't sound like pipe to me. Pipe ain't solid, you know? None the pipe I've seen, at least. Pipes got a hole in the middle. They're hollow, so the water and stuff can go through. I was thinking more like a wrench or something, you know? Not that I ever saw a circular wrench, or an oval one, either. All the ones I've seen're flat. Except socket wrench handles, now I think of it. Could've been one of those. Solid, you know? Something like a wrench.' He took out his ballpoint and wrote 'socket wrench' in the margin.

" 'Jack handle, maybe?' Mark said.

" 'Could be a jack handle,' Deese said. 'Those're sort of circular. Could've been one of those. I didn't think of that, Mark. That's a very good idea.' And he stopped reading for a second and wrote 'Jack Handel' in the margin of the report. 'H,A,N,D,E,L.' "

"Like the composer," Gates said.

"Uh huh," Logan said. "Then he went on. ' "Wound measurements approximately six to eight inches in length . . . , struck from above . . . . " ' And he stopped and frowned. He looked back at Mel. 'Although I got to say here, Mel, it sounds like he agrees with you. Doctor Colt, I mean. Because here he says: "most likely a length of common steel, brass, or lead pipe, which because of its evident weight and the force with which the blow was struck, and the absence of indications that the murder instrument was deformed by the blow that it struck, could not have been a soft or malleable metal, such as aluminum." ' "

" 'Well,' I said, 'that wouldn't rule out what Mark said, Chief. After all, whatever it was, wasn't found. It could have been a jack handle or a tire iron, or maybe a pry bar like they use to open crates, you know?'

" 'You mean,' Deese said, 'like a pinch bar or something like that?'

" 'Yeah,' I said." He hesitated. "See what we were doing?" Logan said to Gates. "We were all competing, all playing Sherlock and showing off for the folks. This was exciting, right? This was really fun. And Professor Moriarty himself, disguised as Mel Shaw, was sitting right there with us, playing right along. The Chief took out his ballpoint again and wrote 'tire iron' and 'prybar' and 'pinch bar' in the margin of the page where the doctor had said 'pipe.' Now everybody had contributed a theory to the investigation on the nature of the murder weapon. Except, of course, that Mel, who knew what it was, had not contributed the truth."

"What was it, then?" Gates said.

"A winch handle, of course," Logan said. "Mel kept his catboat down at Dyson's landing, tied up at the dock. He covered it when he left it. But he gave me a ride once in his car when mine was being serviced at the garage up on Route Four — he had this little mustard-colored MGB roadster — and there was barely room enough in it for both of us, with all the junk in it. Life jackets, little picnic cooler, slickers, all kinds of boating stuff. And I said to him: 'You always carry all this equipment around with you?' And he said: 'Bet your ass I do. This shit is expensive. Lots of people who have boats'd rather take somebody else's, 'n go and buy their own.' And when he had to stop short because a car came out of a side street on the way to the garage, these two long metal things came sliding out from under the passenger seat. And I didn't know anything. I picked them up and said: 'What the hell're these, Mel?' And he said: 'Winch handles. You use them to trim the sail. And you never leave them on the boat. They're made of solid brass and chromed, and they cost forty bucks apiece.'

"So," Logan said, "except for the unfortunate fact that no one, including present company, thought of that possibility in Nineteen-sixty-three, when quick investigative work would probably have resulted in scooping those winch handles out of Mel's car, and having them examined for traces of blood and hair, and skin and bone, or not finding one of them at all and thus raising some questions Mel might've found difficult to answer, that solved the Lavalle case. As far as I'm concerned, at least. Lavalle and Mel both'd had Sunday off. Mel because as bureau chief he had Saturday and Sunday off, the real weekend, Lavalle because Jay didn't open the grille side of the place on Sunday. Nobody looked for Timmy on his day off, because nobody cared anything about him. Nobody wondered where Mel was all day, because his family and everybody else who might have been interested knew he spent every available minute out sailing. By himself.

"That Sunday'd been a beautiful day on the water," Logan said. "Right in the middle of that hot spell we'd been having. It was after Labor Day, so the summer people who kept their boats in the cove'd gone home. There was no one around to see Mel and his boyfriend come down and go for a sail, and then come back and load the gear in the car. Which was just the way Mel and Timmy wanted it, and why nobody'd ever seen the two of them together around town, or had any inkling that they were involved. Because neither of them wanted that to happen, and they'd both been damned careful to see that it did not.

"Driving up from the river," Logan said, "they decided for some reason or other to make a U-turn into the rest area on the west side of Four and walk in the woods. My guess is Timmy thought he was going into the bushes for a pleasant *al fresco* blow job or two on a late summer evening. He turned around to look at his companion, and Mel bashed him with the winch handle. Went back to his car, probably went back to the cove, rinsed off the winch handle in the water — nobody would've thought anything about it if they happened to see Mel puttering around his boat there, or connected it to the murder. Nobody was concerned when Timmy didn't get back to Ma Doherty's boarding house on his day off, because he didn't have any friends there, and the only roomers Ma paid attention to were the ones that drank in their rooms, tried to bring women in, or didn't pay their rent. It worked out perfectly."

"Yeah, I know," she said. "That's what you said on the tape I got from Taves. And it sounds plausible enough. But Taves says it's not enough for Keane to indict Shaw today. Because they didn't get the winch handle in time. And nobody asked around to see if anyone down at the cove that day might've happened to see Shaw, and whether he had somebody with him. What Taves said to me was: 'It sounds real great, the way Joe tells it. It's even probably true. But twenty years after the dirty deed, you know, it's not enough to move. And there's no way to check it out now. Those possible leads're long gone.'

" 'Besides,' Taves said," Gates said, " 'Logan's whole theory here is that Shaw first of all's a fairy. And was a fairy then. Even if we can prove he talks with his mouth full now, we can't prove he did then. And in the second place,' he said, 'the guy who did this had to have a motive. Which we can guess at, I suppose: Timmy was shaking him down for dough, or Timmy'd found somebody else, something along that line. But that we can't prove either. And in the third place, Shaw had to be violent. Had to be a violent person.

" 'Joe can't give us a motive — can't prove one, at least,' is what Taves said to me," she said. " 'And Shaw never did anything to anybody else that'd make you think he'd kill a person, if it suited him. Joe says he's a mean prick, and he probably is. Or was. And Joe says some business with a deer that a cop shot showed that side of Shaw. But, I mean, no judge is gonna let you bring that in, if you try Shaw for something. That he liked it when a cop shot a deer? "Come on, Mister Taves," the judge is going to say. The cop shot the deer, not Shaw. That doesn't prove a thing.' "

"Oh, I know all that," Logan said. "It doesn't prove a thing. In court. But I know Shaw was queer, and I know what it meant when he reacted the way he did, when Peabody shot the doe."

"How?" she said.

"I was there when the doe got shot," Logan said. "Rosemary figured out Mel."

42

"One Sunday night in the middle of September in Sixty-four," Logan said, "a deer came into the village. There were a few deer out in the woods around the Indian Swamps — this was before all the development started out there and probably drove them south into the Myles Standish Reservation — but the Route Three construction had dispersed them. And most likely frightened them as well. The one that came into town was young. A doe, maybe a year or two old at the most.

"When the old police station'd been built in the Fifties," he said, "that two-story cinder block building on the lot behind where the Town Hall used to be?"

"Where they keep the snowplows and the lawnmowers and the Public Works trucks now," she said.

"Right," he said. "Well, that was the police station, twenty-odd years ago. Before the new complex went up on Route Four. And there was a clump of small maples and brush that grew up on the west side of the road that ran between Quentin's building and the Town Hall up to the police station parking lot. Jay never developed that back lot of his, and when the construction'd been going on, he let the town dump fill from the excavation on it. So it was sort of hilly, you know? The maples and the brush and some tall weeds, and the deer wandered into town one night and I suppose got further confused by the feeling of the pavement under its hooves, and it went into the underbrush on Quentin's back lot and hid.

"Dan Munroe's office was on the second floor," Logan said. "Around ten-thirty the next morning, he happened to look out his window and there was this deer standing there in the tall grass. 'I'm telling you,' he told me, 'that poor deer looked just like I feel when I get up in the morning and I've had too many beers the night before and I don't know where the hell I am.'

"I had Dan well-trained by then," Logan said. "Before he alerted anyone downstairs, he called me at the office and told me to get my ass over there with a camera. Mel asked me what I was doing when I grabbed the Mamiya that worked, and I told him, and Didi got the one that didn't always work, and Mel himself grabbed the old Speed Graphic and six or eight film carriers, and we all went tearing across Union Street, hellbent for leather, and up the road to the station.

"I was in the lead," Logan said. "Didi was right behind me, and Mel was behind her. I was probably about a hundred yards away from the front door of the police station, still between the east side of Quentin's and the west side of the Town Hall, hadn't gotten to the lot yet, and Ronnie Peabody came out of the station like he'd been launched.

"Now, Ronnie's stupidity stood out, even in the company he kept on that force. They called him 'Cruiser.' That was because Ronnie in Fifty-nine or Sixty, dunno which, had assisted a motorist whose car started boiling over on a summer weekend afternoon at the Route Four intersection about a mile north of town. And the way Ronnie assisted him was to push him with the cruiser into the first shady place that was handy. Which happened to be just around the bend of a tight curve at the bottom of the next steep hill.

"Ronnie did not push the tourist's car off the road. Ronnie deduced correctly that to do so would be to push it into a muddy place from which it would not emerge without a wrecker being called. What Ronnie did not deduce was that therefore he needed a different shady place, one where the car's engine could cool down without the car being parked on a blind curve of a heavily-traveled two-lane blacktop. Instead he stopped on that curve and parked his cruiser on the same blind curve, behind the tourist's car. And about three minutes later another tourist came over the hill too fast, and down around the curve, and totaled Ronnie's new cruiser. The second tourist and his family were cut up pretty well, and their car wasn't improved either, but fortunately no one was killed or permanently injured. Unless you count the damage to Ronnie's reputation, that is.

"Ronnie's reward for that from Deese was to be assigned all the scut work in the department. That included being Animal Control Officer. 'Dog Officer,' as the job was more widely known. Now and then some terrified citizen'd find a water moccasin in his basement, and Ronnie'd get called to come shoot it, which was work that he enjoyed because Ronnie was a good shot, and proud of his marksmanship. But most of the time his Animal Control duties consisted of ministering to injured dogs that'd gotten run over, and either putting them out of their misery or getting them to the vet — stuff like that.

"The police station had a regular aluminum storm-and-screen door," Logan said, "Because of the amount of use it got, it was bent out of shape. So it banged when you closed it and you had to kick it to open it from the inside. Ronnie kicked it open, which made a loud noise, and I guess that spooked the doe. She wasn't about to run west toward Route Four, where the traffic was. She had Quentin's building behind her to the south, as long as she was in the back lot, and Ronnie coming at her like the U.S. Marines from the north with his service pistol drawn. She did the only sensible thing, under the circumstances, which was head east, out of the back lot and toward the roadway between the buildings. She came out of the vacant lot, all flying legs and fear, and apparently she remembered the pavement, and that she didn't like it. She jumped it to get to the lawn of the Town Hall on the other side. For once I was ready to take a picture. I took it when she had all four feet off the ground and Peabody shot her in mid-air. I took the picture just as Peabody fired."

"Oh, no," Gates said.

"Oh, yes," Logan said. "Like I said, Ronnie had his faults, but he was a crack shot. Naturally he only wounded her. Can't kill a deer, even a little one, particularly one all adrenalized by terror like this one was, with a thirty-eight. But he wounded her. Got her in the side. And she twisted slightly in mid air. She landed on the grass and her front legs buckled. Her head hit the ground. Her back legs shook and spraddled, but they stayed straight. She struggled to get up. He didn't kill her with that shot, but he hurt her. Yes, he did.

"He let out this whoop," Logan said. "I was scared of him myself. Didi was right behind me, also screaming: '*No, you bastard, no.*' I stopped to advance the film in my camera. No motor drives in those bygone days. Didi ran by me toward the deer on the lawn. Deese came out of the station door, with another crash. I took another picture, Peabody running toward the animal with his gun in his hand, Deese too far in the background behind him for a clear view of his mouth wide open as he yelled at Peabody not to do it.

"Peabody didn't hear him," Logan said. "Peabody was inflamed by the thrill of the hunt. Peabody ran up to the animal, crouched, aimed, and shot it point blank in the ear. Didi took a picture of him that instant, his face all distorted, his eyes bulging, the deer all crumpled up on its forelegs with its back legs still straight but spread out. The back end of the deer tipped over to the right, so that she lay on her right side, and I took another picture as Peabody fired again. The deer convulsed a couple of times, and blood started to come out of her mouth. She didn't move after that. I got closer and finished off the roll of film in my camera, Peabody holstering his gun, looking grim and satisfied and exhilarated, all at once.

"When I finished and looked around," Logan said, "I saw Marie and Jay at the corner of the restaurant, down by Union Street. And Didi was standing about ten feet from Peabody and the deer. And Oscar in slow motion, coming down the driveway. And Doctor Penn at the corner of the vacant lot — he'd apparently come down the back stairs. And Mel, just behind me, with this wild light in his eyes. That same excitement he showed in the office. He was enjoying it, reveling in it. And in front of me there was Oscar, who's moving in slow motion, while the rest of us are all in freeze frame, you know? Paralyzed in approximately the same positions we'd been in when the deer died. There wasn't a sound in the world.

"Until Oscar spoke, that is," Logan said. " 'Peabody, you asshole,' he said, in the oldest voice he had, 'get your ass in the station. And gimme that damned gun.' Then we all resumed breathing and speaking and living again. And Peabody said: 'But Chief, this meat. We got to get this deer gutted here, and then take her down and butcher her, this is good venison.' And Oscar said: 'Ronnie, you asshole, do what I told you.' And Peabody gave him the gun, and started back for the station, dejected as he could be."

"Ruined his whole day, probably," Gates said.

"Ruined more'n his day," Logan said. "Ruined the next several years of his life. Didi's picture was damned near perfect. Technically, that is. Her angle showed Peabody and the deer almost filling the frame, and the lens opening was no more'n F-four — might've been F-three-five. So everything in the foreground was sharply focused, and everything in the background was blurred, and the shutter speed was one-five-hundredth, so if you couldn't quite see the bullet coming out the muzzle of the gun, you could sure see the puff of powder residue that followed it. And there was an excellent view of this stricken little deer looking up at her killer with these beseeching eyes, and Ronnie implacable over her, firing his damned gun.

"Naturally the photo desk in Boston ran it three columns wide above the fold on the front page, all editions. Naturally there was a combination gun-control nut and animal lover writing captions who titled it 'Coup Disgrace.' Of course the AP picked it up and ran it worldwide, along with a truncated version of my indignant story about a cop shooting a panicked deer. My grainy, somewhat out-of-focus shot of the deer in mid-air ran on the front page of the second section, the regional edition of the paper, and UPI serviced that around the world. Of course those pictures only appealed to photo editors everywhere whose practice was to snag the heartstrings every chance they got, which is not more than ninety, ninety-five percent of those usually at work. The mail from outraged readers started to come into Chief Deese's office in carload lots, some of it written in crayon, all of it demanding that Ronnie be summarily lynched for what many of the writers seemed to have taken as the crime of killing Bambi. Or Rudolph, or Donder, or Blitzen. None of which had been a doe, of course, but that was beside the point. None of the letter writers seemed to have considered what the Animal Control officer in Waterford should have done instead of shooting a terrified deer that was loose in a populated area, within four hundred yards of a heavily-traveled secondary road. On which, if she'd wheeled and run that way, she'd almost certainly have been killed, maybe with human fatalities. No one thought about that."

"Well," Gates said, "should they have?"

"Well, now I think so," Logan said. "I didn't think so then, at least not when I wrote the story. But then, nobody else did, either. Be that as it may, the volume and intensity of the mail made the Selectmen decide, reasonably enough, that they'd better call a special meeting to consider Ronnie's case. Otherwise there might have been an invasion force bent on burning the town flat. So they convened as a committee of the whole, sitting as the Police Commission. And that started a jurisdictional dispute between Didi and me.

"Mark had left by then," Logan said. "Promoted to Boston after his fishing series had attracted national attention. Mark's replacement hadn't arrived. There wasn't that much going on anyway, so

Mel'd been pinch-hitting on Mark's beats, among the Selectmen. Didi claimed it was her picture that had caused all the ruckus, so she should cover the meeting instead of Mel. My argument was that when the Selectmen sat as the Police Commission, they came under my jurisdiction on the Police beat. See how silly we all were, in the days when we were young?

"Mel was Solomon. That deer story was the most fun he'd had in a long time. All that attention focused on his bureau. Made him a big man. That light never left his eyes until the thing'd run its course. It made him a new man. He said that since Didi's picture had been such a fine piece of work, she could cover the meeting with the camera. He said that since Mark was no longer available to cover the Selectmen, he would write the main story himself. He said that since I'd done the original story about the deer, and the follow-up reaction stories out of the department, I would do the sidebars and the reaction stories to the Selectmen's decision, whatever it happened to be.

"Didi was furious. Insubordinate, too. But clever enough not to get herself fired for it, which Mel would've cheerfully done. What she did on the afternoon of the night of the meeting was plead 'cramps,' and ask to be excused from attending the meeting. Mel knew she was faking it, and he knew also that he couldn't challenge her. So I got the camera job, as well as the sidebar assignment.

"I'm sure Didi felt pretty smug about that dodge she'd pulled," Logan said. "She figured she'd not only thwarted Mel but also seriously complicated my performance, because it's very hard to do both good pictures and a good story of the same assignment. But in fact, it was the best favor she'd ever done me.

"The meeting attracted a flock of out-of-town reporters. Two Boston TV stations had crews there. The AP sent its New England feature writer, Walter Foy, whose experience included war correspondent in Korea, much gadding about with Kennedys, America's Cup competitions — he'd done everything. Ted Williams gave interviews to Walter Foy when Foy went to All Star games, all right? And Ted Williams hated all reporters, except for Walter Foy. Guy was in his early fifties, for heaven's sake, and he was a working legend. Looked just like the old Pontiac he drove; he was presentable enough, and so was it, but there was no question both of them'd had to have a lot of dents banged out of them over the years.

"Walter never sat with the working press. What he did was barge in among the photographers and jot down his notes from there. 'Any goddamned fool,' he said, 'can write down what some jerk says. The story's how he looks when he's saying it. Get close enough to see the bastard's face. That tells you what he's thinking while he's running his mouth, and that's how you decide what the tone of your story's going to be.'

"I went afterwards with Walter to Quentin's Bar. We both got filled up with beer, while I picked his brains. By midnight, when he left, we were the best of friends. 'Tell you what you do,' he said. 'Give me a call sometime, you're ever up in Boston. And come around the bureau. Meet some of the guys.'

"A week after that hearing," Logan said, "Mel spiked my anniversary story of the Lavalle case. I went home and told Rosemary what he'd said."

"Everything?" Gates said.

"Yeah, everything," Logan said. "Look, I loved her dearly. She was my life to me. But when Mel said she was 'used goods,' meaning it as an insult, he had no idea how right he was. Rosemary'd had an instructive life. She'd started out in nursing right out of high school. She went from Somerville Hospital to Boston City, and then to Quincy. She'd worked mostly in emergency rooms — that was why she moved to Quincy, as a matter of fact, to get out of the ERs and into something a little less hectic. She divorced her first husband, whom she never should've married, because he hurt her. She finally threw him out because her gynecologist told her she'd need reconstructive surgery pretty soon if she couldn't make him stop."

"I see," Gates said. "And she needed her doctor to tell her this?"

"Connie," Logan said, "Rosemary's background was different from yours. Girls raised by people like her parents did not get divorces because their husbands were inattentive, or failed to help with housework. Girls from that background didn't get divorced for *any* reason, from random adultery up to and including outright brutality. It was a very courageous act for the former Rosemary Feeley to divorce her husband because he was treating her like the lead character in some sadistic porno novel."

"Okay," Gates said, "okay. But it's still hard for me to believe."

"I went home and I told her what Mel'd said to me," Logan said. "Now, you've got to keep in mind that I hadn't met Rosemary when

Tim Lavalle got killed. So she didn't know much about the case, except generalities I told her while I was working on the anniversary piece. So she asked me that night if I had the story with me, and I didn't, and she asked me to bring it home so she could read it. And then she told me I might as well face it, I had to get the hell out of Waterford and away from Melvin Shaw. 'That guy is sick,' she said. 'He's got something wrong with him.' I reminded her I had at least nine more months to serve in the Waterford bureau before I had even a remote chance of a transfer. 'Get another job,' she said. I told her if I did that, I might have to move. 'So, we move,' she said. 'I'm adaptable.' The following Tuesday I went to see Walter Foy at the AP. That Wednesday I had an appointment with Jack Sampson, the chief of the Boston AP bureau. He offered me the job in Worcester, which I took, and that's how I happened to meet Jack Mahler and Bill Glass in Nineteen-sixty-six, looking for talent in news as they put together their little empire of New England broadcasting properties.

"From which experience," he said, grinning, "I developed Logan's Law of Success in the News Business: 'When in a tight spot, get very lucky.' It's infallible."

"It's also ten-fifteen," she said, as the fourth tape ran out.

"You want to stop?" he said. "It won't matter to me."

"No, no," she said. "But I would like to change chairs. You think we could move to the living room?"

"We can do that," he said, getting up. "Let me get you some more wine."

43

"I don't know if you've ever noticed this," Logan said, when they once again sat facing each other on the two living room couches, "but time moves at various speeds."

"Passing quickly when you're having fun, you mean," she said, turning on the recorder with the fifth tape inside.

He snickered. "Well," he said, "that's the usual scenario. But not always. And it doesn't always drag when you're miserable, either. It doesn't seem to have much to do with whether you're happy or sad. Not in my case, at least. I should've been miserable, for example, for the two weeks I had to put in in Waterford after I gave my notice. Mel was on my back constantly, ridiculing me for my sexual susceptibility, often implying that because I had a couple dimies with my lunch, I was a beer drunk, and never had any real prospects for promotion to Boston anyway. Sniping at me all the time, just doing everything he could to make my life a Hell on earth."

"And what did you do?" she said.

"I laughed at him," Logan said. "I laughed in his face. I was as happy as that lark we've all heard so much about. Which of course was the best strategy I could possibly have adopted — it made him much madder'n if I'd gotten angry.

"The trouble with that was," he said, "it made me inattentive. You have got to pay attention in this world, every damned minute. No matter what you're doing. Or else something gets by you and it's liable to be something important. And that's what I did then.

"Rosemary read the Lavalle story Mel'd spiked," Logan said. "She doped it out immediately. 'Fag fight,' she said. 'This was a fight between two fags. Lovers' quarrel, I'll bet. I'd bet ten bucks on it.' Which, at a time when she was clearing a hundred and three a week at Quincy Hospital, and I was grossing a nifty seventy-six bucks a week, was no small amount.'

"But how would she've known that?" Gates said.

"Well," Logan said, "she didn't *know* it. It was just a guess. But it was a shrewd guess, an informed one. Lavalle had no friends the cops could find. No acquaintances, either. Lots of people are a little short on real friends, although if they're lucky they never find that out, but everybody knows somebody, hangs around with them, talks to them, whatever you want to call it. Lavalle had nobody. Nobody from the time before he went to prison. Nobody from prison. Nobody from Waterford. Which meant that he did have somebody, maybe several somebodies, but neither he nor they wanted anyone to know about it.

" 'Which fags do,' she said. 'The only people who know who their friends are, are other fags.' Keep in mind, Connie, this was over twenty years ago. The closet door was locked and bolted shut. 'It's protection. The only time they surface for what they are in the world outside is when something happens that forces them to.

" 'Weekend nights were the busy times at BCH,' she said. 'Busy nights for fights, I mean. Guys shot by the cops in the course of hold-ups; guys shot by other guys in little arguments; people cut up in car crashes; attempted suicides; heart attacks; people hurt in fires: we got those every night and they were not pleasant, either. But the weekends were the nights for lovers. Friday nights and Saturday nights we'd get these people cut up, beat up, whacked around with teeth out, mostly women but some men, all of them pissed off. And we'd say to them, hem-stitching their lips, putting splints on their arms, repairing their puncture wounds: "You know who did this to you?" Because the Boston cops liked us to do that, you know, make a little harmless conversation with the bleeding citizens. Helped the policemen later, when they grabbed somebody two or three days after he and the victim'd kissed and made up, and didn't want to say anymore that this was the guy who'd done it. Or the girl, as far as that goes — some of those victims were men, and the ladies carried knives. Helped the cops a lot if the victim'd already said: "Well, it was Sammy." Or: "It was June."

" 'Sunday nights were fag nights,' she told me. 'That's when they go out. And therefore when they fight. Sunday nights guys came in with flashlights up their ass. Ballpoint pens, rolls of dimes and bars of soap. Things they couldn't possibly've inserted in themselves. And they always said they did. Nobody ever helped them.

" 'We had one kid that came in one week and he was cut all over his scalp. Bleeding like a waterfall. And he didn't know who did it. And the cops said to him, he did know. And he said he didn't, know. And they said it was Jesse, wasn't it. It was Jesse that did that to him. 'No sir, it was not Jesse, Not Jesse at all.' He didn't even know a Jesse, but if he'd known a Jesse, it would not have been him. And the cops're laughing at him, that he doesn't know Jesse. And one of the cops says: "Tiny, you've been sucking Jesse's cock for years. And you mean to say you don't know him? Didn't anybody ever introduce you two guys, after all this time?" And the kid says he doesn't know Jesse. And the cop says: "Well, you better get straight with Jesse, if you happen to meet somebody by that name, because it looks to us like Jesse's done found out you've been messing with some other Jesse, and he don't like that a bit." So we got Tiny repaired and back out on the street before midnight. And around two o'clock, this enormous black man comes in on a stretcher and his penis'd been nearly bitten off. He was losing blood by the gallon. Barely conscious. Which was also partly because he was high on something fairly strong, but mostly because he was losing blood so fast. So we got him stabilized, and the cop came in and said: "Jesse, my man. Did Tiny do this to you?" Now this guy is barely conscious, like I say. This guy is barely *alive*. But he's still not telling, no sirree. "I don't know no Tiny," he says. Never heard of him.

" 'Now this Lavalle kid,' she said. 'He'd been in the slammer. And when he was in the slammer, he was at the age when most guys are young and pretty horny. And the cops can't find anybody he ran with in the can? He was somebody's doll, then. And if the cops in Waterford can't find that out, it's because they don't want to. Prison guards know everything.'

"I laid that on Dan," Logan said. "I was a short-timer by then, week and a half to go on the *Commoner*, and I just did it by way of no harm. I asked him whether he'd made any effort to push the guards at MCI Concord on whether Lavalle'd had a fairy godmother, while he was in the cooler 'I didn't,' Dan said. 'Oscar might've. He was the one, handled that request for information. He knows somebody up there in the superintendent's office, he was in the army with. You could ask him.'

"But I didn't," Logan said. "I had other things on my mind, as I said. And besides, in my next-to-last week on the job there, the Selectmen'd rendered their decision on Peabody. Suspended him for thirty days without pay, finding he'd discharged his service revolver without good cause, in a reckless and willfully negligent manner. Further imposed two hundred hours of punishment duty: work with no pay, accrual of vacation benefits, or credit toward seniority in grade. And made a gratuitous finding that his explanation for his actions were specious, and showed a lack of repentance.

"They entered that judgment on a Tuesday night," Logan said. "Nine days later, I saw Ronnie in the police station, in uniform except for his gun, working at the typewriter outside Deese's office. 'What is this?' I said to Deese. 'This guy has been suspended. You gonna tell me in a week this guy's served a thirty-day suspension?'

" 'His suspension's over,' Deese said. 'He had forty-one days' sick leave with pay he didn't use, and I let him apply that. Which, he's never sick, guy loves his job too much, still leaves him eleven.'

" 'You can't do that,' I said. 'The Board said "Thirty days." Thirty days is . . . .' "

" '. . . anything I say it is,' Deese said. 'In this department, son. I say I can do it and I say I have done it, and you can say what you want.'

" 'But what about the punishment duty?' I said. 'He's got five weeks of punishment duty. Is straightening your files a punishment, Oscar?'

" 'You would think so,' Oscar said, 'if you ever saw my files. He had four and a half weeks of vacation time, because he never takes them neither, plus he had in the week before the deer alone eighteen hours of overtime we hadn't paid him for, so I let him lump all that stuff together. And we added it up and that come to a hundred and seventy-eight hours of credits that he had, and therefore he owed the department twenty-two hours' duty without compensation, which he did twenty on Tuesday and Wednesday while you were off duty, you fresh bastard, and at ten-thirty this morning he is back on the clock and back on the payroll.'

" 'You're going to have fun when the paper comes out in the morning, Oscar,' I said. And I got up to leave. And Oscar said: 'Not because of this, I'm not.'

" 'That's what you think,' I said. 'When I print this, you're going to have people all over your neck.'

" 'You're not going to print it,' Oscar said.

" 'Like hell, I'm not,' I said, and I stormed out of there, full of fire and brimstone and my First Amendment rights, and I went back to my office, and Mel was sitting there.

"I didn't get the first words out of my mouth before Mel said: 'Siddown. I don't want to hear about it. Oscar called me already, and he told me about the tussle you had with him just now, and I agree with him, and we're not printing it. Now, you got something to say?'

" 'Yes, I have,' I said. I said Oscar's decision was a direct contradiction of what the Selectmen'd ordered, that the public had a right to know about it, and that if we didn't print it we were in dereliction of our duty as the press. And I asked him, did he think Oscar had a right to pull this stunt, with the Selectmen not even consulted? Or informed?

"He got this weary look on his face," Logan said. " 'Joe,' he said, 'goddamnit, will you hurry up and finish out your string here, before you drive me nuts? Don't take things so seriously. The Selectmen do know. Dick Badger knows. Oscar talked to all of them on the phone before he did this. They hit Peabody too hard. This guy has a family that he has to support. You add up all that punishment they gave him, he's not going to get any pay for seven goddamned weeks. He'll lose his house, for Christ sake. You can't do that to a young man with a family. The Board went overboard.

" 'The reason they went overboard,' Mel said, 'in Oscar's opinion is that we overplayed the story. What he said to me was: "Those guys were hamming it up for the press the night they had that hearing, and then they'd put on such a show in public that they had to justify it. So they kicked the poor son of a bitch in the nuts. And I told them that."

" ' "Now," Oscar said to me just now, "now after I get them to agree we got to help this kid — Ronnie maybe isn't very bright but he works hard and loves his job and I could use ten like him — now, after I do that, I get this punk reporter in here and he's reading me the riot act, and says he's gonna print it in the fucking newspaper. And I'm telling you, if he does that, it'll start the whole goddamned uproar all over again and you guys'll have another goddamned circus for yourselves, and you'll sell a lot of papers, and those spineless bastards'll reverse themselves and blame it all on me. And I will lose my job.

" ' "Now," Oscar said,' Mel said, leaning 'way back in his chair and getting the magisterial look on his face, ' "if I lose my job,"

Oscar said, "your boy's pal Munroe will be acting chief, police. Is that what you want, Shaw? You want that in this town? Danny Munroe's a good kid. His heart's in the right place. But Danny don't know shit from Shinola yet, and God help him if his mummy dies and I retire before we get him trained. God help this town, too, if that happens. Dan is not ready."

" 'So,' Mel said, 'Oscar said all that, and I agree with him, and we're not printing the story. The stupid bastard shot a deer, for God's sake. Not a human. Not a law-abiding citizen. Two months later, with a shotgun and a license, what he does is legal. There's a doe season this year.

" 'Now,' Mel said, 'if you want to argue with me, you can go ahead. And when you get all through, we're still not printing that story, all right? We're still not printing that story. You're leaving here pretty soon. You're going someplace else. But Oscar's got to live here, Joe, and so does old Mel Shaw. And you're not going to leave the two of us with a blivit to juggle while you traipse off somewhere else.' "

"What's a 'blivit'?" Gates said.

"Five pounds of shit in a two-pound bag," Logan said. "Mel kept his word. We didn't print the story. And in a few more days I was gone, without ever seeing the point. Oscar Deese could keep things out of the papers if he wanted to. Didn't matter whether he was right, which now I think he probably was. What mattered was that he could overrule Mel Shaw, substitute his judgment for Mel's. Who didn't tell Jay Quentin, like he told everybody else, when his land was up for sale for delinquent taxes. Who didn't send Mark's replacement, and my replacement, and about six months later, Didi's replacement, out to find out who was buying up all the land in town, and how much they were paying for it, and what was going on. And who went to work for those people later on, at a sizeable increase in pay."

"Munroe says Deese could do that," Gates said, "because he collaborated with Mel Shaw to scuttle Baldwin's rape case. He says the fix was in for years before the land deals started."

"Sure the fix was in," Logan said. "Mel covered for the group. And he did it because one of the group, which was good old Oscar, had Mel right by the balls. Oscar covered Mel, and Mel returned the favor. And they all got away with it because nobody cared enough to see what they were doing." He inhaled deeply. "One of the biggest mistakes we make, people in the news," he said, "is spending so much time out in public yelling about how important the job is that we do. It gets to sound like bragging, which of course it is, but it also happens to be true. And when we get corrupt along with everybody else, it matters. It really does. People get away with things all over the place. You let people operate in the dark, in secrecy, and they will follow their natural instincts. Which are to lie and cheat and steal and kill each other. If you make it clear that nobody cares what's going on, what goes on will scare the living bejesus out of you. And that's what Mel Shaw did."

She leaned forward and stared at him. "So what you're doing now," she said "is retroactive caring."

"I suppose so," he said.

"You gain nothing from this, yourself," she said.

"No," he said, "I don't. As a matter of fact, I lose quite a lot."

"Like what?"

"Like fifteen or twenty years of my life, for openers," he said.

"Which you've already told me is worthless," she said.

"Well," he said, "it isn't much fun. But in terms of money, it's not worthless. It's worth quite a lot. The house. What we saved. The insurance. I'm not going to lose all of that, but until I'm in my sixties, I'm not going to enjoy it."

"The insurance," she said.

"Rosemary and I agreed, very early in the game," he said, "that the last thing people who love each other like we did should do to each other is leave them back in a hole like we were both in when we met. So we carried a lot of insurance. If one of us died, the other one was not going to have to say to Rick: 'Well, forget about going to college, because there isn't money enough.' It was double indemnity for accidental death."

"So you are rich," she said.

"By my standards, sure," he said. "By Mark Baldwin's standards, I'm penniless, but by mine, quite comfortable."

"And you can have your old job back, any time you want," she said.

"Well," he said, "or a variant of it. Laura's News Director, but what chiefly interests her is anchoring. She's told me many times she hates 'administrivia,' as she calls it, and would like nothing better'n have me come back to relieve her of those chores."

"Nobody in the community, your community," Gates said, "hates you. For what you've done."

"I don't know about that," he said. "I'd be surprised if everybody approved of me shooting an unarmed man, no matter how extreme the reason."

"Mister Taves does," she said. "Mister Taves thinks he knows, at least. He told me himself he thinks that there's a real possibility that any jury he gets in your case will acquit you, no matter what he proves, or how gory the pictures are, or what the judge tells them to do."

He laughed. "Mister Taves is full of shit. 'Walking Eagle,' as the cops call him behind his back. 'So full of shit he can't fly.' He's got an election coming up. He's priming the pump with the press, feeding everybody a load of bullshit so when he does win the case, he looks like a hero. But: a compassionate, reluctant hero, who only brought the case because I broke the law and he has to enforce that law. Because there are *some* people who still like me, and he doesn't want them mad at him either. Billy Taves wants the world to love him. Everybody in it. He looks like he ought to be running a dice game in Detroit, and he talks like a long-haul truckdriver. But he thinks he's Mother Teresa, and that's how he wants to be seen."

"You're wrong," she said.

"I know him," he said. "You don't."

"I know you're wrong," she said. "He told me, flat-out, on tape, with me taking notes, that the best thing that could happen in this case — for him, never mind you — would be if you came in and pleaded temporary insanity."

"I wasn't insane," Logan said. "I wasn't thinking as clearly as I am now, no question about that, but I wasn't insane. Doctor Gibbs would tell you that. He'd tell the jury, too."

"Doctor Gibbs would not," she said. "Doctor Gibbs told me if he could've held you against your will for another month at Finisterre, he would've. He told me: 'Even better, if I could've gotten him committed to a mental hospital, like McLean's, against his will, for six or eight weeks, I would've done that. But you can't do that any more. People have a legal right to be crazy now. So long as they pose no evident danger to themselves or others, they're free to walk the streets. Joe was very crafty. He never acted suicidal. He gave no conclusive hint of homicidal tendencies.' "

"I didn't have them when I was there," Logan said. "When I was at Finisterre, I didn't know Brutus was out on the highways again."

"That's essentially what Gibbs said," she said. " 'When Joe got out of here, he got out in the first place because he was free to leave at any time. And in the second place because he was in here for physical therapy, and to get sober. And when he checked out, he was ambulatory and dry. We never said we let him out because we thought he was on an even keel. Sane. We didn't think that. He wasn't. We just couldn't keep the guy.' That's what Gibbs would say."

"That's what Gibbs told you he would say," Logan said. "If Taves subpoenaed him, he'd sing a different song."

"That isn't true," she said. "If he wanted to, he couldn't. I've got the tapes of him talking. I've got my notes. As a matter of fact, I mentioned that to him, that he was locking himself into a position, and he said: 'I know that. It doesn't matter. What I'm telling you is my honest opinion. It's what I'd say on the witness stand. When Joe went out of here, I fully expected to see him back within three months. Or in some other facility, if his luck held. Otherwise: dead. I didn't project him shooting someone, but that's only because I don't think he had, either. After all, he'd never done it before, and that's what you look for in a fugue state: what the patient's done before.' "

"Well," Logan said, "he's right there. I'd never shot a man before. I'd never shot anything."

"Is that why you fired three times?" she said.

"That's exactly why," he said. "Hunting, using a shotgun, was not something Rick learned from me. Or from his mother. His pals at school went hunting, and he picked it up from them. Ducks in the marshes. Pheasants in the cranberry bogs. Stuff like that. His first year in college, he took it to Maine with him and hunted deer. Didn't get one, though. All I knew about firearms, the day I came home from seeing Brutus at the wheel, was: You can't kill a hundred-pound deer with a thirty-eight, and; Rick's shotgun was still in his closet. Along with several boxes of shells. I didn't know which kind to use. I chose buckshot because of Peabody's deer. If that's what you use on an animal the size of a deer, that's probably what you use on a man. And when I took it out of the 'Vette and started in on that bastard, I'd programmed myself. 'Make sure. Otherwise some damned doctor with more skill'n sense'll save the son of a bitch, and then he'll drive again.' I thought three'd probably do it. 'Fire.

Reload. Fire. Reload, and fire again.' And that is what I did." He paused. "You have got to admit," he said, "I did get the job done."

"That you did," she said. "But what I have to ask you is: Would you do it again?"

He stared at her. "I've been candid with you," he said.

"That you have," she said. "Don't stop now."

He shook his head. "You're asking too much," he said.

"No argument," she said. "Answer anyway."

He took a deep breath. "No," he said.

" 'No,' " she said. "Why not? You said you did it for revenge. You got revenge. You said you did it to stop Brutus from driving again, and killing somebody else. You said you wouldn't plead guilty because you want to ruin Mel Shaw, and get some more revenge. I've seen the TV tapes, keep in mind. The ones of you being questioned. I can't argue with your logic. If I grant your basic premise, that the system doesn't work, that the only way for victims to get retribution is by doing it themselves, everything you did was right.

"Except, of course," she said, "for what happens next, as they used to say on *Sesame Street* when I was still married and my kids were little, and I watched it with them. What happens next, in this case, is that you go to prison."

"Well," he said, "if you shoot someone and kill him, and you don't have a claim of self-defense, you go to prison. That's the law, I think. When I conned Jack Mahler into thinking I was easing back into SET, guiding Tommy Silva in his van to the processing plant so that Tommy'd be able to recognize Brutus's car, and take pictures of him in it, driving home, I wasn't under the impression that I'd escape punishment. You do what I did, you go to jail. That's the goddamned law."

"Which, you've also said, I think, doesn't work," she said.

"Plainly doesn't," he said. "Plainly doesn't work."

"Now," she said, "you're in a situation where unless something's done, it *is* going to work. At least Taves thinks it will, and I have to go with him. You're going to go prison for a long time, when you could have at least a comfortable life, and you won't have fun in there."

"This is true," he said. "I've already told you: If I could take back those three rounds of buckshot, I would do it. If I hadn't taken that final step — if I'd done what Jack Mahler thought I was doing when he sent Tommy Silva out that day, to take pictures of Brutus driving home to be shown on the evening news — Brutus would've been hauled in as a parole violator. He was an old man. He most likely would've died in jail. Now, instead, there is a possibility that I will die in jail. It doesn't make much sense."

"The system doesn't work," she said.

"That's what I've been saying," he said. "That's what I have said."

"So," she said, "why not put a wrench into it?"

"I don't follow," he said.

"Collude with Taves," she said. "I believe him when he says that all he wants is a way out of this case. Give him one. Get yourself a lawyer. Let him plead temporary insanity. Nobody's going to argue with him. Cut a goddamned deal. Get yourself out of this."

He studied her. "Do, in other words," he said, "exactly what Shaw, and Deese, and Brutus, several times — do what all of those other people that I despise did for so many years."

"That's about it," she said.

"No," he said.

"Why not?" she said. "What makes you think you're better than they are?"

"I know I am," he said.

She hunched forward. "I've done some work for a lawyer named Gleason," she said. "He's got a favorite story, about Abraham Lincoln throwing a corrupter down a flight of stairs after the bribe offer doubled the second time. Guy lands on his duff at the bottom and says: 'Why did you do that? You didn't throw me out when I made the first two offers.' And Lincoln says from the top of the stairs: 'You were getting close to my price.'

"I think,' she said, "I may be wrong, but I think that they're getting close to your price. You look good. You know you can rebuild your life, or could if you weren't going to jail. You're fixing up this place, that you obviously love. You're ready to resume your life. And except for this little matter of a homicide, you could."

She reached forward and shut off the tape recorder. "I don't want to write this story," she said.

He stared at her. "Then why'd you come here, then?" he said.

"When I came here," she said, "I wanted to write the story. Now,

I don't. I've changed my mind. If I write this story, it'll be because you've gone through with it, finished wrecking a life that was almost back together. Thrown everything away. For nothing. It's a sad story, and maybe it's a good one, but I don't want to write it.

"The only way I can *not* write this story," she said, "is if you don't do that. If you take what maybe you would call 'the easy way out,' and beat the same system that's beaten you. And therefore that's what I want you to do."

"Why should I do that?" he said. "What you want me to do."

"Because you want to go to bed with me," she said. "Admit it. I dare you."

"The thought has crossed my mind." he said. He grinned. "Ten or eleven times."

"Damned right it has," she said. "It has mine, too, to go to bed with you."

"Is this a charity fuck?" he said. "I don't want one of those."

"For you it may be," she said. "Not from my side. I've had the course with a very nice guy who's determined to kill himself. I was married to a man with the sensitivity of a stone; and I lived with a man who was partially nuts. I had my fling with the press mogul there, and I've done some slumming, too."

"With Dan Munroe," he said.

"I'm not telling," she said. "More specifics than you've got, you're not going to get. The summary of the story is that since I got emancipated, I've put more miles on the engine than might be a good idea. I'm getting to the point where I'm getting slightly scared. Maybe the Marines are right, saying they have trouble finding just a few good men. I haven't seen a flock, at least — they've eluded me. There don't seem to be a hell of lot of them around.

"You are clearly one of them," she said. "You've got your little imperfections, such as shooting people, but you won't do that again. Considering the bums I've known, you look very promising. So, you may look at me and think: 'A one-night stand.' But I have got to tell you, Joe, I've got more than that in mind."

44

On Thursday morning Constance Gates in her grey silk suit, carrying her attaché case, entered the foyer of North American Group on the twentieth floor of 200 Federal Street in Boston and presented herself at the reception desk. The woman at the desk had auburn hair and wore eyeglasses and earphones. She was running an IBM Correcting Selectric faster than it had been designed to operate, and it was hyphenating when she did not wish to have hyphens inserted in what she was typing. She whispered. "Damn" each time the hyphens came up, cranking the ball back and eliminating the mark. Gates stood there for three "Damns" before she cleared her throat.

The woman looked up and took off her earphones, all in the same motion. She smiled at Gates. "I'm sorry," she said. "I'm filling in here, and I still have my regular work to do for Mister Lacey, and I will be *so* glad when this outfit moves into the twentieth century and gets rid of these damned things. Can I help you?"

Gates smiled at her. "My name is Constance Gates," she said. "I'm here to see Mister Baldwin."

The woman reached for the phone. "Do you have an appointment?" she said.

"No, I don't," Gates said. "But that's my fault, not his. I'm pretty sure he'll see me."

The woman looked troubled. "I don't know," she said, glancing back at Gates. "Things've been a little hectic around here lately. You may have to wait."

"I'll do that," Gates said. "He can't start without me."

The receptionist looked grim but nodded. She punched the number on the call director. She frowned more deeply while the phone rang. She said: "Anne? Yes. I have a woman named Gates, here to see Mister Baldwin. She doesn't have an appointment." She paused. "Oh," she said, "I see. Yes, I will." She hung up the phone. She looked at Gates. "Miss Leeds says you know where he is," she said, "and: 'She should come right down.' "

"Thank you," Gates said. She started for the door on the left.

"For what it's worth," the receptionist said, "she also said he's been wondering where the hell you were. You might be in for it." She smiled. "He has not been a joy in the Christian home these past few days."

"Thanks," Gates said. She opened the door and went down the corridor to the northeast corner of the building. Anne Leeds was not at her desk behind the glass door of Mark Baldwin's office when Gates opened it, but she emerged from his office as Gates entered the room. Leeds had a steno pad in her hand, and a dour look on her face. She shut the door to Baldwin's office and studied Gates for a moment before she went behind her desk. She put the pad on her desk. She said: "Whew."

"Something up?" Gates said.

"*Ohh*," Leeds said. " 'Is something up?' she asks? He's on a tear, Miss Gates. He's been on a tear for the past two days. And you're a good part of the reason. Soon's he gets off this call, you can find out for yourself."

"What did I do?" Gates said.

"You didn't return his calls," Leeds said. "You didn't return my calls, I mean." She exhaled.

"I was out of town," Gates said. "On the job he gave me. So I didn't purge my answering machine for a couple days. This is a crime, perhaps?"

"Hey," Leeds said, "don't snap at me. I've had my share of that. And don't get all upset, either. You're just part of the reason. It's probably not going to matter much to you, when he gets off the phone and you go in the lion's den with the beast himself, foaming at the mouth. But I warn you, throw a steak in first, to keep him occupied. He isn't nice today."

Gates sat down on the couch "It's none of my business," she said, "but can I ask what happened? Since I'm going to get roasted, I mean. I'd like to be prepared."

Leeds sat down. "Oh," she said, "it's mostly . . . , Sylvia Francis killed herself, all right?"

"The receptionist?" Gates said.

"That's the one," Leeds said. She sat down hard on her chair. She lifted her handbag off the floor and took out a pack of Taryetons and a gold-toned Colibri lighter. She lighted a cigarette. She exhaled smoke in a cloud. She dropped the cigarette pack and the lighter back in her bag, glanced at the board of her call director, and took another drag.

"I'm sorry to hear that," Gates said.

Leeds lowered her cigarette. She stared at Gates through the smoke. "You are?" she said. She smiled.

"Yes, I am," Gates said defensively. "Person killing herself? Why wouldn't I be sorry? She must have been under some terrible stress, to do a thing like that."

Leeds took another deep drag and looked at the director board again. She exhaled smoke. "Still on," she said. She looked back at Gates. She grinned. " 'Under terrible stress,' you said."

"Yes, I did," Gates said. "To do a thing like that."

"Well," Leeds said, "you're right on the money. But of course that would figure. You being the terrible stress."

"Me?" Gates said.

Leeds stubbed the cigarette out in the ashtray on her desk. She nodded vigorously. "You," she said.

"What did I do to her?" Gates said.

Leeds looked up and smiled. "She hated your guts," she said.

"But what did I do to her?" Gates said.

Leeds looked at the director board. "He's off his call," she said with satisfaction. "You can go right in."

"Not 'till you answer my question," Gates said, standing up. "What did I do to Sylvia Francis, that'd make her kill herself?"

The buzzer sounded on the call director. Leeds glanced at it with annoyance. "Had an affair with him," she said, jerking her right thumb toward the door to Baldwin's office, "and she found out about it."

Gates sat down fast on the couch. "She found *out* about it?" she said. "How does what I do, whatever it happens to be, how is that her business?"

The buzzer sounded again. "Look," Leeds said, "I'll let him explain that. You don't get your tail in there, he'll be out here in a minute and he'll drag it in."

"The fuck he will," Gates said.

"What?" Leeds said.

"I said: 'The fuck he will,' " Gates said. She nodded toward the call director. "Buzz up the Emperor Caesar there. Tell him you and I're having a discussion, and if he wants to hear it he can get his ass out here."

Leeds stared at Gates. The buzzer sounded again. Leeds looked down at the board again. She looked back up at Gates. "No," she said, "I won't."

"Then I'm not going in," Gates said. She folded her hands in her lap and pressed her knees together.

The buzzer sounded again. Leeds looked at the board and back at Gates. Her expression became anxious. "Look," she said, "I've got to live with this guy, all right? This is my job. My husband's in law school and I need it, all right? Will you go in and see him? Sylvia left some kind of a note. Her husband . . . , I don't know what the hell her husband's doing, but whatever it is, the boss doesn't like it. And it's got something to do with the note. Which has something to do with you. And that's all I know. So will you go in now, please?"

Gates stood up. She straightened her skirt. She picked up her attaché case. She started for the door to Baldwin's office. She said very primly: "Thank you, Miss Leeds." She opened the door and went in.

Baldwin was coming out of his chair. "Close the door, if you would," he said. "Where the hell've you been?"

Gates released the doorknob and started across the room. "Stick the door up your ass, if you would," she said. "I've been anywhere I want." She sat down in the chair to the left of his desk and put her case on the floor.

"You're taking all the fun out of this," he said, sitting down in his chair. "Close the door, Anne, please?" he said loudly. The door to his office closed. He steepled his fingers. He frowned. "What I want you in here for," he said, "was to warn you that a bad moon's on the rise. Sylvia Francis killed herself."

"That I know," she said. "I just heard. Your secretary told me that, and then she gave me the old horselaugh. She said I was the reason. Which I find incredible. I scarcely knew the woman. If she killed herself over me, she would've killed herself over a passing Volkswagen. I never did anything to her."

Baldwin nodded. "No," he said, "you didn't. But she left a note saying you did. She said that she was doing what she did because you had stolen me from her."

At first Gates looked astonished. Then she began to laugh. "Let me get this straight," she said, " '*I* stole *you* from *her*?' "

"That's what she wrote," he said.

"What else did she write?" Gates said. "Did I steal Einstein from Germany?"

"Look," he said. "Sylvia and I'd been having an on-and-off affair for several years. She was jealous. She was very possessive."

"She was a lunatic," Gates said. "And a thief. Shouldn't leave those things out."

"Be that as it may," he said, "I have got a problem here, and therefore so have you. Before she died Monday night, her husband was going through her purse to see whether there was anything in it that might tell the doctors exactly what she'd taken. And he found the note. And he didn't tell anyone. Which was all he found. And then she died.

"The doctors," Baldwin said, "were perfectly agreeable to calling it accidental death. And that is what they did. But if the note comes out, there is going to be a scandal, for everyone concerned.

"I could not care less," she said.

"I could," he said. "And that's why I needed to see you. Her husband's lawyer's Richard Pond. Richard is my cousin, and I hate his filthy guts. I know you and Richard've had conversations. I also know that if Richard doesn't get what Richard wants, he will do what he says. He's the queen of the hop, maybe, but he's a dangerous man as well."

"What does he want?" she said.

"He wants the Logan story killed," Baldwin said. "If your story about Waterford gets printed, Jason's company, which Richard also represents, will have a scandal on its hands. If that happens, so will you, and so will I. If I kill your story, Jason Francis will burn the note. Richard knows I can kill your story, because you showed him our contract."

"That sounds a lot like blackmail," she said. "To these shell-pink ears, at least."

"Does to me as well," Baldwin said.

"But it doesn't seem to bother you too much," she said.

"I've been through this sort of foolishness before, with suicides," Baldwin said. "They're kamikazes, all of them. The reason that they do what they do is to cause maximum harm to their survivors. When they succeed in their attempts, the only sensible thing to do is cut your losses. Dead as they are, they don't know it, but you're alive, and do. You've frustrated them at last."

"So you're killing the story," she said.

"Yes, I am," he said.

She inhaled deeply. She exhaled. "Okay," she said, picking up her case and starting to rise. "Mister Pond told me you'd have that right, if I signed that paper. And I signed it. So you do."

She stood up. "Look," he said. "I feel bad about this."

"No need to," she said. "I'd probably do the same thing myself, in the same circumstnces."

"I'll have Anne draw up a voucher," he said, "for the other ten grand."

"That's not necessary," she said. "Come to think of it, though, this is." She opened her purse. She took out her wallet. "This is definitely necessary," she said, extracting the credit cards. She tossed them on his desk. "Cut 'em up,' she said. "I think I'm through with them."

"I want to do it," he said. "Pay you the money. It'd make me feel better." He smiled. "I mean it when I say I really regret this, Connie. For a while I thought we might have something nice going for us. Something that'd outlast this assignment."

"Oh, come on," she said. "You set me up. You set me up from the beginning. You set me up to answer that woman's call. Before that, you set me up with Taves. You set me up with Logan, and now, goddamnit, you're trying to set me up again. And you know something, Mister Baldwin? I'm letting you do it. Have Anne draw the voucher. I need the damned money."

45

At 12:15 on Thursday afternoon, Baldwin and Roger Kidd followed the hostess of the Charter Club down the space between the tables in the center of the room and the row placed at the western windows. John Flaherty, Robert Doran, and a man Baldwin did not recognize were seated at the third window table from the northwest corner, engaged in earnest conversation. Doran and Flaherty wore dark business suits and blue shirts with repp strip ties. They leaned forward over their plates and their martinis. The third man wore white suede boating shoes, tan chino pants, a red polo shirt and a black blazer that did not fit him. He had long blond hair and a deep tan.

Doran and Baldwin exchanged small waves of recognition. Flaherty, momentarily distracted from what he had been saying to the third man, looked up expectantly. His face looked haggard and drawn. The expression on it tightened. He looked down into his lap and straightened his napkin. He did not raise his eyes again until Baldwin and Kidd had passed the table.

The hostess seated Baldwin and Kidd at the table in the northeast corner. She asked whether they would like drinks.

"Sprite," Kidd said firmly.

"I'll have a Kronenbourg, please," Baldwin said.

"Beer?" Kidd said. "Seldom see you drink beer."

"For a change," Baldwin said. He nodded toward Doran's table. "Who's the guy with Bobby Doran and John Flaherty there, you know? The one in the house blazer?"

"Mike Russell," Kidd said absently, studying the menu. "Guy's got more money than he knows what to do with, and I bet he doesn't own one suit. Always looks like a bum."

"The sailmaker," Baldwin said.

"That's the one," Kidd said. "He's heading up the *Fortitude* syndicate for the Eighty-eight America's Cup trials. So naturally

Flaherty and Doran're pitching him today for the licensing rights. Tee-shirts, jackets, watches — you name it. Could be a good account."

"How do you know all this?" Baldwin said.

Kidd snapped the menu shut. "I think I'll go with the veal again," he said. "Know about it," he said, "because Mister Flaherty had to get my permission to meet with Mister Russell today. I had him noticed for further depositions beginning ten o'clock this morning. He begged off for this conference. And being a nice guy, I let him do it."

"He didn't seem too grateful," Baldwin said. "From the way he reacted just now, I'd say he's not grateful at all. He doesn't seem to like you."

Kidd unfolded his napkin and spread it in his lap as the waitress brought their drinks. She set them down and left. "Ah," Kidd said, "I can't blame him for that. Jane's playing the usual vindictive client's game: Order your lawyers to pound the living daylights out of the other party, and then when the other guy gets hurt, blame it all on your lawyers. I can just hear her, when he howls. Puts on that sweet little maiden act of hers and says she can't imagine what's gotten into Mister Kidd, but he just won't listen to a word she says. Then as soon as he's out of sight, runs for the phone with some new suggestions to clobber him again. Notice his mother for deposition. Call in the woman who was his secretary two years ago and lives in Chicago now. Anything and everything that will inconvenience him, embarrass him with his friends and business associates, and, not incidentally at all, also run up Kincaid, Bailey's bill, which he will end up paying when she finally gets tired of this idiocy and gives him his divorce. I don't blame that guy for not liking me. He probably figures I came here for lunch today just to check up on him. I wouldn't like me either."

"She's a real bitch, huh?" Baldwin said.

"They all are," Kidd said with distaste. "The men and the women, both. Divorce work is the pits. I wish we didn't do it. I can't tell you how many arguments I've had with Bayliss that we should stop doing it, farm it out, get rid of it and quit. It's nasty and it's time-consuming and we don't make that much money on it, and at the same time we create a hell of a lot of new enemies for ourselves. Usually new enemies who still have plenty of money left after we get through screwing them, and lots of legal business to place, but who will never bring a dime of it into our shop, not after what we've done. They'd hire Satan, Esquire, before they'd come to us. And Bayliss fobs me off with the same old explanation: It's something we do as a service to the clients who are beneficiaries of our trusts, and we have to keep it up even though it's unpleasant.

" 'It's not a matter of making money on the divorces,' Bayliss says. 'It's a matter of not losing the money we make from those clients' other work. They expect us to help when they encounter these problems. They come to us for assistance when their marriages collapse because they know and trust us, and we know their situations. They don't have to expose themselves and their families' business to some outsider, someone whose discretion and trustworthiness they're unfamiliar with. If we don't succor them as they wish, if we farm out these problems, pretty soon we'll find that whoever gave them the help we refused them is succeeding us as trustees.' Then he claps me on the back and tells me to keep my chin up. 'Law's not always nice, Roger,' is what he says to me. 'Sometimes we have to get down in the mud and do a dirty job.' It really stinks."

The waitress returned. Kidd ordered veal marsala. Baldwin ordered chicken Kiev, and a half bottle of Côtes du Rhône.

"Why don't you hire another lawyer, then?" Baldwin said. "You've certainly got enough money in the firm to do it. Get some hungry kid in from Suffolk Law and let him do the muggings."

"Oh, can't do that," Kidd said. "Bayliss'd be horrified. Don't you understand the reason that the Baldwin family trust is still with us, after all these years? It's because we're men of breeding and discretion. When you got divorced from Lucille, you know, with all that nastiness, none of it found its way into the papers by way of some loose-tongued, vulgar person that our firm employed. Oh, horrors, no. The firm not only has to keep doing the work — the people who own the damned firm have to do it themselves."

He put his elbows on the table. "You know what I've done to John Flaherty to date?" he said. "You know what I've done to a perfectly nice man whom I'd probably like, if I didn't represent his wife — whom I don't like at all? I have come pretty near to destroying his life. That's what I have done. Jane's family trust will remain with Kincaid, Bailey and Kincaid when John at last gets shed of her, but no matter how many generations it stays afterwards, it won't outlast the bad taste I've gotten in my mouth from what I've done to keep it."

"Like what, for example?" Baldwin said. The waitress delivered their salads.

Kidd looked down at the tablecloth. "Oh, hell," he said, "I'm going to eat. I don't want to talk about it."

"Oh," Baldwin said.

Kidd looked up. "Oh, I know," he said. "It's just that it's all so damned pointless. John Flaherty fell in love. Illicitly. Poor judgment on his part. And that was just the beginning. The opening round, as it were. We've learned he set the lady up in a condominium on Horizon Wharf. Which cost him seventy grand when he bought it, practically a steal ten months later, when they're going for one-twenty-five. And the monthly maintenance charges, which he's been paying, come to twelve hundred bucks.

"Where he made his mistake, doing that," Kidd said, "and believe me, it was only one of many, but where he made his mistake there was buying the place in his own name, not hers. So, up go his total assets by the current market value of the hideaway, and up go Jane's demands, by a like amount."

"Which of course means," Baldwin said, "that unless he's got liquid capital squirreled away someplace else, the condo has to be sold."

Kidd nodded, digging away at his salad. "That's what it means," he said. "And he hasn't got the other assets, so the place has to be sold. Which it will be, according to the purchase and sale agreement he signed last week with the new occupants, as of August fifteenth."

"And what happens to the lady?" Baldwin said.

"A very good question," Kidd said. "One she put to me, oddly enough, through her tears, when I took her deposition. Her status in this country is precarious as it is. Emma Sung is not a citizen. She's here on a green card from Hong Kong. As long as she keeps her job, playing the piano at the Reef, she'll be able to get by. But no more than that. And she won't be getting by at Horizon Wharf. She'll be lucky if she can get a place in Medford, for God's sake. Comes here to make her career in American music, among other things, and ends up living in a walk-up in Medford. Because Jane Flaherty is mad."

"Well," Baldwin said, "if Flaherty's getting divorced, can't she move in with him? You're not going to beggar the guy after all, no matter how you try. He'll have to have something left. And he'll still have his job."

Kidd finished his salad as the waitress brought their entrées and Baldwin's wine. "She could but she won't," he said. "She declined to be specific, and I didn't press her on it, but for some reason or another, she will not do that. Apparently he disappointed her in some way since their relationship became the focus of this unpleasantness, and she wants nothing more to do with him. But I don't know what he did." He sawed away at his veal. "As a matter of fact," he said, "if I were to make an educated guess, I'd say there's more than a slight possibility she might sue John for palimony, after Jane gets through having us clean his clock. He's truly offended Emma."

"Maybe by suddenly putting himself in a position where he's going to lose all his money?" Baldwin said.

Kidd shrugged. "Could be," he said. "Could be. As I say, I didn't press her. Things were bad enough at that session. She's an exquisite little creature, and I'd reduced her to tears as it was. I felt enough a brute without piling Pelion on Ossa by asking her if she'd been fortune-hunting when she went to bed with him."

"You're getting fastidious in your old age," Baldwin said, eating chicken.

"I know it," Kidd said. "I've got to watch that, or pretty soon I won't be fit for duty any more." He chewed veal strenuously. "Is this stuff tough today?" he said.

"Been known to be," Baldwin said. "Calves are like people, you know. Some're tougher than others."

"Yeah," Kidd said. "Pity you can't tell from the outside what you're getting, before you order one."

"Which brings us," Baldwin said, "to your protégée, Miss Gates."

"Well," Kidd said, "now there you're certainly not going to complain. I told you she was tough."

"Oh," Baldwin said, "no quarrel on that score. She's tougher'n John Wayne, I've found. If she'd played Sergeant Stryker in *The Sands of Iwo Jima*, there would've been no movie — the Japanese would've left, regardless of the script."

"She worked out well, then," Kidd said. "Well, that's some good news, at least, in a week when it's been short." He paused in cutting his veal. "I assume you slept with her," he said, looking at Baldwin from under his brows.

"You can assume anything you like, Roger," Baldwin said. "She's a very attractive woman, unattached and unafraid. I enjoyed her company."

"Yes," Kidd said. He frowned as he studied the veal on his fork. "And as I assume you slept with her, so, apparently, did the late Mrs. Francis." He put the veal in his mouth and chewed vigorously, gazing at Baldwin. "As you, ah, predicted she would?"

Baldwin poured wine. He also frowned. "If my dear cousin Richard wasn't making things up," he said, lifting his glass, "as Richard has been known to do when it suited his purposes, but if Richard was reading to me the actual contents of the note he says her husband found, she did indeed make that assumption. Very much so, yes."

"And this note," Kidd said, looking troubled, "just what does Richard propose to do with it?"

"He was vague on that point," Baldwin said. "Vague, but threatening. Basically what he proposed was an exchange of hostages. The note destroyed in exchange for my decision to cancel the story Miss Gates had. Prevention of some awkwardness for me, with my board, in return for prevention of some embarrassment to his clients, Mister Francis and Appalachian investments."

"What did you say," Kidd said. "Did you agree to that?"

"Did I have much choice?" Baldwin said. "No, I didn't really agree to it. Not right off, at least. Tell you the truth, Roger, I didn't know if I could carry out such an agreement if I made it. Constance Gates is a resolute person. I could raise hell if I ordered her to drop the story and she got mad and sold it somewhere else, but about all I could do in that event would be sue her and the other publication after it was printed. By which time, of course, Richard and Mister Francis would've long since retaliated by releasing the contents of the note."

"Well," Kidd said, hacking away at the veal again, "but not if they kept their word and destroyed it."

Baldwin laughed. "Roger," he said, "really. Did you fall in the shower this morning and crack your head or something? Do you seriously think Richard would destroy the original without running it through the Xerox eight or ten times, and putting the copies in a safe deposit box? Would Richard Pond do that?"

Kidd chewed slowly and with effort. "No," he said, "I don't guess he would,"

"Of course you don't," Baldwin said. "Richard Pond is a man utterly without scruples. He'd rather climb a tree and lie to you than stay on the ground and tell the truth."

"Well," Kidd said, raising his glass of Sprite, "only if there was something in it for him."

"Money, you mean?" Baldwin said. Kidd nodded once. "You underestimate him, Roger," Baldwin said. "Richard will distort the truth for almost any reason. And he's hated me all his life. When my brother was killed in the accident, do you know what Richard did? He came up to me after the memorial service and as much as accused me of engineering the explosion that killed Cal."

"You're not serious," Kidd said.

"I am serious," Baldwin said, "He stood there outside the church and said I'd deliberately failed to fire the Argentinian kid on the crew because I knew sooner or later he'd make some stupid mistake that would result in Cal's death. As of course, he did. He should've seen that the pump on the fuel supply was faulty, that it surged from time to time, and told me, and replaced it. And he didn't, and the car exploded. And perhaps I should've known from other blunders he committed that he should be fired before something fatal happened. But I didn't know it, and I did leave him in place until fate took its course."

"But why would Richard say you planned it?" Kidd said, putting his fork down. "What would your motive be?"

"Ah," Baldwin said, "that's where Richard's true nature shows. He said within earshot of perhaps a dozen people that I did it because he'd slept with Cal, and I hated Cal for that."

"Oh, my Lord," Kidd said.

"Absolutely," Baldwin said. He drank wine. He wiped his lips.

"That's unforgiveable," Kidd said.

"No," Baldwin said, "although it took me a while to come to that conclusion. Richard was terribly upset that day. To the rest of us, I must say, that diminishing band of family that remained when Cal finally got his wish and perished while still young, the death didn't come as a great surprise. Cal'd shown a decidedly self-destructive tendency ever since he was twelve. If it hadn't been a fuel explosion, it would've been something else. But to Richard, obviously, it was completely unexpected. His grief was genuine. Most likely because he *had* slept with Cal. I don't know that he had, but Cal was eclectic in his search for excitements. He was capable of homosexual seduction, actively or passively. He ruled nothing out."

"Dear me," Kidd said. "Thank heavens for my sheltered life."

"Yes," Baldwin said. He finished his chicken as the waitress arrived to remove the plates and inquire if coffee was wanted. Kidd ordered tea. Baldwin accepted coffee. "Anyway," he said, "having all that in mind, I was not about to question Richard's firmness of intention, or commit myself either to an agreement that I couldn't carry out. Which I wouldn't know until I called Connie in and saw how she reacted.

"And we couldn't find her," Baldwin said. "Here is the whole uproar in the office over Sylvia killing herself, and people giving me sidelong glances and whispering suspicions that Richard will confirm in spades if I don't get to Gates, and we can't find the woman.

"This morning she came in," Baldwin said, "truculent as Patton, loaded for bear, you know? And I thought to myself: 'Oh-oh, we may have some trouble here.' And I told her I'd decided to kill the Logan story, not knowing what the hell I'm going to do when she gets up on her high horse and tells me she'll take it somewhere else, and she said: 'Okay.' She didn't even want the second ten grand on the contract. Which I gave her anyway. Just stood up, gave me another ration of shit, and walked out of my life."

"Well," Kidd said, as the waitress brought the tea and coffee, "that's certainly odd enough. I know Connie's short of cash all the time, but all the same, I would've expected her to resist. She takes a lot of pride in her work."

"Couldn't figure it out," Baldwin said. "She stomped out of the office, and I called Richard up and told him he had his deal, and then I just sat there and looked out the window and made my head hurt, thinking.

"I was getting nowhere fast," Baldwin said, "when the thought crossed my mind to call Bill Taves. Who, after all, got me involved in the whole mess in the first place because he was in it too. Anne got him on the phone down in New Bedford, and I started to tell him the story was deader than the murder victim, and before I could get a word out of my mouth, he said: 'Baldwin, you son of a bitch, I got to hand it to you.' And I said: 'What?' And he said: 'Got a call this morning from Jake Tenney. Says he's representing Logan. Wants he should come here and maybe we can cut a deal. You did it, Baldwin, you smart bastard. Got to admit I never liked you, but you are a fuckin' genius, there's no getting around that.'

"I'd thought I was baffled when Gates left the office," Baldwin said. "Now I was all at sea. 'I don't follow you,' I said. 'The broad you picked,' he said. 'The broad that talked to me? Tenney comes into the office, and we're working the thing out, voluntary manslaughter, ten years' suspended, has to get psychiatric care, all the usual ribbons and bows you tie on a package of shit you're gonna dump, and we get all through and I ask him: "Jake, I say, the fuck is going on here with this guy? For weeks he's a goddamned rock, he won't budge how hard you hit him, and now all of a sudden he's gonna blow this damned thing out? What the hell is going on?" And Jake says: "Simple. He's in love. Now he don't want to go to jail. He wants to go to bed." And I say: "Jesus Christ," all right? "Who the hell's this broad he's got. that gets me out of this?" And Jakes says: "Some lady reporter, that's been working on the case? She come down to see him Monday and they don't come up for air, I guess, until he got me out of bed at seven today, sends me over here." So, I got to thank you, Baldwin, for your great idea. You are a smart bastard, Marcus. I would not have thought of that.'

"As, of course," Baldwin said, "I had not myself."

"Then how did he know?" Kidd said.

"Precisely what I asked him," Baldwin said. " 'Simple,' he said. 'Jake Tenney's goddamned kid works this painter guy, kid the name of Barry. Painting contractor. And they're doing a job at Logan's house. And they're there in the afternoon, this's Monday, and it's starting to rain, and Logan's telling them, they gotta lay off, anna broad shows up. So they come back on Tuesday, right? 'Cause they gotta finish the job. And the car's still inna driveway, and the broad is still there, all right? And the same thing on Wednesday. Car's still inna yard. Broad's therefore prolly still inna house. So they're painting the eaves or something, on Wednesday afternoon, I guess, and they move the ladders around, the back of the house, and they get up the scaffolding and everything, and they start up the ladders and look in the windows. Which is natural enough, am I right? And they look inna bedroom window there onna first floor, when they're climbing up, and there's Logan anna broad naked onna bed, goin' at it like a coupla fuckin' dogs. Hump, hump, hump.

" 'So, they don't say nothing,' Taves said to me," Baldwin said, grinning. " 'They keep on climbing up the ladders and they get onna boards, and they paint the fuckin' eaves. And they get through paintin' eaves, and they come down again, which is probably an hour or so later, they got to move the ladders again, and the boards and everything, and naturally they look back inna windows. And Logan anna broard're lyin' bare-ass onna bed, and she's playin' with his dick. And I guess they made some noise or something, because all a sudden, she looks up, and she sees them and smiles. And she blows them this big kiss, all right? And Logan opens up one eye and, you know how the fighters do, put both hands in the air and shake them, when they won the fight? That is what he does. And he is also grinning.

" 'I tell you something,' Taves told me, 'I wished I knew a broad like that, just one time in my life. She really must be something. She must know what's going on.' "

"Connie Gates is a smart woman," Kidd said.

"She's very smart," Baldwin said. "Out of that assignment she got herself a new man and a twenty-thousand-dollar dowry to start her new life with him. Of course, you are pretty smart yourself. She was your idea."

"Well," Kidd said, "I have to be modest here. I really didn't know about her talents besides research. But I'm glad it all worked out."

"I'm sure you are," Baldwin said. "Now, let me ask you something else. A hypothetical. When you called up this morning and invited yourself to lunch, might you have been working on a file by any chance?"

"Certainly," Kidd said, dabbing at his lips. "We have a busy office. No idleness at all."

"And that file," Baldwin said. "Might it have been the Flaherty divorce case on your desk?"

"Yes, it was," Kidd said. There was a suspicion of a smile at the corners of his mouth.

"Which of course contained the deposition you had taken from Emma Sung," Baldwin said.

"Among other things," Kidd said, smiling openly.

"And the thought occurred to you," Baldwin said, "that there might be a way to wipe at least some of the crap off your hands in that disagreeable case, and perhaps avoid a second proceeding that would splatter more scandal all over your client, Jane, by doing a good deed."

"Well, after all, Mark," Kidd said, "where possible we always strive for the best result for all of the parties involved in these dreary triangles. Our clients have to come first, but if everyone emerges reasonably happy, well, it's better all around."

"Would I be mistaken," Baldwin said, "if I surmised that while browsing through Miss Sung's deposition, and considering what might happen to Jane, not to mention her estranged husband, if Miss Sung got herself a mean lawyer and also went to court, it occurred to you that things would be neater if Miss Sung found a new place to live, and a new man to keep her?"

"Not seriously mistaken, Mark," Kidd said. "As I said, I felt pity for Miss Sung, and I was sorry for her trouble. But she is an exquisite creature, and . . . . Well, let's just say there's room in her testimony for the inference that she's aware of her attractiveness, likes to be taken care of, and understands that her skill as a musician won't suffice by itself to provide her with the comforts she requires."

"You didn't happen to jot down any telephone numbers that you might've acquired in the course of your inquiries, did you?" Baldwin said.

Kidd reached into his left inside pocket. He took out a slip of paper. "This is unpublished," he said. "Not unlisted, though. So you could've gotten it through Information." He looked up at Baldwin. "If you follow me."

"Your name will not be used," Baldwin said. He took out his pocket secretary and a ballpoint pen.

"Oh, you can have this," Kidd said, handing him the paper. "I have no need for it."

Baldwin put it in the notepad. He put the notepad and the pen back in his pocket. He grinned at Kidd. "You're a thoughtful man, Roger," he said. "Thanks in large part to you, Connie Gates, Joe Logan, Billy Taves and I are all having much better days today than we would have without you." Kidd smiled. "Which of course also means," Baldwin said, "that you're having a pretty fine day for yourself."

Kidd plucked his napkin out of his lap and dropped it on the table. "Except for the veal, Mark," he said. "The veal was rather tough."